ADVERSE IMPACT

*Merry Christmas
Lauren —

Hope you
enjoy!*

ADVERSE IMPACT

Best Wishes,

PHILLIP TOMASSO, III

[signature]
11/03

Quiet Storm Publishing • Martinsburg, WV

Published by Quiet Storm Publishing
PO BOX 1666
Martinsburg, WV 25402

www.quietstormpublishing.com

Cover by Clint Gaige

ISBN: 0-9728819-4-8

Library of Congress Control Number: 2003090664

OTHER BOOKS BY PHILLIP TOMASSO III

JOHNNY BLADE
THIRD RING
TENTH HOUSE
MIND PLAY

**Children books under the pen name
Grant R. Philips:**

KING GAUTHIER & THE LITTLE DRAGON SLAYER

Be sure to look for:

PIGEON DROP

COMING SUMMER 2004
FROM QUIET STORM PUBLISHING

DEDICATION

This is for all of my family and friends. For your constant love and enthusiastic support, I'm grateful...

ACKNOWLEDGMENTS

Many people want to be writers, but it takes a certain person to actually become a writer. Writing is oftentimes a lonely and solitary job, with hours and hours spent by yourself in front of a computer. You've got to love what you're doing. And I do. I love telling stories. But I could never do it alone. Wouldn't dream of it. For this, I would like to thank some many people, but if I leave anyone out, it is unintentional. Thank you Christine Wrzos-Lucacci, Greg Palmer, (Aunt) Linda DeCarlis, Corrine Chorney and Marian Gowen. These poor souls suffer through endless drafts of my work. And for some reason, are still talking to me. They provide insightful input on storyline glitches and editing and you name it, they're there to help fix it. I would also like to thank all the people who have read and reviewed this novel. I want to thank my publisher, Clint Gaige, and his wife Darla. They are energetic, helpful and maintain constant contact with their talented pool of authors over at Quiet Storm Publishing. I would also like to thank Liza Marshall, my editor, who I think did a wonderful job shaping up and polishing off the manuscript. And, as always, I would like to thank God for everything.

Prologue
Denver, Colorado 11:54 PM

It was a noise just loud enough to wake her from a sound sleep. With everything happening—the obscene letters, the phone pranks—maybe she was not as sound asleep as she might have imagined. Upon awakening, an immediate sensation of terror filled her body. Her eyes opened wide, straining to see the shape of someone in the dark bedroom with her. She silently cursed at having closed the curtains before falling asleep. With the curtains open, the bright winter moon would have lit her room better than a naked hundred-watt bulb.

She forced herself to breathe slowly and quietly. Fairly confident she was alone in the room, she lay listening for other noises to break the silence. For three long minutes she listened, waiting, but no other sounds came. The fear of the moment had not left her body. She knew reaching out to turn on the lamp on the nightstand would chase the darkness away, but she couldn't do it. She felt paralyzed under the bedspread. The muscles in her arms and legs felt tight. She was sweating behind the knees and on the back of her neck where her bunched up hair touched skin.

Closing her eyes and falling back asleep did not seem like an option. On a normal night, maybe she would have been able to do so. The way things had been going lately, she did not think comfortable sleep would ever be possible again. Whoever was stalking her had made his point perfectly clear. If he couldn't have her, then no one could. It had started out like some romantic, secret admirer only a few months ago. The casual love letters made her feel special and attractive. Soon after, though, all that changed. The cute little love notes that she found herself looking forward to abruptly turned graphic and obscene. Once the police became involved, she felt sure the undesired attention would come to an immediate end. The exact opposite happened. The sadistic admirer became even more compulsive and obsessive and then the physical threats started.

A sound in the night would rarely be more than a sound in the night to most. To her, any noise she heard in the middle of the night was the stalker trying to break in. It felt impossible not to take the madman's threats seriously. He knew how to get to her and had proved it time and again. When she changed her phone number, he had been sure to call the next day and let her know he had the new, unlisted number. The police had traced calls. The traces always led to pay phones from all over the city, never the same phone twice. When she drove a rental car to keep him from leaving perverted, and sometimes threatening letters of a sexual nature under her windshield wiper blade, she would end up finding the same type of explicit items on the front seat of the rental when she was one hundred percent positive the doors had been locked. Eventually the police assigned a young detective to the case. He worked on trying to figure out who might be harassing her, but seemed to spend more time trying to get her to go out with him.

After ten minutes of listening to small noises a house is almost obligated to make, she decided she needed to do something. Lying in her dark bedroom unable to fall asleep was not going to accomplish anything. She needed to switch on a light and search the rooms of her place or she had to close her eyes and pray to God that she could fall asleep. Regardless which option she chose, she had to go to work in the morning. She had missed more than her share of days over the past several weeks. Stress from being stalked had taken a toll. Her therapist was in the process of finding her the right anti-depressant. The first two medications she tried made her stomach upset, her mouth cotton-ball dry and gave her an appetite like an elephant. The one her doctor prescribed last week seemed to have none of those side effects. She wouldn't swear she felt any differently since taking the new pills, but neither did they make her feel sick or make her feel as if she were putting on ten pounds just by looking at food.

Finally, she thought, *that's it,* and took a deep breath. *I can't stand this anymore.* She counted silently in her head. *One. Two. Three.* She turned on her side and reached for the lamp on the nightstand and turned the switch all in one fluid motion. The light came on. She rolled over and searched every corner with wide, expecting eyes. Just as she'd thought, just as she'd hoped, no one was in her room, no one. *This is silly*, she thought. *Silly!*

"Silly, but I still can't sleep," she said to the empty room.

Knowing she would not be able to fall back to sleep she reached for the telephone. Though it was close to midnight and she had no right to make this call, she also felt as if she had no other option. She hesitated for a few more seconds but decided to dial. She listened anxiously as the telephone rang a few times. Losing her nerve, she hung up. What did she expect? She calls someone and they rush right over and hold her hand until she can fall back to sleep? *Ridiculous*. Besides, she had broken it off with him. He owed her nothing.

There seemed few options left. Stay up the rest of the night and wait for the false security of daylight to comfort her—get dressed and go to work dead on her feet, or try to get some sleep. If someone had gotten in the house she found it hard to believe the burglar, or whatever you might call him, could be quiet for fifteen minutes. Although, with her lamp on and the rest of the house being dark, an intruder would see the light from the crease under the door. Maybe the light would scare him away. Maybe not. *Unless it was her stalker*, she thought. He didn't seem like the type to get scared off easily. The idea of having the police trying to find him didn't deter him, why would a light showing under a door? If anything, she feared it might encourage him.

She looked at the telephone again. She picked it up. The line was dead. It didn't make sense. A moment ago the line was not dead. She had made a call. She hung up the telephone, waited a few seconds and picked it up again. The line was still dead.

"No, no! This isn't happening," she said. Her heart was beating so fast she feared it might erupt inside her chest. First a noise and now the phone line's dead.

Outside her bedroom window she could hear the sound of a winter storm. The wind was howling. It could be that a tree had fallen and taken out a telephone cable.

She got out of bed and went to the window. She parted the curtains. With her bedroom light on she could not see out into the darkness. She could only see her own reflection in the glass. She cupped her hands and pressed her face in close. It was snowing hard. The winter moon and stars had to be hidden under blankets of stormy clouds. Though she was only on the second level, she was unable to see the ground around her house. She was looking for footprints in the snow. *With the phone dead*, she wondered, *what would I even do if I saw footprints?*

Someone started pounding on the front door downstairs and calling out her name. She screamed from the unexpected pounding, but then thought she recognized the voice and felt overcome with relief. She picked up her robe and slid her feet into slippers. "I'm coming," she hollered, pulling open her bedroom door and bounding down the stairs.

From one switch, she turned on the foyer and living room lights all at once. At the door she looked through the peephole. No one was on the front step. Cautiously she disengaged the two dead bolts and opened the door a crack, but no one was there.

She felt uncomfortable and quickly shut the door, engaging all the locks. She had had enough. She was going to call the police. She picked up the telephone on the end table and nearly screamed. There was still no dial tone.

All the lights went out in the house. She screamed again. Panic racking her body. She was not sure what to do next. She looked aimlessly around the dark room, eyes wide in a futile attempt to search for something, anything that might be used to help her. She saw nothing.

The sound of glass shattering came from another room. It sounded as if someone had thrown a large rock through the kitchen window. A surge of adrenaline sped through her body. As quickly as she could, fumbling with the locks, she pulled open the front door and ran out into the wintry night. She lost her slippers almost immediately as her feet sank into the mounting snow banks. She did her best to ignore the icy cold sensation when her bare feet touched the snow and ran as fast as she could toward the main road.

She knew she needed help. She would never be able to outrun anyone in these conditions. The pinecones under the freshly fallen snow were like agitated crabs under the sand, pinching relentlessly at the soles of her feet. Thankfully, her feet were quickly going numb from the cold. The falling snow was accompanied by a harsh, bitter wind that bit at her exposed flesh making her thighs feet as if they were getting stung by a swarm of angry, killer bees. As she ran, her quick, shallow breaths appeared in front of her face in moist vapors. The cold air filled her lungs which felt like they would explode from the burning sensation. She did her best to ignore all these feelings and just concentrated on running to the end of her pine tree-lined driveway, which twisted for nearly two hundred yards before reaching the main road.

She knew screaming would be useless. Her closest neighbor was two acres to her left.

She wanted to turn and see if she were being chased. Every instinct inside her screamed she should not. Keep running, keep heading for the road. *Run as fast as you can*, she kept telling herself. The faster she ran the more she felt she'd be tackled from behind. She knew she was being chased. She was barefoot, cold and did not know what she would do next even if she did make it to the end of her driveway.

Suddenly, she was jarred forward from a push behind and felt a warm, intense sensation in her back as if she might be on fire. Her shoulder blades protruded in a thwarted attempt to shield her skin from the serrated edge of a blade slicing its way through her flesh. She wanted to scream, but could not get enough air inside her lungs to do so.

When the knife was pulled out it felt as if a chunk of her innards had been pulled out with it. She felt suddenly empty and hollow. The pain subsided some. The reality that her sick admirer was going to kill her was a little surprising. She'd been afraid of the threats, terrified even, but never expected any of it to lead to this.

She fell forward into the snow. The blood spilling from her wound spread into a puddle resembling an obscene, cherry flavored snow cone.

She rolled onto her back. Her robe was open and she hated that she was dressed in only a silk pajama top. Her bare legs were cold and instinctively, vulnerably, she drew them in. "Why?" she asked.

Panting. Huffing. Clouds of breath exhaled from her attacker like plumes of smoke from a dragon's nostrils. "Why? Why? Do you really have to ask? Was it not plainly clear how much I loved you?"

No. It hadn't been clear. It wasn't clear to her at all. It wasn't clear until this moment. Even now that she knew, she still didn't truly understand *why*. She shook her head. "Why … why are you doing *this*?" She felt like a pool with a hole in it. The warmth of her seeping blood was a thick, sticky puddle pooling inside the fabric of her robe.

As if extremely tired, her eyes grew heavy. She fought to keep them open. This didn't seem right; it didn't feel right. She couldn't believe this was the way her life was supposed to end.

"You've got to understand something," the killer said, bending down, cradling her head. "None of this *had* to happen. It's your fault really. All of this could have been avoided. You were a tease, a little tease the way you flaunted and showcased. You had to know it would catch up to you. Not everyone wants to play the games you play. Not everyone was going to follow your rules. I didn't want it to end this way. I expected a different ending. I wanted a different ending. I wanted us to be together. We'd have been happy together. It worked between us. We worked well together."

"You're sick," she managed to say. Just those few words took a tremendous amount of effort. Everything the pursuer had said did nothing to provide closure. Besides, what if everything were true and it had all been her fault?

And then, none of it mattered, not really, not anymore. She could no longer keep her eyes open. They were heavy and closing and she was tired. She could hear the wind whipping violently around her, howling in her ear, though not nearly as vicious a sound as the last words she'd ever hear.

"I love you," were the last, disgusting words she heard as a chilling cold overtook her and a complete and permanent darkness enveloped her body and soul.

Chapter 1
Rochester, New York—Thirteen Months Later
Tuesday, January 14

"Joey, where did this come from?" Linda Genova said, sitting across from Joey Viglucci. Linda had been dating Joey seriously for the last six months. He was one of the most handsome men she'd ever met. He kept his silky black hair all one length and wore it pulled back in a ponytail. He had thick, dark brows that framed piercing, intense blue eyes. His skin was dark with a Mediterranean olive tint that made him look all that much more exotic.

Using the cloth napkin to dab at spaghetti sauce around the corner of his mouth, Joey shrugged. "Linda, we've been together a long time." He spoke with confidence, in a slow calculated way.

It wasn't a ring, but that was his point, wasn't it. "I don't know about this," Linda said. "Moving in together?" She wasn't sure how she felt about it. She loved being with Joey. They didn't just go to restaurants; they went to *the* restaurants. People everywhere seemed to know Joey. They never waited in any lines.

"You want time to think about it?" Joey asked. "You can take time to think about it." Calm and cool. Linda admired that about him. He never seemed to get anxious or ruffled.

Working as a paralegal in a large law firm, Linda thought getting anxious and struggling to keep her cool seemed like part of the written job expectations. Linda knew better than to make a knee-jerk decision. He was offering her time to think about it. She would be foolish not to use that time to sift through the pros and cons. She already knew Joey made her feel special. Not to mention, anywhere they went women stared at him, but he never acknowledged them. Linda knew he saw them, too. He'd have to be blind to miss the blatant ogling. But even though his attention never wavered, she still had to ask herself if she loved him.

He made it sound as if their six-month relationship was a long time to be together, but she knew it wasn't. Linda had been in relationships that lasted years before going sour. Perhaps they had gone sour because they needed to extend to the next level, a greater commitment level, but instead fell flat at a stagnate dead-end.

"Yes, I think I would like to think about it," Linda said finally. She immediately saw the hurt look in his expression, but also noted how quickly he recovered.

"Certainly," Joey said, setting down his napkin. "Care for dessert?"

She no longer felt hungry. The thoughts in her mind spun out of control in a mental whirlwind. "I'm stuffed from the meal. That was fantastic veal."

"What did I tell you? I don't know how they prepare their sauce, but it's something special here," Joey said. He held a finger in the air. A waiter appeared. "I would like a cappuccino. Linda?"

The waiter looked at Linda and she nodded. "Sounds good."

"What's wrong, Linda?" Joey asked. He sounded concerned. "Are you upset?"

"Upset? No. You just invited me to move in with you and now we're going to drink cappuccino. I just feel a bit confused," Linda said, laughing. She did not want Joey to think she was confused in a bad way. She just felt strange going from having to make a serious decision to what she will now drink.

As if reading her mind, he said, "We can talk a little about it now if you'd like. " Joey leaned back so the waiter could remove his empty dinner plate. "Please, Vincent, let Chef Andrea know how much the meal was enjoyed."

"I will, Mr. Viglucci. Thank you." The waiter removed the empty plate from in front of Linda. "Ma'am."

"Thank you." Linda folded her hands in her lap.

Oftentimes Linda felt the way Joey treated people was odd, but more often she thought it odd how people treated Joey. There was a respect thing that always reminded Linda of those old *Godfather* films. People catered to Joey, and he tipped nearly everyone he came in contact with.

Joey ran the family construction company, which was passed down after his father was killed in a freak accident at a construction site nearly ten years ago. She also knew, aside from the strange way Joey's father died that it was hard to find a building in Rochester not built by Viglucci Construction. And although Linda knew the Mafia didn't exist anymore, she felt pretty confident that if investigated, Joey's family tree would branch back to mob ties. That thought bothered her a bit. Every family has a history. Why should she worry that his grandfather and great uncles might have been in the, as she has heard it referred to, Family Business. What mattered was that Joey was not involved in any criminal activity. And he wasn't, as far as she could tell.

"What are you thinking," Joey asked.

Whenever she was silent too long he always wanted to know what she was thinking. He never made the question sound as if he were being nosey. *He always seems to sound sincere*, Linda thought. *He seems like an all around great guy. So why am I having trouble deciding whether or not to live with him?* "I was thinking about us."

"About my proposition?" Joey said coolly.

Maybe she thought that was part of the problem. He was too cool all of the time. In the six months they had been dating she has seen him display three different emotions: cool, horny and tired. Could that be real? Could that be all there was to Joey? If it were, was it really a problem or was it hard to admit that she liked all three images?

Then her thoughts went to the word "proposition." It was close to proposal, but not close enough. Joey made this sound like a business deal. *Would I need to sign a contract*, she wondered. He was forcing her to examine and scrutinize the relationship. "What about my house?"

"You can do with it what you like. Rent it out, or sell it." Joey took a sip from his cup. His little pinkie was raised just enough in the air to give him a literary, artsy-fartsy look. "You can play landlord. You know I own some property and I love being a landlord."

"That's you, Joey. And you don't just own some property, you own most of the double houses in the city," Linda said. "What if I get a poor family, some young couple with a few kids and they have trouble coming up with the rent?"

"There is a term that comes to mind for that kind of situation," Joey said, taking another sip of his cappuccino. "Eviction. You have it as a clause in the contract. You have it say something like, if rent is paid later than 30 days from the day it is due then gather your belongings and pack your bags and start looking for another place." Joey smiled. "I'll let my attorney draw up papers. I'm not good with all that legal mumbo-jumbo."

"You're rotten," Linda said. She knew Joey was kidding around. "I'm serious. Have you ever run into that type of situation?"

"A few times," Joey said.

This was another thing Linda wondered about. Joey rarely talked about his work. Sometimes he would call her from work and they'd meet for lunch. They discussed her job, or she did, anyway, but whenever she asked him about his job, he'd shrug, or vaguely respond with something generic, like how busy he was, or that one guy who's always giving him crap about one thing or another. Expertly, Joey always managed to change the subject, or reroute the conversation back to Linda.

Why am I so critically analyzing everything about this man now? Linda wondered. *It's because Joey is getting serious and wants to move the relationship along,* she tried to tell herself. In a way she was comforted by her ability to think a situation through thoroughly before reacting.

"So what did you do?"

Joey was silent for a moment. He looked uncomfortable. The attention was on him. This was perhaps the most she had ever pressed him about his job before. It seemed oddly clear that he did not like it. "I had to evict them, Linda."

Linda tried not to gasp. She knew her facial expression had to be giving away the shock she felt. "You evicted people before?"

"Only a few times," Joey said. He quickly continued on. "Once around Christmas, this guy and his family were stringing me along. The guy kept telling me he'd pay. I knew he was out of a job. He was working for the city as a pipe fitter. It snowed in early October that year, and there wasn't much work and his unemployment checks were not even a quarter of what he'd been bringing in so he went through those checks buying groceries and stuff. He was three months behind in rent though, you know?"

"Christmastime?" Linda asked. She studied Joey's face. He didn't look upset, and only appeared slightly embarrassed. Having trouble making eye contact, Joey kept looking down at his miniature coffee cup. His finger traced the edge of the saucer. "Joey, you didn't? Did you? How?" Linda asked.

"Look Linda, it's a business," Joey said, his voice strong and commanding. He had no trouble staring at her now, but more than that, he appeared to be staring her down. She felt challenged, but accepted it and did not look away.

"You evicted people at Christmastime, sending a family out into the streets?"

"Linda, I was there, in his house. He had a tree with presents under it. Where was he getting the money for presents, huh?" Joey asked. A new side of him was coming out, his shell, cool and calm, was cracking.

"He had children, Joey? How many?"

"I don't know. Three, four?" Joey said. Linda watched him clench his teeth and grind them, his jaw muscles looked like rippling waves of skin along his cheeks. "Linda, this is crazy. What are we doing here? Huh? Why are we doing this?"

"We're talking Joey. And this is not crazy. I want to know more about this eviction. Why couldn't you give the guy a job with one of your construction crews?" Linda asked. "You're always saying how you don't have enough good employees."

"This guy was a bum, Linda. He was milking the system and getting a free ride at my expense," Joey said. He had started to raise his voice, but brought it back under control. There was something different in those piercing and intense blue eyes that Linda was seeing for the first time. Ice.

Linda could not believe the way the events of the date were unfolding. She suddenly felt as if she might be sharing a meal with a stranger. "At your expense? Joey, it seems like you have more money than anyone else in Rochester," Linda said.

"That has nothing to do with running a business and running it properly," Joey argued. He spoke through clenched teeth, again. He was clearly agitated and perhaps angry. "Linda…"

"Don't you think there has to be some kind of line between running a business and just being human and compassionate toward others?" Linda said.

"Yes. And that was exactly where I drew the line." He spoke in a matter of fact tone. It sounded like he wanted to end the conversation. As far as Linda was concerned, all he accomplished was planting his foot firmly in his mouth.

Linda did not appreciate the way Joey thought he could control the conversation, as if he could just brush aside her concerns. "You know what? I don't agree with what you did. Right now, I'm not too thrilled to be with you. I honestly had no idea you could be so cold."

"Me cold? What about you? You work at a big law firm, surrounded by bloodthirsty, ambulance chasing sharks," Joey said, trying to punch below the belt.

Linda knew the blow stung, but she found it easy to shake off. "The people I work with try to help people. My job is to investigate complaints from people who think big companies aren't treating them properly." Linda's approach to an investigation was to never assume that a company is right, but rather to ensure every complainant receives an impartial and complete review of the situation. "It might sound idealistic…"

Joey sat back in his chair and crossed his arms. "Some speech, Linda. It means nothing to me. To me, what you're saying is that you sold out to the man. You work for some big law firm, representing big companies who concentrate on squashing the little person. Am I close on that one, Lin?"

Those words stung. She said, "You couldn't be any further from the truth!"

How could what she had just said mean nothing to him? Her job was more than a job. It was part of the way in which she defined herself. Linda believed everything she just said. She spent close to sixty hours a week helping those less fortunate. Or was she wrong? Could he have been very close to the truth? Was this fight about the eviction at all? It could be over something more basic. How could she move in with a man she did not love? Maybe that was what was at the heart of the argument. She didn't think she was in love.

All at once, Linda stood up. "You know what? Not only do I *not* want to move in with you, I don't think we should see each other anymore, either."

"Linda, sit down and stop raising your voice." Joey was commanding her to do as he ordered, and she did not like it at all. "Linda, please, sit."

"This side of you, this part of you, it came out of nowhere tonight. I never saw it before," Linda said, shaking her head. She stood rigidly with her hands balled into fists and her arms stiff at her sides. "It's like you are two different people, and I don't like the one I am seeing now."

"Linda, sit down," Joey said. He was trying to smile. It was obvious he did not like the attention Linda was drawing. "Now."

That did it. *Now? Who does he think he is?* Linda wondered. In all her life, she had never done what she was about to do. She picked up her wine and splashed it into Joey's face. "Don't you ever tell me what to do. You don't own me," Linda said in a stern whisper. She had not intended to create such a scene, or any scene for that matter.

As she turned to leave, she felt him grab her arm with a strong hand. He was on his feet, digging his fingers into her flesh. "You're hurting me," she said. As he dug his fingers in he seemed to be squashing the meat under her skin against her bones. She felt hot tears coming, but fought back the urge to cry. "Stop it."

Joey was standing right next to her. His face was in front of hers and the way he looked at her made Linda think that he might be possessed. She was shocked by everything that had taken place, but was most of all taken aback by his exhibition of violence. "Let go of me right now," Linda said, demanding a courage and strength of herself that she did not know existed.

Instinctively, Linda felt eyes on them. Everyone in the restaurant had to be watching them.

"Ma'am, are you all right?" Two guys stood next to Linda. She looked over at them. They were men smaller than Joey, but she respected their desire to help. Joey let go of her arm and hissed. "There's no problem, gentlemen. I was just leaving."

"Good," one of the men said. Linda was not sure which one.

Linda watched Joey throw a large bill on the table. "That should cover the meal and tip. Have a nice, lonely and pathetic life." His sneer reminded Linda of a wolf, a rabid wolf. She almost flinched at his words. Almost. He wasn't about to hurt her, not anymore, not in front of all these people. Not ever.

When Joey Viglucci left the restaurant, the two men helped Linda sit back down. "Are you all right?" they both asked.

"I'm fine." Linda knew she was not fine. Her mind was in a panic mode. The fight, as it replayed itself back in her memory, seemed frivolous and insignificant. Joey was a landlord. He had a job to do and collecting rent was the most essential function of that job. *Why did I let things get out of control like that?* she wondered.

"Do you need anything? A ride home?"

"No. I'm going to call a friend. I appreciate what both of you did. Thank you," Linda said, dismissing her saviors. Did the argument make sense? *Did I pick a fight because I was disappointed when he asked me to move in and not to get married? But if I didn't think I love him, what would have happened if he had asked me to marry him?*

Linda pulled out her cell phone. She hated to call for a ride, but it was that, or pay for a cab. "Patty?" she said when her friend answered. "Are you busy right now?"

Chapter 2
Wednesday, January 15

Linda Genova, an employment law paralegal at Hartzman, Cross, Lacy & Bierman, sat in a chair in Patrick Bierman's office. The firm represented many employers in the area. Linda did more than a fair share of the legwork involved with these employers, whether it is was a workers compensation claim, an unemployment insurance hearing, or a charge filed against a company with either the New York State Division of Human Rights or the Equal Employment Opportunity Commission. Companies appreciated paying fees to cover a competent paralegal, which would work their issues, as opposed to a lawyer whose billable hours were considerably more. As an investigative paralegal, Linda considered herself an asset to the firm. She learned all she could about the employment laws and even provided presentations for an array of supervisory and human resource staffs.

Patrick Bierman had been on the phone, keeping Linda impatiently waiting. When he ended his telephone conversation, he gave Linda a warm smile. "I'm sorry, that was an important call that couldn't keep." He laced his fingers together and set them on his desk. Bierman was just less than six feet tall. Linda guessed he had to be in his late thirties, even though he looked older. His hair was thin and receding, an aerial view of the top of his head resembled a triangular shaped bicycle seat. Though he was not fat, he was clearly out of shape with a soft midsection that jutted out a few inches past his belt buckle. "You have a ten o'clock over at MCT, tomorrow?"

MCT stood for Mason Chemical Technologies, located on State Street for whom the law firm provided advice and counsel on employment matters. It stood in the shadow of Rochester's icon, the Kodak tower.

"Yes, a former employee, Jason Kenmore, filed a discrimination complaint against them," Linda said.

"Alleging?"

"Race, age and retaliation." She could feel her heartbeat increase. She enjoyed her job. She could not help feeling like a private investigator.

With or without merit, it is nothing at all for a current or former employee of a company to go down to Monroe Avenue where the government office is located and file a charge, known as a discrimination complaint. The New York State Human Rights Law includes the provision that a complainant pays nothing to bring a complaint against an employer. Yet it could cost a company thousands if the charge leads to a full-fledged lawsuit. This makes Linda's job even more important—to dispose of as many frivolous complaints in the early stages, so the more serious matters can be addressed. The New York State Division of Human Rights, whose responsibility it is to uphold the NYS Human Rights Law, is impartial and will examine the charge filed by the individual, launching an investigation. The first step is to put the employer on notice that a charge has been filed against them. They give the employer a few weeks to conduct their own internal investigation. Generally this is, or already has been performed by a supervisor and a human resource representative.

"You see any merit to the charge?" Bierman asked

"Yeah. There is some merit, but the issue is complex," Linda said, truthfully. She knew often times, a company is not previously aware or warned that a problem may exist. Regardless, once the company writes a paper stating its position, the investigator at the Division may do further digging, requiring additional information. Eventually the Division will respond to both the employer and the person who filed the charge, either finding probable cause, meaning the company has potentially done something wrong; or a No Probable Cause, dismissing the charges completely. Either way, the person who filed the charge may have the option to appeal the decision through New York State law or pursue the matter in Federal court.

The New York State Human Rights Law was passed in 1945, twenty years before Title VII of the Civil Rights Act of 1964, being one of the first, if not *the first*, state human right laws. When the Division issues a No Probable Cause it isn't likely the person alleging some type of violation of his rights will continue. However, it has happened. Litigation is always a threat. No employer wants to be sued for violating a person's rights. Courts like to make examples of employers caught doing so. Companies try to avoid the adverse publicity at all cost.

"Well," Patrick said calmly. "Let's talk about what's going on. Have you had a chance to look at anything?"

"I received the Jason Kenmore file and some other documents on Monday. I've read through them," Linda said. "Kenmore is an African American and was an employee of MCT for eleven years. Two years ago in September he had been verbally warned about inappropriate behavior. It seems he was harassing a female coworker. The team leader, who was available at the time, never reported it to her supervisor. Then, last summer, he did the same thing with a different female employee. Now the team leader informed the supervisor of both incidents right away. The supervisor, after speaking with Kenmore, wrote him up and put a memo in his file that, no doubt, would influence his year's performance evaluation. However, there was a slight problem. Kenmore claimed that the second woman he'd been allegedly harassing, had been giving it right back to him."

"Okay, I'm with you," Patrick said, seeming to be a bit more interested. "What do we have by way of documentation on this?"

"Some. The memo that Kenmore and the supervisor signed also had a statement attached to it written by the team leader explaining the first and second harassment behavior issues. The woman alleging to have been harassed by Kenmore also signed a statement explaining her actions. She thought by 'giving it back to him,' he would leave her alone," Linda said. "Kenmore says he was treated this way, a memo put in his file, because the woman alleging the harassment is white and does not like black people. He says that the team leader and supervisor do not like black people. That's the race part of it."

"Now, here's why the charge was filed, in my opinion," Linda said. "MCT was in the process of going through a severe restructuring. It put in place a plan to cut its workforce by nearly twenty percent."

"I helped them write that plan," Patrick interrupted. "I'm sorry, continue."

"The employees were inspected in cohort groups and compared against one another. When Jason Kenmore's yearly assessments did not rise to the levels of his peers, perhaps because of what his team leader had input on the documents used for the evaluation, it was decided he would be one of the twenty percent impacted," Linda said.

Patrick said, "So Kenmore went to the State Division and filed his charge. The age and retaliation issues? Kenmore's over forty, so he's in a protected group, right?"

"Exactly. And the retaliation, he says, came when he was terminated and not the woman harassing him," Linda said.

"When did MCT receive the charge?"

"Last week, then they faxed a copy of the charge immediately to me. And as I said, I have Jason Kenmore's personnel file sitting on the center of my desk," Linda said. "Tomorrow morning I will meet with the supervisor and human resource associate assigned to the work group Kenmore came from," Linda said. "The paper is due next Tuesday." Linda needed to investigate the substantive issues of the allegations. This took time. Everything needed to be in order before she could write a paper stating the company's position. Any time she represented a company, whether a charge was filed with the state or the EEOC, out of Buffalo, Linda knew the work would be challenging. She needed to conduct a thorough investigation to decide whether or not the company violated an employee's protected rights. She knew she needed to remain unbiased. Sometimes it was more difficult than it should have been.

"Sounds tight, can you manage it?"

"I think so."

"Good. Why don't we plan to meet some time this week after you get into the investigation and see where we stand?" Patrick said.

Linda thanked him and left the office, closing the attorney's door on her way out. She walked briskly down the hall. Her secretary was not at her desk, so Linda went into her own office and closed the door. It was nine. She had nearly an hour to sort through Kenmore's file before other scheduled meetings occupied the bulk of her day.

A soft knock on the door interrupted her reading. "Oh, come in Patty," Linda said.

Since March of the previous year, Patty Dent had been Linda's secretary, having moved to Rochester from Texas. However, in that short time a strong friendship had formed. As tightly bonded as they were, Patty and Linda were exact opposites. At five ten, Linda was a good five inches taller than Patty. Linda's hair was … to call it dirty blond would be incorrect, but to call it brown would also not accurately describe the color. It was closer to blond than brown. She wore it short, just past the nape of her neck. It curled in, cupping her earlobes while stray strands kept falling in front of her face. Patty, on the other hand, possessed raven black hair, kept it long and sensually straight. They were similar in that they were both slim and in solid physical shape; members at the same gym, it was ritual for them to exercise together on Mondays, Wednesdays and Fridays.

"I have today's mail," Patty said tentatively. She chewed at her lower lip. This was a clear sign to Linda that more was on her friend's mind than the day's mail.

"But that's not it all, is it?" Linda asked.

"No. That's not it."

"Come in then. Close the door," Linda said, reaching for her bottled water.

Patty sat down in one of the two chairs opposite Linda's desk. Linda's office was the largest office occupied by a paralegal in the firm. Linda optioned for the large office when a lawyer retired and the decision was made *not* to hire another, but to instead hire three paralegal employees. Aside from the mahogany desk, four filing cabinets and credenza, there was a large potted plant that was almost five feet tall, a standup lamp, a small, round table with four chairs set around it and two windows providing a wonderful view of the city. The firm rented the top three floors in the Reynolds Arcade building on East Main. The Reynolds Arcade, built in 1828 as a five story architectural masterpiece, was perhaps the finest building in western New York at the time. It was on a tract of land known as Rochesterville. It housed, aside from office space, a post office, barbershop and the first Rochester weather office opened by the U.S. Signal Corps on October 12, 1870. It is now a prestigious landmark. Linda has always loved the building. It possessed an atmosphere of class and elegance that the more modern buildings lacked.

"Are you all right?" Linda asked. The worried look was evident in Patty's facial expression. It was more than the chewing of the lower lip; it was the creased brow and sad eyes, all very uncharacteristic in Patty's usual personality traits. "Is something wrong?"

"With me? No," Patty said. She set the small stack of mail on the edge of Linda's desk in front of the weighted, gold nameplate. "I know you've been busy, but I was worried about the other night, you know, with Joey."

Linda sighed. For a flitting moment Linda almost felt irritated with Patty for bringing him up. After all, she had been burying herself in work all morning long. She knew she was doing everything possible to keep from thinking about Joey. "I'm fine. I'm all right."

"Are you sure, because you didn't seem to feel that way last night," Patty said. "I offered to take you out for ice cream cones and you passed. That is not the Linda I know."

Linda had to admit she'd been down. Reflecting, she wondered if she hadn't overreacted. Joey was a great catch. He liked her enough to want her to move in with him. That was a compliment. Should she have been flattered and jumped at the idea?

"What? What are you thinking," Patty probed, leaning forward.

"Nothing. I guess I was just questioning my behavior. Do you think I overreacted?" Linda asked. Though Patty did little dating, Linda often went to her for advice.

"From what you told me, I gather you were upset that he asked you to move in, and not to get married. Right?" Patty asked.

"Very insightful."

"Then when he started telling you about his work, and you were already a little hurt and upset, you had a hard time accepting the things he was saying," Patty said.

"So you think I overreacted?"

"I didn't say that. Let me ask you this, now that you have had time to think a little, how do you feel knowing Joey had a family removed from one of his many rental properties near Christmastime?" The question was like an arrow re-piercing a wound.

"I hate him for it." The thought of bickering over a few hundred dollars around the holidays sounded just as cruel and ludicrous now as it had the other night. "But did I overreact?"

"Did you throw a glass of wine in his face?"

Linda laughed. "I did, didn't I?"

Patty was laughing but stopped. "He hurt you, didn't he?"

"He hurt me, yes." But did I start the fight because I did not want to move in with him and feared telling him so, she wondered.

"That's not good. It's better that you realize this about him now, before making a decision to move in with him," Patty said.

Linda knew Patty was right. Regardless of what the argument had been over, Joey had physically hurt her. And though it may have been subtle, the other night he had also messed with her mind, playing some kind of mental power game. She did not like that.

"In my opinion, he might be good looking, he might be rich ... okay, no might about it, he is rich and good looking, but as far as personality, he has nothing to offer you. You deserve better than that," Patty said as she stood up. "Besides, the answer is simple. Do you love him?" She waited a beat. When Linda stayed silent, she clucked her tongue against the roof of her mouth. "Settled."

Linda sighed.

"I know you have a ten o'clock meeting at MCT tomorrow, but if you think you're going to wrap up by noon or so, would you want to meet for lunch? My treat."

Linda smiled. "I have no idea how long that meeting might last, but I'll keep the offer in mind. But don't plan to wait around for me."

"I won't. If I don't hear from you by noon, I'll just eat alone." Patty walked over to the door, placed her hand on the knob and looked back at Linda. "You going to be all right?"

"Joey and I were together for several months," Linda said. "He might have turned into a jerk, but he had also been a big part of my life." She thought she might cry and did not want to do so, especially in front of Patty.

"I know what you're saying," Patty said.

Linda did not like this attention. It was too focused on her emotions. As good a friendship as they might have together, Linda did not consider herself an open person. Right now she felt vulnerable and weak and these were two feelings she never wanted to face up to.

"There are thousands of people better suited for you, Linda. When you realize that you've found that special one, you'll understand just how right you were about leaving Joey," Patty said with a smile.

"I hope you're right," Linda said.

"I know I am."

Chapter 3
Wednesday Night

He knew the one thing he hated, regardless of what state he was in, was winter. It was barely seven P.M. and everything around looked gloomy and gray. People, bulked out in heavy clothing, resembled dark colored, earth walking, puffy clouds. Smoke exhaust seemed to stain and harden the snow lining the street curbs. One word came to mind summing up his feelings about the season, *ominous*.

He drove up and down Lyell Avenue, and back and forth past the small church several times before deciding to pull into the tiny parking lot behind the cathedral. There were five other cars in the lot. He parked alongside a car in worse shape than his, rust eating away at the doors and fenders, dents that made him wonder if there had been a car accident, or if a rhinoceros had battered the body at one of those drive-thru zoos.

Getting out of the car at a place like this was never easy. However, sometimes the hardest part was just pulling into the parking lot. With that leg of the journey already completed, it should get easier from this point on. It should, but such was not always the case. He took a deep breath and let out a long desperate sigh.

Two people, huddled close and bundled up warmly, walked past his car. He watched them make their way to the church doors. He continued to watch them enter the sanctuary. The clock on his dash told him it was five minutes to seven. He knew if he waited in the car for three more minutes, he'd never go in. Aside from winter, he hated being late. Normally he was early to everything, other than an event of this type of gathering. If he waited five more minutes he could start his car and drive a few blocks away to his apartment on Avery Street.

It started snowing. Large flakes fell from an invisible, *ominous* sky. The wind, thankfully, was not blowing so the snow fell like feathers, floating in the air and swirling on what currents carried them. Once landing on his windshield, the flakes slid down the warm glass, melting, leaving a wet snail-like trail.

"Forget this," he said, turning his key. The engine coughed and groaned, but refused to start. Relentlessly, he tried and tried again, turning the key and stepping hard on the gas pedal. The clock said two minutes to seven.

When someone knocked on his window, he jumped. Rolling down the window he saw a large black man with a gray streaked beard wearing a Buffalo Bills knit ski hat and fingertip-rotted imitation leather gloves. "Yeah?" he said.

"I think it's flooded," the large man said. "Were you going inside?"

"I was thinking about it."

"Ought to come in out of the cold for a while then. Let the old thing sit for a while. Should start by the time this is over," the man said, rubbing his gloved palms together.

"Yeah," he said. "I guess you're right."

Ray got out of the car and the two of them walked toward the church. The man in the Bills hat moved ahead to pull open the doors as he introduced himself. "Name's Malcolm."

"Raymond. Ray," he said. They shook hands and went into the haven, leaving the cold winter night where it belonged, alone in the ominous outdoors.

* * * * *

A meeting in a church basement on Lyell Avenue, or anywhere else in the city, or anywhere else in the country, for that matter, might be said to look exactly the same. Sure the rooms were different sizes, decorated differently, some damp, others dry, some cinderblock, some paneled. It didn't matter. They were all the same. Coffee urns. Coffeepots. Styrofoam cups. There was a bowl holding tea bags and a cup with stir sticks. You could count on white packets of sugar sharing space with pink packets of Sweet-n-Low, just as much as finding milk in a quart cartoon and a cup with a spoon containing non-dairy cream powder. The choices were the same across the country.

Ray stood next to Malcolm, waiting to fill his cup with coffee.

Malcolm was like a tower at close to six five, a good six inches taller than Ray. Where Malcolm wore a ring of fat around his midsection, Ray was proud of his washboard abs. He worked hard each morning doing two hundred crunch-style sit-ups and an additional two hundred every night. Since he quit drinking, focusing his time and energy on exercising seemed a natural, productive way to keep busy. The results, he'd admit, gave him incentive to stay sober.

Malcolm took a sip. "Strong. The way it should be, I guess."

Ray just nodded. He added three packets of sugar and two teaspoons of powdered cream, stirred it together and sucked on the end of his stir stick. Ray and Malcolm both had tight curly hair. Malcolm's was mostly gray, but in places seemed cotton-ball white. It looked as soft and fluffy. Ray's hair was a Hershey wrapper brown, like his eyes.

"My goodness, man, that coffee or melted caramel you're drinking?" Malcolm asked, showing Ray his cup of black coffee.

"I like it this way. What can I say?" Ray said. He didn't want to say anything. He was appreciative that Malcolm had gotten him out of his car, but he did not plan to make friends here.

An empty coffee can sat on the edge of the table with money inside. Ray dug into his pocket and pulled out a dollar bill. He dropped it into the can and moved away from the table to find an empty folding chair. Without being asked, Malcolm followed and sat in the chair next to him.

"First time here, huh?" Malcolm asked.

The small talk. Ray hated small talk. And the list of things he hated seemed to keep getting longer. Ray looked at some of the others in the room. Only one guy was dressed up, wearing a white collared shirt with a red necktie. The man had loosened the knot and the top button had been undone. There was also a woman—a girl, really—sitting across from him. Ray tried not to stare, but could not help it. She was nursing half a cup of coffee and pathetically staring at the ground. She looked haggard and worn with her greasy blond hair. Her mascara ran in streaks down her cheeks as if she had recently been crying. She could not be more than seventeen years old.

"First time, yeah," Ray said. He took a sip of coffee. Damn, it was strong. He needed a fourth packet of sugar. He was not going to get up, though. There was a line at the coffee table. He didn't want to get up and risk losing his chair. He'd do without the extra sugar.

The room was pretty full, and it was two minutes past seven. He would not enter a movie late, even if only coming attractions were playing. He hated when other people did not respect time the way he did. Add it to the list. "Where's the person running the show?"

With a smile, Malcolm stood up. "Hello, everyone. My name is Malcolm and I'm an alcoholic."

"Hello Malcolm," everyone said together.

Malcolm moved past where Ray was sitting to the front of the room. He took off his coat and hat and gloves and set them on a folding chair. He rubbed his hands together, cupped them, and blew into his palms. "It's a cold one tonight. I'm glad to see so many people here. Shall we get this meeting underway?"

Most people just nodded. Ray watched everyone. He watched Malcolm intently.

"I started drinking when I was eleven," Malcolm began. He tucked his hands into his pockets and his shoulders were slouching forward while he spoke. "Why? I don't know, really. It was fun. We'd be at a friend's house and his parents would be out for the night and we'd raid the liquor cabinet. Wild Turkey and Southern Comfort, beer, wine, whatever was there, we'd drink it. Taking sips from this bottle and that one. Talk about your mixed drinks!" Malcolm said, getting a laugh from those listening. "We did this nearly every weekend. Sometimes during the week, too. And during the summer, my friend's parents went to work and left him home alone. Let me tell you—I never left him alone. No sir.

"Things got bad, though, when I was in high school. I began suspecting I had a problem when I couldn't make it through a full day of classes. Not without sneaking off to the boy's room for a swig of vodka, if you know what I mean. We all know how difficult it was supposed to be to smell vodka on someone's breath. So for those of us in school—or later in life, like for me at work—vodka was my drink. I downed it straight, or with orange juice. I used to drink it in my office, at my desk. I thought no one would think it odd if I had a large glass of orange juice on my desk. Who's gonna know it's a screwdriver, right? Forget the fact that vodka was not supposed to be on your breath after drinking it. Forget the fact that no one would find it funny to see a grown man drinking a glass of orange juice in his office after lunch. So you know who I was fooling? Nobody! Teachers, bosses, secretaries, classmates … maybe they couldn't smell the alcohol on my breath, and they saw the orange juice and thought it odd …but guess what? When I was stumbling down the halls and my speech was slurred, they knew what was going on. I was fooling nobody. Everybody knew I was drunk. It was so damned obvious to everyone . . . everyone, that is, but me," Malcolm said.

"Looking back on it, I had to look so stupid trying to write a math problem on the chalk board, or explaining something during a meeting to a room full of important business people. I had a good job too, damn it. A man, a black man like myself, with just a high school diploma. I was damned lucky to have the job I had. I wore a shirt and tie to work. I had an office with a window. I had a secretary," Malcolm said, turning very emotional all of a sudden. "I had a family," in a whisper Malcolm said. "A family."

Malcolm took a moment to regain composure, but did nothing to wipe away the tears that had rolled down his cheeks. He took a deep breath. "But it has been almost five years, it has been fifty-six months, since I've had a drink."

Someone yelled out, "Yeah, man!"

People clapped.

"Already, I'm a better person because of it." Malcolm did not mention if he was able to patch things up with his family. Ray assumed this not to be the case. Otherwise, he guessed, Malcolm would have said as much.

Malcolm sat back down. The floor was open. For a moment, no one said a thing.

Ray did not say a word at meetings. He sat. He listened. He pictured himself standing up and introducing himself. He imagined telling people about the job he'd start in the morning, but opening himself up and communicating was never easy for him. He was a very private person, lonely and private. *My name's Ray and I'm an alcoholic. Like Malcolm, I started drinking when I was young, but not before I was a teenager. It was in high school. I'm thirty now, and in fourteen years I have completely ruined my life. But I don't want to dwell on that. Instead, I want to tell everybody; tomorrow morning I start a new job. I've been sober for nearly three months.* There was a chip for each month of sobriety in Ray's pocket. He carried them everywhere.

After an hour and a half of listening to relatively the same story with different characters, told time and time again, the meeting was brought to a close. Ray wished he had stood up and talked. He knew when he left he would feel depressed for having missed an opportunity to share his story. He had always been told that talking about a problem helps. It might be true, but it didn't matter. Again, he kept his thoughts, his feelings, his life, private, even after knowing and seeing how destructive such behavior can be.

Malcolm stood up again and brought the meeting to an official end. As a group they recited the Serenity Prayer. Ray closed his eyes and recited the meaningful words with the others.

God, grant me the serenity to accept the things I cannot change,
Courage to change the things I can,
And Wisdom to know the difference.
Living one day at a time,
Enjoying one moment at a time,
Accepting hardship as the pathway to peace.
Taking, as He did, this sinful world as it is, not as I would have it.
Trusting that He will make all things right if I surrender to His will.
That I may be reasonably happy in this life,
And supremely happy with Him forever in the next.
Amen.

Ray couldn't put his finger on it, but there was something about the Serenity Prayer that he truly could relate to. It made sense to him. It was one of the few things in his life at the moment that did make sense to him.

There are many theories as to how this prayer came into existence. Some believe it had been written by Dr. Reinhold Niebuhr. Others think Neibuhr credited the prayer's writing to an 18th century theologian named Friedrich Oetinger. Regardless, one way or another, the co-founder of Alcoholics Anonymous, Bill Wilson, wound up using the Serenity Prayer because it seemed like such a perfect fit to sum up his efforts.

It had been at Ray's third meetings that he had been given a laminated business card with the prayer printed on one side and the name and phone number of the man who'd given him the card on the opposite side. "You ever want to call me, you call me," the man had told him. Unfortunately, that man had died in a drunk driving accident the following week. The ironic thing about the tragedy was that Ray's friend had been sober and the driver of the vehicle that struck him had been the one who had been drinking.

Everyone pitched in, folding up chairs and putting away the coffee supplies, Ray was ready to head home. On his way to the door he was not surprised to feel a hand on his shoulder. Ray was even less surprised to see Malcolm smiling at him. "Feel like going for coffee? Stuff here is brutal."

"Normally, I'd say yes. I've got to be up early tomorrow morning and I get the feeling it isn't going to be easy falling asleep," Ray said. "Maybe next time."

"We meet Wednesdays and Fridays here. Same time."

"I'll keep that in mind." Ray zipped up his coat. "Have a good night."

"You, too man. One good night at a time," Malcolm said.

Ray went out into the cold night alone. The wind howled like a mob of spirited ghosts, flying lifelessly through the city, scaring and painting the town, not red, but white. Snow white. And aside from the screaming of the blowing wind, it had a bite to it. Any exposed flesh would feel the burn of the cold. As if he might suffer frostbite from immediate exposure, Ray jogged toward his car, climbed in and slammed the door shut. It was cold in the car, but he was safe from the winter teeth of the relentless, harsh wind.

"Now start for me, baby. Start," Ray said to his steering wheel as he inserted his key into the ignition. "Come on."

He turned the key and his piece of junk automobile came to life. "That's a girl. That's my girl. I'm gonna reward you when I get my first paycheck. You'll see. Nothing but some high octane gas for you." Laughing, Ray started to pull out of the parking lot. He stopped laughing when he saw Malcolm leave the church, turning up his coat collar to brace against the evil night elements.

Going for coffee might not have been so bad. "But I've got to get home to sleep," Ray said, as anxious about starting his new job as a child the night before the first day of school.

Chapter 4

Linda thought her legs might explode. Her ass felt numb. Her lungs kept her breathing, despite feeling as if they might combust and burst into flames. She ignored the sweat dripping down her forehead and streaking down her cheeks. She kept her hands fisted and her attention focused. Though she could not see Patty on her right side, she knew her friend would be experiencing the same murderous torture.

Ignoring the pain, thinking of how great she would look in that new dress she bought last weekend at Greece Ridge Mall, Linda pumped her legs a little harder, walking on the treadmill a little faster. Her leg muscles felt like tightly coiled steel springs. One twist more and it felt like every tone muscle in her leg would unwind and shred and leave her crumbled on the floor unable to walk. But still she pressed on walking for another full five minutes before she finally lowered the treadmill speed and slowed the uphill climb, to a slow steady walk while she cooled down.

"I've been waiting for you to do that," Patty said, huffing and puffing, seriously winded from the intense workout. "I didn't want to be first."

The gym where they exercised was located at the Elm Ridge Center, off West Ridge Road in Greece and was exclusively for women. Linda and Patty had both worked out at places where men and women were members and detested the environment for multiple reasons. They were there to work on their body, not have it ogled while they lay on their back doing bench presses. Working out was not easy. It was hard work. There was sweat and grunting involved. Linda felt if there were a guy there who might appear interesting, she did not want him to see her looking the way she normally looked after a solid workout.

Linda smiled. "A little competitive are we?"

"No. A *lot* competitive," Patty said. "Let's go get some water.

I'm so thirsty."

Linda used her hand towel to absorb the sweat off her face, neck and arms. "We did good today."

"Real good. Look how late it is," Patty said. "Think you worked us so hard to get out some aggressions?"

"Worked *us* so hard? You could have stopped any time you wanted," Linda said as they approached the juice bar. She needed a drink before showering, a chance to just unwind and let her muscles cool off. "Two waters," she told the young lady dressed in a navy blue and white striped exercise suit, working behind the bar.

"Quit? Never," Patty said, finally seeming to catch her breath. "I liked how we worked out today. I'm going to pay for it in the morning, though. My legs feel three feet thick."

"Mine, too," Linda said, sitting on a barstool. She rubbed her thigh. "I already ache." For the few hours while they worked out Linda was able to escape from the pressures of work and her personal life. She was able to focus on toning the muscles in her body and burning calories to keep the fat and flab away from under her arms. She kept her belly slim and cut. Her legs and butt were like iron and she was proud of them. She felt good and invigorated.

Patty paid for the waters. It was her turn, so Linda did not protest.

"Oh boy," Patty said, suddenly, jumping up to sit on the barstool next to Linda.

"What?" Linda asked.

"Don't look now, but…"

"Linda, we need to talk," a male voice suddenly said.

Linda turned to see Joey Viglucci standing behind them. "You're not supposed to be here. Men are not allowed," Linda said. He wore a pair of pointed toe cowboy boots, tight blue jeans, a too tight black T-shirt with the muscles in his chest and abdomen visible and rippling beneath the thin cotton fabric, and an ankle length, black trench coat. Passively, his arms lay limp by his sides. Though it was only the other day, he looked as if he had been going through hell since the breakup.

"Joey, I'm not sure there is anything for us to talk about," Linda said. She had been feeling good a moment ago, and was disappointed how quickly that mood changed. She was also annoyed that he had invaded her safe haven so easily. She had never seen any men at the juice bar, and assumed they were somehow kept out. Obviously, she was wrong.

"Excuse me," Patty said, getting off the barstool with her bottled water. "I'm going to shower."

Linda wanted to tell Patty to stay. There was no reason Joey should ruin their night out. "I think you should go," Linda told him.

"Listen Linda, you let everything spiral out of proportion the other night, you know? Maybe you were tired, or you had a bad day at work, but I'm not mad at you. It was just a little..."

"You're not mad at *me*?" Linda said. "I don't believe you. You have no reason to be mad at me and I resent what you just implied!"

"Honey, dear, you're the one who dumped your drink on me, angel face," Joey said. He looked past Linda, toward the barmaid. "Does it even look like this conversation concerns you?"

"You leave her alone, Joey. And I want you to leave," Linda said with more force this time. "I really believe there is nothing between us."

"See, but you're wrong. Whatever happened the other night, I want to let it go. We can start all over, if you'd like. I'll even apologize," Joey said, earnestly.

"Apologize? Why would you apologize?" Linda asked. She anticipated the answer.

"Because you want me to," he said.

"But do you know why? What is it you'd be sorry for?" Linda questioned Joey.

"I have no idea, but if it makes you happy to hear me say I'm sorry and it will get us back together, then I am sorry. I am and it will never happen again," Joey said. He sounded like he was begging, only seconds from getting down on his knees.

"How can you tell me it will never happen again if you're apologizing without knowing what it is you did wrong?" Linda asked. She felt more frustrated and aggravated with every passing second.

"How am I supposed to know? This is your game, your rules. I'm trying to learn. You don't want me catching on. I'm ready to do whatever you ask, whether I know why I'm doing it, or not. But you're not willing to even give me a chance, are you? You know what? You think you're some quick talking, shyster lawyer, but you're not. You're a paralegal, a glorified secretary really," Joey

40

said, his words loaded with venom.

Linda let the insult pass. It didn't matter what he thought of her job, regardless of how wrong he was. His perception couldn't be any further from the truth. A glorified secretary! That would be like calling a nurse a glorified maid. Damn him. Damn it. *Damn him!* "You just helped me make my decision. Thank you," Linda said.

"Good," Joey said, relaxing. "Good, great. Okay. What do you say we run and get a pizza or something? I haven't really eaten anything yet today, except for lunch. I had a few burgers."

Linda just laughed. She glanced at the barmaid stocking juice bottles into a cooler, obviously listening. "You don't get it. We are through. It's over. Now please, I'm asking you to leave."

"You still want me to leave?" Joey asked, reminding Linda of a tiger the way he was baring his teeth, his upper lip curled into a snarl. He started pacing back and forth in a small area, as if trapped behind a barred cage, except there was no cage. "You're not staying here. You're coming with me."

When Joey reached out and grabbed her arm, Linda thought she'd shrug his hand off and walk away. His hand was like a vise and it held her wrist in a death grip that she could not shake out of. His fingers were like teeth. "You're hurting me."

The barmaid flinched, her hands disappearing under the countertop.

"I'd never hurt you, Linda, and you know that," Joey said, visibly seething.

But he was hurting her. The color had disappeared in the flesh where he tightly held onto her. "Let me go," Linda tried, her heartbeat racing. She actually felt scared. She had never been in an abusive relationship. She knew she was lucky to be getting out of this one, and was thankful she had not decided to move in with him. However, even though she was ending it between them, or was desperately trying to, he was not respecting her decision. This realization frightened her. She did not want him hounding and harassing her. "Joey, damn you, let me go," she said, unable to control her emotions. She began to cry and hated Joey for making her do so. She closed her eyes. Joey was squeezing her wrists so tightly she actually feared her bones might crumble. "Let me go," she managed to say again.

"Let her go," a man's voice said.

The grip on Linda's wrist loosened, briefly, and she opened her eyes to see Matthew. He was the gym's owner, and a big man! If he had been green, you might mistake him for The Incredible Hulk. Linda was embarrassed to have Matt see her crying, but knew the barmaid must have pressed a panic button, hidden somewhere under the counter. At the same time she was thankful, she was humiliated.

"You know what, this don't concern you," Joey said.

Matt was a black belt, trophy-winning karate expert. The trophies were on display in the front of the gym, along with pictures of Matt in his white uniform, the black belt knotted around his waist— which Joey must not have noticed on his way in, or he might have recognized the potential for danger.

"See, but it does," Matt said placing a large, thick hand on Joey's shoulder. Joey let go of Linda and spun around to face Matt. "I don't want any trouble with you. I would just like for you to apologize to Ms. Genova and then leave my place, and never come near it again."

"You don't want any trouble with me? Then you should have thought about that before you stuck your crooked nose into our business," Joey said. He sounded like an Italian in some Mafia movie. It was a thick slang-sounding accent that Linda knew was faked because normally, Joey did not talk or sound that way.

Linda sensed the punch before it was thrown, but so did Matt. He caught Joey's arm, moving his head out of the way. He twisted Joey's arm around to his back and easily pinned Joey to the countertop. Like a lever, he lifted the arm up so Joey's hand moved closer to the back of his head.

Joey moaned in pain. "You're going to break it, freak!"

"I would like you to apologize to Ms. Genova and then leave my establishment. Do you understand?"

Joey did not reply. He just stared at Linda. She wanted to look away, but couldn't. Joey's face was pressed hard against the counter, drool oozed out of his mouth. She hated this, wanted it all to end. Still crying, she begged Matt to stop.

"I want him to say he's sorry," Matt said. He applied more pressure to Joey's restrained arm. "Say it!"

"Sorry. I'm sorry. Okay, now get off me," Joey said, trying to yell, trying to sound cool, tough and in control, despite his position. Did he know his face was turnip-red?

Matt let go of Joey's arm and took two quick steps back. He did not look afraid, he looked ready. And when Joey swung at Matt again, Matt sidestepped the punch and delivered three of his own, fast and hard. The first hit Joey square in the nose. The second and third crashed into Joey's stomach, doubling him over. Matt grabbed onto Joey and led him away from the juice bar toward the front of the gym.

"I'm so sorry," the barmaid said. "I'm so sorry."

Linda wanted to thank the barmaid for calling Matt. She wanted to apologize for everything that just happened, but she was unable to talk. Sobbing, she rested her elbows on the counter and buried her face in her hands.

When Matt returned, Linda had fought to regain her composure. He did not deserve to see her this way. No one did. She wanted to go home and be alone, she felt so ashamed. "Thank you, Matt," she said, surprised at how difficult it was to speak. She decided to keep silent. She did not need to start crying all over again.

"It's okay, Linda. You okay?" Matt asked. For a man so large, you wouldn't expect him to have such a gentle sounding voice. He was married though. Linda realized it just might be possible that all the good ones were.

"I'm okay."

"Sure?"

"Yeah, I'm all right," Linda said, and was finally able to thank the woman behind the counter. Matt left and Linda excused herself.

In the locker room, Linda found Patty sitting on a bench between rows of lockers tying her laces. Her hair was wet. She had a gym towel draped around her neck. She looked up and smiled. "Jerk-face gone?" Patty asked.

Linda shrugged and started crying. It did not take much coaxing. Linda told Patty what had transpired. Patty did not say anything. She just listened. When Linda was done, Patty nodded her head and held out her arms.

* * * * *

"Way I see it, the guy's an idiot and finally out of your life," Patty said as the two left the gym and headed out to the parking lot.

Cars were everywhere. It might be late, but the plaza did wonderful business nearly every night of the week. It was packed full with stores selling shoes, party supplies, knickknacks and cards, as well as hair salons, a car rental place, a few restaurants and both ends of the mall sidewalk were home to chain stores.

The lot was well lit. Linda did not want Patty to notice how uneasy she felt. Joey's violent behavior unsettled her. She never knew him to be that way. For the six months they had been dating, he had completely fooled her. *Shame on me*, she thought.

They walked carefully, using each other for support. Slush covered the lot and patches of slippery black ice hid under some of it, like waiting mines. Linda looked at the sky and saw that the moon was blanketed behind a spread of clouds. Only a month into winter and already she missed seeing colors, like green grass, blue and white skies and leaves on the trees. Everything looked drab and colorless, especially with Christmas being over and no one using the colorful lights strung around their homes anymore. She missed seeing the lights.

"At least that part of my life is over," Linda said in a non-convincing way.

"It's over," Patty said. "I just wish I could have seen Matt beat him up."

Linda stopped walking. She did not like seeing Patty getting pleasure out of this. "You would not have liked it. I hate fighting. I hate it."

Patty shrugged. "I'm not so sure. I think I would have liked seeing it."

"Well, it was awful," Linda said, walking again. "I hope I never have to see anything like that again."

Patty did not respond. Instead she walked a little faster. She stopped walking when she reached Linda's car and gasped. "That bastard!"

"What?" Linda asked, but knew who Patty was talking about when she saw the flat tire. "Maybe it wasn't him."

"Why are you sticking up for him? Don't you think it's a little odd, your ex-boyfriend gets beat up because of you and then you have a flat tire? Doesn't that seem a little too coincidental?" Patty sounded angry and upset.

"Why are you yelling at me?" Linda shouted back. "And what do you mean Joey got beat up because of me?"

"That's not what I meant," Patty said.

"It's what you said," Linda added.

"I'm looking at it the way Joey might look at it," Patty explained.

It made sense. Linda let her shoulders droop. She wanted to sit down in the middle of the parking lot and just cry. This was too much. When would the day end? "How much longer will today last," Linda said out loud, but to no one.

"What?"

"I want to go home," Linda said.

"But your car. I think we should call the police."

"I don't want to call the police, I want to go home," Linda said, sure she would collapse soon. She did not want to be in the middle of a parking lot on a cold wintry night.

"What are you talking about? You have to call the police," Patty insisted. She removed a phone from her purse and dialed before handing it over to Linda. "Tell the police."

Linda did not want the phone despite knowing Patty was right. Reluctantly she took the phone and waited for someone to answer. "Yes. I have reason to believe someone cut the tire on my car." Linda told the police operator where she was and gave the station some information. She was told an officer would be there within the next fifteen minutes. Linda hung up and used Patty's phone to call triple A.

Handing back the phone, Linda said, "You know, you can go. You don't have to stay."

"I know I don't," Patty said. "I want to stay."

"At least it's not snowing," Linda said, hugging herself.

As if on cue, it started snowing. "Too perfect," Patty said.

Laughing, the ladies waited nearly an hour before a police officer arrived.

Chapter 5
Thursday, January 16

Ray Telfer removed and unfolded a scrap of paper from his pocket. It told him that at nine, he was supposed to meet with Barbara Cunningham, the human resources liaison at Hartzman, Cross, Lacy & Bierman. She was one of the people he interviewed with last week. Ray walked the length of the long foyer to the bank of elevators. The red arrow pointing up was already lit. People huddled around the sets of doors, patiently waiting for the next available car. He watched as impatient people repeatedly pushed the button, as if it would make the elevator arrive any sooner. Ray knew that, like vultures, they'd pounce, every person for themselves, as soon as the doors to an elevator opened.

Glad he'd worn dress slacks and a tie, Ray did not feel nearly as out of place as he'd thought he would. However, his ski jacket, all puffy and silky looking, did not resemble the cashmere coats of the others around him. Feeling a little self-conscious, Ray looked around casually, trying to see if people might be sizing him up. He felt only a little worse when he realized no one was even looking at him.

An elevator came, and the doors opened. The car was empty, but not for long. As Ray had suspected, people pushed into the car as if it were the last one for the day and anyone not on it would be forced to use the stairs. Ray stood back, smiling to himself.

Ray took the next elevator to the first of the three stories owned by the law firm. Stepping off the elevator, he was greeted by the woman sitting behind the front desk. Smiling, she said hello.

"Good morning. I'm supposed to meet … I'm sorry, my name is, I'm Ray Telfer. Raymond Telfer," Ray said. He felt his cheeks and earlobes beginning to feel hot. He hoped he wasn't turning red. *Calm down*, he told himself. *Take a deep breath.* "I'm sorry. I'm supposed to see a Ms. Cunningham. Barbara Cunningham."

The lady stood up. "You must be our new server administrator?"

"That's right," Ray said. Every muscle in his stomach seemed to be churning and grinding against everything else in his stomach. He thought he might throw up. Ray concentrated on not fidgeting. He shrugged out of his ski jacket and held it with a hooked finger by the collar. When he had interviewed, he was given a tour. At this point, it didn't matter. None of it looked familiar. He felt as if he were lost in a maze.

"Barbara will be right with you. If you'd like, you can hang your things in there," the woman said pointing to a closet. "And there is coffee and doughnuts just around the corner. I'll have Barbara look for you in there."

Ray nodded and smiled. "Thank you. Thanks," he said, feeling a little relieved. If everyone at this law office was as friendly, Ray did not think he'd have a problem adjusting. For some reason he kept thinking of lawyers, paralegals and legal secretaries as a higher class of people. He knew they were not. They just had jobs revolving around things Ray knew little about. He was sure he would feel the same way working for doctors, but perhaps not as strongly. Maybe because doctors chose a profession where they could actually help other people. But then he remembered an old saying. *Nobody likes a lawyer, until they need one.* As he hung up his jacket and went around the corner for a cup of coffee, he wondered if there might be a word for his phobia of attorneys. *Largebillsaphobia?*

Ray entered a small room with a few round tables and cafeteria chairs, a microwave, a refrigerator, a television set, and a small coffeepot tucked into the corner of the counter. He pulled a Styrofoam cup off a stack and filled it with coffee. Stirring in cream and sugar, Ray wondered what he should do. He could sit, but that seemed awkward. He did not want to look bored sitting in a chair waiting for his contact to arrive. Instead he walked over to a corkboard mounted on a wall. The board was full of photos from a holiday party. A man dressed as Santa Claus, the beard pulled down under his chin, managed to find his way into most of the pictures. Ray found himself smiling. He remembered the job he had had before leaving for Rochester. It had been a fat and happy advertising firm. There were challenging times, but for the most part, much like this law office, everyone seemed to get along and have a good time working together.

"Mr. Telfer?" A woman's voice asked.

Startled, Ray spun around spilling hot coffee onto his shirt. The unexpected burn caught Ray off guard and he jumped back a step, holding the coffee cup away from his body. The coffee sloshed around the rim of the cup and splashed out, burning Ray's hand. He set the cup down, went to wipe his hand on his pants, but stopped himself. "I'm sorry, sorry," he said, his eyes scanning the countertop for a napkin or paper towel.

"No, I'm sorry. I didn't mean to startle you like that," the woman said, making her way toward the counter.

The woman unrolled a few sheets of paper toweling and handed them to Ray. "Thank you," he said. "First day jitters, I guess."

"Are you all right? Did you get burned?" she asked.

"Not really. It was hot, but I … I'm not burned, no." Ray felt like an idiot. His shirt had a large, upside-down tear drop shaped coffee stain. His tie looked like it might be ruined. There were even coffee spots on his slacks.

"We've all been there," the woman said, graciously. Ray seriously doubted it. He'd love to meet the person with a life similar to his. "I'm Barbara Cunningham."

They shook hands.

"What's that old commercial for that shampoo? You only get one chance to make a first impression?" Ray said. "How am I doing so far?"

Barbara smiled. "You're doing fine. This is nothing. If you want, take a few minutes and go into the men's room, or are you all right?"

"Is there a hand dryer in there?"

"There is."

"Okay. That sounds great."

"Let me show you where my office is. When you're all set, you can come right there," Barbara said. As she led him down the center corridor, Ray could not have felt more embarrassed. It seemed like one of the longest walks of his life. Of course, everyone wanted a good look at the new guy. People seemed to stop Barbara for any reason they could think of, just for an opportunity to stare. Barbara did a wonderful job introducing Ray and explaining about the incident with the coffee. Ray shook hands and smiled helplessly like the village idiot.

Once in the men's room, Ray unraveled. "Damn it, damn it. What a jerk I am. What a clumsy jerk." He looked at himself in the mirror. The stain was larger than he'd thought. The coffee was working its way through the fabric of his shirt, spreading in mass like a hungry mold on cheese. "Don't you just look like a big dummy."

Ray smiled at his reflection. He thought, *At least my day can't get any worse than this.* As he pulled his shirt out of his waistband and stuck the coffee-wet part under the air dryer, a toilet flushed behind one of the closed stall doors. The stall door opened. A man in a three-piece suit emerged, eyeing Ray rather suspiciously.

Great. Ray thought, *just great.*

Chapter 6

Linda gathered the charge file and her portfolio; made sure she had a pen, her personal calendar and cell phone, then tucked everything into her briefcase. She removed a palm-sized mirror from a desk drawer and checked her teeth for seeds from the morning's bagel. She ran her tongue over her teeth, put the mirror away and lifted her keys off a hook from the inside corner of her desk. Checking her watch, she knew she had time before her meeting with MCT, but the weather made her apprehensive. If traffic or the roads were bad, she did not want to be running behind.

Leaving her office, Linda stopped at Patty's desk and watched as her secretary retyped a brief for the Unemployment Insurance Appeal Board. "Patty, I'm sorry. Excuse me?" Linda said, hating to interrupt.

Patty stopped typing and turned around. "Yes, Linda? Leaving for your meeting at MCT?"

"Yes. That's where I'm heading now. I just wanted to let you know, in case anyone was looking for me," Linda said. She was aware of an aching in her arm. Her briefcase felt like it might be filled with led bricks. The hardcore workout from the other night was taking its toll. "You still want to meet for lunch?"

"Sure," Patty said. "Want to meet at Empire Brewery, on State?"

The restaurant was walking distance from MCT and across from Kodak Office and Frontier Field. Empire did a nice business, in part because of its prime location. At lunchtime, the place was usually packed with business suits. During the summer and fall, after a Red Wings baseball or Knighthawks lacrosse game, people walking through the parking lot stopped for a beer or a meal. Empire was known for its onsite microbrewery and the place offered a varied selection of fine micro-brewed beers. What's more, the prices were good, the food excellent and the staff responsive and enthusiastic. "Sounds good. We can say noon, but what if I'm late?"

"I'll eat," Patty said, smiling.

"Call for reservations?"

"You got it," Patty said.

Linda went to the elevator bank, left the building, walked through the parking garage and climbed into her car. She started the engine and turned the heater on as high as it would go. At first it insisted on blowing out cold air, but it eventually turned warmer.

Traffic was light and the drive to MCT took less than ten minutes. It was 9:40 when she arrived in the MCT parking lot, directly across the street from Empire Brewery. She gathered her things and braced herself for the cold as she trekked across the parking lot and State Street and into the front lobby of MCT.

There was a security guard sitting like a receptionist behind a counter. "Good morning, ma'am."

"Hello," Linda said. "I have a ten o'clock meeting with Jolene Davids, in human resources, and Nicole Thomas, a MCT manager?"

"And your name?" the guard grunted. She told him. She noticed corners of a newspaper and knew she had obviously caught him off guard. "You can have a seat. Someone will be down to get you." He handed her a Visitor ID Badge.

"Pretty tight security," she said.

"It's a chemical plant," he said. "Many of the chemicals used, and the waste of the chemicals used, are highly dangerous, toxic. No one can just walk in to the plant. And if you're walking around the plant as an employee or as a visitor you need to wear that ID where it's visible." He went back to his paper.

It took only a few minutes before a buzzer sounded and the main door leading into the plant opened. Linda stood up, recognizing Jolene Davids. "I'm a little early," Linda said. "The roads weren't as bad as I'd expected."

"Well, that's good to hear," Jolene said. Like Linda, she was tall, thin and athletic looking. Her long straight hair was the color of high polished mahogany wood. Large, round eyes, perfect white teeth, full lips and not a day over twenty-seven. Linda felt envious.

"And we'll be meeting with Nicole Thomas?"

"She's in a conference room waiting for us." Jolene handed

Linda a pair of thick, clear, plastic safety glasses. "You'll need to wear these." Jolene's pair dangled around the front of her neck. She put hers on as well and held open the door. "After you."

Linda entered the plant. Her nostrils were assaulted by the pungent odor of burning plastic. "Do you ever get use to that smell?"

"Yes, you do," Jolene said, laughing. "You must, because either I'm use to it, or I just can't smell anything anymore."

Linda smiled, but knew Jolene was being serious. She could not imagine coming here to work every day, entering an environment where she knew her senses would be getting fried.

* * * * *

The conference room was plain and nondescript. The bare walls were eggshell white. A four-foot table with six chairs around it sat in the center of the room. Nicole Thomas sat in one of the chairs flipping through documents in a thick manila file and looked up from the papers as Linda and Jolene entered the room.

Linda and Nicole shook hands. "The two of you look like you might be related," Linda said. Nicole resembled Jolene with long straight and shiny brown hair, large round eyes and full lips.

Nicole smiled. "We're sisters."

"That explains it," Linda said. Everyone sat down around the table, making small talk as they got comfortable. Linda hoisted the charge book Patty had created for her. It was a black, three-ring binder, divided into multiple sections for easy reference. She opened to the charge received from the Division of Human Rights. "Shall we get started?"

"Linda, this is Jason Kenmore," Nicole said, passing Kenmore's employee ID badge to her. "He was required to return this when he was laid off."

Linda examined the man's face. Prominent features. Short, black, curly hair, slight graying around the temples. A thin, gray mustache. Dark eyes like a cup of strong coffee. A distinguished, nice looking man. "Can I get a copy of this?"

"You can have it. We have his picture on a security server," Jolene said.

Linda thanked Jolene. "Okay, Nicole, what is your position with MCT?"

"I'm a manager for the research labs. I've been with the company six years, hired right out of college with degrees in chemical engineering and business management," Nicole said, proudly.

"And Jason Kenmore worked for you?"

"Yes. He did not report directly to me. He worked under a team leader, who reported to a supervisor, who reported to me."

"How many supervisors report to you?" Linda asked, pen poised, ready to continue writing.

"Three. An A shift, a B shift, and a C shift supervisor. Then each supervisor has a team leader on the crew. Each crew has roughly twenty additional employees. So, roughly, sixty-six employees report to me all together," Nicole explained. She was an animated speaker, waving her hands around while she talked.

"And Kenmore's team leader?" Linda asked.

"Roger Gaston," Jolene said.

Linda wrote it down.

"So how does it look?" Nicole asked.

"We have some room to work here. Why don't we start at the beginning and see if we can reconstruct everything that took place and develop some kind of a chronology of events?" Linda suggested. She started scribbling notes onto her yellow legal pad. "Let's start with you, Nicole. Have there ever been any other complaints by any other employees made to you suggesting a problem with Kenmore?"

Chapter 7

Linda did everything possible not to look at her watch though she knew it had to be close to noon. The sisters, Nicole and Jolene, talked in great detail, describing the way the company's lay-off process worked. Her stomach kept threatening to rumble with hunger pains. She knew Patty would be sitting at a table, patiently waiting.

"The policy of ranking employees for the purpose of a downsizing has been in place for close to eight years. The attorney you work for, Beamen?" Nicole asked.

"Bierman. Patrick Bierman," Jolene corrected. "He spent a lot of time here helping us write a business plan prior to any ranking. See, this way it's fair. We set up a process before we even look at the employees. First, as a business, we needed to come up with the total number of employees we needed to let go. Then we offered a retirement package to any and all retirement eligible employees," Jolene said. "Once those who were offered a package made a decision, then we knew how many employees would need to be involuntarily separated from the company."

Linda took notes. She was very familiar with the way the plan worked. She had reviewed drafts of the procedure with Bierman. However, she wanted to make sure those implementing the plan had as solid an understanding of how things were supposed to work. "After those retirement eligible people decided to retire, how many more employees would be involuntarily impacted?"

Jolene, without looking at her notes, said, "One hundred and three."

Linda pursed her lips. She knew MCT was not a large operation. "How many employees in the company, total?"

"About seventeen hundred."

"Lost a lot of people," Linda said.

"We will more than likely lose more," Jolene said. "With Kodak moving away from film and more and more into digital, we are slowly losing one of our biggest customers. Not to mention, they keep reducing their workforce size and shutting down departments, and that affects us as well as the rest of the community."

"So, what criteria did you use to rank employees against each other?" Linda asked.

"We have three things we look at. A person's performance ratings, attendance records and skills set," Jolene explained counting on her fingertips. "And that is something I think is important to mention about Jason."

"What's that?" Linda asked.

"Jason's performance," Nicole said. "Well, obviously he was in the process of progressive counseling for his behavior issues, but also for performance. In his file you see the memo and documents about the harassment issue, but you'll also note some on the fact that the quality and quantity of his work is consistently not up to par. He wasn't a bad performer, but he wasn't good, either."

"Bad enough performance that he was documented for it though," Linda wanted to state for clarity.

"That's right. And in addition there were numerous verbal warnings," Jolene said, sighing. They all knew that verbal warnings made things difficult. Documentation was a key when things leaned toward litigation. Without it, everything became a credibility issue. He said, she said.

"Let's talk about the behavior issues a little more. What was going on?" Linda asked.

"Jason had an argument with a peer. He called the woman a pig and a slut. There was one witness to the exchange," Nicole said. "Again, we in management didn't know anything about it until well after the fact."

"At least the team leader was consistently inconsistent following policies," Linda said jokingly.

"Well, that information was used on Jason's performance rating, and he was rated low because of it," Jolene explained. "It may have been an important factor in where he fell in the rankings."

Linda smiled, nodding her head up and down. She knew with a discrimination charge a person's performance rating could be considered tainted to the state agency. If a boss is accused of discriminating against an employee, the agency will wonder how objective the performance rating could have been. To make matters more complicated, in this case, the first incident was never documented so the state investigator might infer it could not have been that significant. Still it was information that Linda would want to incorporate into the position paper. "Has Kenmore ever exhibited other signs of hostility?"

"Toward women?" Jolene asked.

"Toward anyone," Linda clarified.

Someone knocked on the door. Jolene stood up and opened the door. "Yes?"

Jolene stepped out into the hall to talk privately with the person who interrupted the meeting. A moment later, Jolene came back into the room, closing the door behind her. "It seems Jason Kenmore is in the front lobby asking to talk with both you and me," Jolene said to Nicole.

"Should we?" Nicole asked Linda.

"Would you normally talk to an ex-employee?" Linda asked. "Forget about the fact he has filed a charge."

"More than likely, yes," Jolene said.

"Then I don't see why not," Linda said. She was conscious of the conversation and clearly knew Nicole was asking for legal advice. As a paralegal, she was not allowed to provide any legal advice. To do so would be breaking the law. She then added, "That is just my opinion, though."

"I would hate to cut this meeting short, but I have another appointment right after lunch and I am starving," Jolene said. "Do you think we can schedule another meeting and continue where we left off?"

Linda glanced at her watch. It was ten to twelve. "I think that would be fine."

"Me, too," Nicole agreed. She looked at Jolene. "Should we go to the lobby?"

The three women went back to the lobby. Linda recognized Jason Kenmore immediately. He was dressed fashionably in an oversized knit sweater, leather coat, dress slacks and loafers. His feet had to be wet and cold if he walked through the parking lot.

Kenmore stood up and smiled warmly. Shaking hands with Jolene and Nicole, he said. "Hello Mrs. Davids, Mrs. Thomas."

Linda preferred not to be introduced. She cringed when Nicole stepped aside and made introductions. "It's a pleasure to meet you," Linda said, pleasantly. She shook hands with the Complainant.

"Linda Genova. That's a pretty name. Are you new with the company?" Kenmore asked. "It's a wonderful company."

Jolene must have noticed the uncomfortable expression on Linda's face and quickly interjected. "Jason, what can we do for you?"

"I'd like my job back. I was always a good worker, wasn't I?" Kenmore wasted no time. He started out begging. "None of this was my fault, none of it. If you bring me back then there's no problem. I'll do my job. I've always done my job, and everything can go back to the way it was, back to normal."

"Jason, you were not let go for one single thing. There was an evaluation ranking you and your peers. Business needs change. We are cutting back to try and save this company. We need a leaner workforce to better compete. You know that. You saw the work schedules slipping," Jolene said.

"You don't understand. I've got responsibilities, a wife, three children, bills ... I have a house with a huge mortgage payment, I have credit card bills, orthodontist bills for my daughter ... Mrs. Davids, please. I'm asking you, help me get my job back," Kenmore said, pleading. His hands were tightly pressed together as if in deep prayer. "I know that you know I filed a charge with the New York State Agency, the Division of Human Rights ... but I'll drop that, I'll call it off if you consider giving me my job back."

At this moment, Linda hated to think this man was out of work. She felt sympathetic for this grown man groveling for his job, but what could be done? The company he worked for went through a series of layoffs and Jolene had indicated more were to follow.

When both Nicole and Jolene turned to look at Linda, she gasped. Linda did not want Kenmore to know she was involved with his case in any way, but it only took a moment for him to catch on.

Kenmore's demeanor changed quickly. He asked, "What's going on here? Why are you looking at her? What does she have to do with anything?"

He kept shaking his head up and down with his hands on his hips. Linda glanced to the right. The security guard was watching the exchange. However, seeing the guard did nothing to relieve the knot of tension growing in her stomach. The guard was old and out of shape. The most he could do would be to call 911 in case of an emergency.

"You an attorney? You the lawyer they hired to fight my charge?"

A Complainant had never confronted Linda before. She was not sure how to respond or react. She did not want to lie because if there was ever a fact finding session between the two parties and an administrative law judge for the state, they'd meet again and he would know she had lied to him.

"I am a paralegal investigating the merits of your allegations," Linda said, hoping she sounded calm and professional.

"Uh-huh. Then are you in a position to negotiate a deal, Ms. Genova?" Kenmore asked, staring intensely at Linda.

She shuddered when Kenmore used her name. She did not like the way he said it. She might be overreacting, but it sounded menacing, as if he wanted her to understand that he knew who she was. "That is not a position I am in, no."

"Then who is the person I need to talk to?" Kenmore said. He removed his hands from his hips and rolled his fingers into tightly clenched fists. "Huh? Who?"

"I think we need to cut this conversation off right now. You are not in a position to talk calmly, and you do not have an appointment. If you would like to call me, Jason, that would be fine. Right now, I would like for you to leave," Jolene said, firmly. She had that Human Resource authority that made employees feel as if they were being scolded by a loving parent.

For a moment, Linda did not think Jolene's brief lecture worked. Kenmore stood his ground for several long seconds just staring at each of them. Linda wanted to see what the guard was doing during the standoff, but did not feel comfortable looking away from Kenmore.

"All right. I get what you're saying. I'm not looking for any trouble. I'm not. I just need work, okay? I just want to be able to take care of my family. Forget it. Forget I was here. We'll just let the courts decide what's best," Kenmore said. His tone of voice had changed. He sounded calmer. Linda still did not feel comfortable.

"Thank you, Jason. Now, if you would, please leave," Jolene

said, sounding like steel, her voice steady and stern.

Linda found herself admiring the woman. Watching Jason decide to retreat, she cringed as his eyes strayed over her body. He stared too long at her chest. The tip of his tongue wet his upper lip in a repulsive attempt at seduction.

"Good-bye, Jason," Jolene said assertively.

Jason pulled up his coat collar and bowed his head. "Have a wonderful life, ladies." Jason Kenmore opened the door and stepped out onto State Street. The cold and bitter wind entered the foyer in a rush, sending shivers up and down Linda's spine.

"God, that was awful," Nicole said. She seemed to be hugging herself. It could have been from the sudden burst of cold air, but Linda did not think so. She felt the same way, as if Jason Kenmore's eyes had invaded her. She felt dirty and angry. He had made her feel more uneasy than anyone else had ever made her feel, maybe even more so than Joey.

Linda talked with Nicole and Jolene for a few moments in the MCT foyer. She was a little upset with the security guard. He came over only after Kenmore was gone to see if there had been a problem. Linda tried to let those feelings go. The guard looked old and was, perhaps, retired trying to earn an extra income to supplement a compact pension.

* * * * *

Linda left MCT and took a deep breath of fresh air. She welcomed the cold as it filled her lungs. She despised the way the factory smelled. She thought she could actually feel a chemical build-up on her skin and it made her feel itchy. It might all be psychosomatic, but she did not think so.

Looking at her watch, Linda realized she would only be a few minutes late for her lunch date with Patty. She walked along the sidewalk, by the Kodak Office tower toward the crosswalk. On her right was a marble bus stop dugout with a bench secured to the cement, installed by Kodak. Linda grimaced when she saw Jason Kenmore sitting on the bench, his collar turned up against the cold.

She winced when he saw her and stood up.

"So, Ms. Genova, you are representing MCT against my charge?"

"Yes, I am," Linda said, silently cursing for even replying.

"You waiting for the bus, too?" Jason Kenmore asked. He smiled a broad and wicked smile. His straight, white teeth were perfect. "I'd think an elegant and beautiful woman like you would have a fancy, expensive car, especially being a lawyer."

"I am not a lawyer, and don't you have a wife?" Linda spat. She was in a dilemma. She could not walk across the street to the Empire Brewery in front of Kenmore. He might follow her. He might wait for Linda and Patty to leave. He might follow Patty. It would not be fair to subject Patty to this man's obscene behavior.

"I'm married. Yes, but so what? We have an open relationship. I can do what ever I want and she accepts that," Kenmore said sounding conceited and obnoxious.

"I would like you to leave me alone," Linda said. She hoped she sounded like Jolene. She knew she did not. She could hear it in her own voice, the uncertainty and the quiver. "I'm serious."

"Serious about what? I'm not doing anything to you. I haven't touched you," Kenmore said.

Linda tried unsuccessfully to repress the shiver. *I haven't touched you.* The thought of it made her feel ill. No one had said anything about touching. It had been obvious, but now it was blatant and obvious. Linda knew what was on Kenmore's mind. She needed to get away from him, but could not seem to walk. She could go back to her car, but did not want this man to see what her vehicle looked like. It was bad enough he already knew her name. She did not want just to walk aimlessly down the sidewalk. He might walk with, or behind her. Then where should she go?

She heard a blast of compressed air being discharged and the squeal and squeaking of brakes and sighed when she saw a city bus come to a stop at the crosswalk. The doors swooshed open. Silently she watched as Kenmore insisted on undressing her with his eyes as he walked around her toward the bus.

"You know what, Linda Genova? You're kinda cute when you get all ruffled like you are now. I think I'll be seeing more of you. What do you think? I think you'll like that." Kenmore blew her a kiss as the bus doors closed on him.

On shaky legs, Linda stood like a statute. She could feel her heartbeat pulsing like a bass drum in her ears. The throbbing worked its way up to her temples and took the shape of a dull headache.

No longer hungry, Linda just wanted to go home.

"Linda! Linda!"

Linda looked around, holding her breath. She feared Kenmore might have got off the bus at the next stop and was walking back toward her, but smiled when she saw Patty, wrapped in her coat, standing on the sidewalk on the other side of State Street.

"I just got here, had to finish some things up at the office!" Patty was yelling.

Linda smiled and ran across the street.

"Things at the office got pretty hectic," Patty said. "I thought I would have missed you."

"I was just heading over," Linda said.

"Is everything all right?"

"Fine. Everything is fine," Linda said. "Let's get out of the cold."

Chapter 8

Ray loved his office. It was a tiny space, not much larger than a prison cell, but it was his. There was no window and the walls were bare. The desk was old with scratched up wood, but it didn't matter. Not really. He was going to get a nameplate that hung outside the office door and that thought excited him. It had been a long, long time since he felt this good about working. He was going to work with one other computer administrative assistant and his boss. His cohort, Gwendolyn, whom he had never met, was out recovering from an unfortunate car accident. His boss, Mark Ling, the main person who had interviewed him for the job, worked out of an office on the tenth floor.

He did everything he could to let the morning's confusion go. He felt invigorated. Barbara's tour around the office meeting everyone had been stressful. Lots of names. He knew he'd never remember any of them. He knew that after a time it would come to him as he grew to know each person a little more personally. Right now he just wished they all had to wear nametags.

Moments ago Barbara stuck her head into Ray's office, just after lunch to make sure he was adjusting all right. He had assured her he was doing just fine. She had given him so much information, an overload amount, really, but like with the names of the others in the firm, he was sure it would all come to him eventually.

Right now he was familiarizing himself with the law firm's databases. All of the computers were connected to a large server with three separate databases. Each employee had two separate drives. One was confidential and password protected, the other was less confidential, but password protected as well. Ray had access to all the files in each of the drives. He could also log onto his computer and go through each employee's desktop and view the personal drives, as well. However, to do so would be unethical and an abuse of his position. Ray tucked the hint of temptation into the back of his mind.

When his telephone buzzed, Ray realized the one thing he had not been trained to do was answer the telephone. He stared at it and tried to remember how the telephone had been answered when he called responding to their ad in the newspaper. "Cross, Hartzman, Lacy & Bierman, I mean, Hartzman, Bierman, Cross & Lacy." *Damn it.*

"You mean, Hartzman, Cross, Lacy and Bierman?" a woman's voice said, and Ray could hear the amused and teasing tone in her words.

Feeling relieved that the caller was friendly, he sighed. "Yes, that's what I mean. First day, but it's no excuse. I'm sorry."

"Nothing to be sorry about. When I first started, I got the names mixed up, and there were only two to remember."

Ray just realized that his telephone had not rung. It had buzzed. The call was coming from somewhere on one of the three floors in the building. It was not a customer, or a client, or whatever lawyers call the people they represent. The person had to be an employee of the firm. "What can I do for you?" Ray asked, certain he should not take up anyone's time at the firm with meaningless small talk, feeling certain everyone was busy.

"Actually, I was calling for two reasons. My name is Linda Genova, an employment law paralegal. First, I wanted to say hello and welcome you to the company. My secretary told me Barbara brought you around for introductions, but I was away at a meeting. So, hello and welcome," Linda said.

"Thank you. I appreciate it," Ray said, feeling immediately uncomfortable with the attention. Here he was just having a telephone conversation and yet he could feel his forehead dampen with perspiration. Ridiculous. This Linda wasn't even an attorney.

"And the second reason I'm calling, my Internet connection isn't working. Do you think you can give me a hand?"

"Ah, now we get down to the true reason behind the phone call," Ray said jokingly. He regretted it the minute the words were spoken. Why should Linda appreciate his dry sense of humor?

Linda laughed. "You got me. But you've got to admit, the introducing myself and saying hello was a nice touch."

"I agree. A nice touch," Ray said feeling relieved. He let out a large lung-full of used air. He did not realize he had been holding his breath. "Where do you sit? I'll come right over."

Linda gave Ray directions. He hung up the phone and left his office. Fixing Linda Genova's Internet connection was his first assignment with the firm. His heart felt so swollen with a sudden burst of pride he feared it might explode. He also feared his emotional condition. He thought he might cry. It sounded silly and absurd, but he could not deny the feelings. It had been some time since he felt needed. Working while intoxicated had been a much different experience. Phone calls from people needing computers looked at was annoying and had made him angry. Right now he felt as if he were at the opposite end of the rainbow. He thought he might actually be swimming in a pot of gold. Being sober for nearly the first time in a long time felt like such a rush. It was hard to believe he was actually enjoying the physical change. One day at a time, that's what they preach at those meetings. At first, getting through a single day without a drink seemed like an impossible task. Though it was not easy, it had gotten easier. Each day of sobriety Ray could stack behind him made him that much stronger and that much more determined to make it through the next day. He stuck a hand into his pocket and fingered his AA chips. Next week he would earn his third.

* * * * *

Ray stopped at the desk outside Linda's office. "Hello Ms. Dent," he said. He was rubbing his index fingers nervously against his thumbs. He hated fidgeting, but he could not help it.

"Ms. Dent? Please, don't call me that. We're informal around here. It's Patty, all right?" Patty said. "You're here to help Linda with her computer?"

"Yep. Yes," Ray said. "She gave me a call a second ago and I rushed right over."

Ray knew he sounded overzealous. He needed to relax. The day was going fine. He was doing fine. Relax.

"She's waiting for you, go on in," Patty said.

Ray thanked Patty, but knocked on Linda's open door just the same. He saw the back of Linda. She was sitting in her chair facing the window. Slowly she rotated to face him and Ray was caught off guard.

Linda was strikingly beautiful with large, dark eyes and dark blond hair. He cleared his throat. "You still having trouble getting online?"

"Ray? How are you?" Linda said, standing up and reaching out her hand.

"I'm sorry, excuse me. Yes. I'm Ray. It's a pleasure to meet you." Ray crossed the room and shook hands with Linda, feeling self-conscious of his suddenly warm and sweaty palms. It took tremendous energy not to wipe his hands on his pants. He wondered if she wanted to do the same.

"You know, Ray, it's really no secret that my computer hates me," Linda said, laughing. She moved away from her desk. She pointed at her computer with both hands the way a model showcases a prize on a game show. "It's all yours."

Ray sat in Linda's chair and rolled himself in front of her terminal. Now he was in his element. He used the mouse and worked his way around the databases, getting familiar with the firm's set-up as he worked. After a moment of clicking all over the place, he stopped and tried to figure out what might be the problem.

"You go to school for this?" Linda asked.

"Not college. I took classes and earned software certifications. I have to renew the certifications annually so I read a lot of computer and software magazines to keep current," Ray said. He felt like he was rambling. She didn't care that he read technical journals.

"Do you take classes now, too?"

"Some. But they cost quite a bit of money," Ray said.

"The firm supports educational efforts. You should talk with Barb and see about having her enroll you in some classes,' Linda said.

Ray nodded. "That sounds like a wonderful opportunity."

"It is. I wouldn't pass on it, if I were you," Linda said, encouragingly.

Ray slid off the chair onto his knees. He crawled under Linda's desk to get a better look at the CPU. He wiggled the wires connecting to it. He heard a click, and smiled. "Got it," he said, coming out from under the desk. "Try logging on now."

Linda sat down in her chair. Ray stood next to her, his arms folded contentedly. He watched as she double clicked on her Internet browser icon and the link to the service was made. "Loose wire?" Linda said, as if embarrassed.

"Loose wire," Ray said. "I'll be right back with a fix."

There was this certain friendliness about Linda that Ray liked. She seemed easygoing and down to earth. If things were different, he would have considered entertaining the idea of eventually asking her out. Things weren't different, though. He might be a week from three months sobriety, but that did not eliminate his past. It did nothing to take away the pain he felt from the mess that he'd left, abandoned really, back in his hometown. Would he ever really be able to get over what he had done? Deep down it wasn't exactly a secret that he hated himself. He had acted in an unforgivable way, and then had run away. *What kind of a man am I*, he thought?

I am the kind of man that may finally have learned his lesson.

I know better than to even consider Linda in any other way than professional.

I know better than to even think about getting romantically involved with anyone. No matter what, no matter how much time passes, I am still a loser. I might be sober, and sober is better than being drunk, but it doesn't change the truth. I know who I was. I know what I did. Running away didn't change the past. Getting clean and sober won't make things right. I don't deserve to be with another woman, not after what happened, not after what I did to ... her.

Still, Linda is so beautiful ...

Chapter 9

Linda poured herself a cold glass of white Zinfandel. She kept the lights in her home dim. Her head throbbed. The dull headache started sometime before lunch with Patty and progressively got worse. She had taken aspirin a little over an hour ago. The pills did not seem to be working. Dim lights and white wine seemed like the perfect medicine. At her home entertainment center, she turned on the CD player. The CD cartridge was loaded and ready with a variety of music. She was not in the mood for country, nor was she in the mood for dance. She selected a mellow alternative CD made up of a compilation of artists.

Sitting on the sofa with her feet up on the coffee table, Linda thought only a hot bubble bath could make the night better. When the telephone rang she debated on letting the answering machine get it. Instead, she reluctantly leaned over and picked up the receiver by the end of the third ring. "Hello?"

Linda could hear someone breathing on the other end of the line. "Hello?" Linda said. "I can hear you breathing."

Linda was no stranger to obscene phone calls. She was not quick to hurl insults at a caller for a number of reasons. She remembered a time when someone called, but did not talk to her when she answered. Immediately she had started name-calling, only to find it had been her mother on the other end. Her mother had been about to sneeze, which was why she had been silent when her daughter answered the phone. Another reason was because she had always been taught doing so would fuel the caller's purpose. Ignore them and they will get bored and hang up. Obscene callers like to get the *prankee* bent out of shape. Linda already felt bent out of shape enough. She hung up the telephone. "I don't need this," she said and took a satisfying sip of wine.

There were not many nights where Linda sat and did nothing. Quickly, she thought about how much work she had left behind at the office and how usually she brought it home. It was normal for her to sit at the kitchen table reviewing files and preparing for up-coming unemployment insurance hearings until late at night. But she must admit this relaxing thing felt great and she promised her-self that she would set aside one night a week for it. In fact, taking an evening just to sip wine and listen to soft music sounded so good that she couldn't wait for the following week when she could do it all over again.

Slouching comfortably, snuggling into the cushions, Linda closed her eyes and let the rhythm of the music caress her soul. She cringed when the telephone started ringing again. She knew she had been close to falling into a peaceful sleep. Irritated, she picked up the telephone. "Hello?"

No one answered. Linda could hear breathing from the other end, and knew someone was listening. "Look, creep. Quit call-ing." Linda hung up but held the receiver in her hand for a moment, then decided to dial *69. She listened to the prerecorded voice of an operator telling her that the phone call she had just received was from outside the calling area and no number was available. "It figures," Linda said, hanging up the phone.

Determined not to have anything spoil this evening she thought it was time for the bath. A special bath. A tub filled with hot water, a skin moisturizer and bubbles. Linda stopped the music, removed the CD and took it along with her glass of wine to the kitchen for a refill. She climbed the stairs to the upstairs bathroom, off the mas-ter bedroom and set her glass down on the counter next to the sink. Linda inserted the CD she had been listening to into a portable player she kept in the bathroom. She waited for the music to start, then decided to turn up the volume.

She started the water, adding a perfect blend of soaps to it and watched as the foam filled the tub. She could hardly wait to climb inside. Then suddenly, the two prank phone calls came to her mind and they were beginning to bother her. Not just because they com-pletely interfered with her privacy, but because her meeting Jason Kenmore had unnerved her. She kept imagining that somehow he'd managed to get a hold of her unlisted home number. She could picture him in a bar somewhere, drunk, using his cell phone to call her.

Linda quickly removed her clothing and set the glass of wine on the tub's edge. Stepping into the tub sent a wave of calmness through her toes and feet. The wave continued up her legs and across her back and belly as she lowered herself into the water. She kept her eyes closed as she sank back in the tub and extended her legs to the opposite end. The sound of the music and of the water filling the tub was more relaxing than she ever could have imagined.

Until the doorbell rang.

"If it's not the phone," Linda said as she sat up, turned off the water and climbed out of the tub. She reached for the red and white terrycloth robe and wrapped it snuggly around her body. She descended the stairs and went toward the front door. She stopped at the bowed picture window and parted the curtain with the back of her hand. Peering out into the night, she saw only her car in the driveway. From her angle, she could not see the front step.

At the door she stood on tiptoes and looked out the peephole. No one was on the step. She looked at the locks. They were engaged. She could feel her heartbeat increase some. "This is crazy," she said, beginning to doubt whether or not she had even heard the doorbell ring in the first place.

She stood still by the door listening for sounds. Her eyes scanned the rooms around her. She knew the door in the kitchen was locked, but thought she ought to check it just to be sure. She looked out the peephole again, saw nothing, and went to the kitchen doors. Just as she had thought, everything was locked up securely.

It was nothing more than the events of the day that made her this jumpy, she knew. She was letting everything get to her. The bath, the wine, the music was all waiting for her upstairs. She decided to hurry back before the entire mood was lost.

She disrobed and stepped into the tub. The water was still hot and felt even better than it had last time. The silkiness of the moisturizers in the water made her skin tingle in a pleasurable way.

The combination of everything worked and Linda felt better and more importantly, relaxed. After the bath, she made an extra trip to the kitchen for a refill and then went up to her room where she dressed in a comfortable pair of flannel pajamas. She switched on the television and watched a sitcom while sipping wine.

With the television on, the empty wineglass on the nightstand, Linda fell asleep before ten o'clock. The prank phone calls and the ding-dong-ditch, for the night, forgotten.

* * * * *

When Linda woke up, she immediately knew that something was wrong. Everything around her seemed impossibly dark, confining, foreboding. The air felt too thin to breathe and tasted stale inside her mouth. She tried to sit up, but banged her head on something hard, but silky, only inches above her. She went to lift her arms, but couldn't, realizing she was trapped inside something. Frantically, with her arms at her sides, she felt around the box-like prison. Her skin brushed along the silk lining as she began panicking and gasping for air.

She knew where she was. She was in a coffin. She kicked her legs uselessly. She ran her hands over her body, bringing them up to her face. She used her fists to pound on the coffin's lid. If someone were around, they'd hear her making noise. Kicking, punching and screaming did not bring anyone to the rescue.

The air continued to get thinner. She was exerting all of her energy, using up all of her oxygen. Feeling paralyzed with fear and anxiety, she struggled to move, but there was no room in the tight confinement. The complete sense of helplessness felt overwhelming. She thought she might die from it long before the disappearing air supply.

She thought she might throw up.

She used her fingernails to scratch at the silk lining, no longer strong enough to pound on the inside of the casket lid. "Help me, please. Someone, help me!" she said in a gravely whisper.

The air was nearly gone. The coffin felt as if it were closing in on itself. Linda's mind went wild trying to figure out how this happened. How did she wind up in a coffin buried six feet in the earth? How had she gone from sleeping in her bed to suffocating to death?

A last burst of energy gripped her and she went to pound on the coffin lid, she felt something wet and slimy slither across her neck. Worms. The worms had made their way through the coffin wood.

She tried to scream, but there was no more air. She had used it up. She could feel the tremendous pressure building behind her temples, as she ineffectually attempted to suck in air when there was none available.

And all at once, she sprang up into a sitting position. Her body was covered in a thin sheet of sweat. She was breathing rapidly, sucking in quick shallow breaths of air, close to hyperventilating.

She touched her fingertips to her chest, unsure what to believe. She looked around her bedroom. Moonlight filtered through her curtains, lighting the room. Slowly she realized what had happened had been nothing more than a dream, a terrible nightmare. Knowing it had all been a nightmare did nothing to make the experience any less real.

Trying to get comfortable in bed, knowing she needed some sleep, Linda snuggled under the blankets after fluffing her pillow. She stayed on her back, suspiciously fearing falling asleep. She irrationally expected the dream to be waiting for her. It was the wine. It was the phone calls. It was some neighborhood kid playing ding-dong-ditch. It was meeting Jason Kenmore—no, being unnerved by meeting Kenmore. It was, after all, only a nightmare, a dream and nothing else. Close to an hour later, Linda fell into a fitful sleep.

Chapter 10
Friday, January 17

He slept like shit. Tossing and turning. The truth was, he hadn't felt tired. He had been wound up. Excited. He'd gone to an AA meeting around eight, but could not concentrate on what people had been saying. He had felt so good. All he wanted to do was get back to work. He had been that thrilled with the new job.

Maybe there had been more, a little something else. However, Ray forced himself not to think about Linda, not to associate Linda with his feelings. They were separate from one another. Ray felt good because he possessed a sense of worth with the new job. No one at the law firm knew he had a drinking problem, or that he was running away from his past. This was why he felt so good and not because he met some woman whom he found attractive. That had nothing at all to do with it.

He had, perhaps, finally fallen asleep around three. When his alarm clock went off at seven-thirty, he thought he'd feel groggy. Instead, he got right out of bed and into the shower. The hot spray was refreshing enough to rejuvenate any tiredness lurking in his mind or body.

He dressed, ate a quick breakfast and left for work.

* * * * *

Linda's car was covered in snow. She unlocked her car doors, started the engine and cranked up the front and rear-defrost knobs on the dash. She picked up her snowbrush and left the sanctuary of the car to face the whipping, bitter, wintry wind. She started brushing away the snow from the driver side and rear windows before making her way around to the passenger side and front windshield. As she brushed the snow off the car and scraped away the ice from the glass, she found a business size envelope placed under the driver side, windshield wiper blade.

Cautiously, she regarded the plain envelope. She looked around her yard and the yards around her suspiciously. She looked around her driveway for footprints in the snow, but saw only her own, leading from her front step to the car.

Swallowing uneasily, Linda climbed into her car and locked the doors.

The envelope felt cold. She opened the sealed envelope and removed the folded sheet of printer paper. Had the temperature dropped and the snow melted any, she suspected everything would have been wet and ruined. Instead, everything felt cool and crisp. She read the type written message.

Dear Linda,

This seems strange, writing to you like this. I think you are beautiful, maybe one of the most beautiful people I have ever seen. Please don't think of me as a coward, but approaching you scares me. I guess I just want you to know I'm thinking about you, dreaming of some wonderful time when it will no longer be you and I, but of a time when it might be "us".

I promise I will not keep my identity a secret forever, but I will keep it this way for a while longer. I will let you know who I am when I feel the time is right. Right now is not that time. I feel too nervous and self-conscious. Some day, some day soon, I promise, you will know who I am. I just pray when that day comes that you will, if not feel the same way, at least take the time to give "us" a chance.

Your Secret Admirer

Linda felt a wave of mixed emotions. She had never had a secret admirer before. Still, the idea of someone noticing her and watching her, all the while keeping at a safe distance was weird. It made her a little uncomfortable. She immediately wondered if this admirer had been the person calling her last night. It had to be. It had to have been the admirer who had rung her doorbell, as well. He must have put the envelope under her windshield wiper blade then rang her doorbell, perhaps had run and hid behind a tree watching the door, hoping Linda would come outside and see the envelope.

Linda shivered. The thought of someone hiding behind a tree watching her felt eerie and just a little bizarre. She might like the idea of having a secret admirer, but at the same time, she did not like the idea of being stalked. Not one little bit.

She stuffed the letter into her briefcase and backed out of her driveway. As she drove to work her thoughts were all over the place. In a way she felt better about last night, but then thought maybe Jason Kenmore had found out her telephone number and home address and was harassing her.

Linda stopped at a red light as another, more disturbing, thought came to mind. If it were not Kenmore, then who was it and how did he get her unlisted number and address. No. She did not like being stalked, not at all. And that's what this boiled down to, a stalking. In essence, a secret admirer is nothing but a stalker, taunting its prey with unsigned letters...

"You're overreacting," Linda told herself. The car behind Linda beeped and she looked up to see the light had changed from red to green. Linda thought she might feel too shaken and uneasy to drive. Another long blast of a car horn got her moving. Linda drove down State Street to Corinthian Street and made a left, driving past the rear entrance of the Reynolds Arcade building and into the multi-leveled parking garage. She found a spot, shut off the engine and sat in the car for a moment trying to sort through her thoughts.

Linda finally left her car and the parking garage. She crossed Corinthian Street and entered her building through the back door. She ignored the marble floors and the plaque mounted to the wall between a set of elevator doors that told how Bausch & Lomb started as a company in a basement office back in 1857. She just pressed the arrow pointing up. Waiting for the next car, she kept one hand on the strap of her shoulder slung briefcase and the other tucked warmly in her coat pocket. Linda replayed the events of last evening in her mind. She kept trying to recall seeing someone out in the yard. She remembered parting the curtains and looking at the driveway, to see if she had company, but only her car had been in the driveway. The snow had been trampled on, she could remember that, but it had to have been trampled on before, too. She tried to focus her concentration on the car itself. Could she recall looking at the windshield and seeing something tucked under a wiper blade? Of course not. Had she noticed it last night, she would have gone outside to get it. Or if it had been there, she just did not notice it. She closed her eyes tight and tried to remember every little detail. The doorbell had rung. She had gone downstairs, parted the curtains, had seen her car in the driveway … yes, yes, there was definitely something under the wiper blade. No. No. She was just seeing it now because she knew it was there. Frustrated, she opened her eyes as the elevator chimed, signaling the arrival of a car going up. The doors parted and Linda walked on. When she turned around, the new guy, Ray, was getting on behind her.

"Good morning, Ray," she said politely, thankful for something to take her mind off the anonymously written letter.

"Hello, Linda. I was going to say good morning while we waited for the elevator, but you looked like you were concentrating pretty hard," Ray said, smiling.

"I'm sorry, I was preoccupied," Linda admitted.

"Don't worry about it. You're a busy lady," Ray said.

"How was your first day?" Linda asked. The elevator stopped. A moment later, the doors opened. She and Ray stepped off the car. "Tough meeting so many new people?"

"It was a pretty good first day, but you're right. Learning all the names might prove to be the most challenging part of the job," Ray said.

"Well, you got my name down," Linda said. She then thought about what she had said. Ray had called her by name on the elevator. It seemed odd that he claimed learning names to be the most challenging part of the job.

"That was easy. You were the first person to call me to fix something with your computer," Ray said. "You are like that first dollar bill a corner grocery store makes and they frame it and hang it on the wall over the cash register."

"Framed and hung. That's how you think of me?" Linda said. She was teasing. She wished she had not said anything. Ray's friendly and warm smile disappeared.

"No. No, that's not at all what I mean," Ray said. He sounded very apologetic, not at all defensive.

Linda reached out and touched Ray's shoulder. "Ray, I was only kidding. I knew what you meant. I was just making a joke," Linda explained. *He looks so uncomfortable talking to me*, Linda thought. Ray kept shifting his weight from foot to foot. He kept his thumbs hooked in the corners of his pants pockets.

Ray looked as if he were about to say something, but stopped as the elevator chimed and the doors slid open. Linda watched Ray's eyes lower as Patrick Bierman stepped on to the elevator. "Good morning, Linda, Ron," Bierman said. He was dressed, as usual, in a dark three-piece suit. He wore his long, heavy overcoat and goulashes over his expensive Italian shoes.

"It's Ray," Linda said, casually.

Patrick Bierman stood between Ray and Linda, his hands on his hips and regarded Linda for a moment, as if pondering over the possible truth of her statement. He then turned to Ray and cocked his head to one side, the way a dog might. "Is it Ray, Ron?"

"Yes. It's Ray, but that's okay," Ray said waving his hand to dismiss the confusion. His weak smile clearly conveyed how uncomfortable he was with the discussion. Linda looked at Patrick and thought she could detect the faintest hint of a smile, the bastard.

Chapter 11

Linda and Patty talked briefly before Linda went into her office. She debated telling Patty about the letter she found on her car windshield this morning, but decided against it. Until she decided what she planned to do, she thought it best not to tell anyone.

In her office, Linda turned on the computer. The message light on her telephone was lit, signaling a host of calls that needed her attention. She took off her coat and hung it on the hanger on the back of the office door. Before she did anything else, she needed a cup of coffee.

In the break room she fixed a cup of coffee and was glancing at the headlines on the front page of the morning paper when Patrick Bierman came in. Linda watched the lawyer pour a cup of coffee. He left the coffee black and took a sip, silently standing next to the same table Linda was near. He began fingering his way through the newspaper. The silence made Linda uncomfortable.

"I had that meeting at MCT yesterday," she said, breaking the silence.

"Oh? How did it go?" he asked, not looking at her. He appeared to be only half-listening as he read an article in the sports section.

Talking about something serious to a lawyer not paying attention to you seemed a little worse than standing next to a lawyer in an otherwise empty room in complete silence. Now she wished she'd just taken her cup of coffee and left the room. She couldn't. She'd brought up the meeting and whether he was listening or not, she would need to brief him. "It was interesting," she said.

"Oh? How so?" Bierman said, turning the page. He had mastered the art of half-listening.

She felt embarrassed, but had no reason to feel that way. It was Bierman who made her feel unimportant. She knew her cheeks had to be turning red and could feel the heat radiate from her skin. First embarrassed and now angry. He had no right treating her that way.

"You know what? It's kind of involved. I'll have your secretary set up a meeting for us and we can discuss it then," she said, wanting to get out of this room, away from him and back to her office.

"Okay. Sounds like a good idea," he said.

She took her coffee and started out of the room when Bierman called to her. "Yes?"

"I was thinking," he said. He had a funny look to his expression. He could not make eye contact with Linda and his smile was crooked. "I am pretty busy all day today."

"Well, it's Friday anyway. I figured we'd set something up for early next week," she said.

"Well, that's not exactly what I meant. I have meetings most of the day, but I have lunchtime free. Maybe we could make it a working lunch, grab a sandwich and salad somewhere and discuss the MCT issue. We bill the lunch to the client, of course," he said, trying to laugh.

Linda could feel the tension in the room thicken around her. A partner in the law firm had just asked her out. He knew it was more than a business lunch and he had to know she knew it was more than a business lunch. Linda did not like the way he did this. It was sneaky. Now she felt trapped. Bierman had protected himself, ever the smart attorney. If she said no, it would look like she was shirking job responsibilities. How do you tell a partner that you don't want to have lunch and work on a case, especially when you could bill the client for the time and meal? If she wanted to complain about him asking her out, he could deny any romantic intentions. He had made it clear it was a business lunch to discuss the MCT issues because the rest of his day was so busy. If she said yes, Bierman could get the wrong idea. He might think there was some kind of attraction between the two of them. That couldn't be any further from the truth. He might be a nice guy, a wealthy man, but Linda only thought of him as one of her bosses.

"Lunch? Sure," Linda said.

"Great. I'll have my secretary call and make some reservations for around noon," he said, sitting down at the table and concentrated more intently on the article he'd been reading. She watched him for a moment longer and then went back to her office.

* * * * *

After her lunch with Bierman, Linda was on the telephone with Joanne, a human resource representative at the auto parts factory the firm represented. "And you hired an investigator?" Linda said. She was making notes on a legal pad.

"Not yet. We weren't sure what to do, exactly," Joanne said. "The guy's been out of work for three weeks on a workers' compensation claim. He claims he hurt his back mopping the floors on the C shift. I don't know, rumor has it he had fallen asleep on one of the benches and rolled off it. Maybe he had a nightmare or something."

"But that's not really the issue. The issue right now is someone saw him tending bar at a place on Buffalo Road?" Linda asked.

"Yeah, on the corner of Buffalo and Mt. Read," Joanne said. "It was last Saturday night."

"And the person who saw him, knew for sure it was the same person?"

"Yeah. He talked to the guy. The guy had smiled at him, gave him and his date free drinks all night, then asked him to keep quiet about it."

"But the employee came and reported it?" Linda asked.

"This morning. Said he'd been thinking about it all week long. He kept going back and forth saying it wasn't any of his business what this other guy did. Then he would feel guilty because he knew this guy was screwing the company. Eventually he couldn't take it anymore and told me what had happened."

Linda wrote down some notes. It sounded easy enough to resolve. The man scamming the insurance companies and collecting a workers compensation check was committing a crime. The proper authorities needed to be notified. "So you want a private eye to go to the bar and secretly film him working or something?"

"I'm sure once we contact the insurance company it will be out of our hands and they'll handle it."

"So I'm not sure I understand the problem," Linda said.

"The guy that came forward, that told me what was going on, he's afraid if this other guy gets in any trouble then he's going to know who turned him in," Joanne said.

"Ah. I see." Linda said. It made sense. "Is this guy, the bartending thief, prone to violence?"

"He's a big guy. If he gets charged with insurance fraud, or whatever happens, if he loses his job … I guess anyone might be prone to some type of retaliation, don't you think?"

"I hate to think so, but I suppose you're right. But I still don't think it's an issue. Insurance companies hire private detectives all the time to follow people out of work on a compensation claim. It's even possible when you tip them off that they will already have assigned an investigator to follow the guy. What the investigator will do is follow him for several days, weeks, maybe, taking video footage of him everywhere, not just at work. Maybe they'll get him shoveling his driveway, too. See what I mean? This guy may think he knows who turned him in, but he won't know for sure. In the back of his mind he has to know there's a chance he'll get caught," Linda explained.

"What about the bar? You think they're paying him under the table?"

"I'm positive of it. The insurance company will contact the Department of Labor. Let them worry about that. If you want, I can run this by an attorney here at the firm and see what they think," Linda said, careful not to give the impression she was giving legal advice.

"No. That's all right. I just wanted to run this by someone else, get a feel for the situation. I think I am going to contact the insurance company," Joanne said.

"Okay. If you have any other questions, or if you want to talk with one of our attorneys just give me a call, all right?" Linda said.

"Okay. Thank you," Joanne said.

Linda made some additional notes on the legal pad. She wanted to document the fact that Joanne did not want her to run the scenario by any of the attorneys, that Joanne planned to contact the insurance company and would call for actual legal advice if she needed it.

When someone knocked on the door Linda looked up and saw Patty with a funny look on her face. "What?" Linda asked.

"We haven't had any Chatty-Kathy time. Everything around here has been so busy," Patty said, lingering in the doorway.

Chatty-Kathy was time during the day the two set aside, ten or fifteen minutes, just to talk or gossip. "Why? What's on you mind?" Linda asked, knowing exactly what the topic would be about.

"Lunch with Bierman. How'd it go?"

"It went all right," Linda said.

"I should think it was a little more than all right," Patty said. She disappeared from the doorway and returned a half-second later holding a beautiful flower arrangement. "These just came," Patty said, smiling suspiciously. "I have no idea who they are from. The envelope is sealed." She put the arrangement on Linda's small conference table.

It should have been exciting to receive flowers at work. Linda tried to smile, but knew she could not hide her surprise. Patty gave her a funny look. Linda wanted to tell her about last night, but decided against it.

"They're not from Bierman, are they?" Linda asked. Bierman had been out of line at lunch, a little too forward. She had thought she set him straight.

"I'm telling you the card is inside a sealed envelope."

"Get in here, shut the door," Linda said.

"What's going on?" Patty asked.

"At lunch, Bierman takes me to this real nice Italian restaurant, Carbone's, near the Blue Cross Arena."

"Nice place," Patty said.

"Tell me about it, too nice for an innocent business lunch. He orders us some red wine and for a while we look over the menu. On my menu, there were no prices. You know what that means."

"Expensive."

"Exactly. At this point, I'm trying not to let my imagination get away from me. I get the feeling he's making some kind of move. But the guy's married, so I keep telling myself this is how bigwig lawyers eat lunch," Linda said.

"Not likely. They're cheap when it comes to spending their own money."

"Actually, Bierman said he planned to bill MCT for the lunch, since it was a working lunch. But by the food he ordered, I don't know how he'd explain the expense to the client.

"So he gets a phone call right after the waiter takes our order. I'm not purposely trying to listen in, but I'm sitting right across from him. What am I supposed to do? Anyway, it's his wife. They're arguing. He hangs up, right, and he says to me, he says, you know my wife and I are in the middle of separating."

"Slam. Expensive restaurant," Patty said.

"Wine."

"Working lunch with just the two of you."

"Exactly. So I know right away what's going on," Linda said. "What am I supposed to do though? He's a senior partner in the firm. We have a legitimate reason for this lunch," Linda said.

"Did you talk about the Kenmore charge?"

"Not once. We ate, and all the while he talked about starting his life over, how he felt like a new man. He said to me, 'You're not married, are you Linda?' I almost choked on my manicotti. He wants to know if I can take him around on the weekend, show him the places to hit in the city for a good time."

"Did he come onto you more than that?"

"A little. He wanted to know if it would be all right for us to go out tomorrow night," Linda said.

"And? What did you tell him?" Patty asked.

"He's not a bad looking guy," Linda said.

"But he's married."

"Separated."

"Separating."

"Same difference," Linda said.

"Not even close. Did you tell him yes? You're not going to be dating Patrick Bierman, are you?"

"No. I told him no. I told him it would be too weird, having to work together all the time."

"And he let it go?"

"Not right away," Linda said. "He tried a few more times to persuade me, and I had to tell him flat out that I was not interested."

"How'd he take it?"

"He asked for the check."

Patty plucked the envelope out of the bouquet and handed it over to Linda. Linda cringed. She did not want to read the card in front of Patty, but how could she ask Patty to leave. They were friends. Linda read the card quietly to herself.

"Well? Come on," Patty asked impatiently. "What does Bierman say? Is he sorry?"

"I'm not sure they're from him." Linda took a deep breath. "I think I have a secret admirer."

Patty laughed. "Get out of here? Are you serious? How cool."

Linda raised an eyebrow. "You think so?"

"Do I?" Patty sat down at the table. "I always wanted a secret admirer. I remember being in school wishing I'd had one. Someone seeing me pass by them in the halls, taking one look and knowing they were in love with me, but too shy to say anything about it. The only way to express their passion was in an unsigned letter slipped into my locker."

"Hello? Earth to Patty," Linda said and laughed.

"You never thought of things like that in school?" Patty asked.

"I might have, I don't know. I don't remember, really." Linda said. She did not feel like talking. She wanted to sit down and read the card again. Despite the beauty the flowers brought to her office, she wanted to throw out the arrangement. They made her uncomfortable.

"What kind of a romantic were you?"

"Who said I was any kind of a romantic?" Linda retorted. "I had some boyfriends, went to some dances, but I never let myself fall into some fantasy like Romeo and Juliet."

"A secret admirer has nothing to do with Romeo and Juliet. That's a tragedy. This is something different, something romantic," Patty said. "Do you have any idea who they might be from?"

Linda hoped to God they were not from Jason Kenmore. First the letter on her windshield, now this. Kenmore had come on strong. When they had met he had been raw and cocky. He might have been truly attracted to her, but it was lust driven and threatening. Besides, he was married and he had to be angry with her for representing MCT against his charge.

"I don't know," Linda said.

"What about Joey? That jerk might be trying to fix things up between the two of you," Patty said.

Linda cocked her head to one side. "You know what? I hadn't thought of him. It makes sense, too." And it did make sense. The phone calls, the knock on the door, the envelope left on the windshield, the flowers … it all reeked of Joey Viglucci. He wanted to smooth things over, to patch up the relationship.

"Well?" Patty asked.

"Well, what?"

"If those are from him," Patty said, pointing at the flowers on Linda's desk, "are you going to give him another chance?"

Linda smiled easily. "Not on his life."

Linda regarded the flowers suspiciously.

"What? You don't want them?" Patty asked, rubbing a rose petal between her fingers. "Because, let me tell you, they will look wonderful on my desk."

"No, I'm sorry. Of course I want them. I just got so much … work going on, it's sometimes hard to stop thinking about it," Linda said.

Chapter 12

Linda answered her telephone on the second ring. "Hartzman, Cross, Lacy and Bierman, Linda speaking?"

"Ms. Genova? This is Andrew Egert, with the New York State Division of Human Rights?" Egert said.

"How are you, Mr. Egert?" Linda asked. She knew Andrew Egert was the investigator assigned to the Jason Kenmore charge. She looked at the clock on her computer. It was getting late.

"I'm fine, Ms. Genova. I'm calling about the Jason Kenmore charge. I believe you are working on it?"

"I am."

"I would like to have a meeting with both parties to discuss this. I think we may be able to resolve this charge fairly quickly if I can have the company representatives sit down with Mr. Kenmore. I would like Jolene Davids and Nicole Thomas at the meeting."

"When were you thinking of holding this meeting?" Linda asked.

"Sometime next week, if at all possible."

Linda chewed her lip. "You know Mr. Egert, we have not submitted a position paper yet." This bothered Linda. She had met with an investigator from the state agency on many different occasions. The meetings always occurred some time after the submission of a position paper, the formal written response to the charge.

"I understand. However, the paper is due on Tuesday. If you bring two copies with you, we should be all set." Egert sounded tired and a little bored. "That sound all right?"

"Should be fine," Linda said.

"And because it is a fact-finding, Mr. Kenmore will have the right to be present," Egert added.

She told Egert she would need to contact MCT and verify that the day was okay. Egert said that any time Tuesday would be okay. Linda told him she would call back with a time.

It took Linda the better part of a half-hour to coordinate the meeting for Tuesday. Nicole, Jolene and Linda would drive to the state agency Tuesday morning at ten. Egert was fine with the time.

Linda, concentrating on reading through what she had written of the position paper for grammatical errors, did not notice Patty standing in front of her desk until her friend cleared her throat to get her attention. "Have you been standing there long?" Linda asked.

"Just since lunch," Patty said with her hands on her hips. Linda knew she was kidding and smiled. "I was thinking since it's five and it's Friday..."

Friday. The gym. "You know what, Patty, I am just not in the mood to workout today. Work has been a little overwhelming," Linda said. She had much more to add to the list, but decided to keep it short.

"That's the whole point of going, to workout that build up of tension and aggression and get it out of your system, not to mention burning up some calories while we're at it." Patty had her hands in fists. She looked like she was boxing. She seemed purely energized by the thought of exercising.

Linda wanted to *want* to go, but shook her head. "I can't. Not tonight. I'm just not in any mood. Don't be mad."

"Mad? Not at all. I'm still going to go," Patty said. Linda could hear the disappointment in Patty's tone.

"You should," Linda said tucking the position paper neatly into its manila file. "Is Bierman still here?"

"Just went to the elevator, which is where I'm headed if you don't need anything else?" Patty said.

"No. I'm all set."

Patty leaned forward and smelled the roses. "Great flowers. Expensive flowers. I don't know, whoever sent them..."

"Want them?" Linda said. "You're absolutely right, they'd look great on your desk."

"They would have, not now. Everyone in the office knows they're yours. It would look weird on my desk."

"Everyone knows I got flowers?" Linda asked. It was a stupid question. An out of the ordinary delivery like a large bouquet of flowers demands attention. "Did anyone ask who the flowers were from?"

"Only everyone," Patty said. "Don't worry. I told them you were being all secretive about it. I didn't think you'd want everyone knowing you had a secret admirer."

Relieved, Linda sighed. "Thanks Patty."

"You leaving? I'll walk out with you," Patty offered.

"I am, but not just yet. Go on and enjoy your workout. I know I should be going with you," Linda said.

"Can still change your mind," Patty said.

"I know I can, but I don't think so. Monday I'll be ready," Linda said. Patty shrugged and left.

Linda sat back in her chair and just stared at the flowers. Patty was right; it looked like an expensive arrangement. It sure smelled wonderful, but none of this mattered. Linda was not comfortable with the idea of someone admiring her from afar. It just felt eerie and icky. Even if Joey were behind all of this, she still felt uneasy. She did not want him following her, calling her house and hanging up. She did not want to find love letters on her car, or to receive flowers at work.

Linda jumped as something made a thumping sound outside her office.

"Patty?" Linda said, tentatively. She stood up, one hand pressed to her chest. "Patty?"

No one answered. Thought it was a little after five it was too early for everyone at the office to have gone home, even on a Friday. Linda came out from around her desk and went out into the hall. Patty was not at her desk and the computer was off. Everything looked neat and orderly. Linda looked all around. No one seemed to be on the floor. Doors were shut. Lights were off.

So what made the thump sound? Linda went back into her office and began shutting down her computer. She gathered the things on her desk and locked them away in filing cabinets. She put on her coat and picked her keys up off the desk.

Closing her door as she left the office, she glanced around looking for anyone still at work. Linda could not believe how apprehensive she felt. For some reason this feeling made her remember being a little girl visiting her grandmother, who lived in a big house on Hague Street, off Jay in the city. Her older cousins would tease her about bats and monsters and dead people living in the attic. She was frightened of the second level of the house and each time she had to go to the bathroom she would ask her mother to go upstairs with her. Since she was having coffee with Grandma, Linda's mother would insist that one of the cousins go with her. They would then go up the stairs, but that would be as far as any of them went. They would stop and sit on the top step. "Go on already. Hurry up," they would say.

"You're going to stay right there, right where I can see you?" Linda would always ask.

"Duh. Just hurry up," they would say.

Linda would never shut the bathroom door all the way. She always wanted to be able to see some part of her cousins on the top step. Then as soon as she'd sit on the toilet they would start to tease her.

"What was that Linda? It's a, it's a, it's a dead person!" And she would hear them run down the stairs, screaming.

She, herself, would scream as if someone was killing her and suddenly she would jump off the toilet with her panties around her ankles, whether she was urinating or not. She would throw open the door, ready to run down the hall to the stairs. However, at the top of the stairs would be her cousins, laughing. Then her screams would fade into sobs and she would yell, "Mom! Mommy!"

Linda could not believe that same fear went through her at this very moment leaving the office. Many nights she had been the last one to leave. It never bothered her before. It never bothered her until today.

Walking toward the outer office doors, she felt her imagination getting wild, teasing her. She kept envisioning someone behind her, sneaking up on her. It was a terrible feeling. It made her heart beat faster than normal. She felt clammy and shaky. She walked faster toward the door until she couldn't take it any longer and spun around to face an empty office. Amid the maze of neck-high cubicle walls, Linda felt confident no one was there. At least she didn't see anyone.

Linda could not deny this feeling. The hairs on the back of her neck were raised. Someone had to be back there, watching her. She left the firm, closed and locked the doors behind her. She took a long deep breath, relieved to be out of the office. In the hall she waited patiently for the elevator.

When the doors finally opened and she entered the elevator

car to stand with five other people, she almost started laughing. The more she thought about it, the more ridiculous and childish she felt. It took a lot of self-control to keep from bursting out in laughter. Everyone would think she was crazy.

Linda left the Reynolds Arcade building and walked into the parking garage. Most of the cars were gone from the multi-tiered lot. She walked down the first row of cars toward where she remembered parking. When she heard someone behind her cough she turned to look. The tall man nodded and she smiled, but she tried to figure out where he had come from. A moment ago, no one had been behind her.

It's a garage. People park their cars here, she told herself. *Stop it. You're acting like a scaredy cat. So just stop it.*

Regardless, she walked a little faster. She wanted to look over her shoulder to see if the man following her was also walking faster.

He's not following you!

She wanted to get to her car. A strong sense of panic was overtaking her and running wild with her emotions. Nearly running, she chanced a look over her shoulder. The man in the garage had not picked up his pace. He was walking slowly, reaching into his pocket.

He's got a gun. He's going to shoot me!

Running now, waddling from side to side because of her purse and briefcase, Linda made it to her car. She felt winded. She turned to look behind her, but the man was gone. He had disappeared.

Linda dug through her purse. She couldn't find her keys. She looked all around at the cars parked in the garage, expecting to see the man pop up with a gun in his hand. Her pocket! Linda stuck her hand into her coat pocket and pulled out her key ring. She went to unlock the car door but dropped the keys.

"Damn it!" She said, bending over to pick them up. She fumbled with the ring in her hand, looking for the right key.

"Is everything all right?"

Linda screamed at the sound of a man's voice. She stood up straight and spun around. The guy that had been following her was standing in the row of cars behind hers.

"Linda, right? It's me, Ray," he said as if he thought this would be comforting. She could feel every nerve in her fingers trembling.

She kept spinning the keys on the ring searching for the one that would unlock the door. "The computer guy."

Linda let this sink in and for a moment, shut her eyes. Ray. The computer guy.

"I need a drink," Linda said out loud.

"Are you all right?" Ray asked, walking toward her.

Linda saw a set of keys in his hand, not a gun. "I am. I wasn't. I mean, I was, just…"

"Spooked?"

"Yeah, spooked." Linda felt so stupid. She could not look Ray in the eyes.

Chapter 13

"I'm sorry I scared you," Ray said.

"You didn't scare me. I mean, you did, but it wasn't you. Does that make sense?" Linda asked. She started to laugh. "I feel so, I don't know, ridiculous. You should have seen me leaving the office. I practically ran out of there."

"I don't mean to laugh," Ray said, covering his mouth.

"It's okay. It's funny. I'm laughing," Linda said.

Ray looked at his watch and Linda stopped laughing. "I'm sorry. It's Friday night and you have some place to be. Anyway, thanks for making sure I was okay."

"That's no problem, but I was looking at the time because I have somewhere to be in about an hour," Ray said.

"I understand. And again, thanks," Linda said. Here was a very nice looking guy, no wedding band and she was annoying him with stories of how she thought the bogeyman was going to get her. *God, how stupid am I?*

"I need to get something to eat, I worked through lunch. Would you be interested in a burger or something?" Ray asked.

Linda felt her entire mood change. Here she had been getting ready to go home alone but instead she was being asked out. Everything inside her seemed to shift. Her heart was still beating at an irregular rate, but to a different tune. She could feel the palms of her hands get a little sweaty. First she had been afraid, now she feared some adolescent excitement run through her.

"I'm sorry if I've offended you. I suppose I was out of line," Ray said putting his hands into his pockets.

"No. I'm not offended. As a matter of fact, I'm starving," Linda said. She watched Ray smile and thought it might just be the cutest smile she had ever seen. "Where would you like to go?"

"You know, I'm pretty new in town. I heard some people talking about a place called Nick Tahou's?"

Linda laughed. "I can't remember the last time I went down there to eat. There's two. One on West Main and one over on Lyell Avenue. You know where it is?"

"Lyell Avenue, yes. That was the one I wanted to go to," Ray said.

"Want me to follow you?"

"I'll still get lost. Why don't I follow you?"

* * * * *

The Nick Tahou's on Lyell Avenue was an old renovated Kentucky Fried Chicken building. The restaurant sat on a small lot across the street from a Wegman's grocery store. Cars parked in front and along the east side of the building. Linda parked and Ray pulled in to the empty spot next to her.

As they got out of their cars, Ray looked excited. "I'm going to feel stupid if I say this and I have no clue what I'm talking about."

"After every stupid thing I told you, I doubt it," Linda said. Inside her head she was trying to figure out what was going on. For some reason there just seemed to be a click between the two of them. She felt almost immediately comfortable with Ray; once she realized he wasn't carrying a gun and trying to catch her alone in the parking garage.

"The people I heard talking about this place," Ray said as they walked to the front entrance, "said if I ended up coming here for dinner I needed to order something called the Garbage Plate." Ray shrugged to show just how uncertain he was, but his smile never wavered.

Linda laughed. "Nope. You got it right. In fact, I was going to insist you order one."

"Are you getting one?" Ray asked.

"Any respectable Rochestarian will order one," Linda said.

* * * * *

Ray held the door for Linda as they entered. They moved up to a break in the crowd along the counter. When a woman in a red sweatshirt and blue jeans approached them, Linda gave her order. "Can I get a cheeseburger plate with macaroni salad and home fries, heavy sauce on the whole thing, no onions and a large soda?"

"Here or to go?"

"Here," answered Linda.

The lady nodded and looked at Ray. Ray looked at Linda and shrugged. "Same."

The woman turned and shouted the order to the cook, who was barraged with orders from two other counter workers. He never flinched or acknowledged them, and his spatula never faltered as it flipped and pushed and pulled and speared a whole grill full of meat. She then set a tray on the counter with two paper plates. She wrapped two chunks of fresh Italian bread with a couple of butter packets inside what looked like freezer paper. She then grabbed plastic utensils and placed everything on the tray. Then she filled their drink order.

Ray slid the drinks over to Linda. "This place is packed. Why don't you find a seat and I'll wait for the food."

Linda offered money. "Use this," she said.

"Find a seat, we'll worry about that later," he said, turning his attention away from the money in her hand. He intently watched the operation. The cook had people calling out orders and changing them and calling out reorders and he never once indicated if he heard the order being recited. Instead he just whistled while he cooked. None of the counter help people wrote down orders. No one seemed to be complaining.

Ray watched the lady who took their order scoop out a large ladle full of macaroni salad into each plate. She then used a spatula and added a large helping of home fries. She held the plates near the cook who dropped the two burgers into each plate. The lady took the plates to a large vat. She used the ladle and poured a hearty, sloppy amount of hot sauce over everything.

After paying for two plates, Ray was then bumped out of the way by those behind him waiting to order. The food looked disgusting all tossed together like that, and yet he could not wait to dig in.

"Well?" Linda asked. She had found a booth in the back of the restaurant.

Ray looked around. There was an array of diners: bikers, construction workers, people in suits, a mother with three children. "This place is something else."

Sitting down, Ray took one of the plates off the tray and passed it to Linda. He looked at his own and wondered where to begin. He then watched Linda use a knife and fork and followed suit. After chewing a mouthful, Ray shook his head and laughed. "A Garbage Plate. Who'd have thought that type of a name would be on a menu in a restaurant? This is fantastic."

Linda laughed, too. "It's kind of crazy, isn't it? But I'm glad you like it."

"I do. I love it," Ray said.

They ate in silence. Ray felt thankful. He had no idea what to talk about. Despite loving every minute spent with Linda, he worried about being with her. Eventually they would spend time talking, even if just filling silent moments with small talk. Ray never considered himself much of a talker. Little in his past made him proud, so he did not share things with anyone. Unfortunately, when people want to get to know each other better, what else but the past is there to talk about?

That's why a situation like this or maybe a relationship between him and Linda, could never work. Never.

Ray put down his fork and knife. "Wasn't sure if I could finish it."

"Well, I can't," Linda said, having eaten only half of her meal.

Ray knew he had to cut this short and leave. His meeting, only just down the road, would start in twenty minutes. Perhaps an abrupt departure would annoy Linda enough so that she could see he was not worth getting to know.

Ray would have given anything not to have this dinner end. He looked at his watch and immediately regretted doing so.

"Oh, that's right, you have plans for this evening and I am so full all I want to do is go home and pass out on the sofa," Linda said.

He could deny having plans, but she would know he was lying. He did not want her to leave and did not feel ready to say good night. Religiously he had attended AA meetings, many times taking in two the same night. Missing one couldn't hurt.

But it could. It is even recommended not getting into a relationship while working through recovery. And a relationship was the last thing Ray wanted or needed. Moving to a new city, starting a new job, that was all enough change, perhaps more than enough.

Even if Linda showed signs of being interested, eventually she would want to know all about him. Women were like that. She would want to know about his childhood, family and upbringing. She would want to hear about the women in his life.

"I wish I could get out of my plans, but I don't think I can," Ray said. He felt so confused. He was grinding his front row of teeth anxiously. At this point an AA meeting felt like the exact thing he needed.

"I didn't expect you to break plans," Linda said, graciously. They stood up. Ray put the plates onto the tray and took it to the garbage receptacles, keeping his soda.

"I appreciate you bringing me here," Ray said.

Linda gasped and pulled out money. "I forgot all about this," she said, offering it to him.

Ray smiled and turned away from her. "You can catch the bill next time."

Ray wondered why he'd said that. He didn't want there to be a next time. There shouldn't be a next time. There should not have been a *this* time. He wondered, for that matter, why he had paid the bill. That could be misconstrued as an *I'm-interested-signal*. What right did he have spending money, anyway? He had quickly dwindled away most of his savings to buy that beat up bucket he used as a car, front and back rent for his apartment, not to mention the clothing he had to buy for the job. Of course, financially things would be different after he started receiving a steady check from the firm, but until then, he needed to watch his spending.

Too much. It was all too much and moving too fast. Things needed to slow down. He knew what happened when things moved with too much speed. Things got out of control. This was a new beginning. He couldn't risk having things get out of control. Not ever again.

Chapter 14

Linda was too excited to go home. She did not really want to pass out on the sofa, though she had eaten way too much and felt extremely full. As she left Nick Tahou's parking lot she just enjoyed the feeling of not being able to remove the smile from her expression.

She remembered when she had first started dating Joey Viglucci. She had been swept off her feet with his hard and handsome looks, charm and she had to admit it, his money. Dating Joey had brought her a certain amount of prestige, as shallow a relationship as it had turned out to be. The good looks were just the shell, the charm a façade. As far as the money, even though he spent it on her freely, it did nothing to increase her feelings for him.

Linda sensed she might not have realized all of this until just this moment. Perhaps the only reason she was able to understand her past relationship with Joey was because she could see how completely different he was compared to Ray.

Something about Ray intrigued her. He was handsome in his own way. She loved looking into his chocolate colored eyes, and wondered why he had trouble looking back. The mysterious man. She wanted to explore this some more. She wanted to take things slowly.

"What am I thinking," Linda said, slapping the steering wheel as she drove toward the expressway.

"How many times did the guy check his watch?" *That's because he had plans. He didn't want to be late.*

"A date is more like it," Linda said. *I can't believe I'm getting jealous.*

She took I-390 north until she reached the West Ridge Road exit. Traffic became more congested as she got closer to Greece Ridge Mall, one of the largest malls in western New York. She knew that after working out, Patty would sit at the juice bar at the gym and rest her over-worked muscles. Linda parked in the lot at the Elm Ridge Center and went into the gym looking for Patty.

She saw her secretary using a Nautilus machine to work her abdomen, twisting and bending, burning away any flab and strengthening the sets of muscles. When Patty looked over toward the window, Linda waved.

When Patty finished her set, she picked up her towel and wiped the perspiration off her face and neck. Linda went into the weight room to say hello.

"Change your mind?" Patty asked, sounding winded.

"About exercising? No. It's too late now," she said.

"So what's going on? Look at you. You look like a little kid who caught Santa putting presents under the Christmas tree." Patty looked excited, too, as if she could not wait to hear Linda's news.

"I had dinner with a guy," Linda said.

Patty looked at the clock on the wall. "When?"

"Just now."

"Where?"

"Nick Tahou's," Linda said knowing immediately how it must have sounded to Patty. "It wasn't really a date. We just started talking in the parking garage."

"At work?"

"Yes. You know who it is?" Linda asked.

"No. How would I? Tell me. You're killing me here with the suspense!" Patty looked like she could hardly contain herself.

"Ray. He just started at the firm. The computer guy," Linda said.

"The computer guy? Ray?" Patty said, mulling it over in her mind. She raised an eyebrow and smiled. "He's kind of cute."

"He sure is," Linda said.

"I think we better get some juice and sit down. I want to hear everything," Patty said. They left the gym and walked over to the juice bar.

"Not much to tell. I mean, it's not like he said he likes me or anything. We just went to get something to eat. Patty, I don't know what to think. I feel like this little junior high girl all of a sudden," Linda said as they approached the juice bar.

"Want me to give him a note from you? You can ask him if he likes you to check yes or no in the box and give it back to me?"

Patty said.

Linda laughed. "Would you?"

"Well, if anything, this beats the hell out of Joey," Patty said.

Linda just smiled. She could care less about Joey. He was sick anyway. She would consider calling the cops the next time he bothered her, whether with a prank phone call or a delivery. She was not going to tolerate being harassed by the macho jerk even if he thought he was acting sensitive and sincere. "You know what, I guess we do have a lot to talk about."

Chapter 15

Ray saw Malcolm standing by the coffee table, stirring sugar and cream into his cup, wearing his Buffalo Bills knit hat and worn gloves. He was such a big guy, Ray found it hard to accept the man's gentle mannerisms. He watched Malcolm discard the stir stick and inwardly cringed when he had been caught staring.

"Ray, how are you?" Malcolm asked. He crossed the room and shook hands. "Glad to see you're back."

"How are you, Malcolm?" Ray asked. Despite the confusion and his continued attempts to dissuade himself, Ray could not suppress the tingling sensation he felt in his fingertips and toes. All of this seemed clearly attributable to the meal he had just shared with Linda.

"Apparently not as good as you," Malcolm said, smiling. He patted Ray on the back. "Have a good day?"

"Actually, I did," Ray said. A small part of him wanted to tell Malcolm that he had started a new job. An even smaller part wanted to talk about Linda. For some reason Ray could never open up at these meetings. He never felt comfortable enough to do so. And he didn't know Malcolm. Sure they shared a common denominator and that formed a certain bond between them, but they weren't friends. Not really.

Ray knew why he kept his silence. He could stand up and introduce himself and say he was an alcoholic. He had managed to stay sober and was collecting his chips. These were wonderful things, all things a recovering alcoholic could be proud of.

Did any of this heal him? Was he being cured of his illness?

Ray didn't think so. In the back of his mind, he knew he needed something more before he could get better.

He might have started drinking because he was young and stupid. This might have been the time the dependency started. It had nothing to do with why Ray drank now, or why the guilt he carried around made him think about drinking every day.

Each morning should get easier and easier to stay away from bars and booze. It wasn't so. Each morning was still a challenge. Some might be easier than others, but none were easy.

Since moving to Rochester, Ray felt an even stronger urge boil within him to give up the fight. For some reason, some higher power, perhaps, Ray had stayed sober.

Ray knew the day he could open up and talk about the past, about the things he was running from, he would begin to heal. Only then. Only when he could stand up at an AA meeting and tell everyone that he was done running, would he start truly to recover.

Ray had no idea when that day would come. Standing next to Malcolm, however, he knew it was not today.

Admitting to everyone that he had a troubled past, and that he was not going to run away anymore meant he would have to go back home and face up to things. Somehow he would have to right his wrongs. That was a scary thought. It was that realization that kept him from getting better. He knew he was not man enough; not brave enough to do this.

"Want to share your day with the others?" Malcolm asked.

"I don't think so," Ray said, suddenly solemn.

"You know, usually when people talk here they dwell on the past, on the bad. We could all use an uplifting story. I have no idea what happened to you, for all I know you got laid, but even that might make those around you feel a little better. Think about it?"

Ray shrugged passively. He did not want to appear argumentative. There was no way he'd talk. "I better get some coffee," Ray said pointing at his watch. "It's just about seven."

Malcolm pursed his lips, as if he knew Ray would not participate. "Maybe after the meeting you and I can stop somewhere for a real cup of coffee. What do you think?"

"I'll think about it," Ray said. He knew what was coming. Malcolm would want to know if he had a sponsor. He did not. He knew Malcolm was going to want to volunteer to fill that position. Ray was not ready for a sponsor. He didn't need one. He was making his meetings. He was doing what was expected. He was staying sober.

Chapter 16

Linda was surprised to see that it was already two in the morning. She would have sworn she had just closed her eyes. That had been four hours ago. Lying on her side in bed, looking at the alarm clock, she wondered why she had awoken. She could not remember having a nightmare, or any dream for that matter. Her eyelids felt heavy, fluttered and closed as a thick sense of sleep encased her.

They sprang back open when, just before she fell back to sleep, she heard the creaking noise. This was one disadvantage to living alone. Otherwise, she enjoyed the freedom and privacy. She could not elbow a husband and tell him to go check the noise. She didn't even have a barking dog. Instead, if she wanted piece of mind, she would have to get out of bed and investigate.

She stayed silent in bed for nearly two full minutes. The creaking noise did not come again. She tried closing her eyes, but sleep would not come. She did not feel comfortable falling asleep without at least making a cursory check. Reluctantly Linda turned on the lamp as she got out of bed. She put on her robe and stepped into cold, but fuzzy slippers. From the nightstand drawer Linda removed a large flashlight. It resembled the ones used by security guards not licensed to carry a gun. The flashlight was metal and held five "D" batteries. For all intents and purposes, it could easily be used as a weapon.

Holding the flashlight like a baseball bat Linda opened her bedroom door and flipped on the hall light. She checked the two rooms and the bathroom and finding nothing decided to check downstairs as well. She could feel her heart beating wildly behind her ribcage. She was very conscious of the sound of her breathing. Perspiration wet her skin. Loose strands of hair stuck to her cheeks. She stepped on the first stair and it creaked.

Then she felt the cold.

Freezing air chilled the exposed part of her legs.

Linda turned on the flashlight and aimed the powerful beam downstairs. The front door stood wide open. Wind was sending snow into the foyer in miniature whirlwinds like tornadoes.

Someone is in the house.

Linda ran into her room and closed the door. Crying, she picked up the telephone and called the police. On the third ring, an operator answered. "I think someone is in my house," Linda said. She tried to whisper, to talk quietly. Having never felt this afraid before in her life, Linda could not control her emotions. "Someone is in my house."

"Okay ma'am," the female dispatcher said. "Stay calm. Where are you?"

"In my house. I'm in my house." Linda held the telephone up to her ear, but her eyes kept darting around her room as if expecting to see the intruder pass through the wall.

The door.

"I understand you are in your house. What is your name?"

"Linda. Linda Genova." Linda gave the dispatcher her address before being asked. She backed away from the bedroom door and went to the side of her bed furthest from it. She knelt down, then laid down on her belly. She felt certain someone was going to come through the door and find her.

The light. She knew shutting the bedroom light would be better. If someone came in the room looking for her … the light wouldn't matter. "Please, please, send someone," Linda said.

"Honey, stay right where you are. Police cars are already on the way. Where are you in the house," the woman asked.

Biting down on her lower lip, Linda fought back sobs. "In my bedroom," she said, trembling.

"Are you in a ranch style home?"

"No, a colonial. I'm upstairs," Linda managed. Time seemed to be moving in slow motion. It felt like more than an hour had passed. The constant calm voice of the dispatcher on the line was the only thing keeping her sane. She heard more noise coming from downstairs and screamed. "Someone is downstairs! I hear them. Someone is downstairs."

The lady dispatcher was trying to talk, but Linda could not calm down.

"It is a police officer, Linda. A police officer just entered your house and is walking up the stairs. Can you see him Linda?"

Linda got up on her knees. "No. My bedroom door is closed. I'm so scared. Please help me."

"Everything is all right now, honey. The policeman is going to knock on your door right now."

Knock. Knock.

"Okay Linda? Tell the police officer to come in."

"Come in," Linda said and watched, feeling paralyzed with fear as her bedroom door slowly opened.

Linda screamed again.

"Linda? Is everything all right? Linda?" The dispatcher asked.

Linda saw the police officer and dropped the phone. She stood up, shaking; her hands up near her face.

Within ten minutes, a horde of police officers filled Linda's house. Linda sat on the stairs talking with a Lieutenant O'Neil. "So you didn't actually see anyone in the house?"

"No," Linda said. "I heard them."

"You heard a creaking floorboard?"

"Right."

"Let me show you something," Officer O'Neil said. He led Linda to the front door. "Do you think it's possible when you came home you didn't lock the door? It's pretty windy out. Maybe it was not shut tight. Maybe the door blew open?"

"I don't think that it happened that way. Someone was in my house."

"The door doesn't look jimmied. Do many people have a key to your home?"

Linda thought. "My mom. My neighbor ... Joey."

"Joey?"

"An ex-boyfriend," Linda said and watched O'Neil write something in his notepad planner after asking for Joey's last name. She debated telling the police officer about the phone pranks, the letter on her windshield and the flowers at work.

"When I arrived here, I took a quick look around the house. There were no footprints in the snow. Of course your driveway and sidewalk are shoveled free of snow. However, when I entered your house, the first thing I looked at was the carpeting. Anyone walking up the driveway and down the sidewalk would have some wet, snowy shoes. The carpeting when I arrived, unlike now, did not have any prints. Sorry about what I and the others tracked in here," O'Neil said.

Linda was trying to absorb everything the officer was telling her. He was saying a lot, with out coming out and saying anything. "You think I imagined someone in my house tonight?"

"I didn't say that. I am just pointing out some possibilities," O'Neil said.

"Yeah, I understand what you're saying. You're trying to say the flighty woman living in a house all by her little o'l self heard a thump in the night, panicked and called the police," Linda said. She knew she might be overacting and treating the police officer unfairly, but she couldn't help it.

"Ms. Genova, ma'am, that is not what I am saying. What I am saying is, I see no signs of a forced entry. I found no signs that anyone has been in or around your home. Unless the intruder removed his shoes when he entered your house, I cannot imagine how…"

"I'm sorry. Sorry. I know what you're saying, but it doesn't make me feel any better. I feel all, I don't know, weirded out." Linda looked at the police officer who just kept staring at her empathetically. "I guess it is possible that I did not shut the door all the way, highly, highly unlikely, but possible."

"I'll tell you what we're going to do. For tonight and the next several nights, we'll make sure a police cruiser frequently passes by the house, okay? You have anyone you can call? Someone you can go and stay with?" Officer O'Neil asked.

"I'm all right."

"Sure?"

"With police officers like you protecting the neighborhood, what do I have to worry about?" Linda asked, feeling suddenly tired. At the same time she wanted the night to be over.

O'Neil smiled.

When the police officers left, Linda sat in the living room holding her long metal flashlight, with the television set on, but the volume off. She strained to hear any sound, and at first everything sounded like a burglar trying to break into the house—the howling wind running like a freight train against the siding, the rumbling furnace shaking the house as it kicked on, the impossibly loud hum of her refrigerator. But nothing unnerved her more than when the wind died, the furnace shut down, and the refrigerator quieted. The silence became deafening.

Eventually, morning came. When a person passed by the front window Linda panicked. She saw the shadow of the person through the curtains. Linda jumped to her feet and ran to the door. She was not going to be a prisoner in her own home. She pulled open the door, raised the flashlight over her head as if it were a hatchet and screamed, "What do you want from me!"

The expression on the boy's face was one of utter shock. His mouth and eyes seemed frozen wide open. "Nothing, Ms. Genova. I don't … nothing. I'm just delivering your morning paper."

Chapter 17
Saturday, January 18

Ray Telfer woke up around nine. After showering and getting dressed he decided to go out for breakfast. He wanted eggs, bacon, rye toast, coffee and juice. Only white bread was in the breadbox. The fridge had no juice, eggs or bacon. He could make the coffee, but without everything else, he did not see the point. He needed to go shopping.

Ray put on his coat. One tough thing about moving to a new city was that he did not know anyone. He did not like the idea of going to a restaurant and eating alone. He reached into his pockets for his gloves. When he pulled them out, a square piece of paper fell to the floor.

Picking it up, Ray did not need to look at it to know what it was. Malcolm, after the AA meeting last night, after Ray had passed on going out for coffee, had given him his home telephone number. Ray looked at the telephone number. As much as he did not want to eat breakfast alone, inviting Malcolm to go with him would be like opening an invitation for trouble.

Ray decided against calling him. He set the square of paper on the end table next to the lamp and telephone, picked up his car keys and went to the door. He opened the door and paused, looking back at the telephone. *I could call him and he might not even want to go. At least then I tried*, Ray thought. He closed the door and walked back over to the phone. *Or I'll call him and he'll want to go. Then he'll talk my ear off like some politician, telling me why I should let him be my sponsor. Forget that!* Ray went back to the door, but stopped as he put his hand on the doorknob.

"Or I'll look like a loser sitting alone in a booth for four. I could bring the paper…"

* * * * *

"Man this is a good idea," Malcolm said, sitting next to Ray in the car. "I don't usually go out to eat. I'm not a bad cook, really. Every once in a while though, going out with a friend for breakfast, it just sounds like a good idea."

Ray was not sure what to say so he said, "Glad you could make it."

"I like this place, too. They have great breakfast specials," Malcolm said as Ray pulled into the Peppermill parking lot, on Dewey and Ridge.

They went inside and were seated immediately. The waitress handed them menus. They both asked for coffee to start with.

"You like football?" Malcolm asked.

"Yes. I haven't watched that much this year though," Ray said.

"You a Buffalo fan?" Malcolm asked.

"No. Not at all. I like the Denver Bronco's—I was a huge John Elway fan." Ray looked over the long list of meals; there was quite a variety. His initial cravings would not be detoured. Eggs, bacon, rye toast and juice.

"Now he was a great quarterback. Him and Dan Marino, they were the best out there for their time."

"No arguments there. You know what's funny? They almost never played against each other. That's weird isn't it?"

When the meal came, they ate and continued to talk about football and cars. Ray knew little about cars, but Malcolm had a passion for them. He went on and on about a Barracuda he once owned.

"The thing was what you might call a plum crazy purple," Malcolm said.

"Like a metallic purple," Ray asked.

"You could say that. It had the scoop on the hood sitting between two fat rows of racing stripes. The engine was sweet. I'd take it to shows and pop the hood and even people like yourself, people who know nothing about cars, would just stop and stare at the beautiful engine. The chrome was always polished up to a high quality shine, and I kept a mirror on the ground, under it, so people could see how immaculate I kept the undercarriage. Man, she was sweet. I called her Sea King, you know like after the Hans Christian story?" Malcolm asked, adding an extra few shakes of pepper over his scrambled eggs.

"No. What story?"

"Sea King? The Little Mermaid?"

"Oh, yeah. Sounds really wild," Ray said. "Still got it?" Ray knew the question sounded stupid as soon as he asked it. The man sitting across from him had gloves with holes in every fingertip.

"Sold it. Had to. When you get divorced you wind up losing much more than just your spouse," Malcolm said, solemnly. "I don't even just mean all the personal belongings, though let me tell you, I lost more than my share of all that. Had me a gorgeous house in Ogden. If she had cheated on me, if she had been mean, or even inconsiderate, I'd have fought her tooth and nail for that house and for everything else we accumulated in the marriage. I would have fought for my girls."

Ray bowed his head. Malcolm seemed like he might start crying. "Pretty tough?"

"Tough doesn't even get close to describing it. Not even close. But you see, my ex-wife, she wasn't any of those things. She gave me so many chances to get my act together. All I ever did was make a fool out of her. I made her look stupid in front of her family and mine. She was a tough lady, let me tell you. She stuck by my side for so much longer than she ever needed to. Maybe she did it for our kids. Maybe she loved me enough she thought she could change me. Leave it to a woman, always thinking they can change a sick, stubborn man," Malcolm said, letting out a little laugh.

"But look at you. You've changed."

"A little too late. My wife and I were divorced nearly ten years ago. Like I said at that meeting, I've only been sober for the last five. My ex, she remarried. I see my girls every other weekend. I love that time with them more than anything in the world. I cherish it. But you know what? I can see it in their eyes. They don't really want to be with me. They'd rather be home with their mother, spending time with her or with their friends. They live in the rich part of Webster, you know. Why would my girls want to come and spend a weekend with me, trapped in my stinky city apartment where I don't even earn enough money to have digital television? I don't have money to take them out and buy them things. Ray, I don't even own a car. Why would my girls want to spend time like that with me?"

"Because you are their father," Ray said.

"That's bullshit. They know as well as I do that I was never a father to them. I had my alcohol and my car. I spent more time out in the garage waxing the car and changing parts that didn't need changing than I ever spent talking with my kids, or with my wife. I was no father to them then, and even though I want to be a father to them now, they don't want me. It's like that Cats and the Cradle song. I didn't have time for them when they wanted to spend time with me, so now that I want to be with them, they don't have the time. Except they are forced by the courts to spend every other weekend with me. And I know in my heart they hate every minute of the visit," Malcolm said. He was looking at Ray with a severe intense look. The pain was evident in his expression.

"I don't know what to say." Ray poked at his eggs with his fork. He was thankful he had already eaten most of his meal. Listening to Malcolm had made him lose any appetite that might have been left.

"Man, forget about it. I'm sorry to have dumped on you like that. It was inconsiderate of me." Malcolm took a long sip of orange juice. Ray knew the man had to be imagining the taste of vodka in that swig. When Malcolm set down his glass the two exchanged a knowingly look. "You don't have to worry about me. There's no going back now. I've come way to far and it's taken way too long to get here. I've wasted a good part of my life on this journey and I have no intentions of throwing anymore of it away."

Ray just nodded; surprised to find himself relieved to hear Malcolm say all of that. He found that he actually was enjoying this time with Malcolm. It should only make sense that the two of them would get along. Their lives might be different, but the similar links were like bonds tying them together and possibly providing a base for the beginnings of a friendship.

"How about you, Ray. Were you married?" Malcolm asked after a long awkward silence.

"Married? No. Came close a few times. Came real close, once. But I guess you could say things didn't work out between us."

Malcolm just nodded. He must have thought he understood what Ray meant, even though Ray had not elaborated.

When Ray dropped Malcolm off, he stopped Malcolm from

getting out of the car. "I've got to ask you something."

"Shoot."

"I was convinced you'd ask me if I needed a sponsor for AA."

"Did you want me to ask you?"

"No. I didn't," Ray said.

"Well, Ray, I figure when you are ready, and if you want, you'll ask me. I used to ask people if they wanted a sponsor, but not any more. Being someone's sponsor is demanding and often disappointing. It is hard not to take it personally when someone you sponsor falls off the wagon, know what I mean? I'm not saying I won't help someone who asks for it. I'm all for helping whoever asks. At least then I know that the person asking at least thinks they are serious about getting better. Someone who doesn't ask for help … maybe isn't ready for help. See what I'm saying?"

Ray nodded. "I see what you are saying."

"And Ray, thanks for asking me to go with you for breakfast. I enjoyed your company."

"We'll have to do this again," Ray said, and meant it.

"I'd like that."

PHILLIP TOMASSO, III

Chapter 18

Linda paid for her groceries at the checkout and stuffed the receipt into her purse. She enjoyed shopping on Saturday mornings, it was a long-standing tradition for her. She wheeled the shopping cart outside, thankful to see that it was no longer snowing and the sun in a blue sky. There was something known in Western New York as the January thaw. It was a brief period of time where spring-like weather conditions interrupted winter's feverish dominance. Linda hoped this would be the beginning of some more pleasant days.

"Hey, Linda," someone said. Linda turned to see Ray Telfer about to enter the store. "Nice morning, huh?"

"It's wonderful. I was just thinking about it. I can't believe how tired I am of the cold and the snow," Linda said. She wondered why she had said so much. Ray had merely said hello and made a generic comment on the weather. He might as well have said, 'How are you'.

"Is it crowded in there? I am so out of food at home, but hate shopping, I think, even more than I enjoy eating."

They laughed. "It's a Saturday morning. Need I say more?"

"I guess not," Ray said. He took a deep breath and looked at the store. "I guess I'm going to have to be strong, go in and get this over."

Again, Ray seemed to want to get away from her. She felt hurt and rejected. She struggled to keep the knee-jerk emotions from her expression. Linda just smiled. "Don't let me hold you up."

"Hold me up? You're not." Ray looked at the ground and stuffed his hands into his pockets, reminding Linda of a shy schoolboy. "If this sounds at all out of line, just say so, all right? I'd enjoy it if you and I could do something together tonight."

"Seriously?" she asked.

"I'm out of line. I'm sorry," he said.

"No. You're not out of line. Not at all. I just kept getting the feeling that you were brushing me off." Linda shook her head. She hated how insecure she felt. She hated even more how easily she shared this weakness with Ray. She did not want him to think less of her.

"How could you think that? I had a great time at Nick Tahou's last night. I hated having to leave."

"You did?" Linda said. She could hardly believe what she was hearing. "You know what? I'd love to get together with you."

"I have no idea how long it's going to take me in there, but it should be safe to set something up for around, I don't know, seven?" Ray asked.

"Seven sounds great." Linda wrote her phone number down on the back of a firm business card and gave it to Ray. "Call me around five?" She asked, resting her hand on his forearm.

"What's this? Who's this?" Joey Viglucci asked. He was standing on the opposite side of Linda, dressed in black, sporting a goatee.

"Joey," Linda said. She almost asked him what he was doing here, as if she had been caught doing something wrong giving Ray her home phone number. She had to remind herself that Joey was not a part of her life. He did not deserve an explanation.

"So who is this guy, Linda? We been separated a few days and you already latched on to another guy? That's pathetic. You're pathetic," Joey said.

"Like slashing my tires?" Linda said, accusingly.

"Hey buddy," Ray said.

Linda held up a hand. She did not want Ray getting involved. She knew Joey enjoyed fighting and was good at it. He was solid layers of muscle and fighting was one way he could utilize all the dedicated work he put into forming the size and shape of his body.

It seemed too late.

Joey walked briskly around the shopping cart and stood in front of Ray. "Did you say something, assface?"

"Assface?" Ray asked, and laughed.

"You think this is funny?" Joey asked.

"No. I think assface is funny. I've never heard that before." Ray laughed a little harder.

Linda watched Joey. Somehow Ray's laughing confused her

ex-boyfriend. One, Ray exhibited no sign of fear. He did not appear intimidated by Joey. Two, she thought Joey might be smiling. Linda also thought assface was a funny word.

"You stay away from Linda, got that?" Joey said and turned around.

"I don't think I can do that," Ray said.

"Oh damn it," Linda said. They had almost avoided an incident. If Ray could have just agreed with Joey, then nothing would have happened.

* * * * *

Ray could feel his stomach doing flips inside his body. He felt the adrenaline surging through his veins. It had been some time since he had been in a real fight. There had been many bar fights, but those were different. This would almost be a clean fight. No one was drunk. This Joey wanted to show off for Linda. For some reason, he thought beating on Ray would impress her.

"You looking for trouble, ass ... hole?" Joey asked. He kept his fists at his sides. He wore leather gloves.

Ray knew the type. Tough guy. Street fighter. It would be a dirty fight. He knew if he fell, this guy would start kicking him. There would be no honor in this fight. Joey would do anything to win. Even a sucker punch ...

Which came like a lightening bolt toward Ray's stomach.

Ray was ready for it, and knocked his forearm down onto Joey's. Simultaneously, Ray threw a punch, putting all of his weight into the swing and hit Joey in the face. He went for the nose, but wound up smacking his teeth. Ray's bloodied knuckles hurt as if he'd hit a brick wall. He could not tell if the blood was from Joey's gums, or his own split skin.

"You bastard," Joey said, barely phased by the blow.

"Stop this. Stop it," Linda was screaming. Ray hated to hear her sounding so upset. "Joey, it's over between us. Over!"

Joey threw three quick punches, whacking Ray in the arm, the stomach and the forehead. Ray felt dizzy. His arm and gut ached. He thought he might throw up. There was no time. Joey seemed far from done with the round. Two more punches connected with Ray's face, and he went down hard. He could feel blood oozing from his nose.

"Stop it!" Linda continued to yell. People walking stopped and stared.

A siren sounded.

A man in uniform got out of a car that resembled a police cruiser, but was simply white with SECURITY written across the door panel. "Gentleman? We have a problem here?"

"Problem?" Joey asked, looking down at Ray.

Ray held out his hand. Joey took it and helped him to his feet.

"No problem," Ray said. "Slipped on some black ice. Might want to salt this area better."

It must have been obvious to the security guard what had been going on. "I'll check into sprinkling salt. Right now, I think the three of you better get moving out of here."

No one moved. Ray stood by Linda, holding onto her shopping cart for balance. She put her hand over his. He looked at her and smiled.

Joey looked at their hands and over at Ray.

"Guys? I mean get moving now or I'll call the police," the guard said. He had a CB radio in his hand.

"I'll see you around," Joey promised before walking out toward the parking lot.

"I guess I'll have to shop later," Ray said to Linda.

"I'm sorry this happened," Linda said.

Ray looked at the guard. "We're going."

The guard didn't seem completely satisfied, but must have figured the fight was over since one of the men involved had left. He got back into his marked cruiser and continued to patrol the parking lot.

"Are you all right?" Linda asked.

"Wasn't too bad. Guy's solid as a building," Ray said. He looked at his knuckles. The skin was split. The blood was coming from his hand. "A brick building."

Chapter 19

Ray wanted to surprise Linda with something special planned for their first date. He didn't want to do the dinner and a movie thing. Optimistic, he spent nearly an hour looking through a newspaper and the yellow pages in the phone book hoping to find something different for them to do—something that would make the night memorable. What he had learned was that Rochester could be a damned-boring city if you didn't drink. Ladies night at this bar, dollar drafts at another. Comedians are entertaining on stage at a prime club ... with a two-drink minimum, or course. Eventually Ray decided on a less than extraordinary, and less than original idea.

At five, Ray called Linda. "I thought we'd go bowling," Ray said. He wanted to sound confident, as if these were the plans he had in mind all along. He debated telling Linda how much time he spent trying to find something for them to do, but did not want her to think he had trouble coming up with ideas, or was too indecisive. At the same time, he had no intention of telling her about his recovery, at least not right away.

"I haven't been bowling ... It sounds like so much fun. I can't even remember the last time I went bowling," Linda said, sounding genuinely excited.

"I'll pick you up at seven, then. All right?" Ray said. Linda gave him directions to her house. He did not write them down. When she asked if he understood how to get to her house, Ray recited the directions back to her.

Hanging up the telephone, he almost laughed. Ray could not recall a time when he had felt more apprehensive and excited. The way he felt when he was talking with Linda on the telephone reminded him of early high school days. He remembered being fourteen and having his first real girlfriend, resulting in some of his most awkward memories. He never knew what to do on the weekends. See a movie; hang out at the mall; watch television at each other's house. During school it had been easier. They both had friends around. Still, there was kissing in the halls between classes, carrying her books to class and then winding up being late to his own. It had seemed that only after sex did the awkward tension in the relationship begin to vanish. The experience behind losing his virginity had been awkward in an entirely different way though. Still, something between them had changed. They had grown closer. The confidence increased, on both parts. Everything they had done together felt more natural, especially the kissing.

The thoughts that kept returning to the scene with that jerk from the supermarket insisted on trying to ruin everything. He could not get the incident out of his mind. He did not like being made to look like a jerk, especially in front of Linda. This guy had to have been out of his mind, looking for trouble. Ray did not consider himself a fighter, but knew how to defend himself and did not consider himself afraid of any man. He had not grown up in a tough neighborhood, but during his drinking years he had been involved in a fair share of barroom brawls.

Ray's emotions were running strong inside of him. In a way, he feared such feelings. Staying in control over all aspects of his life was more than a bit challenging. It dominated each day.

He decided he needed to make one more phone call. He felt funny making it. Things were going very well. Maybe because everything seemed to be going well, making the phone call became that much more important. Almost reluctantly, he picked up the phone and dialed slowly.

* * * * *

Linda had just gotten off the telephone with Ray when it rang again. "Hello?"

No one answered. "Hello?" Linda said, again. She could hear the person breathing on the other end. "You know what? I don't appreciate this kind of phone call." She slammed the phone down.

Screw them, she thought. She felt too good about tonight, was too excited, to let a prank phone call ruin the rest of the day. Joey Viglucci had already ruined her morning. If that had been him calling, she had no intentions of letting him ruin her evening. She wondered if she should call the police. Maybe the next time Joey bothered her she could warn him that he was leaving her no option but to call the police. Not that he deserved the chance, but this way she'd know she gave him every opportunity to quit harassing her.

* * * * *

When the doorbell rang, Linda looked at her alarm clock on the nightstand next to her bed. It read, 6:50. "He's early," she muttered even though she was ready, she couldn't help feeling panicked and anxious. There were twisting knots of apprehension in her stomach and she felt shaky. She had been sitting in front of the mirror for the last five minutes. Her hair was brushed and she wore a light application of make-up. She had painted her nails with a clear polish and wore a pair of slightly tight blue jeans with white sneakers. The hardest thing had been finding the right top to go with the casual outfit. After sorting through her closet and dresser drawers several times, in the hopes of having missed something absolutely perfect during the previous search, Linda had finally settled on a burgundy colored, long sleeve, low "v" cut shirt.

With Ray at the door, however, she wasn't confident that she had made the right outfit decision. She looked in the mirror and sighed. "Forget it," she said to her reflection. "You look fine."

Forcing herself to get up, Linda went downstairs and opened the front door. Inwardly, she sighed a second time. Ray was dressed in jeans and sneakers. His top looked nice, a pullover with three buttons, but was nothing special.

"I'm a little early," Ray said apologetically. He had his hands behind his back.

"That's all right. I'm just about ready." Linda said, stepping aside. "Come on in."

Ray entered the house, looking over the place quickly. Then he showed Linda what he had been hiding behind his back.

She grinned.

"Ray, you shouldn't have," she said taking the flowers. "They're beautiful. I'm going to run and put them in some water. Why don't you have a seat in the living room, turn on the television if you'd like. I'll be all set in a minute."

"Okay," Ray said.

Linda started toward the kitchen, feeling really good inside. She had not been looking for a new relationship to jump into. If anything she needed a nice long breather after Joey. That's how love seemed to work. It came upon you when you were least likely to be looking for it.

Love, a little strong of a word. However, she could feel its powerful potential. She looked back and saw Ray leaning against the wall in the foyer, untying his shoelaces, removing his sneakers and setting them on the Welcome mat next to hers. In his socks, he caught her watching him.

"Everything all right?" Ray asked.

"Perfect," Linda said, and went into the kitchen. She felt giddy after being caught.

Chapter 20

Ray held open the door to the bowling alley and felt self-conscious about his decision. Maybe bowling had been a completely wrong choice for a first date. Maybe he should have stuck with something a little more traditional. With a movie and dinner, the date would last maybe three-and-a-half-hours, but for two of the hours, they would be watching a film and there would be no pressure to find things to talk about. After the film, while they ate, they could talk about the movie they had just seen. With bowling, damn it, he would need to provide a steady flow of topics to keep a conversation alive.

If anything, he repeatedly warned himself, *do not talk about work.*

They walked from the silent parking lot into an explosion of light and sound. The place was dark, while the actual lanes were brightly lit with spotlights on the pins at the end of each alley. Video game noises, speaker music and announcements could barely compete with the sound of balls rolling down oil-slicked alleys and smashing into pins, like the whistle of a falling bomb before it explodes.

"Ray, this is going to be so much fun," Linda said.

Ray felt it too. The place was lively. It definitely possessed atmosphere. The loudness, the lights … the place possessed excitement.

They went up to the front counter and Ray told the guy he had called earlier about a lane.

"Sorry, buddy. We're booked with leagues," the man said, turning his back to Ray.

"Where's Scott?" Ray asked, demanding attention. His voice was not loud, but the man behind the counter must have known the question had been directed at him. He looked at Ray, who asked the question again. "Because you're not Scott, right?"

"That's okay, Ray. Let's go," Linda said.

Ray was not going to go. Linda said she had been excited about going bowling. Hell, he felt excited about bowling. Scott had been the guy he talked with earlier. The man had agreed to let him use a lane until nine when the lane would be needed the night league.

"No, I'm not Scott. Scott's on a break. Sorry." The man looked like he might turn away from Ray again.

"Page him," Ray said.

The guy gave Ray a smile that said, *I can't believe this asshole.* "I don't know if he took his break here, or if he went out for something to eat."

"So if you page him and he doesn't show, we'll wait until he gets back," Ray said.

"Really Ray," Linda said, tugging on his arm.

Ray was sure she did not want to see any more trouble for the day. Her ex-boyfriend had already caused enough.

"You should listen to her," the guy said to Ray, as if thinking he was tough.

"Page him," Ray said. He stared intently at the guy behind the counter. The way he spoke this last time contained impact.

The guy picked up a microphone and held it up to his mouth. "Scott to the front desk," he said, his voice booming like God's over the thundering noises of bowling. "Scott to the front desk, please." He replaced the microphone under the counter, never losing eye contact with Ray.

"Thank you," Ray said, politely.

Within thirty seconds, a tall thin man with a brown beard and mustache approached the counter, wiping his hands on a paper napkin. "What's up Benny?"

Benny, Ray thought. *Figures.*

"This guy says you promised him a lane?" Benny said.

Scott looked at Ray and Linda. "Ray? You the guy I talked to earlier?"

"Yes. That's me," Ray said, holding out his hand.

Scott rolled the napkin up in his palm, then quickly wiped his hand down the side of his own jeans before shaking. "Just eating Buffalo chicken wings," he said apologizing for any messy sauce that might have transferred onto Ray's hand.

"Benny, give them a lane, and when the nine o'clock teams

show, he'll leave. Right Ray?" Scott said, still looking at Benny with scolding eyes.

"Of course," Ray said.

"Got it," Benny said. "Sorry to bother you on your lunch."

"Forget about it," Scott said. He looked at Ray. "Have fun bowling."

Ray shook hands one more time with Scott. He'd palmed a tip. Scott fisted the money and nodded appreciatively. "We will. Thank you."

* * * * *

Linda was not sure what had just taken place at the front counter. That Benny guy had been a creep. Though she did not like the direction the exchange seemed to be headed between Benny and Ray, she felt relieved to see Ray get things under control. She thought she tasted a flavor of Joey Viglucci in what had just happened however, and it made her wary. After Joey, she obviously couldn't completely trust her own judge of character, and she didn't want to make the same mistake twice.

After they selected black house bowling balls, they went to their lane down into the settee area and set their balls in the return rack and sat down to put on their multi-colored bowling shoes.

"You know, as ugly as these things are, there is something attractive about them," Linda said, tying a big bow with her laces, then admiring the red and blue paneled sides of her shoe.

"I guess," Ray said. "I sometimes can't get past the fact that nearly half the city probably wore this pair of shoes. Smelly feet inside sweaty socks all inside these shoes."

Linda grimaced. "You would think of that," she said, laughing. "They spray them after you give them back."

"Oh sure. Benny looks like a very hard working and dedicated employee," Ray said, nodding in the direction of the front counter.

"Great. Now I feel like bowling in my socks."

"I used to be on a league. I owned my own shoes," Ray said.

"Oh, is that when you first moved to Rochester? Is that when you met Scott?" Linda asked.

"No. It was a different city. But its how I know the type of men Scott and Benny are. There are, like, the same people work-

121

ing at bowling alleys all over the world. Go anywhere and you'll find a Scott and Benny," Ray said smiling.

Someone behind them cleared their throat. Linda turned and saw a cocktail waitress dressed in black slacks, a black vest and white blouse. "Can I get anything for either of you?"

Linda shrugged. "A Genny Light?" She looked at Ray.

"I'll take a Coke."

Linda saw something in Ray's face that made her change her order. "Know what, make it two," she told the waitress.

When the waitress was gone, Linda felt uncomfortable. She found it difficult to make eye contact with Ray, but was not sure why. She had merely ordered a beer. It was the way he had ordered his soda that told her something was, maybe not wrong, but different.

"I don't drink," Ray said, indicating that he too had been thinking about what just happened. "But there is no reason why you can't have a beer."

Linda smiled thinly. "I don't need the extra calories," Linda said, patting her flat belly.

"I'm a recovering alcoholic," Ray said. Linda knew he was telling her this reluctantly. "I didn't intend to discuss this tonight. It's something you should know, I thought. But I guess it's something that is a little embarrassing to bring up."

It must have taken tremendous courage for Ray to share this with her, but to be honest she was not sure how this made her feel. She hated to admit it, but it did alter her point of view. "How long?" she asked. She hated getting so personal, but she had to know.

"I'm close to three months," Ray said, as if he knew he was taking a test. He dug into his pocket and showed her some colored coins. "I get one for every month I am sober. I get my third next week."

Linda could hear in his voice the proud sense of accomplishment. She watched his face while he spoke. He had a look in his eyes, an intense look that spoke volumes. She could not look away. "I will never go back to drinking," he told her. "I'm sorry I didn't tell you this sooner. I was wrong. I didn't plan to keep it a secret; I just didn't plan to bring it up so soon. At the time, that made perfect sense. But now, right now, I know how bad a decision that was. If you want me to take you home, if you want to call things off, believe me, I understand."

Linda knew she did not want to make a knee-jerk reaction, either way. Dating someone, perhaps getting serious with a person she already knew had a drinking problem could be dangerous. Not giving someone a chance, someone she thought she already cared about, might be a mistake. "Let's just see how things go," Linda said honestly.

Ray pursed his lips and nodded. "That sounds good."

Linda actually had so many questions that at first, she found it difficult to concentrate. She wanted to know when and why he started drinking. She wanted to know what kind of a drinker he was. She wanted to know maybe more than anything, the reason he decided to get sober. All these questions swirled around in her mind, at first.

"Now, I've got to warn you, I've bowled on leagues nearly all my life," he said, picking his ball up out of the rack. His tone was strained. She could tell he was trying very hard to make things as normal as possible.

"So you're not going to let me win?" Linda asked. She sat at the scorekeeping table. She entered their names into the computer, Ray's first.

"That would be insulting," Ray said. "Don't you think?"

"Oh, so very insulting," Linda said, laughing. She watched Ray on his approach. He showed nice form, and his little rear end looked cute from where she was sitting.

Ray released the ball, and a second later it crashed into the gutter. She laughed as he clapped his hands to his head in disbelief. "So all those years of bowling didn't do anything to increase your talent."

"I said I've been bowling since I was little, I never said I was any good." Ray stood by the ball return waiting for his ball. When the machine spat it out, he picked it up and winked at Linda.

Linda watched Ray roll his second ball. This time he managed to avoid the gutter, and miraculously, the ball curved two thirds of the way down the lane. It struck the pins at an angle between the first and third pin, sending all ten pins into a fury. Ray threw his arms up into the air in celebration. "Spare!" he shouted.

Linda stood up. "Nice recovery," she said and cringed.

Ray put his hands on her shoulders. She looked into his eyes.

"Thank you," he said. He leaned forward and gently kissed her lips. *I didn't mean to say recovery*, she thought. "I'm sorry."

"For what? It's your turn," Ray said. "Let's see what you got."

The waitress returned with their drinks. Ray paid for the drinks and tipped the lady. "Can we get a bowl of popcorn when you have a chance?"

Despite everything, Linda had to admit she was having a good time. She was truly enjoying herself. She enjoyed being with Ray. There was just something about him that seemed right, that felt right. She was glad she had not decided to go home.

Linda stared at the pins, concentrating. She could count the times she had bowled in her life. She always had a good time when she went; she just didn't go often. She rolled the ball straight down the center of the lane. The ball struck the first pin, head-on. Almost in slow motion pins fell in a domino like fashion, knocking over all ten pins. Linda jumped up and down. "I got a strike!"

"I see you're out for blood, eh? Merciless."

"You know it," Linda said. "Do I get to go again?"

"You just got a strike," Ray said.

"You had two turns," Linda said, teasing.

"Can I ask you something?" Ray said sounding serious all at once.

"I guess."

"This Joey, what's the story?"

"He and I had been seeing each other. I just broke it off with him, not too long ago," Linda said. She knew Ray would ask about Joey sooner or later. If he didn't, then she would have wound up telling him anyway. "We were together about six months, borderline serious, you know?"

"I know the six month mark. It makes or breaks the relationship," Ray said.

"So I've heard. Ours broke. He had two faces, but managed to keep that second one hidden from me for a long time. When I saw it, it was so ugly, there was no way I could stay with him. When I left him, he didn't take it too well. He's been harassing me," Linda said and immediately regretted her words.

"Harassing?" Ray asked.

"He calls my house and hangs up when I answer. He left a love letter for me on my car and sent flowers to the office," Linda said. "At least I think it's him. He's trying to be romantic, something he had never really been when we had been dating. He was flashy and threw around money, but he was never romantic. So now he's pretending to be my secret admirer."

"And is it working?" Ray asked.

"Is what working?"

"Is he being romantic?"

"You know, the idea of a secret admirer might seem romantic to some people," Linda said.

"And to you?"

"To me? It's kind of weird. I feel paranoid, like I'm being watched," she said.

"I guess you are, in a way," Ray said.

"But no," Linda said.

"No what?"

"I don't think Joey's technique is working. I don't feel anything for him. Truth is, I don't think I really ever did." Linda watched Ray as his mind went to work on that information. He seemed relieved to hear those words. "Your turn," she said, diverting attention.

Chapter 21
Monday, January 20

Linda spent most of the first half of her morning working on the position paper on the Jason Kenmore charge. The meeting with the state agency was in the morning. She needed to wrap up her final draft and get it in to Patrick Bierman for review before submitting it to Andrew Egert at the fact-finding session.

Finding it difficult to concentrate, Linda decided she needed a cup of coffee. When she returned to her office, Patty stopped typing. "Bierman was just down to see if you were in. I told him you had an empty coffee cup in your hand."

"He wants to see me?" Linda asked knowing he must have found out about the interview at the state agency. She had meant to tell him, but had not managed to find the time.

"He said to send you over when you got back," Patty said, shrugging.

Linda took the latest draft off the printer and headed toward Bierman's office, a little annoyed that the fresh cup of coffee would be cold by the time she returned.

Bierman's door was open. His secretary was not at her post. She lightly rapped her knuckles on the doorjamb to get his attention. She did not want to startle him. He looked intent on the documents he appeared to be reading.

"Come on in, Linda. Close the door please," Bierman said, setting down the papers he'd been reading. He smiled as Linda took a seat across from him. He folded his hands and leaned onto the desk. "How's everything with the Kenmore charge going?"

Linda told him about the meeting in the morning. She gave him the draft of the position paper. Bierman said he'd review it immediately. "After you do, I'll make changes, then I'd like to fax it to Egert at the state agency. This way he'll have time to review it before our meeting."

"Need me to accompany you?" Bierman asked. He had that

way of asking things that should have sounded sincere, but instead came out demeaning. Even if Linda did require his assistance, she would have felt uncomfortable asking after the way that he offered it.

"I've got it," Linda said. "I'm familiar with these types of meetings."

"Good. Everything else going all right?" Bierman asked.

Linda could not guess where the attorney was headed with his line of questioning. It seemed obvious that something was on his mind. She figured it had something to do with the other day, at lunch. She wanted to forget his behavior. She wanted to act as if the entire thing had never happened. "Seems to be, yes."

"Good. Great. Listen the reason I wanted to see you has to do with last week," he said.

Linda held up a hand. "Please. It's forgotten," Linda said. The moment felt intense for her. She did not want to discuss this. She had rejected her boss. She figured he was worried she might file a complaint, or something.

"I'm sorry?" Bierman said, cocking his head to one side. He looked like a confused puppy.

Linda felt self-conscious, wondering if she had spoken out of line. "I thought you were talking about our business lunch," Linda said, purposely substituting the words lunch date with business lunch.

He shrugged, as if he had no idea what she might be referring to. "Anyway," he said, dismissing her perspective entirely. "It was brought to my attention that you were out with a firm employee the other day. Is this true?"

Her boss' demeanor shocked Linda. He sounded accusatory. What could he be talking about? Ray? "You mean Ray?"

"The new computer admin, yes." Patrick Bierman now leaned back in his chair, crossing his arms across his chest.

"We went bowling, if that's what you mean," Linda said. "What does this have to do with anything?" Her emotions surged and she felt her cheeks and ears reddening.

"I just want to remind you about the firm's policy on dating between employees," Bierman said with a seriousness that made Linda' stomach roll.

The dirty bastard, she thought. "I don't understand what you're talking about. Ray and I went bowling. That's hardly dating." She wanted to ask him how he might have handled the situation, had she agreed to go out with *him!*

Patrick Bierman stood up and walked toward his window. He stuffed his hands into his pockets, and after a few silent moments, turned to face Linda. "Listen, I'm not trying to tell you what to do. I am merely reacting to some information I was given," he said smugly.

"Who gave you the information?" Linda wanted to know.

"I don't see why that's important," Patrick said.

Linda knew not to let this get out of hand. She was angry. She wanted to yell. She knew she would not let Bierman get away with this kind of treatment, but she needed to keep her head. "It's important because someone is ..." What? Lying? It wasn't a lie. She had been out with Ray, and though no one else could know for sure, it was something of a date.

Secret Admirer. Joey—the true bastard. He must be aware of the firm's policy and decided to make waves. *He must be following me,* Linda thought. This was getting absurd, completely, and irrationally out of hand.

"Someone is *what,* Linda?"

"Nothing," she said and stood up. She wanted to storm out of the office, but did not want to be insubordinate. She wanted to handle this the right way. T's crossed. I's dotted. Bierman, of all people, should know better. He appeared to be doing this because she refused to go out with him. "Are we done?"

"Do we understand each other?" Bierman asked. He stood in a way that he must have thought made him look cool. His hands were in his pockets, all the weight on his left leg, while his right leg extended casually, as if he were posing for a catalogue ad.

"I think we do, yes," Linda said and left. She realized her hands were balled into tightly clenched fists. She felt so hot she thought her head might explode, or as in the cartoons her skullcap would shoot into the air from the tremendous build up of steam inside her head.

When she made it back to her office she asked Patty to schedule a meeting for her with Barbara Cunningham, the firms human resource associate.

"Why? What's the matter?" Patty asked.

"Nothing. I'm going to be busy in there," Linda said, pointing toward her office. "Except for that meeting, I prefer not to be disturbed."

"Is everything all right?" Patty asked. Her face looked wounded. "Linda, talk to me."

Linda led Patty into her office. She closed the door. Linda told Patty what had taken place. "So what do you think I should do? Should I report his behavior?"

"Damn right you should. This guy wants you. It's obvious. He must have a mad crush on you. He can't treat you that way. I'm going to go out there and set up a meeting right away for you. She'll take care of things. There is no reason you should have to be abused by him," Patty said, full of fire.

"We'll talk tonight, okay? At the gym."

"We're on? You sure you still feel like going?" Patty asked.

Linda smiled. "Of course."

Chapter 22

Linda left Barbara Cunningham's office not feeling much better than she had after the absurd meeting with Patrick Bierman. Of course, after Linda described the way the business lunch went between herself and Bierman, Barbara insisted she would look into the matter. However, she was not sure she saw anything wrong with Bierman reminding Linda about the firm's rules on dating.

"It is a company policy," Barbara had said, pursing her lips and batting her eyes. Her tone of voice sounded an octave higher than condescending.

"We were bowling," Linda had explained. "The lawyers meet for golf all the time. Are they dating?" Most of the attorneys were men. She did not know if any of the women attorneys golfed. It made her question more of a dig.

"You know, and I know, there is nothing wrong with bowling. We just need to make sure it stays as platonic as that," Barbara had said.

"Of course," Linda said, feeling like she was in one of those dreams where you were being chased, but could not move because the floor was made of glue. "But what about retaliation?"

"At this point, I can't comment. I'll have to look into things."

"And what does that mean? I mean, Patrick and I were the only ones at the restaurant when he asked me out," Linda said, realizing a little too late what was going to happen. "You're not going to talk to Patrick, are you?"

"I have to," Barbara said. "You've raised an issue of harassment. I have an obligation to react and respond." The smile had to be condescending now. It said, *You handle this type of thing all day long, Linda, you should know exactly what's expected of me.*

She thought she might be getting sick. Her stomach acids churned. She thought she could taste bile in her throat. "So what do I do?"

"You carry on normally. You did the right thing coming to see me. I'll look into everything," Barbara said.

"And you'll keep me informed?" Linda asked.

"As much as I can, yes."

Walking back to her office, Linda thought she could taste unemployment. It was after five, but people were still working. It was much different working past five on a Monday. On a Friday, everyone wanted to get out as soon as possible, natural human instinct.

Patty's area was closed up. Stuck to her monitor screen, Linda saw a yellow Post-It from Patty:

> *Linda*
> *Had a few errands to run. Will meet you at the gym by six.*
> *Patty*

Linda put files away and locked drawers while her computer shut down. Aside from the need to workout, Linda was in the mood for a drink. Her head felt as if it were spinning just fast enough to make everything blurry. Bierman had started a process that could make her continued employment with the firm challenging in the least, especially once Barbara started her investigation.

Regardless, there was nothing she could do at this point. The situation was out of her hands. Though she might feel weary about the process, she knew she had done the right thing. She could not allow Bierman to treat her disrespectfully, out of spite, or otherwise.

Linda put on her coat and left the office. In the parking garage, she was too preoccupied with her thoughts to notice the white envelope on her windshield under the wiper until she'd climbed into her car and was about to start the engine.

She opened the door and got out of the car, picked up the unmarked envelope. It wasn't sealed; the flap was tucked into the back. Inside was a single piece of plain white computer paper with a printed message.

Reading the message enraged Linda at first, too much all at once. Tightly clenching the letter in one hand, the envelope in the other, she briskly walked toward the guard manning the booth at the garage entrance. He must have seen her coming. He stepped out of the booth and slowly walked toward her with his thumbs hooked through his waistband.

"Problem, ma'am?" He was a tall lanky African American dressed in a navy blue security guard uniform complete with a square badge pinned to his coat. He wore a blue security baseball cap, which he removed in Linda's presence, revealing a hairless and shiny head.

"Do you have cameras that watch the garage?" Linda asked.

"We do," he said. He shifted his weight from one to the other foot. "Someone hit your car?"

"No. Someone did not hit my car," Linda said. She knew she had no right taking her frustration out on the man in front of her, but could not help it. "Someone put this under my wiper."

The man reached for it.

"No. You can't read it. I want to know who put it there, though," Linda said. She could feel her body shaking. The anger did not seem to be subsiding, but a sense of panic and perhaps fear ebbed its way into her emotions, demanding some attention. She thought she might cry. She did not want to cry.

"I'm not sure I can just show you the…"

"I want you to call the police for me," Linda said. "Please, call the police for me."

She read the letter again:

Linda,

I keep thinking about you, about the two of us making love. I keep picturing us naked, together, touching, kissing, licking, screwing. I get excited thinking about this, about you, about us … so excited I have to touch myself, close my eyes and pretend it is you touching me. Soon I will tell you who I am. I know you'll feel the same way, or learn to, and when we touch the way I imagine us touching, it will only turn out to be better than I ever dreamed it could be.

Love,
Me

* * * * *

Linda sat in the front seat of the police cruiser to keep from getting cold. The car sat parked by the back entrance to the Reynolds Arcade Building. At the moment, the officer was talking to the security guard. The police radio kept crackling to life and some toneless voice would talk, telling officers about incoming 911 calls and recite addresses and street names. The responding police were a lot more difficult to understand. Regardless, everyone talked politely, and Linda found it a little disturbing that no one seemed in any kind of a rush. She could not detect any urgency in any of the voices she heard.

The driver door opened and the police officer climbed into his car. "How are you, Ms. Genova?"

"I'm okay. Angry and a little scared, but I'm all right." She had told the police officer all about her secret admirer. He listened without taking notes. He kept great eye contact while she talked.

"We're getting a copy of the digital surveillance set up. My guess is this case is going to be assigned to an investigator who will review the data and then get back in touch with you," the police officer said. His buzz cut made him resemble a Marine, but his sky blue eyes made him look like a boy. "You say you had called the police the other night, afraid someone had broken into your home while you were sleeping?"

"That's right."

"But the officers on the scene, they didn't find anything?"

"Right."

"Okay, now it's important if you can try to think of any people who you suspect might be doing this to you," the officer said.

Linda took in a deep breath, held it for a long moment and then sighed.

"Ms. Genova?" the police officer asked.

"I've got two people I suspect could be responsible," she said. "The first is my ex-boyfriend, Joey Viglucci." Linda gave the officer Joey's address and telephone number. She also told him where Joey worked.

"I've heard of the Viglucci's," the police officer said. He wrote the information down on his pad. "How long ago did the two of you separate?"

Linda told him. "It had been a big scene." Linda explained

how Joey had started a fight with a friend at the grocery store.

"And who was that, Ms. Genova?"

"I'm sorry?"

"The person who fought with Mr. Viglucci. What was his name?"

"I don't see why that's important," Linda said.

"And it might not be. I just want my report as clean and as clear as possible. See where I'm coming from?"

"I suppose. Ray Telfer. He works with me at the firm," Linda said, cringing. She did not want to pull Ray into her problems.

"Is he a boyfriend?" the police officer asked.

"Ah—no. He's a friend," Linda explained.

"Okay, anything else about Joe Viglucci?"

"Not that I can think of," Linda said.

"And the other person," the officer said.

Linda could not believe what she was about to do. She closed her eyes. If she thought reporting Patrick Bierman to human resources was going to make her job with the firm difficult, giving the name to a police officer would surely open up an entirely new can of worms.

"And this is a man you work with?"

"He's a lawyer, a partner at the firm. I work for him on many cases," Linda explained. She told the police officer all about Patrick Bierman. With each passing minute she thought for sure this time she would be sick.

"And the letter," the police officer said. "Can I have it and the envelope?"

As Linda handed it over to the police officer, she wondered if she shouldn't make a copy of it for herself. It had to be the paralegal in her. This was her only copy of the sexually obnoxious and suggestive harassment letter. "I guess. But can I get a copy of it?"

"Yes. I'll note it in my report that you gave me an original and are requesting a copy. Because you opened the letter and handled the paper, I'm not sure what type of prints we'll be able to lift, if any other than your own," the officer said.

"So what should I do if I receive another?"

"Don't touch it."

"Then how will I know if it is from this secret admirer or not?"

The police officer just looked at Linda. "You're right. I'll know," Linda said. "When can I expect a call from an investigator?"

"This phone number you gave me?"

"My cell phone," Linda said.

"My guess? You'll receive a call sometime tomorrow." The police officer handed Linda a copy of the report. With his pen he pointed to the top. "My name and number in case you need to get a hold of me."

They got out of the car. She walked around to shake the officer's hand. "Thank you."

"Just call if you don't hear from someone by the end of tomorrow, all right?" the officer said and Linda agreed. She watched him get back into his car. She thought he would pull away immediately. She thought for sure she had taken up too much of his time. When it looked like he wasn't going anywhere, she decided to walk back to her car.

Only once she was back in the garage, and had passed the security guard, did she feel completely exhausted. She was not sure she had the strength to make it to her car.

"Linda," she heard, and turned around to see Ray walking toward her. "Is everything all right? I saw you get out of a police car."

Linda shook her head up and down, but did not say anything. She did not trust herself to talk. She knew that if she opened her mouth she would begin to cry. When Ray caught up to her, she tried to smile, but instead cried anyway.

"What's wrong? What's going on?" Ray asked, hugging her tightly, his hand rubbing her back in big circles. "Is it that Joey? Did that guy do something? Are you all right?"

Linda was thankful he'd stopped asking questions right away and instead focused his attention on comforting her. She quickly regained her composure. "Will you walk me to my car?" she asked.

"Of course. Of course, I will," Ray said. At her car, he asked, "Does this have something to do with that idiot ex-boyfriend of yours?"

"I don't know. I'm not sure what's going on," Linda said. She did not want to talk about this. She appreciated Ray's compassion and was comforted by him wanting to protect her. "I don't want to discuss it right now. All right?"

"Does this have anything to do with Patrick Bierman?"

Linda felt shocked. "Why would you say that?"

"I don't know. He called me into his office today, showing me some policy out of the firm's employee handbook about how I needed to refrain from dating anyone working at the firm, clients of the firm, blah, blah, blah. Apparently," Ray said, raising an eyebrow, "you and I are a hot item, and everyone around the water cooler is talking about us."

Linda swallowed hard. "Are you serious? Everyone is talking about us?"

"No, I'm not serious. But I am serious about Bierman talking to me," Ray said.

Linda became angry. "I'm sorry he did that. He talked to me, too. But I don't appreciate you making jokes about this. It's serious," Linda said.

"I'm sorry. I thought a little humor would lighten the mood," Ray said.

Linda shook her head. "Too much is going on to lighten the mood," she said.

"So what was the deal with the police? If it didn't have anything to do with Bierman … Are you all right?"

"I guess," she said.

"Do you want to go somewhere and talk about it?" Ray asked.

"No. I want to go home. I want to be by myself for a while," she said, knowing there was some edge to her words.

"Okay. I understand. I should be home around nine, ten. If you want to call and talk," he said.

"Ray, I gave the police your name. I gave them Joey's name and told them about the fight the other day. The officer wanted your name, too. I hope you aren't mad," Linda said.

"Mad? No. I'll do whatever I can to help," Ray said.

"Thank you. I appreciate that. I may take you up on the offer to call you," Linda said. She just wanted to get out of the dark parking garage. She just wanted to go home.

Chapter 23

Ray Telfer waited for Linda to get into her car and drive away before he walked to his own vehicle. He walked with his hands in his coat pockets, head down. He knew something had seriously upset Linda and wished he knew what. Despite all his attempts not to get involved, he found he really liked being with her. Bowling, once they had hurdled over the drinking issue, had made for a wonderful evening.

Patrick Bierman was a jerk, plain and simple. Ray did not like the idea of being told whom he could not date. The firm might have a policy, but when it came to, and he hated thinking with such a melodramatic edge, but when it came to *love*, why should a policy stand in the way? Ray knew he needed this job. It was a good job. It would provide him the opportunity to get back on his feet, not just from a financial standpoint, either. Emotionally he still felt the havoc of his past, like heartburn. It came and went, but singed his insides leaving a bitter taste in his mouth.

Driving home, Ray tried to block out the day. Work, except for the talk he had had with Bierman, went well. He was enjoying most aspects of the job. Ray did not want to screw things up. He had been screwing things up most of his life.

Once in his apartment, Ray took the list off the corkboard by the phone and located an AA meeting that started around six. It was in Greece, off Dewey. Ray buttered up a frying pan and set it on the stove. He made two peanut butter and jelly sandwiches and plopped them onto the hot pan. He halfway filled a large glass with milk, then added a handful of ice cubes. He flipped the sandwiches, went into the living room and switched on the television, setting his glass on a coaster on the coffee table in front of the sofa.

The sandwiches were gooey, leaking melted peanut butter onto the plate. Sitting on the sofa and switching on the news, Ray ate his dinner contemplating whether or not to call Linda. He picked up the phone between sandwiches and dialed her number. He let it ring once, and wanted to hang up, but Linda answered. "Hello, Linda? It's me. It's Ray," Ray said, feeling suddenly foolish for calling.

"Ray, I really need some time to sort through some things," Linda said. She sounded depressed to Ray. Her tone of voice was flat and soft, barely audible.

"I know. I understand. I just wanted to call and apologize. I shouldn't have made that joke about everyone talking about us. I just didn't like seeing you upset. I don't like seeing you that way and I thought if I could make you at least smile…" Ray said, stopping. He wasn't sure what else to say. He did not want to babble on and on. He told her the truth. That was what mattered.

"I appreciate your calling to tell me that. I'm really not upset with you. I'm not. I just don't feel like talking about what's going on."

"Is Joey bothering you?" Ray asked. He knew it had to have something to do with the Neanderthal man who he scuffled with in the grocery store parking lot. "What? Did he do something to your car?"

Ray heard Linda sigh, and thought she might be crying. "I'm sorry. I know you said you didn't want to talk about this, but I can't help it." Ray closed his eyes and took a deep breath. "I care about you."

He knew for certain that now she was crying. "Am I making things more difficult?" Ray asked.

"Yes. No. Maybe. Ray," she said, nearly screaming out of frustration. "I told you how someone is harassing me? This time I got a sick, sick letter from whoever it is doing this to me."

Ray ground his teeth.

"You there? Ray?"

"I'm here. I'm just letting what you said sink in. You think it's Joey who's harassing you?" Ray asked. A lot of different questions were going through his mind. Aside from *who*, he wanted to know how else she was being harassed and when it started.

"I don't know. It could be him. It probably is him. I gave his name to the police," she said.

"That's why you were with the police," Ray said, more to himself. "So what happened, exactly?"

"Someone left an obscene letter on my windshield again," Linda said.

"Again?"

"Well, last time it wasn't obscene. It was more like a love letter from a secret admirer," Linda said.

"But this time it was different?"

"Much."

"What did it say?" Ray asked.

"The person who wrote it, he told me the sexual things he'd like to do with me, to me," Linda said. She sounded shaky and scared, as if she had been physically violated. She had been violated, mentally.

"Sick bastard," Ray said. "How are you?"

"I'm coping. I'm going to be getting a call from a police detective," Linda said. "I have a meeting downtown tomorrow, or else I don't think I'd even be going to work."

"I can imagine," Ray said.

When he hung up the phone a minute later, he was not sure if he felt any better. In the back of his mind he started to formulate a plan, but stopped short of implementing it. Attacking Joe—Joey—would not help matters, aside from a personal sense of satisfaction. Battery and assault were serious enough crimes that Ray did not want to take foolish chances. The last thing he wanted, or needed, was to involve the police. No one wanted to get in trouble with the police.

Ray finished his dinner and grabbed his coat on the way out. When he pulled into the church parking lot, he found a spot a few rows back from the doors, never amazed by the high attendance these meetings drew in. Recovering alcoholics were everywhere, could be anyone, and most people wouldn't even know any better; never guessing their physician normally swallowed a fifth of whiskey before work on a daily basis; or that the woman driving kids to school in a big yellow bus used to be so hung over that the only way to stop the pain was to have a few beers first thing in the morning.

He liked to think he could spot them, could point to a person and say, "That seventeen-year-old girl is a recovering alcoholic." But it wasn't that easy. The only thing easy was knowing the side affects of being an alcoholic. The physician, who is always late in the morning and despite the accepted medical chicken scrawl, his handwriting is more dyslexic than legible. The bus driver always chews a huge wad of strong, strong cinnamon flavored gum and slurs her words when she talks on the radio to the garage.

Ray hated his past. He hated how he let his weakness shape his life to the point where his past became something he was forced to hate. Spending time imagining how his life could have been different if he had never become an alcoholic was a waste of time. Looking back, wishing there were a way to change the past was a waste of time. Ray spent many years wasting his time thinking of his bad ways. Most of the time it led him to drink and wallow in his own self-pity. Despicable and pathetic.

Rock bottom. It's when you hit rock bottom, they say, when you see yourself at a level so low, there is obviously no other way to go but up. The person talking at the meeting tonight talked about rock bottom. Ray sat in a cold, metal folding chair, nursing a strong cup of coffee partially listening to a woman in her forties. She was crying so hard while she talked, Ray could not understand everything she said.

"I never had a husband. I had boyfriends, though, a lot of boyfriends. I kept searching for that right man, the one I could marry. Here I was, the mother of three children who desperately needed a father. They needed a father more than I needed or wanted a husband. Maybe that was where I went wrong," the woman said. "I never really gave the men in my life a chance. I based my opinions of them on how they interacted with my kids."

Rock bottom was a place she was only now starting to climb out of. She had only two weeks of sobriety; she was a newlywed to the idea, trapped in a hell she never could have fathomed.

"When this last one left me, I was crushed. He would have made a perfect husband, but he sucked as a father—at least as a father to my kids. He couldn't accept them as part of me. He didn't like them, and was clear about that. He treated them rough and was always punishing them by sending them to their rooms to get them out of his hair," she said. "And I never tried to stop him. I never stuck up for my babies. I would agree with him, because I didn't want to lose him. I never thought that would be me. All these years, I only dated men I thought would make a good father—all those men—and this time, this one time I dated a man because I liked him. I liked him and didn't want to lose him and so

I was blind to everything he did. I let him use a belt on my sons. I would stay in one room and cry while he used a belt on my boys, and he beat them so hard and so often .... I did nothing. I let some man beat up my children because I didn't ... because I ..." She could not continue. What would have been the point? Ray did not think she'd make it through the next weekend.

"When the school nurse called me, said my Tyrone got hurt in gym class and they made him lift his shirt to look at the injury they were shocked by the welts and bruises. They wanted to talk to me right away. I left work and when I arrived at school, there was a child welfare lady there in this business suit, holding a clip board and looking at me like I was some kind of criminal."

Ray sipped his coffee. He thought he could guess where the story was going. He felt his heart going out to the woman. She had a disease. Everyone in the room suffered from a disease, but the woman talking was a mess. He didn't think alcohol was her problem. Not solely. She probably never had a father and ended up spending her life around guys who treated her like shit. He knew the type. It was all too common, really. A woman like this will do anything when they have some guy, any guy, who will show even a shred of interest. Pathetic. The root of her problem wasn't drinking. She used it to camouflage the real problems. *Who am I to psychoanalyze?* he thought.

"At the time, I felt so defensive. I was ready to start telling the lady from welfare and the school nurse just what I thought! I was going to tell them to mind their own damned business. It was right there, on the tip of my tongue. Instead, I just collapsed into a chair and cried," the woman said.

"They took my kids, you know. They took my babies from me. I kicked that bastard out of my home. I told him to leave, and it felt good when he left. I knew it was something I should have done long ago. In the back of my mind, I always knew it. But the state, they wouldn't give me back my kids."

Using alcohol to camouflage the real problems. That was an alcoholic, though, wasn't it? Ray wondered about his own camouflage. He'd been hiding things so long he wasn't sure he could even see through the deceptive color patterns to the truth.

"I been sober two weeks," the woman said, smiling, ignoring the tears still running down her cheeks and dropping off her chin.

"I'm going to stay sober, too. I'm going to get my kids back and I'm going to make everything up to them."

"That's the way," someone called out. A few people clapped.

Ray hated to be a pessimistic person, but nothing is that easy. She might get her kids back, but how could this woman make it up to them? She let a strange man beat them with a belt time and again. Those kids might be thankful when they are sent home to her and they might forgive her, but they would never trust her again. How could they?

Ray finished out the meeting, helped put away folding chairs when it ended and went home.

Back at home with the television on, but ignoring the program, Ray wondered what Linda might be doing. Could she be thinking of him, too?

Chapter 24

Patty Dent was wearing tight fitting jeans and a sweater. She sat on her ankles on Linda's couch sipping a glass of Chardonnay. Linda sat in the recliner across from her, leaning forward, resting her elbows on her knees and holding her wineglass with two hands out in front of her.

Linda had put some music on. It played softly in the background. During the silence, Linda found herself in tune to the melody of the song playing. The wine was working. It relaxed her muscles. Her neck had felt stiff since she had gotten home from work.

When Patty called from the gym, Linda apologized profusely. Once Patty heard what had happened, she insisted on coming over. She brought a pizza. The two had eaten hungrily, without discussing the obscene letter Linda had found.

"So what, you told the police it might be Joey?" Patty asked. She ran her tongue over her teeth like a toothbrush, as if trying to ensure nothing was wedged between them. "I need more wine."

Linda reached for the bottle. Patty held out her glass. "I told them it was possible." Linda explained to Patty about the fight at the grocery store between Joey and Ray Telfer.

"So are you getting serious about this guy?" Patty asked. She had that look in her eyes that reminded Linda of junior high slumber parties. "I mean, what's with the two of you?"

This prompted Linda to tell Patty in more detail about what had taken place between her and Patrick Bierman.

"Get out of here," Patty said. "He called you into the office and actually quoted out of the employee handbook?"

"More or less, yes." Linda stood up. Her legs felt weak. The wine made her feel a little dizzy and lightheaded. She welcomed the feeling. It was slightly surreal and she enjoyed the sense of escape she was experiencing.

"That's why you went to HR, huh?" Patty asked.

"Not just because of that, because of the business lunch the two of us had, as well. Bierman is starting to freak me out," Linda said. "It's like he wants me, and if he can't have me no one else can."

"The guy's still married, besides the point," Patty said in a disgusted tone.

"You don't have to tell me about that," Linda agreed.

"So what about Ray?" Patty asked.

"Officially? There is nothing between us. We went bowling, exactly like I told Bierman, the scumbag," Linda said topping off her glass with more wine. She took a sip and sat back down. She felt as if she could not get comfortable. She couldn't relax enough to unwind, not completely. The wine was helping, no doubt, and having Patty over turned out to be an enjoyable way to spend the rest of the evening. None of this seemed to be enough. She still felt a ball of tension lodged at the base of her neck.

"Blah, blah, blah. How about unofficially?" Patty asked, her interest obviously piqued. Linda could tell by her friend's body language. She had moved forward on the sofa, showing she was ready to give Linda her full attention.

"I don't know. I kind of like him," she said.

"Enough to ignore Bierman's scolding?"

Linda was thoughtfully silent.

"Linda?"

"I guess so, yes."

"My God, you're ready to risk blowing your career over a few games of bowling?" Patty said, smiling in romantic disbelief.

Linda just shrugged. Out of the corner of her eye she saw Patty chewing her lip and shaking her head. Inside though, she was thinking about Ray. Could there be a future for them together? She had no intention of telling Patty about Ray's problems with alcohol. She didn't need to know about that. Ray, she believed, had confided in her. She had no business sharing that type of personal information with anyone. *Would I want to be involved with someone who has this type of a skeleton in his closet,* she wondered?

She decided to play it slow. There would be no need to rush. After all, she had just gotten out of a long, draining relationship. The last thing she wanted to do was jump head over heels into another one. Ray seemed like a good guy, but lately her judge of character could be called into question. She knew Patty had spotted Joey Viglucci for a jerk right from the beginning. Why had she been blind to such an obvious self-centered idiot?

"What do you think of Ray?" Linda asked. She wasn't sure she wanted the opinion of anyone else. She hated to think what someone else thought could sway her own feelings, but they could. She had not asked Patty for her opinion on Joey. Maybe that had been a mistake. Some times you had to, as they say, live and learn.

"My opinion? Me? The one who has not had a date in how long?" Patty asked, pointing an accusatory finger at her own chest.

"Oh stop it," Linda said. Part of her felt sorry for Patty. She was a very attractive looking lady. She wondered why her friend didn't date more often, or at all. Except for when exercising at the gym, Patty was a little reserved and matronly. If anything, Patty was one of the most down to earth people she knew. She would make a great person for the right guy, no doubt about it. "I want your opinion."

"Well, to be truthful, I don't know anything about him, other than he's terribly handsome," Patty said, sheepishly. "In fact, most of the secretaries on our floor think he's handsome."

Linda smiled. It felt something like pride inside her, as if Ray were hers and she had shown him off like a trophy.

"This is all too much," Patty said, sitting back on the sofa, leaning her head back on the cushion. "You turned Bierman into HR today?"

"I did."

"What the hell do you think tomorrow will be like at work?" Patty asked. She shook her head back and forth. "This is going to be an interesting week."

"Interesting? That's an interesting word. Know what else?" Linda asked.

"I'm not sure I can absorb much else," Patty said, looking at Linda.

"I also gave Bierman's name to the police," Linda said. She wondered if that was the right thing to do, but at the same time it felt good having an ally. She needed to confide in someone. Sure she shared some of this with Ray, but only because he had been in the garage and saw how upset she had been.

"Get out of here. I don't believe you," Patty said, clearly believing Linda. "That's too much. Well, if anything, it's been nice working for you."

"You don't think I'd lose my job, do you?"

"Let's see. You turned the partner of the law firm over to human resources and gave his name to the police to investigate for harassment. Hmm. I could have been looking at this from the wrong angle. Maybe you'll be promoted?" Patty said. She picked up the bottle of wine and filled her glass.

"That would be retaliation," Linda said. "They can't retaliate and terminate me because I'm being subjected to a hostile work environment, because one of my bosses wants to sleep with me and I turned him down."

"Good legal words, hostile work environment, retaliate. If anyone knows the system with the state agency, it's you." Patty shrugged. "Firm's got deep pockets. Get a settlement for a few hundred thousand. Set for life."

"You're getting drunk," Linda said.

"I prefer to say tipsy," Patty said.

"You passed tipsy two glasses ago," Linda said.

"Seriously, though Linda, what the hell do you think is going to happen around the office tomorrow?"

"All hell is going to break loose," Linda said.

"Linda, is this thing—are these letters—freaking you out? I mean, the flowers, the phone calls, you thought someone broke into your house... How do you feel?" Patty asked.

How do I feel, Linda wondered. "Distracted," she said. She felt the need to qualify her answer. "I keep thinking this isn't happening to me, or that what is happening isn't serious."

"Do you think it's serious?"

"I think, I should think it's serious. I mean the police were here. They saw no sign that anyone actually came into my house. Maybe if someone had actually come in, I would be freaked out. And that last letter, it was so sexually graphic... It made me so angry," Linda said. "I'm angry and annoyed more than anything."

"Do you feel, I don't know, violated?"

Linda gave Patty a thin smile. She did feel violated. "I don't like to think about it that way."

"You aren't happy that someone is in love with you, admiring you from a far?" Patty asked.

"Admiring me? In love with me? Patty, if you had read this letter you would know that those are the furthest from this maniac's mind. He isn't in love with me," Linda said. "My God, Patty, the creep told me all the sexual things he wanted to do to me with his tongue. I can't handle that. It's ... this whole thing ... it's freaking me out."

"I'm sorry. I didn't mean to upset you," Patty said. "I just think someone writing down all the things they wanted to do to me ... but I guess it's different if you don't know who the person is, huh? If it were someone you loved, it would be kind of a turn on, but not like this. Not this way."

Linda started crying, but stopped herself almost immediately and wiped away the tears. "No, Patty, not this way, and there is nothing to be sorry about. We're talking. It's the stupid wine getting my emotions all stirred up and spinning them out of control. You know, maybe the other way ... me dating the guy ... would be different. Not this way though. I feel paranoid. I don't like feeling that way." Linda reached for the bottle of wine.

"And you're filling your glass," Patty pointed out.

"And I'm filling my glass," Linda agreed. "Ready for more?"

Patty held out her glass, smiling. "Hit me."

Chapter 25
Tuesday, January 21

Linda found it difficult to believe the beauty she was seeing. Driving on I-390 East toward work, the morning sky reminded her of a Thomas Kinkade painting, if Kinkade did city backdrops instead of quaint cottages. The Rochester skyline's most prominent tower said KODAK in big red lights on each side of the building. Aside from the glowing letters, the structure stood like a giant shadow against a canvas-like sky that was smeared with crimson-tinted clouds and streaked with early morning magenta colored light.

Despite the bitter cold of a Rochester winter, mornings like this made up for it. Linda parked in the garage and wearily left her car unattended. She was anxious to talk with a police detective after the security video was reviewed. She was certain the person responsible would be caught on film placing the letter under her windshield wiper. She was both anxious and apprehensive. She wanted to know who was bothering her, but wondered what would happen after everything was revealed. Would she press charges against Joey? Would she press charges against Patrick Bierman?

For the first time in a long time, Linda actually dreaded going into work. She took her time walking to the building's rear entrance. Once on her floor, she noticed Patty was not at her desk. When she had left Linda's the night before, she had seemed all right. *Maybe I shouldn't have let her drive*, she thought.

Linda unlocked her office door and called Patty. There was no answer. She must be on her way to work. Linda hung up her coat and powered up her computer. She leaned back in her chair and waited. Everything she'd need for the meeting at the state agency was in her desk drawer. She would call MCT to see if Jolene and Nicole had any questions prior to their appointment.

When someone knocked on her door, Linda opened her eyes. She expected to see a perturbed partner in the firm wanting to know why in the hell she was causing so much trouble. Instead,

Patty stood at the threshold, smiling, holding up a box of Krispy Kreme doughnuts. "Sorry I'm late. Line at Krispy was huge. They're still hot, want one before I set them in the break room?" Patty asked, shrugging out of her wet winter coat, switching the box of doughnuts from hand to hand.

"Not really, but I'll walk with you. I need a cup of coffee." As they walked, Linda said, "I got worried when I didn't see you in here this morning. I thought maybe I shouldn't have let you drive last night."

"Few glasses of wine. I was fine," Patty said. "Head's a little foggy today. Other than that…"

Linda filled a cup of coffee and watched Patty open the box. "You know what? Those look good." Linda picked up a glazed. When she bit into it, everything melted in her mouth. "Good."

"They are, aren't they?" Patty asked, sucking glaze off her fingertips.

Patrick Bierman entered the break room with an empty coffee mug in his hand. He smiled fleetingly at Linda, then turned his attention to the box of doughnuts. "That's a nice treat," he said. "Linda could you fill this for me?"

Linda assumed Bierman handed her his mug since she was standing next to the pot. Reluctantly she filled it. She'd be damned to add any cream or sugar. He could do it himself. Almost in disgust, she watched him greedily eye the doughnuts, losing the taste for the one she held in her hand.

"Oh Patrick, there you are," Barbara Cunningham said, walking into the break room. "I needed to speak with you and was wondering if you had a free moment this morning to talk?"

"I suppose we can talk now," Patrick said. "My coffee, Linda?"

Linda put the mug of coffee in Bierman's outstretched hand. She could not help but look at Barbara as she did so. Barbara rolled her upper lip into her mouth and bit down with her teeth. Linda felt somewhat relieved. She could not be imagining the odd treatment she was receiving. Patrick must be upset with her for not dating him. She didn't like this. It made everything very tense and uncomfortable.

"Wonderful, if you'll meet me in my office…"

"Your office?" Patrick asked. "What's going on?" Patrick was smiling, but looked confused. He turned his attention from

Barbara to Linda and shrugged.

"Well, that's the point of us meeting and talking," Barbara said. She turned and left.

As Patrick followed behind, a doughnut in one hand, the mug of coffee in the other, he called after Barbara. "The way you make it sound, I feel like I'm in trouble." He laughed as he disappeared around the corner.

"Oh shit," Patty said, giggling.

"This is not funny," Linda pointed out.

"You don't have to tell me," Patty said. "I'm laughing because I'm nervous."

"You think you're nervous, imagine what I'm feeling."

"No, thank you," Patty said.

"You know what I might do? I might leave for my meeting with the state agency just a little bit early," Linda said, trying to smile.

"Can't say I blame you."

"Thanks for the breakfast," Linda said taking a small sip of coffee. "And thank you for coming over last night."

"Forget about it. We're friends. I'm here whenever you need to talk."

Ray Telfer walked in to the room, smiling.

"Hi Ray," Linda said. He looked handsome this morning. She did not realize how much she missed seeing him until seeing him at this moment. "You've met Patty, right?"

Patty smiled. "We've met." She winked at Linda. "I've got to get back to my desk. Ray, help yourself."

"Umm. Doughnuts," Ray said, rubbing his stomach.

Patty, looking at Linda, raised an eyebrow and shrugged, as if wanted to say, 'Help yourself to Linda, but if you prefer doughnuts.'

"I'll be back in a minute," Linda told Patty as her friend left the break room. "How are you, Ray?"

"Me? I was about to ask you the same thing." Ray walked between the tables to the counter. He used a fingertip to trace along the edge of the box.

"Want one?" Linda asked, watching him, knowing something was on his mind.

"Not really. I wanted to ask you something," Ray said. "It's stupid, so I'll understand if you don't want to. In fact, I can't even think of a reason why you…"

"Ray, ask me," Linda said.

"Tomorrow night, at an AA meeting I'm going to receive a chip for three months sober. I was going to ask if you'd like to come with me. You don't have to stay for the whole meeting. I don't know, maybe we could go out for something to eat afterwards?" Ray could barely make eye contact with Linda. He kept looking up at her then down at the doughnuts.

Linda was not ready for the question. She had assumed he would ask her out, but did not think it would be to an AA meeting. She knew it must have taken tremendous courage for him to ask. "I'll go."

"You don't have to you know," Ray said, sounding defensive.

Linda realized she had said she would go with little enthusiasm. The idea scared her. Because Ray had asked her, it meant he must care about her. Because she is willing to go, it meant she must care about him. Did she want to care about him? Could she stop herself if the answer were no?

She reached out putting a hand on his. "I want to go." She spoke while looking into his eyes, demanding he not look away from her. The urge that suddenly filled her was more powerful than she could have thought. She wanted to kiss him, but didn't. Something in his eyes told her he wanted to kiss her, too.

Chapter 26

Linda took the Inner Loop to the Monroe and Clinton Exit. She made a left onto Monroe, heading in the opposite direction of Manhattan Square Park and crossed over South Union. At the large yellow brick building, she turned right and parked in back. The Division of Human Rights, along with a lot of other state agencies, occupied what used to be a Sears department store. The large parking lot, as always, was full. Linda found a place in the back corner of the lot. She took out her briefcase, locked and shut the car door.

"Hey, Linda Genova!"

Linda turned around and saw a man walking toward her. She stopped walking and waited for him to get closer. When she saw his face, she knew he looked familiar, but could not put a name to the face. She ran into a lot of people here and assumed he must work for the state, but then it came to her. "Oh hello, Mr. Kenmore," she said.

"Bad parking, isn't it," Jason Kenmore said. "I even got a worse one than you did."

She had nothing to say. She did not want to talk to the man, regardless of the appropriateness. She walked a little faster toward the rear entrance. She saw some people standing by the doors smoking. There were other people in the parking lot walking to and from their cars. *Why didn't I give the police officer Kenmore's name?*

She knew he was staring at her while they walked. She could just see the edges of his smile out of the corner of her eye.

"I've got to tell you, since we last met, I can't think of anyone but you," Kenmore said softly.

"That's not appropriate," Linda said. She hoped she sounded firm and harsh. She did not want him to realize how terrified she felt. She knew her heartbeat was accelerated, hated the way it felt inside her chest. She was close to panicking. "I want you to leave me alone," she said aggressively, raising her voice.

"What, leave you alone? Linda, I think there is something between us, something that can be beautiful," Kenmore persisted.

Linda stopped walking. The door into the building was less than ten yards away. The people smoking were watching them. She did not want to lose their attention.

Linda heard a honking horn. She turned and saw Jolene and Nicole drive down one aisle over, searching for a spot to park.

"Aren't you coming in?" Kenmore asked, as if they were friends.

"No. I am waiting here for other people," she said staring at him with a hardened look. She hoped her stare would be intimidating, but was deflated when he smiled and laughed at her.

"I'll see you inside in a little while, all right love?" Kenmore walked toward the building. At the glass doors, he turned and waved. Linda was irritated at herself. She should not have given him the satisfaction of still watching him.

Linda pursed her lips together tightly. She had already told him to leave her alone. He wasn't going to listen. She dreaded going inside now. She tried to calm herself. She could feel her arms and hands trembling. Linda shifted the briefcase from one hand to the other. She put her free hand into a coat pocket and turned to see Jolene and Nicole walking toward her. "Find it all right?" Linda asked.

"Good directions," Nicole said. "No problem at all." She had on a long, heavy black trench coat. The belt that should have gone around her waist dangled at her sides. She wore a gray business suit with a below-the-knee skirt, black stockings, high-heel shoes. She walked carefully on the slick pavement.

"Were you just talking with Jason?" Jolene asked. Her black leather coat was just long enough to go past her waist. She wore dark blue slacks and flats. Both women looked elegant.

"I was. Last time, when he showed up at our meeting, he hit on me. I was waiting to cross State and he was waiting for the bus at the same corner," Linda said.

"He hit on you?" Jolene asked.

"It was obnoxious then, and he just did it again," Linda admitted. "I'm not very comfortable around this guy."

"That makes three of us," Nicole said rolling her eyes. "I'm going to be so thrilled when all of this is over."

153

Entering the building, Linda led them down the hall past a small cafeteria, toward the security booth. They made a left at the booth for the elevator and went up to the third floor, all the while making small talk.

Linda felt more nervous than she could ever recall feeling before. She knew it had nothing to do with the purpose of the meeting. She was comfortable around the investigators for the State Division. Her mind just kept rethinking everything that had been going on in her life. Bierman was a jerk, but it didn't seem likely that he would harass her as a secret admirer. And Joey? Get real. The guy was too self-absorbed to care enough about driving her crazy with unsigned, dirty letters.

Jason Kenmore on the other hand…

As they stepped off the elevator, Linda's cell phone rang. "Excuse me," she told Jolene and Nicole as she removed the phone from her purse. "Hello?"

"Ms. Genova? This is Josaiah Valente. I'm with the Rochester Police Department," the police officer said. "Yesterday you reported…"

"Mr. Valente, I'm sorry, this is not a good time for me to talk. I'm just about to go into a meeting," Linda explained.

"I understand, but let me just take a minute here. The security video revealed nothing. Your vehicle was not within its range of view. The system that garage uses is so damned archaic. However, the officer that took the report included some tips I plan to follow up on. There isn't much there that looks promising though," Officer Valente explained.

"You know, about that, I have something I'd like to add," Linda said.

"Okay. I'm listening."

"Only now is not the best time. Is there a way I can reach you? Can I call you after this meeting?" Linda asked. Jolene handed Linda a pen and paper. She wrote down the phone number.

"Before I waste time here, do you still feel that Joseph Viglucci and Patrick Bierman could potentially have left the obscene letter?"

Linda took a deep breath and said, "Yes."

"All right. How about Ray Telfer?"

"No. I just met him," she said.

"And that would rule him out as a secret admirer why?" Officer Valente asked.

Linda felt the wind sucked out of her. "No," she said finally. "It couldn't be him. We're already seeing each other." It was a lie.

"Ma'am, the report says that you says Telfer was just a friend," Valente explained.

"He's a little more than that," she said. Why was she lying to the police officer? What if Ray was the secret admirer and here she was stopping the police from finding anything out?

Ray couldn't be the secret admirer. Not Ray. That didn't even make sense. "I've got to go," she told Josaiah Valente.

"Right. That meeting," he said, almost sarcastically.

Linda didn't have time for this. She hung up and stuck the phone and the officer's number in her purse. "I'm sorry," she told Nicole and Jolene. "We better get going."

Chapter 27

Andrew Egert reminded Linda of an actor. It wasn't that he resembled anybody famous. He just had that look. Linda found Egert very attractive. She knew he could easily have traded in his menial state paychecks for a nominal advance as the leading role in a silver screen production. Brown hair, brown eyes and straight white teeth. "Mr. Egert, how've you been?" Linda asked.

Shaking hands with Linda, Egert shrugged. "Busy. How was your holiday season?"

"Too short. Except for Christmas and New Year's Day, I worked," Linda said. "It would have been nice with a week or so off."

"I hear that. We were open, too," Egert said. "Thank you for faxing the position paper last night. I took it home and read it, so I think we're in a better position to proceed today." He turned his attention on Nicole and Jolene. Linda made introductions. "Wonderful to meet you. Mr. Kenmore and his attorney are talking in a conference room down the hall. If you're set, we can head to that room and get this underway?"

Linda, Jolene and Nicole followed Egert down the hall toward a closed door. Egert knocked and entered. "Mr. Brownstein, this is Linda Genova. She is here representing MCT's position against the charge filed by your client."

Brownstein stood up and shook hands with Linda. They exchanged business cards. Linda introduced the attorney to the ladies with her.

"And Mr. Kenmore, you know everyone here? Have you met Ms. Genova?" Egert asked.

Kenmore smiled, licked his lips, and nodded. "We've met. It's good to see you again."

Linda ignored the comment. She looked away from Kenmore, and saw Egert raising an eyebrow. Inwardly, Linda smiled. The tone of Kenmore's words was not lost on him.

Linda removed a legal pad and Kenmore's file from her brief-case as everyone sat around the large wood table. Andrew Egert made some opening comments. For the next hour and a half, Egert rolled through pages of listed questions, until finally he asked Brownstein and Linda if either had any additional questions.

"Mr. Kenmore is interested in reinstatement with MCT. If this can be achieved, he is willing to forego demanding monies from lost wages, interest earned in his investment account, and the earnings that would have been attributable to increasing his pension," Brownstein said, checking off items on his legal pad. When he was done speaking, he put down his pen and folded his hands. He looked at Jason Kenmore and nodded, as if everything was going to be all right.

Egert smiled and looked at Linda. Linda turned to look at Nicole and Jolene. They looked perplexed. Linda understood. "Mr. Egert, we need a moment to talk about this offer."

"Of course," Egert said. "If you'd like, step into the hall. While you are out of the room, we will not discuss any aspects of the case."

In the hall, Linda crossed her arms. "It's not an option is it?"

Jolene shook her head. "The company is still in the process of downsizing."

"He's not the type of employee I would want to bring back, regardless. There were other employees we let go that I'd feel more comfortable calling in to work," Nicole added.

When they returned, Linda told Egert they were not interested in accepting the offer. "I'm sorry," Linda said.

"Okay then, I want to thank everyone for coming down here this morning. I will work on the case and inform Mr. Brownstein and Ms. Genova of the state's decision as soon as one is reached. Thank you," Egert said standing up and officially ending the meeting.

Linda shook hands with Mr. Brownstein. "It was nice meeting you," she said, and he returned the compliment. Linda was not prepared when Kenmore grabbed her hand. She attempted to pull away, but he was stronger than he looked. "Let go," she said.

Egert, who had been about to leave the room, turned around. Linda felt embarrassed. Brownstein put a hand on his client's shoulder as Kenmore said, "And I hope we get to see each other again."

Brownstein just smiled. Linda knew the attorney had to think Kenmore was slime. She wondered what Egert was thinking. Hopefully everyone in the room was on the same page.

Deciding not to say anything, Linda put her belongings back into her briefcase and left the room, Egert stood holding the door for her. Nicole and Jolene followed.

"Ms. Genova," Egert said.

Linda wanted to walk right to the elevators and out to her car. Twice this man has gotten under her skin. The way he looked at her, the way he talked to her, made her feel so dirty. Talk about feeling violated. "Yes?" she said, slowly turning around.

"Are you all right?" Egert asked.

"To be honest, no. The first time I met Mr. Kenmore, he did something very similar. I imagine in very much the same way he treated the female employee at MCT," Linda said.

Brownstein was coming out of the conference room. "I object to that comment. It is out of line and we have already concluded the fact-finding session. Mr. Egert?"

"I have ignored the comment," Egert said.

"And the employer was not able to produce any documents to support their allegations that my client harassed anyone at work," Brownstein continued, making his case in the hallway.

"But we can bring the woman in as a witness," Nicole said. "We can talk to her anytime you'd like."

Linda held up a hand to politely silence Nicole.

"I have ignored the comment, but cannot ignore the things I have witnessed," Egert said. "I'll be in touch," he said to everyone, then went back into the conference room and closed the door.

Linda knew Egert was just hiding from confrontation. She stared intently at Kenmore, who just smiled at her. Jolene took Linda by the arm. "We're leaving."

As the three of them walked to the elevator, Linda felt like an invalid. Nicole held one arm, Jolene the other. Linda really wanted to run. She wanted to get off the elevator and run to her car. She did not want to go back to the firm. She just wanted to go home. The entire morning made her feel embarrassed.

In the elevator, Linda apologized.

"What are you sorry for? Jason was out of control. He was out of hand," Nicole said. "This is exactly the kind of behavior that was reported to us. I'm the one that's sorry. I wish we had documentation supporting everything."

"Yeah, but at least that investigator guy saw firsthand what Jason is like. He might have told everyone that he was going to ignore the comment about the incident at MCT, but…" Jolene said.

"But he even said he couldn't ignore what he'd just witnessed," Nicole finished. "What do you think that means, Linda? Think that means we won?"

Linda smiled. She was listening to them banter excitedly, finishing sentences for each other. "I think we have a much better chance at getting a no probable cause than we had before."

"We should go and get some lunch," Jolene said, looking at her watch.

"Great idea. Our treat," Jolene said.

Linda shook her head. "I can't. I wish I could, but I have a meeting in forty minutes and I'm not completely prepared for it yet?"

"Are you sure?" Jolene asked. "We can just go somewhere quick and get a small sub or something? It is lunchtime. Aren't you hungry?"

"I am, but skipping lunch often goes with my job," Linda said honestly. "You two go on ahead. Both of you did really well this morning. I think we're going to be okay on this one, so enjoy a good meal. You deserve it. The minute I hear anything, and it could be months, I'll be sure to contact you."

Jolene and Nicole nodded. "You sure you're all right?" Jolene asked.

"He gave me a good spooking, but other than that, I'm fine. I'm just preoccupied with that other meeting I have in a little while. You know how demanding work can be. It never ends." They had reached Linda's car. They shook hands and Linda said goodbye to them as they continued on toward their own car. Linda unlocked her door and climbed in. She locked the door and started the engine. Then she tightly gripped the steering wheel, lowered her head to her knuckles and cried.

Everything happening, everything that was going on was too much. She had been trying desperately not to take the idea of a stalker seriously. Seeing Jason Kenmore today and the way he behaved made her wonder if she wasn't being foolish for not taking things more seriously.

Linda took out her cell phone and called the police station. She asked to speak with Josaiah Valente. He wasn't in. She left a message for him to call her whenever he had the chance.

Chapter 28

Linda called the office before leaving the Division of Human Rights parking lot. "Patty? It's Linda. What's going on?"

"You coming back to work?" Patty asked.

"Actually, I'm thinking about just heading home. I had a rough morning. I didn't have anything else on my calendar, but I figured I'd call to see if anything's going on. I figured Bierman would want to talk, see how things went over here," Linda said.

"I'm not too sure about that," Patty said. "Maybe an hour ago he passed by your office, trying to see if you were here. He was craning his neck to look in, straining to see into your office, so I asked him if he needed help. He totally ignored me. He grunted and left. Next thing you know, his secretary is calling me to see what's up."

"And, what's up?"

"Well, when he got back to his office, he was muttering under his breath, but loud and clear enough for her to hear that he was talking about you. Carrie wouldn't tell me what he was saying, but she said they were not nice words. That Carrie is so prim and proper she drives me nuts sometimes," Patty said. "Anyway, he closed up his office and told Carrie he was taking the rest of the day off."

Linda cringed. "You know what's going on, don't you?"

"Oh yeah," Patty said. "All hell is breaking loose."

"So there's nothing new on my calendar?" Linda asked.

"Barb in HR wants to talk to you, but I set the meeting up for after lunch tomorrow. You plan to come in tomorrow?"

"I'll be in. I just need to go home right now. I wouldn't be worth anything back at the office." Linda thought about a glass of wine, music and another bubble bath. She could not think of the last time that she had treated herself to such a luxury in the middle of the day. "Tomorrow after lunch sounds perfect."

"You all right?" Patty asked.

"I'll call you tonight. We can talk about what happened then," Linda said.

"Something happened?" Patty asked excitedly. Her tone of voice went up two octaves. "What happened?"

"I'll tell you about it tonight, goodbye." Linda hung up her cell phone and set it down on the passenger seat. She started to back out of the parking spot, but slammed on the brakes. Someone was behind the car.

Oh my God, she thought. *I almost backed into someone. I'm not concentrating. I'm not paying attention. I could have killed someone.* She unfastened her seat belt and opened the car door. The legal person inside her knew better than to let emotions get the better of her. The last thing she wanted to do was get out of the car and ramble off a bunch of guilty sounding admissions. "Are you all right?" Linda asked.

"I am now that I can see your pretty face again," Jason Kenmore said, smiling. He had the palms of his hands on Linda's trunk.

"You bastard, leave me alone," Linda said. She hated showing him the way she felt. She did not like the idea of him knowing how easily he could get to her. "Leave me alone," Linda said a second time and got back into her car. She locked the door. She could see Kenmore in the rearview mirror. He remained standing behind the car. She honked her horn over and over until he stepped out of the way.

Calm down, she thought. *Calm down.* She backed out of her spot. She expected Kenmore to be there, waving or blowing her a kiss, but he wasn't. He was gone.

Enraged, Linda drove to the parking lot exit on South Union and waited for a break in traffic. She made a right, drove across Monroe and headed back for the Inner Loop. As she switched lanes, she noticed in her mirror an old, silver Mercedes with black tinted windows approaching too quickly.

She remembered Jason Kenmore taking the city bus last time they had met. However, she had the odd feeling that the person in the silver car was Kenmore. She went a little faster. The Mercedes was directly behind her, increasing its speed to remain right on Linda's ass.

Linda tapped her brakes. She wanted the driver behind her to either slow down, or pass her, but to no avail. The Mercedes continued to match her speed. Linda drove faster, changing lanes to pass the car in front of her. She immediately pulled back into the right-hand lane, leaving no room for the Mercedes between her and the car she had passed.

The Mercedes proceeded into the left lane, then picked up enough speed so that it could position itself side by side with Linda's car.

This was getting dangerous, Linda knew. She was not paying enough attention to the road. She was too worried about the car alongside her. She picked up her cell phone and switched it on as the black-tinted passenger window in the Mercedes went down.

Linda looked over and saw Jason Kenmore smoking a cigarette. He blew out a plume of smoke and flashed her a wide grin. Linda showed him the telephone. She hoped he understood the potential threat of her making a call. To be sure she mouthed the word *police*.

The window in the Mercedes went up as the vintage automobile pulled away.

Linda held onto the cell phone for a moment longer before tossing it back onto the passenger seat. It wasn't until the car behind her honked that she realized she'd reduced her speed to twenty miles under the limit.

Pulling into her driveway, Linda had never felt more relieved or thankful to be home. She entered her house, closed and locked the door. As she leaned her back against the door, she banged her head softly as she started to cry. Sobs overtook her. She began to shake as she cried, burying her face in her hands then slowly sinking to her knees.

* * * * *

A glass of wine sounded most appealing. The bubble bath could wait. While in the kitchen pouring a glass, Linda realized she was hungry and would need to think about fixing something for lunch. She checked the cupboards and decided on a tuna melt. She opened a can of tuna, dumped it into a bowl, mixed in some low fat mayonnaise and diced up some celery. She set the frying pan on the stove, turned the burner on low and dropped in a square of butter.

As she removed a loaf of sliced bread from the breadbox on the counter, Linda's doorbell rang. Taking her glass of wine, Linda went to the living room but stopped, suddenly apprehensive. Jason Kenmore?

She moved to the picture window and parted the curtains with the back of her hand. She recognized the car in the driveway. It was not the aged Mercedes. It was a large white Lincoln.

"Damn it," Linda said. She opened the front door. "I don't think you should be here."

"What the hell are you doing, huh? What the hell do you think you're doing?" an enraged Joey Viglucci asked. He had his arms at his sides, his large hands rolled into giant fists.

Linda knew what he was talking about. Officer Valente must have talked to him. She did not know what to say.

"You sent the police after me? Why would you do that? Is your life so pathetic that you think I feel like wasting my time harassing you?" Joey asked. He talked through clenched teeth. She noticed a strained artery in his neck protruding through the skin like a taut rope.

"Joey," Linda managed to say.

Joey pushed Linda into her house and followed. He closed the door. "This cop shows up at work wanting to talk to me. Know how embarrassing that was? I got clients around and I have to look like some kind of a criminal in front of them? Know what that's like?"

Linda felt panicked. She did not like Joey's aggressive manner. His closing the door set an alarm off in her head. She needed to get him out of her house. She needed to get out of the house. "Joey, now isn't the time to talk about this," she said, searching for the right thing to say to disarm his intemperate mood.

Joey Viglucci slapped the wineglass out of Linda's hand. It shattered against the wall. The shards rained onto the floor. "It's not? It's not the time to talk about it? So when? When, Linda, would be a better time to talk about you ruining my reputation, huh? You tell me. We can check our schedules, pencil it in for some time next week. How's that? How does that sound, Linda?"

With every few words Joey said, he advanced. Linda kept

backing up. They were headed toward the kitchen. She thought about turning and running. She decided against it. The kitchen door was triple locked, the doorknob, a chain and a deadbolt. She would never be able to disengage the locks in time. "Joey, this is not how it seems," she said. She wanted to tell him that this was crazy, that he was acting crazy, that he was overreacting. Saying those things would never calm him down; they could only infuriate him more. "Joey..."

"Not how it seems? Linda, I don't understand you? I don't get one thing about you. Did you break up with me? I remember you breaking up with me. I remember you dumping your drink over my head. Am I wrong? Is my memory obscured? Did you break up with me?" Joey asked, jabbing his finger into the center of his chest. "Answer me."

"Yes. Yes, I broke up with you." Linda knew she was going to get hit. She sensed his intentions like electricity in the air. He wanted to hurt her. That was why he was here. That was why he pushed his way into her house and shut the door. He meant to hurt her. "Joey..."

"So why would I harass you? Why would I want to waste my time with you?"

"I never said..."

"Sure you did. Sure you said. You told the police I was harassing you, that I was still in love with you. You told this dumb old cop that I couldn't live without you. You told this cop that I still needed you. How do you know anything about my feelings? You don't. You never did. So where do you get off making up stories, huh? Your life is pathetic, you're dating that wimpy creep, I'm happy for you. Thrilled. I pity the guy you're dating, but I couldn't be more happy for you," Joey said. His hands were up. He looked tense. He was getting ready to strike.

Linda had no idea what to do. He had backed her into the kitchen. She was by the stove and the door. There was no way out. She knew how a boxer trapped in the corner must feel. She turned away from him, flinching in anticipation.

The cell phone in her purse on the counter rang.

The sound stopped Joey from advancing. He looked at her purse. An uncertainty overcame his facial expression. Linda felt saved by the bell. To ensure her safety, she took his moment of hesitation to reach for the hot frying pan. She held it like a baseball bat, and took a more aggressive stance.

He laughed. "You are pathetic," Joey said. The cell phone kept ringing. "You know what I did? Call me childish, I let the air out of your tire … I flattened your tire at that gym you exercise at, yeah. So sue me. I flattened your tire and I beat up your boyfriend at the grocery store and I admit that. All right? I did those things, but I did not harass you."

For reasons she did not know, Joey raised his hand and waved it at her. "I ain't gonna touch you. Got me? I'm leaving you alone, and I expect the same thing in return. All right? You leave me alone, and keep me out of your delusions, okay? Keep me out of your pathetic fantasies."

Then he was gone, leaving only the reverberation from the thundering echo of the slamming the door.

The cell phone had stopped ringing.

Linda was left alone in a silent, empty house.

Chapter 29

Leaning over the kitchen table crying, Linda wondered what was going on. She wondered how her life could have become so complicated. She shouldn't feel this way, scared. With hands shaking, she pulled out a chair and sat down. None of it made sense. Linda had never been the kind of person to say that life was not fair. She knew it wasn't fair, but for the most part she had been spared any serious cruelties. The idea of Joey threatening her was terrifying. He had been ready to punch her. As big and as strong as he was, that punch would have hurt and it more than likely would have shattered bones. The image of him breaking her nose passed through her mind, causing her to flinch.

Linda wondered about Joey. Could he have been her secret admirer? He sounded adamant about her leaving him alone. That's a laugh. She knew he had to be following her. How else would he have known she was at the grocery store that day? How would he have known she'd have been home from work early today?

How would he have known?

He wouldn't have known. Unless he was following her.

When the telephone on the kitchen wall rang, she nearly screamed. Its shrill ringing pierced the silence as effectively as a sonic boom. Linda stood up and answered the phone. "Hello?"

"Ms. Genova? It's Officer Valente."

"Funny you should call," she said.

"I tried getting a hold of you on your cell phone but there was no answer. I called your office, but your secretary informed me you went home for the day. I hope you don't mind me calling you here?" Valente spoke in tone of voice that Linda had trouble reading. He sounded like a tough cop, as if he didn't really give a damn one way or the other. However, he also seemed to have a more sensitive side to his tone. She could not imagine working as a police officer. The horrors they must see day in and day out had to be difficult to deal with. She figured Valente knew how to keep his professional distance, the I-don't-give-a-damn tone, but was also genuine and interested in helping.

"That's fine, I'm glad you have all my numbers," Linda said. She almost ran right into her story. She had wanted Josaiah Valente to know about Joey Viglucci's visit. She wanted to tell him how he'd charged into her home ready to beat up on her. Joey might have left, but his threatening words still echoed around like punches in her head. Maybe the police warning had been enough and now that he had pulled his macho-shit, he'd stay out of her life. In a way, they'd made a deal. She leaves him alone; he leaves her alone. "What's up?"

"A couple of things. The chief has reviewed your file, all right? I worked as an advocate for you, let me say that much. You never told me your tire was slashed at the Elm Ridge Center," Valente said.

"It wasn't slashed. It was flattened. Yes. That did happen, I had forgotten about that," Linda said. She had been certain Joey had been responsible for that. She remembered how angry and embarrassed he'd been leaving the gym. He'd taken his frustration out on her tire. She could just imagine him squatting by her car, letting air out of the tire and giggling the entire time. *Freaking baby*.

"All right. That was a report with the Greece Police, anyway. We got a copy of the report and put it in your file with the Rochester Police. You're getting yourself a pretty good sized portfolio there, ma'am," Valente said, as if trying to lighten the mood.

"Well, if I ever have the need to job hunt, I'll be sure to call on you for a letter of recommendation," Linda said.

"See, aside from the tire and your unconfirmed suspicion that someone had broken into your house, there is nothing to indicate that your life is in any danger," Valente said.

"But that letter," Linda protested. The mood of the conversation took a drastic turn. Valente had to know the curve was coming, which was why he started it out with a buffer.

"The letter, Ms. Genova, was crude and obnoxious. It was a dirty letter, a little more serious than a prank phone call," Valente said.

"But not much," Linda added.

"No, I'm afraid, not much. But like I said, the tire, the fact that you thought someone entered your house, those are factors we're considering. I'm considering," Valente said.

Linda knew what was happening. The chief didn't see enough to warrant police attention. "I appreciate your help," Linda said. "But what are you telling me? You telling me you can't investigate this anymore?"

"More or less. Less, actually," Valente said.

"And what does that mean?"

"It means I can't put too much into it, but I won't file it, either. All right?"

Linda was surprised she thought she might cry. She had not realized how tense she had been feeling. She knew she kept trying to ignore everything going on, to play it off like it was nothing. She knew she was scared. "I hate having a secret admirer," Linda admitted.

"We don't call them that, ma'am. We call them stalkers. There's nothing cute or romantic about what's going on. Nothing. The guy stalking you is a freak. I wish there was more I could do," Officer Valente said, his frustration evident in his voice.

"But you are. I appreciate what you're doing," Linda said.

There was a moment of silence. Linda thought she might have embarrassed the police officer. She heard him clear his throat.

"When we talked, before that meeting of yours, you indicated there was more to tell me," Valente said.

"I thought of another person who might be doing this to me," Linda said, telling the police officer as much as she could about Jason Kenmore without breaching any confidentiality owed to MCT.

"That's interesting. I find that information very interesting," Valente said. "I talked with that Joseph Viglucci. He's no stranger to police investigations. Shame you were ever even caught up with a guy like that."

Linda had no idea what Josiah Valente meant. "He's been in trouble with the police before?"

"The man has a nasty, violent temper. But he's not man enough to fight other men. He likes to hit women. He ever strike you before, Ms. Genova?" Valente asked.

Linda had an image of Joey all too fresh in her mind. "He's come close," she said. "But no. He's never hit me."

"Let me tell you what, consider yourself lucky. There's Polaroid's in the file of his last victim. She's a mess."

Linda wondered how someone could beat up another person as badly as the police officer was indicating and not wind up in prison.

"The lady he beat up on wouldn't file charges," Valente explained as if he'd been reading her thoughts. "Said she fell down a flight of stairs. If you'd seen the pictures, you'd wonder if the stairs were made out of belt buckles or something, know what I mean?"

Linda left the question alone. She knew what Josaiah Valente meant. She also thought she might understand why the woman didn't press charges. It was for the same reason she neglected to tell Valente about Joey's intrusion earlier. Fear.

"All right, listen, I've got to get running. I'll check into this new guy and I still have to talk with Patrick Bierman," Officer Valente said.

Linda knew at that moment that she could tell the officer to leave Bierman alone. It would certainly make things easier at work. Bierman was already angry with her. She did not look forward to tomorrow morning. The thought of having to go back to the office made her stomach roil. She felt ill. "Okay. Thank you," Linda said, and hung up.

Chapter 30
Wednesday, January 22

What made work even remotely tolerable was the fact the Bierman had called in sick. Had Linda known this would have been the case, she would not have wasted an entire night tossing and turning worried about seeing him at the office. Still, she was thankful when she learned he would not be in at all.

Robert Bell, vice president of a mid sized computer chip manufacturing company was on the phone. Bell sounded frantic. "We have a very bizarre situation here."

Linda poised with pen over legal pad told Bell to explain the bizarre situation.

"We have this male employee. Let's call him John, like John Doe, all right"

"What is it about John that concerns you?" she said.

"Well," he started, "John has been taking estrogen, female hormones?"

"I'm familiar with the term."

"Well, now John wants to use the women's restrooms in the plant."

She furrowed her brow. "I see."

"Look, off the record, I don't care if he's John or Janice, but I can't have some guy doing his business in the women's restrooms without causing a panic."

"I suppose you can't," she agreed, jotting down issues.

"Someone in HR talked to him about this, explaining that we have a policy on restroom usage according to biological gender," he said.

"And you do? You have such a policy?"

"Yes. It's new, a few years old. Lacy, the attorney at your firm, she set it up...thank God."

"And how did John handle this?"

"How? Like a, dare I say it? Like a total bitch," he said and

Linda imagined him suppressing a laugh. "John told HR that we were wrong to put our weight behind a discriminating policy, and that the policy should be based on a person's own self-image of gender. So tell me, Linda, what the hell are we supposed to do?"

"Do you have any single bathrooms, like private bathrooms?"

"We do, and we offered him use of them. He declined. I get the feeling we're going to get sued, or he's going to file a charge with the EEOC or something," Bell said.

"You could be right. I don't recall seeing case law on this, but I'd guess as long as you are treating John differently because of his orientation…"

"Linda—where the hell does he go to the bathroom?" Bell asked. "We're not treating him differently. I don't care if he's gay; you know what I'm saying? It's sex, just sex. I'm a heterosexual; you don't see me running around telling everyone, right? He's a damned good worker. I have no problem with him using the men's room still. He still has all the same equipment, if you know what I'm saying. All that's different is his medication and the fact that he says he feels more like a woman than he does a man. He thinks we're violating his rights because we're not letting him pee standing up in the women's restrooms. Is it me? Am I the crazy one here? I mean what the hell is going on in this country? You know, you wonder if the minorities want equal rights, or if they want to keep pushing segregation and inequality. Now you tell me, do we need a gay Olympics? Gay people are allowed in the Olympics, but are straight people allowed in the Gay Olympics? Isn't that discrimination, *not* letting a guy ski competitively because he prefers to sleep with women?"

Linda refrained from commenting. Bell was venting. Nervous and upset, but venting. "You know what, I'm going to pass this one on to Lacy. She set up your policy, and it isn't my place as a paralegal to give you advice. All right? I'll have Lacy call you back." Linda thought fleetingly about the ramifications if something like this ever went to trial. Restrooms, locker rooms and showers would never be the same. Female, Male and Undecided? Linda knew she didn't seem sympathetic to John's needs, but a part of her realized it didn't make much sense. Had John undergone an operation to complete his transformation from a male to a female, then without question she could see why he would want to use women's restrooms. Until then, just because he was on female hormones, this was a little ridiculous.

A soft knock at the door got Linda's attention. "Hey Patty, come on in," Linda said, hanging up the telephone. "What's up?"

"Just had a free moment, thought I'd see how your day's going," Patty said.

"I'm a little distracted," Linda admitted. "But it's a lot easier knowing, I shouldn't say this, but if Bierman were here…"

"I know what you mean," Patty said. She wore a guilty, gossiping smile. She walked into the office and stood by Linda's desk. "Working out tonight?"

Linda smiled nervously. "You're going to hate me."

Patty sighed and collapsed into a chair. "Not again. You know how long it has been since we've gone working out together? Don't your muscles feel all icky and flabby?"

Linda cradled her forehead between the web of her thumb and pointer finger. "I made other plans for tonight that I can't get out of."

Patty, shaking her head, stood up. "With Ray?"

"Yes, with Ray."

"You really got a thing for him, don't you?"

Linda shrugged. "I'm not sure. He's interesting, mysterious. There's something about him though. He has something special that I just can't put my finger on." Linda knew she was playing her feelings down. What she felt for Ray was a bit more intense than what she explained to Patty. She admitted, "I do like him."

Patty walked to the office door. "Well, I am happy for you. I can't remember the last time I was as lucky as you."

"Oh? How am I lucky?"

Patty tilted her head to one side. "You're never alone."

"Patty," Linda said as Patty left the office, but Patty did not walk back in.

Linda stood up, then sat back down. What could she say? It wasn't her fault Patty didn't date much. Linda knew she needed to set aside time to spend with Patty. Even if something did spawn between her and Ray, she did not want it to become all consuming the way new relationships often did. She wanted to make sure she kept time out for friends, for Patty.

She would have canceled her plans with Ray, if tonight weren't such a special night for him. Three months sober had to be a major accomplishment. If it had been just a date Linda would have backed out of the commitment in a heartbeat, at least she liked to think she would have.

Patty came back into the office with her head hung low. "I'm sorry, Linda."

Linda stood up and walked around her desk. "I don't mean to be neglecting you, you know. I want to workout with you. Tonight is a special night for Ray and he asked me to be there with him."

"Why? What's going on?" Patty asked.

Linda trapped herself. She had said too much and there was no taking it back. "It's something I can't talk about. It's something personal. It's not my place to talk about it," Linda said too quickly. She knew she could tell Patty and the secret would remain safe, but she didn't want to if she didn't have to.

"That's all right. I wouldn't want you to break a confidence," Patty said.

"It's not like that," Linda said. "I trust you…"

"Look, I'm not asking you to tell me anything. I came in here to apologize for acting so immature." Patty crossed her arms.

"We can go workout tomorrow. It's not our regular day, I know, but I'll throw in dinner," Linda said. "How does that sound?"

Patty puckered her lips thoughtfully. "Dinner? Can we go for Chinese?"

Linda pretended to think about it. "I don't see why not."

Looking more content then a few moments ago, Patty turned to leave, but stopped at the door. "Look, it might not be my place to say, but…"

"But what?"

"I just find it interesting that the whole secret admirer thing started about the same time he became employed with the firm," Patty said. She looked hurt by her own comment, as if in making it, she felt the lacerations of its implications. "I just don't want you hurt, Linda. You are my closest friend. Granted, I don't know Ray, I don't know anything about him, but he's awfully mysterious, you said so yourself. Where is he from? Why did he leave? Why did he choose Rochester of all places?"

"Patty…"

"What? You don't think it's a little odd, a little weird? Think about his job, Linda. He has access to everything about you, us and everyone here. He can log onto his computer with his administrative password and find out your address, phone number, how much money you earn, when you started, when you were born ... He has access to everything, and we don't know anything about him. Nothing. That bothers me," Patty said. "It might sound like I'm talking crazy, like I'm overreacting and just wildly accusing someone, but I'm not. I've thought about this. I've thought about it. There is something about him, something he's hiding. Something's is not right with him. I know you like him, and I'm sorry, but it's the way I feel. I'm your friend, Linda."

"I know you are," Linda said. She knew what Ray was hiding. She knew why he was hiding it. Why would he want to tell everyone he had had a drinking problem? He wouldn't. Linda wanted to say, 'Yes, you are overreacting,' or 'You're just getting paranoid.'

"Linda, promise me you'll be careful?" Patty asked.

Linda nodded. "I will."

"A good workout and a good dinner then, tomorrow after work?"

Linda pointed at Patty. "You got it."

Rapping her knuckles on Linda's wall, by the door, Patty smiled. "You mad at me?"

"For what?"

"For saying what I just said about Ray?"

"Mad? No. I guess it's something I should think about," Linda said. A growing pain in the pit of her stomach made itself known with a sharp jab at her innards. She felt gloomy all of a sudden, insecure and unsure of how to proceed.

Sitting back down, Linda tried to remember when Ray started working with the firm.

Chapter 31

Linda noticed something on her drive home from work. It was staying lighter, later. In Rochester, the shortest day of the year came in December. It got dark around four and stayed dark until nearly eight the next morning. There is, some feel, a disease associated with seasonal changes and lack of daylight. The obvious symptom was depression. Forever it has been referred to as *winter blue.* Now psychiatrists have labeled it with something more official sounding, Seasonal Affective Disorder. SAD. How appropriate. Linda did not think she suffered from the disease more than anyone else. She had to admit, driving home with some sunlight left in the day, and knowing that the sun would be out a little longer each day felt good. In fact, it brightened her mood considerably. Who knows, maybe there really was something to the whole SAD theory.

Linda felt too nervous to eat. The idea of going to an AA meeting made her apprehensive. She knew a nice glass of wine before leaving would settle her nerves. She couldn't do that. Showering, she worried about how to react when Ray received his three-month sobriety chip, and what to say. The obvious would be to react genuinely when the time came and not to spend hours worrying about how to respond. The last thing she wanted was for Ray to spot a phony or well-rehearsed performance.

As she dressed, she could not help but replay the conversation she had had with Patty. If Patty had known of Ray's meeting tonight, then she might not have felt so suspicious of the man. However, part of Patty's ranting and raving made sense. She knew very little about Ray. He was new to the firm and allowed nearly unlimited access to information on the computer databases.

More disturbing, though, might be the truth behind the timing of the secret admirer and his employment. Maybe, just maybe, she didn't want it to be Ray. The more she thought about it, the secret admirer-thing started after she broke up with Joey, and after she first met Jason Kenmore, too. As far as Bierman, he just recently separated from his wife.

Then again, why did it even have to be one of those people? This was where it got frightening, and Linda tried not to dwell on it. The secret admirer could be anyone. More than likely it was not the boss, an ex-boyfriend, a complainant or Ray. It could turn out to be anyone. Like an agoraphobic condition, the unlimited population of possibilities was suffocating. This was why Linda chose to ignore it. It might seem childish, but she figured if she left it alone, it would go away.

So far, aside from a strong sexual letter, there was nothing to suggest any danger. It didn't mean she liked what was going on. She wanted it all to stop and felt confident it would. Eventually the guy would want to make his identity known. That thought was a little unnerving, she supposed. The how, when, where, and why questions came to mind. Still, it would provide a certain amount of closure. The other likelihood could be that he would just stop and leave her alone.

Likelihood might be the wrong word, Linda realized. The admirer had already shown a persistent interest and had creatively made his feelings known. There was nothing wrong with hoping he would lose interest and disappear. Nothing at all wrong with thinking like that, except perhaps it was naively optimistic.

Ray would pick her up any minute. She knew they did not have time to hang around before the meeting, but what if after the meeting they wanted to stop back for a soda and a bag of microwave popped popcorn? As efficiently as possible, Linda straightened. She put away clean dishes, swept the linoleum, ran a vacuum over the living room carpet. As she fixed the throw pillows and couch cushions headlight beams shown through her closed curtains. Linda looked over the room and left the house, closing and locking the door behind her.

Ray stepped out of the car when he saw Linda coming down the front step. He leaned against his door, hands in his pockets. He looked like he wanted to say something.

Linda felt awkward already. They weren't officially dating. They had gone out once, and they had kissed. Did she go up and hug him? Did she hug and kiss him? She assumed he would enjoy a hug and a kiss. What guy wouldn't? But did she feel right about it? She couldn't just go to her side of the car and climb in. That would be rude, standoffish.

She went up to him, and stopped, shy-like. Linda said, "Hello."

Ray's lips slowly curled into a smile. He wrapped his arms around her. "I appreciate you coming with me tonight. I'm so nervous. You wouldn't believe," he said, letting go of Linda.

She felt cold outside his embrace. "Nervous? Why?"

Ray laughed, running his fingers through his hair like a brush. He gently took her by the arm and led her around to the passenger door. Opening the door for her, he said, "I don't know really. I think it's because you're coming with me tonight."

Linda hesitated.

"No, that's not how I mean it. I want you there," Ray said. "I just feel so, I don't know, odd. I feel proud, but then I feel funny feeling proud, like why should I feel proud that I haven't gotten drunk?"

Linda put her hands on his shoulders. "I'm proud of you," she said. She rose on tiptoes and kissed him. That felt right, natural. It was genuine and unplanned. The chemistry between them felt amazing. It was too strong, she knew, for only her to sense it.

"Whew," Ray said, closing the door and rushing back around to his side. He climbed into the car and backed out of the driveway. "I drove by some bars on my way here, and I have to admit, it was the first time I didn't have an urge to stop in. All these months, whenever I pass a bar, there is this urge in me, on bad days especially. But on good days, too," Ray said. "When I first got to Rochester, I was driving down Lyell Avenue and I saw a bar named, *Fun Ghouls*. I laughed so hard. I wanted to stop in just to talk to the owner."

"I've seen that place. I don't know how they got away with that name," Linda said. As they drove toward Ray's meeting, Linda sighed. "You know, I'm glad to hear you didn't feel an urge to stop at a bar."

Ray reached over, placing his hand on hers, but said nothing.

Chapter 32

Ray feared getting violently ill. He skipped dinner, knowing food would only upset him more. Driving to pick up Linda had not been as event-free as he'd described. Actually, he had lied to her. He passed by three bars. He passed by the same three bars twice before pulling into one of the parking lots. He had sat in his car, the motor running, the radio on, debating whether or not to go in. Going in would end the three-month streak of sobriety. He couldn't walk in, sit at the bar and order a soda. It wouldn't work that way. He tried to convince himself, not just tonight, but on many nights like tonight, that he was strong enough to go into any bar and just order a soda. Luckily, he never believed himself. Going in would end everything he worked so hard to achieve.

It wasn't just nights, he realized. It was mornings, too. Waking up in a bed all alone, in a city he was not truly comfortable with, wondering why in the world he bothered to wake up at all. What was there worth living for? Ray knew he wasn't suicidal, but he also knew, until tonight, that he wasn't happy. Tonight, leaving the bar's parking lot had been easy. That was what he wanted to tell Linda, but he thought she might not understand the significant difference. Someone who hasn't walked in his shoes misses a lot of significant differences in the life of a recovering alcoholic.

He had lied to Linda and did not feel good about doing so, but he knew the essence of what he had told her had been the truth.

"So, where are you from, Ray?" Linda asked, breaking a long stretch of silence as they drove toward the church.

"Florida, originally," Ray said. "I've spent time here and there. I was in Colorado for a few years, went white water rafting down the Snake River. That was scary. I lived in New York City for a bit, which was even scarier," he laughed. "But, Florida is home. I was born and raised there, maybe three miles from Disneyland in Kissimmee. My parents owned some land. With the most famous mouse in the world right next door, realty in the area is quite a commodity. My father sold it to a developer and made enough money to never have to work again. We stayed in Kissimmee, which at the time was a small town, despite the park. Less than fifty thousand people lived there. I wound up working at a fast food place all through high school until I left. But growing up down there was cool. My friends and I would buy a few cases of beer and drive sixty miles to Cocoa Beach," Ray said, smiled. "I miss those times, not necessarily the beer. You know I haven't seen my parents in years. I miss them. I always want to go down and visit them, but before, the way I was before…they wouldn't want to see me like that. I don't think I'd like them to see me that way, either. But now, maybe with a little more time under my belt, maybe I'll plan a trip down there," Ray said thoughtfully.

Linda said nothing. She just kept looking at him. "How about you?" he asked.

"I've lived in Rochester all my life. I've been to Florida, though," Linda said. "Family vacations, you know. That kind of thing."

"Ever been married?" Ray asked.

Linda shook her head. "I've been asked, once, but never accepted. I don't want to settle when I decide to get married. I can't imagine marrying a guy I wasn't absolutely sure I wanted to spend the rest of my life with. I've met some wonderful people, but none of them have been it, you know?"

Ray nodded. "I sure do."

"How about you? Ever marry?"

"Me? Nah. Like you, I came close. Things just never seemed to work out between us," he said, laughed. "My drinking always got in the way. Of course at the time, I saw it differently," Ray said.

"Of course," Linda said smiling. "What happened?"

"It wasn't so long ago. She was a woman I thought I could spend the rest of my life with. But she wasn't important enough to me to quit drinking for, and she pointed that fact out to me more than once. Each time I would promise I would change, that I would stop. You'd think if I were in love, quitting drinking would be easy," Ray laughed. "It should have been easy, but it wasn't."

They pulled into the small church parking lot. Ray looked at the clock. They had time for him to finish the story. He wasn't sure he felt like telling it. He wasn't sure Linda would want to hear it. It was his secret, the past. He was good at keeping things locked away, especially the things in his life that caused him pain.

"What's funny is, knowing how important this woman was to me, I did the exact opposite of what I should have done. Instead of going to these meetings," Ray said, pointing at the church, "instead of trying to quit drinking, I let it get to me, the pressure. Instead of working at getting sober, I drank more. It doesn't even make sense, but that's what I did. I was so stressed out about her, thinking about our relationship and how miserably I messed things up, that I drank more."

"She left you?" Linda asked. Ray could sense how uncomfortable she was. Still, she asked.

"Actually, I left her," Ray said. "Come on. It's time to go in, that is, if you are interested in a cup of coffee and finding a good seat."

Linda nodded, but made no attempt to get out of the car. "Do you know what's important to me in a relationship?"

"Stunning good looks?" Ray asked, smiling.

"Hardly," Linda said with a straight face. She was serious, not looking for wisecrack replies. "I value honest communication. If that isn't there, then there isn't anything."

Ray just watched her, enjoying the seriousness in her tone, the way she looked when she was this way. Radiant and sexy. He knew not to tell her as much. A woman might want to hear these things, but not at the moment she was exhibiting the characteristics. Ray used to tell his old girlfriend how cute she looked when she was angry, except he'd tell her while she was in the middle of an argument. Sometimes it diffused the fight, most of the time it just pushed her beyond cute and angry, to ugly and monstrous.

Perhaps sensing the new tension, Linda smiled. "I'm not saying I want to be around a babbling idiot. I'm just saying I like to talk, and not just about the weather, and not about your past sex life. But I like meaningful talk. I expect it and I expect honesty to come with it. Does that make sense?"

"Perfect sense."

"Do you appreciate that?"

"I do, I always have," Ray agreed. "And we'll pick up where we left off, maybe over dinner afterwards?"

"Exactly what I wanted to hear," Linda said. "You catch on

quick."

"Nothing to catch on to. I think there are things we need to talk about," Ray said. He got out of the car and ran around to Linda's side, ever the gentleman, and pulled open her door.

Chapter 33

Linda wrapped an arm around Ray as he led her through the parking lot to the church entrance. She ignored the cold. She enjoyed the feeling of being close to Ray. Something between them was clicking. Linda knew she wanted to take things slowly. She knew she was not ready for a new relationship, but who was she to fight the feeling? Why should she fight something that—for whatever reasons—felt …right?

"We're in the basement," Ray said. "These meetings take place in basements all over the world, every night of the week. I wonder what they're trying to tell us?"

"How about that the church wants to help you, so they offer you a room to use, completely rent free and confidential. Isn't that important, confidentiality?" Linda asked. She saw people through the doorway. Having never been to one of these meetings, she had no idea what to expect.

"That's a good, political point," Ray said. "The confidentiality thing, I like it. It almost makes sense."

They entered the basement room, Linda first.

People swarmed a table in the back of the room. Most stood talking together, coats on, arms folded, or stiff straight at their side, while they waited in line for a cup of coffee. Gray folding chairs were set up in a U shape. Some people were sitting already, or winter coats were laid over chairs spoken for.

Linda found it difficult to look around the room. People kept trying to make eye contact with her. The men and women around her were checking her out. She knew they wanted to know who she was and why she was here. They had to be wondering if she was an alcoholic, and if she'd share her story with all of them. By the way they looked at her, she knew they thought she was like them, an alcoholic looking for help to conquer the illness. She felt an almost desperate need to tell everyone that she was not one of them; she did not have a drinking problem. *I have some wine at night, but I am not an alcoholic*, she thought.

Linda couldn't help the way she was feeling. At first she felt guilty. *I shouldn't feel this way*, she told herself. But that wasn't true. This environment was new to her. How could she expect to walk into foreign surroundings and immediately feel at home? She couldn't. She didn't think anyone could.

"Nervous?" Ray asked, placing his hand on the small of her back and guiding her up to the table.

"A little," she admitted. She would have told him she was fine, for his sake, but knew he'd be able to see the truth in her behavior easily enough. She felt like a timid child in a room full of giants. How could she keep her features from reflecting a feeling of anxiety like that? She could feel the muscles in her face fidgeting, eyes downcast, nose wrinkling, jaw working and lips puckering.

"Relax. Believe it or not, these people are all just as nervous about being here as you are. They just come more often, so they think they have a handle on their emotions. They don't. None of us do. Seeing someone new is just a vivid reminder of the constant pressures that are out there waiting to tempt us," Ray said. He sounded deep and enlightened. Linda liked this about him. It showed layers to his personality, complexity. "There's someone I'd like you to meet."

She fixed her coffee while Ray dropped a dollar into a money-filled coffee can.

"I paid for ours," Ray said.

Linda stirred cream and sugar into her coffee as she followed Ray toward two men engaged in light conversation. The laughing stopped when Ray and Linda reached them. The tall black man patted the arm of the person he'd been speaking to, dismissing him politely.

"Ray. Ray. Big night tonight," the black man said, shaking hands with Ray. "I'm proud and excited for you."

"Thank you Malcolm," Ray said, lowering his head as if Malcolm were a royal king honoring a brave knight, christening the knight's shoulders with a royal sword. Linda sensed a special bond between the men standing in front of her, although it was obvious that the two had little in common with each other, other than their parallel battle to stay sober. "Malcolm, I would like to introduce you to a good friend of mine. This is Linda," Ray said, putting a hand on Linda's arm as he still held onto Malcolm's hand.

Malcolm gave Linda a warm, but awkward smile. "It's a pleasure to meet you, Linda."

Linda and he shook hands. "Hello," she said. She could not read Malcolm's face. He seemed as if he might be a little annoyed with her. Could he tell she wasn't an alcoholic? Did he consider her an intruder? *You shouldn't be here interloper!* "I'm Linda Gen…"

Malcolm held up his hand. "We don't use last names here."

Linda clammed up, nodding her head. "Sorry."

"Malcolm is my sponsor," Ray said. "He's my first sponsor. I called and asked him a few nights ago."

Linda knew having a sponsor was significant. It suggested seriousness toward staying sober. "That's wonderful," Linda said. She thought she sounded stupid and wished she hadn't said anything at all.

"Yes," Ray said. "It is."

"Well, it's about time. Why don't I get this started?" Malcolm said. "It was nice meeting you."

Linda just pursed her lips and nodded. Ray led her to a folding chair and asked the guy sitting next to her if he could move down one. They each took off their coats and put them over the backs of the chairs. "Coffee's good," Linda commented.

"It's not bad, a little strong for me," Ray said, taking a sip.

"Nervous?"

"A little," Ray admitted, the roles reversed. "How are you doing? Okay?"

"I don't think your sponsor likes me," Linda said. She didn't want to hurt Ray's feelings. She knew she shouldn't have said anything. The last thing she wanted was to come between Ray and his sponsor. She couldn't help it, though. She sensed Malcolm's feelings toward her, and she didn't like them.

"It's not you he doesn't like," Ray said. "It has to do with me. He's upset with me."

"You? How can you say that?" Linda asked.

"It has to do with some rules to AA. One of them says we, recovering alcoholics, should not get involved in relationships while we're concentrating on getting sober. We're not supposed to do anything extreme, buy a house, get married, get divorced, those types of things. We're not supposed to date within the group, either," Ray explained.

"I'm not in the group," Linda said, as if clearing her of any condemning factors set forth by the anonymous committee.

"It's just the idea. Malcolm was hesitant about sponsoring anyone. He's been a sponsor before, usually to people who were not ready. He told me it was like being a parent. Every Friday and Saturday night he'd be home pacing the floor, waiting for a phone call from the person he was sponsoring, hoping and praying they had managed to stay out of trouble. Being a sponsor is not an easy thing. And, anyway, having a girlfriend is dangerous," Ray said.

A girlfriend, Linda thought. "Well thanks. I'm dangerous, am I?"

"You know what I mean. If we fight, if we split up, Malcolm's afraid I won't know any other way to handle it except drinking. Believe it or not, failed relationships knock more people off the wagon than anything else," Ray explained. "For some, it might just be an excuse, you know? Well, she was the only reason I stopped drinking, so now that she's gone, I'm going out for a beer. See what I'm saying?"

"It does make sense. I could see breaking up with someone and going out and getting drunk, either to celebrate, or mourn," Linda said.

"Right, but for you, or someone else, the next day you'd be fine. For someone like me … or anyone in this room, the next day, we'd still be looking to get drunk. It wouldn't end with the one night. It would consume us. So it isn't that Malcolm doesn't like you, it's that he's afraid, well, he's worried if anything happens between us, that it will interfere with my winning streak," Ray said.

Linda could not avoid the obvious responsibility placed on her. It was a little overwhelming. Now was not the time, but she would need to ask him some questions. How would he handle it if they ever fought, or split up, as he put it? She was not sure she could handle feeling responsible if he started drinking again. *It wouldn't be my fault*, she thought. *I'd still feel guilty, though.*

"Hello, everyone. My name is Malcolm, and I'm an alcoholic," said Malcolm, standing with his hands behind his back at the opening of the U-formation of folding chairs. He smiled warmly, more warmly than he had at Linda, and looked at every single person in the room. Clearly, this man was a leader. People liked him.

As he spoke, and talked about his past, Linda found herself drawn to his charismatic personality. She could tell by the way Malcolm spoke, that he had told his story many times, perhaps word for word. However, it did not sound practiced and bland. It sounded sincere and true. By the time Malcolm stopped talking, she knew Ray was lucky to have this man as his sponsor.

The next person to speak was Brian. He wore a three-piece suit. He was not just an alcoholic, he was also a cocaine abuser. He looked coked up now. Linda noticed the faces of the others in the room. None of them seemed to be watching Brian speak, as if they didn't respect him. They knew he was coked up too.

The man was not making much sense, talking too fast and constantly adjusting his tie. Eventually, Malcolm stood up. "Brian," he said in a tender voice. "Brian?"

Brian stopped talking. He was sweating. Ray took Linda's hand and squeezed it gently. Everyone was silent, watching Malcolm and Brian.

"Are you using right now?" Malcolm asked.

Brain looked disgusted with the question. "No. Nah. No way."

"Brian?"

Brian clenched his hands into fists. He was not threatening Malcolm, he looked as if he were trying to gain control. He shook his head, and shook his fists. When he opened his eyes, they were wet with tears. "I took a little. I did a little in the parking lot. I found it in the glove compartment. I didn't know it was in there. I was just getting something out of the glove compartment and I saw the baggie."

"What was it you were looking for in the glove compartment, Brian?"

"Something. I don't remember what," Brian said. He didn't seem to be fooling anyone. He was lying.

"Brian, I'd like for you to sit down now."

"I don't want to sit down. I want to talk. I have so much to say, so much I need to say," Brian said.

Malcolm touched Brian on the shoulder. Linda feared the contact would result in a fight. However, Brian was immediately calmed. He lurched forward and hugged Malcolm. "I'm sorry

Malcolm. I'm sorry. I'm trying. I try so hard. I can't do this. I want to do this, and I can't. I'm going to lose my job and my wife and everything. I don't want to lose everything. I can't lose everything. If I don't stop, I'll lose everything."

"I want you to help yourself to a cup of coffee, Brian, all right? After the meeting we're going to talk. I want you to consider checking in to an in-patient program at Park Ridge, okay?" Malcolm said, delicately.

"A program? You think I need a program?" Brian asked.

"I think we need to talk about it, and we will, after the meeting."

Chapter 34

Ray felt his stomach tie itself into a knot. For three solid months had been going to these meetings, whether here in Rochester or in other cities, and not once had he ever stood up and talked about his past, about his problems, about his alcoholism. He accepted his first two chips humbly. Having Linda here made things a little different. The other times he had been alone. Tonight he felt pressure. Would she expect him to say something? Would Malcolm?

"Ladies and gentlemen, tonight someone is celebrating a three month anniversary," Malcolm said.

People hooted, clapped and whistled. The attention made Ray uncomfortable. He looked over at Linda. She was smiling, clapping excitedly, caught up in the pep rally enthusiasm. Ray put a hand on her knee and stood up.

Malcolm handed Ray the chip, then held out his hand. Ray looked at the chip, closed his eyes to try to fight back tears. Unsuccessful, he shook Malcolm's hand but felt overwhelmed. He pulled Malcolm into a tight hug and they slapped each other on the back.

Ray did not expect to get emotional, but couldn't help it. He'd been working so hard and the chip represented another thirty-one days of hard work. "Thank you," Ray said in Malcolm's ear. "Thank you."

"Don't thank me, Ray. I had nothing to do with this. Now that I'm your sponsor, though, I'll do all I can to ensure we hit another month," Malcolm whispered.

Ray let go of Malcolm and turned to look at everyone still clapping and cheering in support of his continued success. Linda was crying. Ray went over to her, put his hands on her cheeks, which were as wet as his own. Staring into Linda's eyes, he thought, he might be falling in love with her. When he kissed her, he was surprised by how warm and moist her lips felt, by the heat of the passionate kiss she returned.

Something unlike anything he had ever felt before exploded inside Ray. When the kiss ended and Ray opened his eyes, he loved seeing that hers were still closed.

A few whoops and cheers erupted as a result of the kiss. When Linda opened her eyes, she smiled bashfully, rolling her eyes. Ray held her face in his hands a moment longer.

"All right, lover boy," Malcolm said. "Everyone, that's a night. I hope to see all of you on Friday." The meeting ended. Malcolm patted Ray on the back. "Good job, Ray."

Standing up, he shook hands with Malcolm. "I feel great."

"That's good, Ray, real good. Just do me a favor, all right, stay grounded."

"I will," Ray said.

Ray and Linda closed up a handful of folding chairs and put them away, while others did the same, or put away the coffee supplies. They said goodbye to Malcolm. Ray shook hands with a few people. Some felt moved enough with his accomplishment to want to shake Ray's hand. Others treated the handshake like rubbing Buddha's belly, for luck.

Once outside, walking slowly toward the car, Ray reached for Linda's hand. "Thank you for coming with me tonight. Getting the chip was special, but I'll have to admit, having you here with me when I received it, that made the night twice as special."

"Thank you for inviting me," Linda said.

At the car, Ray unlocked her door. "It's not very late. You hungry?"

"Starved. I skipped dinner," Linda said.

"Me, too," Ray said. "I was too nervous to eat."

"Me, too."

"Why were you too nervous to eat?" Ray asked.

"I don't know. Because of this, your meeting. Going out again with you," Linda said.

Ray leaned closer. He wanted to kiss her again. The moment had been right, moments ago. He wanted any and every moment to be right. He loved the feeling of kissing Linda. It felt risky, leaning in closer still.

The risk died when she closed her eyes.

The kiss, more intense this time, involved heavy breathing.

Linda stopped the kiss. "We'd better get going."

Chapter 35

Linda took Ray to The Brook House on Ridge Road, for a nice Italian dinner. The Brook House had been a part of dining in Rochester for what seemed like forever. Years and years ago, Red, the owner, operated his restaurant out of a small renovated home. Tables were clustered together and the place was always packed. Twenty-five years later when a chain restaurant constructed a magnificent looking building but went under after a year, Red bought the place. Now, still packed all weekend long, Red easily quadrupled his business. His clam sauce was exceptional, the tripe to die for, the veal parmesan was out of this world, Linda had explained.

Sitting in a booth by the window overlooking the multi-tiered deck, Ray and Linda sipped coffee. "Well, I'm stuffed," Linda said.

"I was stuffed after the bread and salad," Ray said. "I love that dressing."

"It is good, isn't it?" Linda agreed. Something about being with Ray made her feel lightheaded and giggly. Again and again she thought of herself as a schoolgirl in love. Not since school had her emotions been so overwhelming and demanding.

"Linda, I have a problem," Ray said in a serious tone that immediately caught Linda's attention. "A confession, really."

Looking Ray dead in the eyes, she could feel her breath catch in her lungs. She felt the palms of her hands grow sweaty. There is no way Ray could be the one. He knew how upset she had been about the secret admirer. Even if it had been him, she didn't want to know the truth. She'd prefer that he just stop. Don't admit to it, just stop doing it.

No. No. That couldn't work. She had lectured about truth and honesty. She must have made him feel obligated to come clean. "Ray?"

"What are we going to do about the firm policy on dating, because if I have to, I'll quit if I can keep on seeing you," he said, still as serious as a moment ago. "I think you feel the same way. If you do, I'll start looking for another job right away."

Linda sighed with relief. Then she smiled. When she started laughing, Ray looked hurt. "No, Ray, I do. I feel the same way. For a minute there, I thought you were going to tell me that you were the secret admirer."

Ray shook his head. "That's what you thought I was going to say?"

The hurt did not completely wash away from his facial expression with Linda's explanation. "I'm sorry Ray. Of course I don't think it's you. It was just the way you started the conversation. Your voice got all deep, and you said, 'Linda, I have a problem, a confession, really'."

Ray bit his upper lip for a second. He smiled, suppressing a laugh. "I said that? I said it that way?"

Linda laughed. "You did."

"Well, I feel strongly about this." Ray folded his hands and set them on the table.

Linda knew this had to have been difficult for him. Ray might be different from most men she had ever met, but he was still a man and men had a tough time talking about their feelings. Sometimes she enjoyed milking it, watching them squirm as she probed for more detail and clarity. Not now. Not with Ray. "Ray, what about the AA rules? I need to be honest. The idea of us being together is very exciting. I feel it between us, but how can I be sure if things don't work out, that you won't go back to drinking. It feels like an awesome responsibility."

Ray took in a deep breath and exhaled softly. "You know what? I'm not sure how to promise that won't happen. What I can promise you though is that while we are together I will not touch a drop of alcohol. If our dating does come to an end at some point, I imagine I'd be pretty devastated. I know it, because if you walked out on me now, after only our two dates, I'd feel crushed."

"You would?" Linda asked, in part in disbelief and in part understanding. She thought she might feel crushed if Ray walked out as well.

"I can promise there is no risk of my drinking as long as we're together. That's all I can promise. I'd like to think I am a strong enough person that should you and I split up I would be able to stay away from drinking. I'd like to think that," Ray said.

"I'd like to think that as well," Linda said. She sat up in the booth and stretched across the table. Ray met her half way and they kissed.

Chapter 36
Thursday, January 23

When Linda arrived at work, Patty was just stepping out of her office. "Morning, Patty," Linda said. She walked into her office, Patty right behind her. While she shrugged out of her coat she noticed the pink phone memo in her "In" basket.

"That was a call from Cannon Hartzman," Patty said, holding her hands in front of her as if in prayer. "He just called a minute ago. He wanted to see you as soon as you got in."

"Hartzman? Cannon Hartzman like in, Hartzman, Cross, Lacy & Bierman?" Linda asked, astonished. Cannon Hartzman's father started the firm nearly seventy years ago, and grew it into one of Rochester's largest, most prestigious law offices. Five years ago, unofficially, Cannon Hartzman retired at fifty-five. He still came to work on a regular basis, but he didn't handle any cases. He worked PR for the firm, talking to the press and media. He was a hard, but fair man. Linda had met him only a few times at company functions. She never said more than hello. In her years with the firm, with the exception of Lacy and Bierman, she never talked with any of the partners. She talked with Bierman on a regular basis because he ran the employment law end of business, while Janet Lacy handled not only employment law, but also litigation that involved Linda's charges after decisions from the state and federal agencies had been reached. "What does he want to see me for?"

"I'll give you, I don't know, how about three guesses and the first two don't count," Patty said.

"Bierman?"

"See. You aren't nearly as dumb as you look," Patty said, smiling. "I don't want to tell you what to do, but I think you ought to get moving."

"We'll talk later," Linda told Patty as she left the office and headed for the stairs. The firm worked on the top three floors of the Reynolds Arcade Building. Hartzman's office sat on the tenth floor. Linda ran the stairs. At a large mahogany desk, Linda stood and waited for Hartzman's secretary to look over from her computer.

Linda politely cleared her throat. The secretary, who wore headphones to type out dictation, stopped what she was doing and looked at Linda. With an apologetic expression, nose wrinkled, a weak smile, she removed her headphones. "I'm sorry, dear. I didn't see you standing there. Cannon's expecting you. Just knock on his door."

Linda thanked the secretary, and went to the large double doors. The knobs were brass, shaped like a large letter S on its side. She knocked, thinking she had knocked hard enough. Hartzman was hard of hearing. After a few soundless seconds, she wondered if she should knock again. Just as she raised her knuckles ready to rap more loudly this time, she heard Cannon Hartzman. "Come in."

Hesitantly, she pushed open the door. Hartzman's office was something she had never seen before. It resembled the type of office she always envisioned the President having in the White House. Everything was wood and wood trimmed. The desk dwarfed the old man who wore an expensive Italian suit, and appeared like a child sitting behind it in his father's chair. The back of the burgundy leather chair went two feet higher than Hartzman's head. Framed pictures of Hartzman on the cover of *Corporate Times*, *Litigation Today* and *Law Journal* magazines, aside from the normal law degrees, plaques and awards, tastefully decorated the wall space. The impressive décor left Linda feeling completely intimidated.

"Linda, how have you been?" he asked. Hartzman had thin gray hair. His features had softened. His chin was not as strong, his neck was dangling skin. His nose looked a little droopy. His eyes had lost their shine. They looked glazed over.

"I've been all right. Busy, but all right." she said. She still stood by the closed office door. He had not yet invited her in, or to sit down. Until he said so, she planned to stay put.

"That's not what I hear," he said. "Come in, Linda. Please, sit down."

Linda walked through the large office to the chair opposite Hartzman's desk. She sat down and the plush leather puffed and blossomed around her back and bottom. "Thank you, Mr. Hartzman."

"Mr. Hartzman? Linda, you can call me Cannon. Everyone in our family does."

Our family? Linda thought.

"As I was saying, I understand there has been a problem between you and Patrick," he said. The way he said it, Linda thought he might be asking a question. She could not find an actual question in his statement, but Cannon's silence told her he expected an explanation.

"There was a problem," she said. "I explained it to Barbara, in HR."

Linda wondered if Barbara should be present at this meeting. Linda was not sure she wanted to continue this talk without having the conversation witnessed.

"Yes, I know," he said. "And normally I'd suggest we talk with Barb, but right now I'd appreciate just talking with you, all right?"

"I guess," she said. "But for the record, I think Barbara should be present."

"For the record lets forget the record, okay? That's the purpose of this meeting. I don't want a record of it. I just want to talk, family member to family member." Cannon smiled. His teeth looked a little ragged and pointy, like a row of vampire teeth.

Forget the record. Linda did not like this, it didn't feel right. She clasped her hands together to keep her fingers from fidgeting. "I'm not sure I understand what you're saying."

"Let's cut the bull, shall we? Patrick Bierman has been an outstanding attorney in this firm for more than a decade. We've never had any problem with his behavior," he said.

"Until now?" she interjected, somewhat hesitantly but with an air of boldness.

Cannon cleared his throat. "Yes, well aside from your complaint against him. I would like to discuss with you how we can make things right."

Linda found it difficult not to feel angry. Cannon had picked sides and it was clear he had not chosen Linda's. She knew her cheeks were flushed, could feel the heat inside them. Cannon's behavior was clearly out of line. No wonder he did not want Barbara Cunningham present that would imply the meeting has rules and boundaries. Cannon did not intend to stay within boundaries or follow rules. She knew Cannon merely wanted a quick and efficient resolution, with minimal adverse impact. He wanted to clean up as much of the mess as possible and sweep the remnants under the rug.

"Is it money?" he asked with a wicked grin. He knew money. He loved money. The crooked smile suggested to Linda that Cannon was a firm believer that money could solve any problem, that every person has a price.

"I don't want money, I want his behavior to stop. Did you know Patrick and his wife separated?" she asked. She wanted, or needed, Cannon to see where she was coming from.

"Yes, and it is unfortunate. These things happen. Relationships are a difficult thing, a challenging aspect of life, don't you agree?" he asked. "Wouldn't you say the crumbling of a marriage nearly ten years old could cause undue distress to a person?"

Linda saw his line of questioning like a bullet aimed at her head. "I think relationships crumble all the time, regardless of how long they survived previously. I think that, as an employee of this firm, it is each person's duty to keep separate the personal life from the business life, especially to refrain from harassing one another, as the employee handbook and harassment policy suggests."

"Well done," he said, still wearing his crooked grin. "You brought your complaint to HR, and have taken it a step further, haven't you?"

The police. "Yes. I want the harassment to stop."

"Of course you do. Why wouldn't you? But you have no proof, aside from the lunch date with Patrick and the reprimanding you received in his office, that he is the person allegedly harassing you, do you?" he said. "Ah yes, Patrick told me about the lunch date. He told me how he had explained to you that his wife and he had parted. He didn't come right out and tell me, of course. I had to tell him to cut the crap and tell me what was going on and he did. He also told me how he had made advances toward you and how you rejected those advances," he said, speaking slowly, looking at his fingernails. "He also explained to me that, because he was jealous, he called you into his office when he had learned you were dating the new computer administrative, Raymond Telfer, regardless of the company policy, mind you," Cannon said, making eye contact with Linda.

She knew he wanted her to know a policy violation is a policy violation, but perhaps not in so many words. She had to admit she was surprised to hear Patrick Bierman had told Cannon so much. Of course, Cannon might have threatened him with his job. It didn't change anything that Cannon knew some of the facts. He had still chosen Patrick over her.

"This firm does not need a lot of aggravation and unnecessary trouble, don't you agree?" Cannon asked.

He's calling me aggravation and trouble, she thought. "I just want everything stopped. That's what I want. If Patrick will apologize to me for …"

"Apologize? Dear, I think you are missing the point," Cannon said. "I am working as a mediator here. I want to settle this here and now. I want there to be a clean slate as of tomorrow morning."

"How is that mediating?"

"Simple. I've talked with Patrick. He is going to leave you alone. He is going to pick up where the relationship between the two of you was before his inappropriate behavior," Cannon said.

At least Cannon admitted there had been inappropriate behavior, she thought. "And you don't think he should have to say he's sorry?"

Cannon sat expressionless in his large chair. Linda knew this might be the best offer she'd get. She did not want to lose her job and did not want to file a charge with state or the EEOC. Like Cannon Hartzman, she just wanted the mess cleaned up.

"I can live with that," she said.

"Then you'll contact the police department and have them remove Bierman from their investigation," he said pointedly. He was not asking. "And Linda, I am sorry for any inconveniences this has caused you. There will be a modest adjustment made to your pay that will take place next week."

"Thank you, Mr. Hartzman," she said, not able to call him Cannon any longer, "but that won't be necessary."

"Nonsense," he said, waving his hand, dismissing her request as if it were pure foolishness. "It isn't what you're thinking. After Bierman and I discussed everything, we talked about your performance on the team. He had nothing but glowing reports. This pay increase may not come at the annually scheduled adjustment, but rest assured, if you are in line for a pay increase at that time, this will have no bearing or effect on what you are already entitled."

A payoff. "Again, thank you, but no thank you," she said adamantly.

"I think you are still misunderstanding the merits of the issues. You earned the pay increase," he said.

"Then I'll accept it in June, when and if increases are awarded. I do not want it now," Linda said.

Cannon pressed his fingertips together and shrugged. "Very well. Thank you for coming up to see me."

Linda stood up, ready to leave. "What about Barbara? Do I need to tell her anything?"

"Already taken care of," he assured her.

Some advocate for the employees, she thought. "Then I'd better get back to work."

"And Linda, as far as any actual relationship you might be having with anyone in the office, as far as I'm concerned, keep it discreet, okay? Don't let it affect your work. That policy was put in place as a safe-hold, most policies are. Of course, we want to consistently follow them, and react to violations of them, but we know that's not always possible, don't we? If it were, every one of us would be fired for using the telephones for personal rather than business need. We'd be fired for sending personal e-mails to a friend, or looking at web sites that have absolutely nothing to do with the law. Do you understand what I'm saying?" Cannon asked.

Linda just nodded. She understood all too well. There was more to his testament than explanation. Policies are like a trump card. They can be manipulated to backbone the reason for termination. In a manner of speaking, she'd been afforded an opportunity to disregard a policy, but who, besides herself and Cannon Hartzman, could ever speak to such an awarded privilege?

Chapter 37

They continued to walk at a brisk pace even after twenty minutes on the treadmill, at a twenty-degree incline. Linda could feel the burning in her thighs and buttocks. She felt dry in the mouth while the rest of her body oozed with perspiration. "God, it hurts," she moaned.

"It's because you haven't been in here in a long time," Patty explained. She walked with a determined look on her face. Her hands were fists, thumbs on top while her arms were bent at right angles at the elbow. She huffed and puffed like a locomotive.

"I missed a week or two," Linda said, feeling that sharp pain in her abdomen that threatened to double her over if she didn't slow down and let her muscles rest a little.

"Long enough. Muscle is hard to get, but too damned easy to lose," Patty said.

For the next ten minutes the women walked in silence. Linda found it difficult. Too many things kept running through her mind. The meeting with Cannon Hartzman troubled her the most. She wondered about her job and whether or not she wanted to stay with that firm or move on to another. No matter how hard she tried, Linda could not imagine things ever being the same, at least not with Bierman. Clean slate, or not, they would never have a completely trusting relationship. Respect was out the window.

"You all right?" Patty finally asked as they both powered down their walk.

"Yes and no. Yes because I'm thankful the harassment is going to stop. Hartzman was going to see to that, and no because I'm not sure I still want to work there anymore," Linda said. She stepped off the treadmill and wiped the sweat from her brow with the end of the towel draped across her neck.

Walking toward the free weights, Linda sat on a red vinyl cushioned bench press.

"So Hartzman told you that Bierman had been leaving you love letters and sending flowers?" Patty asked.

"He didn't come out and say it. He didn't come out and say a lot of things. Everything was implied, though it was as obvious as a stack of bricks falling on my head. He took Bierman's side, and that drives me crazy. I mean look at where we are, what century, and there is still in existence a Good Ol' Boy's Club. What is it with that? Is it because they went to the same law school, or just because they're both attorneys and I'm just a low-life paralegal?" Linda asked, distraught. She rested her elbows on her knees and her chin on her knuckles. "I think I'm going to start looking for a new job."

"You can't go, Linda," Patty said. She took a seat on the nearest, bench press. "What will that leave me with? I'll either get stuck with some new person who I can tell already I'll hate, or they won't replace you and then I'll be out of a job. I'll go hungry without a paycheck. Unemployment checks won't be enough to live on," Patty said, dramatizing the situation with humor. "I'll lose more weight than I want to, which won't be too bad, but I'll be malnourished. I'll be forced to make a sign out of a cardboard box flap, 'Will Work For Food … or Sex,' and spend days and nights standing on a street corner. God, Linda, how can you do this to me?"

Laughing, Linda slapped Patty's leg. "Quit it, just quit it. I haven't done anything yet. I'm just thinking things through. I want to keep my options open right now."

"And Ray?"

"Ray? He's one of my options. If anything, I'm relieved to learn he wasn't responsible for the letters," Linda said, realizing just how close she had come to breaking things off with him the other night.

"And last night?"

"Last night went very well. This sounds silly, crazy really, but I think I might be…"

"Ah, don't even say it," Patty said lying down on her back and sliding up under the weight bar on the support arms of the bench press. She gripped the bar as Linda stood up and walked behind to spot. Grunting, Patty pushed up, lifting the bar. She completed a rep of ten and put the weight bar back in place without Linda's help. "Are you going to say love? Are you telling me you are already in love with the guy?"

Linda smiled sheepishly. "I told you it was silly."

"Crazy was one of your better adjectives," Patty reminded her, panting as she tried to catch her breath. She stood up. Linda lay down and started her ten bench presses with the same weight on the bar while Patty spotted. "You're talking about two dates. Two dates and you think you love him? Have you slept with him?"

Linda set the bar down and sat up quickly. "Patty!"

"What? I'm just asking. It sounds to me like you already slept with him, so it would just be natural for you—for most women—to confuse emotions. If anything, you're justifying, after-the-fact, sleeping with him after just two dates," Patty said.

Linda stood up, and Patty sat on the bench, but Linda did not move to spot. "What?" Patty said.

"That was uncalled for," Linda said. "You are judging me unfairly."

"Look, I'm not saying you're easy because you slept with him," Patty said.

Between clenched teeth, Linda said, "I did not sleep with him. I am a bit more substantial than you are making me out to sound. I know the difference between liking a guy and loving a guy, regardless of sex. The last person I expected to attack me was you," Linda said. She felt like there was more to say, but she couldn't grasp the words. Mostly she wanted to yell at Patty, so instead she turned to leave.

Patty stopped her from walking out with a hand on Linda's shoulder. "Linda, I'm so sorry."

"Leave it alone. Leave me alone," Linda said. She hated crying, but could not stop the tears.

"I was just worried. I still am. The last thing I want is to see you get hurt, and I don't want to see you with another loser like Joey Viglucci," Patty said, explaining.

"Ray is nothing like Joey, nothing at all like him."

"Do you know Ray is an alcoholic, Linda? Has he told you that?"

Linda gasped. Her eyes went wide, but she was speechless.

"You knew?" Patty asked, sounding flabbergasted.

"How did you?" Linda asked.

"A lawyer in the building, not with our firm. He saw him at a meeting," Patty said.

"That is supposed to be confidential, those meetings," Linda said. She felt pain for Ray, wondering how he'd feel knowing people at the meetings betrayed the secrecy.

"I'm sorry, I am truly sorry. Let's not end the night like this, okay? Friends?" Patty held out her hand.

Linda hated fighting. Though Patty had said some cruel and hurtful things, she knew her friend had good intentions, even if she stunk at communicating her concerns. Linda shook Patty's hand. "Friends. I don't feel like working out anymore."

"You're ready for dinner?"

"Dinner sounds perfect."

"You know, Ray had to come over and work on my system this morning. He's kind of cute, I suppose. Knows his computers," Patty said. "I promise, I'll give him a fair chance."

"Patty, that's all I can ask."

When they left the gym, walking out toward the parking lot, a car slowed, then sped away. Linda stopped walking and clutched at Patty's arm.

"What is it?" Patty asked.

Linda shook her head. "That was Patrick Bierman's car."

"Was he in it?"

"Who else would be?"

"So much for Hartzman talking to him," Patty said.

Linda wanted to shout out loud. Hartzman wasn't going to listen to her. What could she tell him, anyway? That she'd seen Bierman driving by in a parking lot? "You know what, Patty? This sucks."

Chapter 38
Friday, January 24

When the telephone rang, Linda refused to believe someone would be calling her in the middle of the night. Forcing her eyes open, she expected to see she had overslept and was late for work. Nearly in disbelief, Linda found that her former speculation had been closer to the truth. Though her alarm clock would go off in another thirty minutes, someone was calling her at seven in the morning.

"Hello," she said, barely audible and even less coherent. She knew the third Long Island Iced Tea with Patty after dinner had been a mistake. She blamed the drink. It was too smooth and went down as easily as iced tea on a hot summer day.

"Ms. Genova? This is Josaiah Valente, with the Rochester Police," Officer Valente said. He did not sound the least bit tired. His voice was deep and serious.

"Yes, officer. What's going on?" Linda asked, sitting up in bed, rubbing the sleep from her eyes with the heel of her left hand. "What's the matter?"

She felt a thunderous boom of anxiety in her stomach, the explosion catching her breath. She could not imagine why the police would be calling her this early in the morning. What could Valente want to tell her about his investigation that couldn't wait until morning?

"Joseph Viglucci is dead," Officer Josaiah Valente said. "His brother found him this morning. Are you still there Ms. Genova?"

"I am, I'm listening," Linda said. "What happened?"

"The brother..."

"John?"

"Yes, John. He said he had some trouble reaching Joseph and decided to stop over this morning. He had a set of house keys on his ring and let himself in when Joseph didn't answer the bell. He found his brother in the Jacuzzi, on the deck in the backyard, a CD player in his lap. The thing was still plugged into an outlet," Officer Valente said.

"Oh my God. Oh my goodness," Linda said, covering her mouth with her hand. Tears rolled down her cheeks. Joey had been so mean to her, had threatened her, had come close to using his fists on her, but she never really hated him. She never wanted to see him dead.

Why was a police officer calling to tell her this? She was not next of kin, or even a girlfriend. "Officer Valente, why … why?"

"I'm calling you for a few reasons, Ms. Genova. One, if Joseph Viglucci was the one harassing you, you can expect the harassing letters will stop," Valente said. It sounded like a sarcastic line, but Linda could detect no humor in the officer's tone of voice. "The second reason, I'm going to be interested in talking with you some time this week, after the coroner is better able to provide a time of death."

"Talk to me?" *But why, she wondered. They can't think … he doesn't think that I … why would I kill Joey?* Linda cried a little harder. "Let me know when, Officer Valente."

"You're not planning any trips, any vacations or anything like that?" Officer Valente asked.

Don't leave town was the phrase that came to Linda's mind. "I don't have any plans to go anywhere outside of Rochester," Linda said. She lowered her upper lip into her mouth and let her teeth gnaw of the fatty flesh. "Officer?"

"Yes?"

"How is John?" Linda asked.

"The brother? He's not so good. When he found the body he vomited all over the place. He's still here, talking with one of the other investigating officers. At this point, we don't consider him a suspect," Officer Valente explained. "Of course, John is Joseph's only brother, and Joseph was a very wealthy man, but I haven't seen the will yet."

Linda knew John pretty well. John and Joey had been close. Joey had been just eighteen months older than John had. "No. That's not right. John would never hurt his brother for money. Check John out, he's just as rich, if not more. If anything, John is going to be lost without his big brother."

"We're going to be checking into everything. I'm sorry to have called so early in the morning. I'll be in touch."

Linda hung up the telephone and fell back on the bed, her head landing in the center of the pillow. With her arm draped across her forehead, she blankly stared at the ceiling. She was done crying. It was terrible that Joey died. The police must have reason to suspect foul play or Officer Valente would not have called her. Perhaps, had she not contacted the police and given them Joey's name, then this death might have been more like an accident, or a suicide, even.

Knowing she would never be able to fall back to sleep, Linda decided to get up. She went down to the kitchen first and started a pot of coffee. Back upstairs she showered and dressed. Pouring a first cup of coffee, she jumped when her telephone rang.

"Linda, my God, have you seen the news? Joey Viglucci is on the news. He's dead," Patty said. She spoke loudly and sounded out of breath. "I turned on R News and there was this picture of Joey."

R News did local twenty-four hour news coverage, running the same segments once every forty minutes or so for an entire day. Linda went to the living room and switched on her set. The newscaster talked about the weather. A snowstorm was brewing in Canada and the wind currents threatened to extend it across Lake Ontario, through Buffalo and into Rochester, picking up ferocious power on its trek. "I must have missed it," Linda said. "What did they say?"

"I only caught a bit of it. They were showing the outside of his house, the police all over the place, and were saying he'd been electrocuted and that the police thought the death was suspect," Patty said. "That's what they said, suspect."

Linda told Patty about her wake-up call. "I'm part of the reason they think his death is *suspect*."

"What? Why? Because of the love letters? Oh holy shit," Patty said. "Did you ever tell them about Joey showing up at your house?"

"No, I never told the police about that. I figured if he was going to stop and leave everything alone, then fine, I'd leave him alone," Linda said. She remembered feeling relieved thinking the harassment would stop. At the time, she'd been certain Joey was responsible. After meeting with Cannon Hartzman, she'd felt certain Patrick Bierman was behind the harassing letters. Maybe Joey had not been writing her sick letters. It would explain why he'd been so enraged when he'd come over that day after the police talked to him. Bierman was a bastard, complicating her life whether he realized what he was doing or not.

"So what, you think the police think you couldn't take it anymore, him bothering you, and you just offed him?" Patty asked. She sounded completely wrapped up in everything. "This is unreal."

"I have no idea what they think," Linda said, but knew Patty's rendition couldn't be far from what might be playing inside Officer Josaiah Valente's brain. "This is awful."

"Tell me about it. What do you do now? Do you go to the funeral?"

Linda had not given funeral attendance any thought. "I can't think about that now."

"You should though, you know. What will the police think if you go? What will they think if you don't? Whether or not you attend might have significant bearing on how they look at you as a suspect," Patty said.

"Stop that. I don't like being called that," Linda said. Her hands trembled so much that she needed to set her coffee cup on the counter. "What should I do? Should I go or not?"

"I have no idea," Patty said.

Great. "Thanks for nothing," Linda said. "Are you going in to work today?"

"Why wouldn't I?" Patty asked. "You thinking about staying home?"

"Yes. I guess so. I'm a mess. I have no idea what's going on in my life. I just keep thinking, if Joey's death wasn't an accident, then did someone out there kill him on purpose?"

"Hard to drop a CD player into the water with you on accident," Patty said. "But it could happen. I can only imagine how relaxing it must be to sit in a Jacuzzi, listening to music. Must be nice. Or, must have been nice. Sorry."

When Linda had started dating Joey in June, he had expressed his love for the Jacuzzi. He soaked in it nearly every night, all summer long. It didn't matter if it were one hundred degrees out. He had said it helped his back, soothed his muscles. Linda did not care for the thing during the summer months, but as their relationship progressed into fall, she began to appreciate Joey's fondness for the Jacuzzi. "Forget it, I know what you meant," Linda said. "It just doesn't feel right, though, you know?"

"I don't know. You're right. It's weird," Patty said. "I don't like it, regardless of which way you look at it. I'll tell you what, stay home. I'm still going in. I hate to sound disrespectful, but I'm not missing work over the guy. I didn't even like him."

"Patty…"

"I know, that comment was uncalled for. I just mean I can understand you wanting to stay home today. If anything important comes up, I'll call you. I don't recall seeing anything on your calendar that couldn't be rescheduled. Let me handle it for you, all right?" Patty said,

"Thank you. If you need me, I'll be here, I'll be home," Linda said and hung up.

Dressed for work, Linda took her coffee with her into the living room and sat on the sofa, her legs curled up under her. She held the remote aimed at the television, but did not change the channel. She waited impatiently for the segment on Joey Viglucci's suspect and untimely death.

After she watched the four-minute piece, she remained on the sofa, her forgotten cup of coffee cold on the end table beside her, and waited another forty minutes in silence for the segment to run again. All morning long Linda sat and watched R News, sometimes sobbing when they talked about Joey, sometimes numb, sometimes so lost in her own memories that she missed the segment all together.

Something bothered her. A persistent nagging that she could not pinpoint. It drove her crazy, because she had no idea how to focus her energy. She had no idea what was bothering her or why. She just knew she felt bothered.

Eventually, she laid her head down on the arm of the couch and fell asleep, too exhausted to watch the news any longer.

Chapter 39

Linda ran as fast as she could. She knew someone was behind her, getting closer, but she couldn't see who it was. Whoever was chasing her meant her harm. She could hear her own heavy breathing, but felt as if she were running in slow motion. She hardly paid any attention to the fact that it was no longer winter, but summer. She was running down a street in a town that did not even vaguely look familiar. Parked cars lined both sides of the street. No one was outside. Looking back, she saw no one behind her. She felt like she might lose her balance and fall as she turned her attention back to the road in front of her. Staying on her feet, but clearly exhausted, Linda ran at an unsteady angle into a parked car, knocking the side mirror to the ground. The glass shattered...

And all at once she came awake to the sound of the telephone ringing. Encased in a thin sheet of cold sweat, her hair sticking to her face, Linda got up and wiped her mouth with the palm of her hand before answering the phone in the kitchen. "Hello?"

"Ms. Genova? It's Officer Valente again," the police officer said.

Linda glanced at her wristwatch. She had slept the morning away. It was nearly three in the afternoon. "Yes?"

"I tried reaching you at the office. Your secretary informed me that you stayed home today, too distraught?"

"Yes, that's right," Linda said. "I've been watching the news, R News only, really. I must have fallen asleep on the sofa." She was talking too much, explaining to the officer things that didn't require explaining. She made a conscious effort to keep quiet, to speak only if spoken to.

"The coroner was able to pinpoint the time of Joseph Viglucci's death somewhere close to ten o'clock last night. By any chance do you recall where you were last night?" Officer Valente spoke in a non-threatening, almost soothing tone. In an interrogation, Linda knew Valente would play the role of 'Good Cop'.

"Yesterday Patty and I worked out, went for dinner, had some drinks and then I came home," Linda said.

"Patty?"

"Dent. My secretary. You just spoke to her apparently," Linda said. "We're pretty close friends."

"I see. And what time do you recall getting home?" Officer Valente asked.

Linda did not want to admit she had driven home heavily under the influence. She barely remembered driving home, much less what time it had been when she walked in the door. "Honestly, no. I can't remember."

"Would Patty recall?" Officer Valente asked.

"She might," Linda said, though her recollection was that Patty was pounding the drinks at an equal pace. "You'd have to ask her."

"How about, where were the two of you before you left for home?"

Linda thought she could see Valente in her mind's eye. He would be sitting at a desk, dressed in suit pants, a white shirt and a plain dark tie. She envisioned a shoulder holster strapped in place; shirtsleeves rolled up to the forearm. "A place called Bottom's Up," she said, remembering when it had once been a dive located in the city. The owner of the establishment moved to a location in Greece—away from the street corner trouble—added a grill, over-sized menus and a team of attractive and friendly servers. Add to that live entertainment all weekend long and the place now maintained a steady flow of customers throughout the week, but really packed them in on the weekends.

"I know the place. Did you sit at a booth, up at the bar?"

"Booth. We had a waitress, though I can't think of her name. But we were against the back wall, right next to the jukebox," Linda said. She tried to picture other people there last night. Short of hypnosis, she could not recall much more about the night, other than drinking and talking with Patty.

"Hair color?"

"Blonde. She was young, late twenties? Big breasted. Wears a thick layer of lipstick, or did last night, anyway." Linda tried to recall as much as possible. She wanted to tell the police officer everything. The sooner he could sort through the facts, the quicker she could be taken out of his line of sight as a possible suspect. "Does any of that help?"

"All of it," Valente said. "I'll be in touch. Thank you."

When Linda hung up the telephone she felt sick to her stomach. Her nerves were frayed. Shaking, she stood up clutching at her belly. She took her cup of coffee to the kitchen and dumped it into the sink, then filled her cup halfway with soda from the fridge. From the cupboard above the fridge she removed a bottle of whiskey which was two-thirds full and filled up her glass of soda. She took a gulp, topped it off with more whiskey then put everything away.

Her mind was a whirlwind. She wondered how things would be with Joey gone. She knew it would not affect her life, and that was a strange feeling. Had they have been together she would have been devastated. If Officer Valente had not called her, if the death had never made the news, would she even have realized he had died? Probably not. Her life would have continued, unchanged. The difference was that she did know Joey was dead. Take it up a notch. On some level the police suspected her involvement with the death.

Is it still a death then, she wondered? When does it become a murder?

Linda did not want to sit in the living room anymore. She did not want to watch the news. She had seen the same segment enough times for the truth to settle in. Joey Viglucci was dead. Nothing would change it. Part of her felt guilty. Maybe the tears kept coming because part of her was relieved.

Chapter 40

Ray left work, deciding to drive to Linda's. Patty had told him about Joey. The terrible news troubled Ray, setting off a pang of unreasonable jealousy. First, the guy had died. Even if Linda wanted him back, that option was no longer available. Secondly, Linda had left Joey Viglucci when he had been alive. She had already moved on. The jealousy felt ridiculous and Ray wished he could dismiss it. Instead, it lingered in minute waves of queasiness inside his stomach.

The sky, dark all day long, resembled rolling black lava. The storm clouds hovered over the city, not so much threatening to unleash fury, as deciding when to begin the wintry pandemonium. The temperatures seemed to drop continually. The DJ on the radio said it was twenty-two degrees with a seven-degree wind chill. Damn cold. Ray cranked the heat up, but felt only cold air blowing in his face. He slowed the speed of the heater fans as he pulled to a stop at a red light.

His throat felt dry, and he worked at it, clearing his throat as the light turned green. He knew the scratchy feeling. It was an insatiable itch. Clutching the steering wheel more tightly, he ignored Mr. Hyde taunting Dr. Jekyll inside his mind. The urges came in waves, some stronger and larger than others, but regardless of size, the tide was constant. Even on placid days, the waves still lapped at the dry sand. One day at a time, he reminded himself. One wave at a time.

He thought about calling Malcolm, one of the perks of having a sponsor. When the waves were a little rougher than normal, you did not have to swim in them alone. And sometimes, like now, just knowing that made tolerating the urge to drink a little easier. From one crutch to the next, Ray decided to bring a pizza with him to Linda's. Like a person who quit smoking is known to chew the hell off the end of a pencil, Ray liked to fight a need to drink with food.

He pulled into the Pontilio's Pizzeria parking lot, went in and placed an order. It would be a half-hour wait. Ray took a seat in the waiting area by a small table littered with advertisement flyers and magazines. A single red rose in a cheap ceramic white vase looked out of place on the table. To pass the time, Ray absently flipped through a classic car magazine, and he thought of Malcolm.

"Ray?" The guy behind the counter said, wiping his flour covered hands onto his red sauce stained apron. "Pizza's ready."

Ray paid for the food and left.

The pizza, hot out of the oven, smelled wonderful. Ray drove as fast as he could toward Linda's house. Realizing she might not want company, Ray wondered if he should have called. It wouldn't have hurt. Except, if he called, she could tell him not to come over. Whereas if he just showed up on her front step with a fresh baked pizza, how could she turn him away?

Getting involved in another relationship had not been a part of Ray's plan. He wanted a new, clean beginning in Rochester. He needed the chance to find himself. It might not have been the only reason he moved to another state, but it was a damned good reason. He knew with his drinking, and with his ex, he had no identity. He had been a loser, plain and simple. So why Linda? Why did he want to get involved with someone and risk losing the person he saw he was becoming?

Because, Ray knew, this time he was sober. He was enjoying being sober. It was a rush like he never thought he could experience. It was an old and worn out saying that came to mind, "Where before he had been blind, now he could see". It might be a cliché, but it rang true. The colors of life were far more vibrant than he ever could have anticipated.

In that spectrum of light and color, Ray realized he did not want to be alone. Maybe he needed to spend a few months alone in order to regroup and dedicate his efforts at getting cleaned up. In thinking about it, Ray realized he had never been alone for a longer period of time, not since he was a boy, before he started dating girls in junior high school. He had always had a girlfriend.

Some might think he was afraid to be alone. He did not think that was true. He knew he just enjoyed a woman's company. He enjoyed being with Linda.

Pulling into Linda's driveway, Ray was relieved to see her car and only her car.

He felt little anxious butterflies flitting around in his stomach. He checked his hair in the rearview mirror, and sampled his breath by breathing into the palm of his hand and taking a sniff. Satisfied, he got out of the car, bringing the pizza with him.

This was not a date. Someone Linda knew intimately had just died, he reminded himself. She might not be in the mood for talking, so he planned to sit silently with her. She might just want to cry, so he was ready to let her rest her head on his shoulder. Linda was hurting, obviously. He didn't like that. He didn't want to see her in any pain. It troubled him to know she was upset. That was how he knew the feelings he felt were strong, because he actually cared.

He cared, and he wanted to be with her. Ray wanted to be the one to comfort her.

On her front step, after ringing the doorbell, Ray reached into the inside pocket on his coat and removed the rose from the pizzeria. He set it on top of the pizza box and waited.

After a few moments of silence, Ray decided to knock. He knew she might be sleeping. He did not want to disturb her, but he did not just want to take the pizza and go home without having tried to see her.

This time he heard someone inside. A thump. Ray strained to listen. The storm door was unlocked. He opened it and knocked twice more on the front door, hard and loud. "Linda?" he called out.

The panic set in at once. Ray's imagination ran wild. Something could have happened to her. She could have been extremely upset about that guy's death and …

He knocked again, actually pounding his fist. "Linda?"

The movement again. Something dropped and shattered. "Linda?"

Ray wanted to break down the door. It seemed over dramatic, but he had no idea what was going on inside. He dropped the pizza box and flower to the ground. He jumped down from the front steps and ran to the picture window. He pressed his face to the glass, cupped his hands around his eyes, but could not see inside. The curtains were closed. He rapped his knuckles on the glass, and said, "Linda?"

The front door opened, startling Ray. He turned and sighed. "My God Linda, I was worried."

"What? I said I was coming," Linda said. Her clothes were wrinkled and her makeup smeared. Large dark ringlets of mascara encircled her eyes; black tear streaks dripped from the mascara down her cheeks.

"I didn't hear you. Oh Linda," Ray said, walking back to the stairs. He picked up the pizza and the flower. He sensed it. He knew what it looked like. He wanted to hold his breath and pretend it wasn't happening, but that wouldn't work.

"Pizza? I'm starved, come on in," Linda said, pushing open the storm door as she disappeared into the house.

Ray walked in, stepped out of his shoes and found Linda in the kitchen. She was scrambling to clean up broken glass. "I dropped it," she said, slurring the three words into one.

Ray easily detected the sweet smell of whiskey, an aroma he knew well. The cupboard door over the fridge was ajar. Dark fluid was on the floor with the glass. He had no doubt Linda had spent the afternoon drinking, perhaps the morning, too.

"I cut myself," Linda said, red droplets of blood rolling down the side of her index finger into her palm. "Damn glass."

Ray put the pizza down on the kitchen table. Carefully he knelt beside Linda, taking her wrist he examined her hand. "A sliver of glass is in there," he said. He held her hand up toward the light. Squinting, he saw the sliver. Using fingernails he plucked the shard out of her flesh. "Go rinse off your hand. I'll get this," Ray instructed.

While Linda stood by the sink cleaning the minuscule wound, Ray took the small garbage-bag-lined can between the fridge and the tall cupboard and brought it near the glass. He found the broom and dustpan in the tall cupboard and swept up the glass. He used toweling paper to wipe up the spilled alcohol. He inspected the linoleum for other small shards, but could find none.

In the cupboard over the counter Ray removed two plates and glasses. From the fridge he removed a water container and filled the glasses, adding ice cubes to both. He put the plates and a roll of paper towels on the table next to the pizza, then brought over the glasses.

"Still hungry?" Ray said. Linda had not moved away from the

faucet. She continued to let the cold water run, perhaps numbing her finger.

"I'm sorry," Linda said, her shoulders shaking. Ray knew she was crying. He approached her and softly placed his hands on her shoulders.

"I understand," he said. It wasn't easy. If it were anyone else, he would have left. He did not need to be around someone drunk, or with people drinking. He might have three months under his belt, but that didn't make everything easy. Temptation is temptation. Linda needed him. How many times had he been drunk and needed someone? A friend to turn to?

It was different when he was drinking. He spent time developing relationships with walls. He never really let anyone get close. How could he? The alcohol came first in his life. It was never a secret to those who loved him, regardless. Women always thought they could change him. He was a challenge. They worked at it while he enjoyed the attention. Did any of them ever know him? Not really.

Linda turned away. "How could you understand? I am so embarrassed that you're here. I don't want you to see me this way. You of all people should not see me this way. What kind of a person am I? I'm a horrible person, a horrible person," she said.

"Listen, Linda, I don't think you're a horrible person," Ray said. "I also don't think you're an alcoholic. Something very upsetting has happened in your life. You didn't know how to deal with it. Getting drunk seemed like the best way. I was different. Nothing upsetting had to happen in my life, I just chose to deal with everyday life by drinking every day."

"You don't hate me?" Linda asked, slowly turning to face Ray.

"Hate you? Linda, I think I love you," Ray said, knowing it was not the right time, or the right place to first tell this woman that he loved her, but he could not keep the truth from her. He needed to say it. She needed to hear it.

"You do? You think you love me?" Linda asked. Fresh rolling black tears slid down her cheeks.

He hugged her, squeezing her tightly to him. He could feel her breasts against his chest, and the rapid beating of her heart. She started kissing his neck. He pulled out of the hug. "Not now," he said. "Now is not the time." He wanted it to be the time, but he also wanted Linda in a better frame of mind.

Linda regarded him for a moment and smiled. "I think I love you, too."

Ray hugged her again. This time, Linda wrapped her arms tightly around his waist. "Pizza's getting cold," Ray said.

Chapter 41

Jason Kenmore took a long hot shower. He washed his body vigorously with both soap and shampoo. He dressed in his best jeans and a red silk shirt. He wore his Sunday church sneakers, the ones with the tags still attached to the laces. He used a pick to fluff up his hair and a splash of cologne to trigger the animal inside of women.

He thought about his wife. She was in the cellar washing laundry. A good wife, a good mother, Jason had no reason to want anything more. At first he had just been harassing her. Linda Genova certainly was attractive, stunning, really, but he never anticipated she might feel the same way about him. He enjoyed making her squirm, staring at her, talking to her like a sex-toy. He enjoyed seeing Miss Snow White's cheeks turn flush. He liked getting under her skin.

It should not surprise him that she was actually interested. Before getting married he had been quite the ladies man. Who could blame them? He was good looking, took care of himself physically, and was charming—in a bad boy kind of way. Women liked that. They wanted a bad boy. Screw this, women are looking for a sensitive man. That was crap. What woman wanted to be with a man crying over a long distance telephone commercial?

When he saw the letter in the mailbox from the law firm he had initially assumed the worst. He thought it would have something to do with his bogus discrimination charge. It was his first time filing a charge against an employer and though the process had been explained to him, he was not positive he understood it. When he opened and read the steamy letter, he had been a little surprised, but in a way he had expected it. Sure, he had been harassing the legal lady, but he'd also been sincere. He wanted her, and it was reassuring to know she wanted him, too. Jason felt the immediate chemistry between them. It did not just spark when they first made eye contact—it exploded. At first he thought, foolishly, that perhaps only he had felt it. Everything was different now. The fact that she had rented a motel room and wanted him to meet her there spoke volumes.

Enjoying his reflection in the full-length mirror, Jason almost had to pry himself away. He walked down the stairs to the living room where his kids sat perched on small chairs in front of the television, playing video games. Had he not gone into the room and cleared his throat, they would not have been aware of his presence. "I'm going out with some friends," Jason said, kissing each of them on the forehead. They seemed annoyed, tilting to the side to see around him and to ensure a clear view of the game unfolding on the screen. "Tell mommy not to wait up, all right?"

"Sure dad," his oldest said. Whether or not they heard or understood him didn't matter. In telling his kids his plans, he knew he was shifting responsibility. It was not uncommon for him to go out for all hours of the night with friends, playing pool and getting drunk. His wife didn't like it, not one bit, but he was the man of the house, the king of the castle. He did not want to go down into the cellar and tell her face to face. She would throw an assault of questions at him, "Who are you going out with? Where are you planning to go? When will you be home?" He didn't need that. She would still attempt to question him in the morning, but by then he would have an excuse in place, calling one or two friends to second and third the truth behind his lie.

He felt a little guilty sneaking out the back door, but not enough to call it off, to turn around and go back in. Instead, like a burglar, he tiptoed across the fenced in back yard to the gate that led to the garage. He opened the garage door slowly. It was heavy. Solid wood. He backed out of the driveway and pulled out into the road, leaving the garage door open. He did not want to get out of the car and shut it. By that time his wife might come to the door looking for him. He was too close to getting away to want to risk getting stopped.

The motel was off Mt. Read Boulevard, down Jay Street. The place was a sleazy dive. It sported a sign on a pole high enough in the air to attract travelers driving along the expressway. The sign looked exotic, as if promising luxurious suites. Anyone exiting the expressway hoping for a pleasant night's sleep at a comfortable and clean motel had to be shocked upon pulling into the parking lot. The place might as well have been roped off in yellow and black police crime scene tape. The paint was chipping. The wood warped. The sidewalk leading along the L-shaped motel was cracked and crumbling. Every single door had scratches and digs near and around the doorknobs, evidence at the attempted illegal entries. What most people would wonder is how many of those attempts were successful?

Regardless, Jason Kenmore pulled into the lot, confident his car would not be identified by any of his wife's family or friends. He did not worry about what *his* friends or family thought. His brothers and even his father were cheaters. If anything, they might be proud of him.

The letter had told him the room number, that the door would be unlocked, and that he should just walk in. He saw a few other cars in the parking lot. None were in front of room 7E. Jason parked in front of the room and got out of the car. The place was alive with parties. He could hear loud music coming from all over the place.

He looked up and down the sidewalk. A door, a few rooms down, opened. A boy, definitely not a man, came out of the room carrying a bottle of beer. He looked at Jason, smiled, held up his beer in an acknowledging salute and then proceeded to unzip his pants and to urinate on the black top.

Jason went up to door 7E and tried the knob. As promised, the door was not locked and he stepped into the dark room. He felt along the wall for a light switch and turned it on. A single lamp near the bed came on. The bed was still made, and women's clothes were neatly laid out on it. Jason heard the shower running. A radio on the nightstand next to the lamp was playing dance music.

He closed and locked the door. Jason was a little disappointed. He was turned on, knowing she was in the shower, perhaps waiting for him to join her, but he had already showered. He wanted Linda to see him clothed, dressed in his sneakers, jeans and silk shirt. He had spent a lot of time picking out just the right outfit.

Really, what difference did it make?

He found the mirror on the one dresser in the room. To the rhythm of the radio tune, Jason began to undress. He undid one button at a time, singing softly with the radio. He smiled at himself, proud as ever of his white teeth. He shrugged out of the sleeves and, carefully handling the expensive shirt, folded it and laid it on the chair next to the dresser. He undid the button on his jeans, unzipped the zipper and stepped out of them. He looked at his muscles, as he had done only minutes ago at home. He flexed, making his pectoral muscles dance alternately. He sang more loudly with the song, as he became more and more excited about what he was doing.

Slipping out of his briefs and neatly putting them on the chair with his shirt, Jason walked toward the closed bathroom door. He pushed open the door and walked in. The shower curtain was solid white, not transparent at all. The mirror over the sink was filled with fog. He walked up to the shower and parted the curtain, anxiously expecting to see a vision of naked beauty.

Instead, he saw an empty tub. Confused, he turned around and screamed, caught off guard by the vicious attack. The knife sliced through his muscled body with ease, silencing his scream as the blade punctured a lung.

Chapter 42

Ray had offered to make coffee while Linda dashed into the bathroom. She had been horrified to see her reflection in the mirror. She scrubbed off the makeup, put her hair back in a clip and changed into a comfortable pair of flannel pajamas. When she returned, Ray sat in the living room on the sofa waiting for her with the television off and only one light, in the back corner of the room, on. Two freshly brewed cups of coffee sat on the coffee table. Linda sat on her feet at the opposite end of the sofa and rubbed her stomach. "That pizza was so good, thank you."

He shrugged. "I was hungry and was afraid to find out what kind of a cook you were."

That deserved a swat with the throw pillow. Laughing, she said, "I cook pretty well. I'm not a great chef, but I enjoy cooking."

"Yeah? Well, we'll have to see about that, won't we," he said, daring her to take the bait.

"I'll cook up a marvelous dinner for Saturday night. I'll make enough for two, if you'll consider joining me," she offered.

"Would be my honor," he said. "You know, I was hoping you'd ask."

"I knew you s hoping," she said, smiling. God, she could not believe how much she liked this guy, his smile, the way he talked, the way he took care of her.

A Kenmore file was on the table. Linda saw Ray regarding it. "Sometimes I bring work home," she said.

Ray opened the file. Linda knew she should stop him. Most everything in the file was privileged. She saw him hold up the photo of Kenmore.

"Nice looking man," he said.

"But he's an asshole," she said, harshly.

Ray must have sensed the nerve he'd struck. He put back the photo, closed the file and smiled. "How's the finger?"

She looked at it. "Good," she said.

"How about you? How are you? What happened to your friend?" he asked, speaking softly.

Linda shook her head. "I really don't want to talk about that, about him. It's terrible what happened, but I don't want to think about it anymore. Not tonight. I want to talk about you, to pick up where we left off from the other night." She watched Ray, noticing the way he shifted uncomfortably on the sofa.

"Me, huh? You want to talk about Tina," he said.

"Her name was Tina?"

Ray nodded. "I wasn't in love with her. It was close. I liked her a lot. I cared about her. She was in love with me. I have no idea why, but she was."

Linda continued to watch him, knowing it was not easy to talk about his past. The inner struggle he seemed to be going through showed in his facial expressions. She knew he had never told anyone what he was about to tell her. He had not told her that this was the case, she just knew it. It was a special moment, and spoke volumes to Linda about Ray's intentions. He was serious and she was thankful. Her feelings toward him were undeniably strong. She did not just *think* she loved Ray. She knew she loved him.

"I'm sure you can guess my drinking was a problem. At first, not for her, not really. Tina thought she could change me. I don't know. She had issues of her own. Not drinking, but other issues. So with me she had these idealistic plans. She was so sure she could get me to quit drinking. I remember laughing at her, like it was something cute, instead of a serious problem," he said. He stood up and paced back and forth, stopping to look out the front window. "It's snowing pretty hard."

Linda crossed her legs, sitting Indian style on the sofa, her elbows in her lap. She didn't want to talk. She was afraid if she said anything that she might break his concentration. Instead she just stared at him, patiently waiting for him to continue.

Ray cleared his throat, kneeled by the coffee table and took a sip of coffee. "It's almost funny now, you know, thinking about it. I cared about Tina, but the truth was I cared about getting drunk more. I told her we were through. I broke things off for her benefit. Not mine. I could have stayed with her, could have kept drinking and who knows, she might have put up with me forever.

My guess, sooner or later she would have seen the hopeless battle and given up. Every woman I have ever been with did the same. I never blamed any of them. Most of the time I was amazed at how long they had actually stayed with me."

Linda was not sure what to expect. She was not thrilled to hear how much he liked this other woman. She felt pangs of jealousy, and that bothered her. She had asked to hear this story, he hadn't volunteered it. He was telling her an honest version about his life. She forced herself to ignore the pangs. "How'd she take it?"

"How'd she take it? Not well. A lot of crying. Believe it or not, she said she could change, she was all ready to change to please me. She thought she had done something wrong, something to ruin the relationship. It didn't matter how many times I told her that it was me and not her. She didn't care. She kept saying that … that's what people always say when they end a relationship, it's me it's not you. She's right, too. I've heard it before, I've used it before," he said.

"It is an old one," she said, knowing that she had both heard and used it before. "It's a classic next to the let's-be-friends line."

He laughed. "Exactly, exactly."

Ray sat on the couch next to Linda. "For a while, after I ended things, she called me every day, all hours of the night. I was less than patient with her. I was a little rude, you know, to get my point across."

"And what happened?"

"What happened? The oddest thing happened. She stopped calling. When she stopped, I missed her. I used to sit by the phone and wait, thinking she'd call any minute. The days became weeks. In those weeks, I spent more time thinking about Tina than I spent thinking about getting drunk," he said. "So I said to myself, I can change. Maybe I can change. That night, about three, three and a half weeks after breaking up with Tina, I went to my first AA meeting."

"So you were sober for three full weeks before going to your first AA meeting?" she asked, impressed.

"Hardly. I said I spent more time thinking about Tina than I spent thinking about getting drunk. That's not even close to the same thing as being sober," he said, smiling.

Ray rubbed his face with the palms of his hands. His fingers worked like a brush in his hair. He slapped at his thighs, then rubbed them vigorously along his legs. Linda guessed this must be a tough part of story. So far it had been interesting, but not unsettling. She knew there had to be something unsettling, or else it would not be so difficult to tell. She did not want to press him. Ray had been talking well on his own, at his own pace. She continued to wait for him to be ready. She put a hand on his hand. He looked at her and smiled, reassuringly.

"I went to a meeting every night for the next few weeks. I was doing great, feeling great. I decided to go and tell Tina that we had a chance and that I had changed. I had a few weeks of sobriety under my belt and I felt good. Real good," he said.

He stood up again, walked over to the picture window and parted the curtains. He seemed agitated and apprehensive. He reminded Linda of a person tossing and turning in a dream, only with Ray she was able to glimpse his nightmare as he narrated. Linda thought she might know where the story was headed.

"So after a meeting one night, a Thursday night, not that it makes a difference, I decided to drive over to her place. When I got there, there was nothing to suggest she wasn't alone. There was only one car in the driveway," he said.

"Ah, Ray," she said. She stood up and walked over to stand next to Ray. From behind she wrapped her arms around his waist. He took hold of her hands. "You don't have to continue."

"I know. I want to," he said. "Unless you want me to stop."

"No. Not if you want to keep going."

"I rang the doorbell and she didn't answer the door. Another guy did. He was wearing her bathrobe. He said hello, you know. He didn't know who I was. He just had this grin, this I-just-had-sex grin. I was speechless. I just stood there, staring at him. My jaw must have dropped," he said.

Linda moved her hands out of his, then rubbed his back and neck with her fingers. She could feel the tension in knots, and worked them out as she firmly gave him a massage. Ray groaned and rolled his head from side to side.

"I should have walked away. I had no business being there. I was unannounced, you know. I was the one that left her. I gave her every reason to think she should get on with her life," he said.

"I should have walked away, but instead, instead of leaving, I punched my hand through the storm door. The glass shattered and I cut my knuckles, but that didn't stop me. It infuriated me."

"Ray, you didn't?" she asked as she stopped massaging his back and rolled her fingers into the palm of her hand.

Ray lowered his head. "Tina came to the door. She was screaming and crying. She had her new guy and was pulling him away from the door, back into the house. I don't know, he thought he was tough, he wanted to show off for Tina. He broke free from her and came after me. It was a terrible fight," Ray said. He remembered nearly every blow delivered and received. With one punch, Ray had broken the other man's nose. When the guy cupped his nose with both hands, Ray kicked the man in the groin. As the man doubled over, Ray grabbed a fistful of hair from the back of the guy's head and as he brought up his knee, he slammed the man's face downward. Tina had been screaming and crying. She had jumped on Ray, trying to get him off her new boyfriend. In a blind rage, Ray had shrugged her off his back. The boyfriend was on the ground. He wasn't moving. It hadn't mattered. Ray kicked him a few times in the ribs, until his anger and energy was spent.

"What happened?" she asked.

"Tina called the cops. Charges were filed against me, but dropped. I have no idea why. I hung around for a wile longer, but then I left," he said. He could tell Linda had questions about the details of the fight, but was refraining from asking. One day he might tell her.

"That's when you came to Rochester?" she asked.

"Not exactly. It wasn't that easy to get over her, you know. I wasn't just jealous that Tina had a new guy in her life, I was crazy about it. I kept calling her, wanting to tell her that I changed, that things could work for us, but when she would answer the phone, I'd hang up," Ray said.

"Why did you hang up? I mean, why didn't you just tell her what you'd done, how you'd gone weeks without drinking?" she asked. She was resting her chin on his shoulder, her fingernails lightly scratching his back.

"I hung up each time, because what I wanted to tell her wasn't true anymore. I went right back to drinking, right back to it. The only reason I kept calling her was because I was drunk every time

I dropped money into the payphone," he said.

"So what happened?"

"Let's sit down," he said.

They went back to the sofa. They sat close to each other. Ray took a deep breath. "Eventually I had to give up on her. I had to forget Tina. It wasn't easy, but I did it. I started going to AA meetings again, more than one a day. At first I was still calling her. Sober, but hanging up, just the same. Then I knew I had to get away from her all together. I knew if I ran into her somewhere, a store or at the movies, I risked falling off the wagon. So I said goodbye to her, goodbye to the town, and I moved. Rochester wasn't the first city I stopped in. I was in Pittsburgh for a while, and over in Syracuse. I planned to come to Rochester, and if things didn't work out, head over to Buffalo."

"But things have worked out?" she asked.

Ray smiled. "So far."

"How did you say goodbye to Tina? You said you had said goodbye to Tina," she said.

"Just in a manner of speaking, you know? I didn't really say goodbye to her," he said. "In a nutshell, that's how I wound up in your neck of the woods."

Linda stood up and went into the kitchen. What she wanted was a stiff drink. She felt drained, as if she had just finished reading a Danielle Steel novel. She removed the jug of water from the fridge and filled a glass. "Want a glass of water?" she called into the living room.

"No, thank you. The coffee is enough," he said. "Linda, I didn't scare you away with that story, did I? I mean, was my story…" He stopped talking and just looked at Linda.

She stood in a seductive stance between the kitchen and the living room, one arm rested against the wall, her hip cocked. Between her lips was the red rose. She removed it. "Where did this come from?" she asked in a deep husky voice.

"I picked it up with … after the pizza," he said, getting to his feet.

"Oh yeah?"

"Yeah," he said, swallowing.

"Want to know what?" Linda said walking into the living room, hips swaying from side to side.

"What?" he asked.

"I'm not drunk anymore," she said, wrapping her arms loosely around his neck.

"You're not?"

"Well, not like I was. I feel good ... want to feel?"

He smiled. "Linda?"

She kissed him. His mouth was moist and hot. His tongue tasted sweet and bitter, like coffee. He kissed her back, wrapping his arms around her, pulling her tight against him. He was strong and she liked the feeling of him holding her. "Have I showed you my room?"

* * * * *

It was close to midnight. Outside Linda's bedroom window the night sky was hidden behind a blanket of storm clouds. The wind blew strong, moaning and whistling as it whipped against Linda's house. In silence, holding each other, warm and cozy on flannel sheets and under a thick, soft comforter, Ray and Linda listened to the brewing storm.

"Will you stay tonight?" Linda asked. She talked so quietly that Ray almost did not hear her words.

"I can't. I have to work tomorrow," he said.

"Tomorrow? Why?"

"I'm running a systems migration. With Gwen still out recovering, Ling's depending on me. I was hired expected to hit the ground running. I don't want to let Ling down. He's pretty good, as far as bosses go. I sent out an email to everyone about the migration, but you weren't at work. It can't really be done during the week because everyone works long, odd hours. Saturday is the only day. Besides, I can't refuse the overtime," Ray said.

"Can you go in late?"

"I don't want to go in too late. It'll eat up our Saturday. I'll go in early and get out just after noon. Maybe we can do something together after?" Ray asked. "I'll just have to stop home for clothes tomorrow."

In a heartbeat he would miss a day of work to spend the night with Linda. He knew in doing so he would risk losing his job. The migration was expected to run in the morning. He knew he would need to have a solid reason for not showing up. If he lost his job he wouldn't feel too good about himself. Feeling that way could lead him into a depression. Not having money was a depressing thought. He had spent too many nights that way, unemployed and depressed. Of course, he had then dedicated his time to renting a barstool and scraping up enough dollars to spend the workweek drunk. It was a self-destructive life he had led. He was away from it now, thankful to be away from it. Damned thankful.

"Get up early, shower here and stop home on your way to work," Linda suggested. "I don't want you to go."

Ray remained quiet. It was a plausible solution. He was in no hurry to leave. He knew he could fall right to sleep with her nestled in his arms. He rationalized sleeping until five, showering and stopping home for a change of clothes. It could work.

"Will you?" she asked.

He kissed the top of her head. "I'd love to."

Chapter 43
Saturday, January 25

Linda hated watching Ray leave so early in the morning, but relished the night they had spent together. He had been a gentle lover, but hungry. It would not have mattered had he not have been as tender and skilled. Still, knowing he could please her did not hurt matters any. If anything, it made the entire situation that much better. She missed him.

As she stepped out of the shower, she smiled at the fogged mirror. He had left a message for her, perhaps written with his fingertip into the steam from his shower. Inside a big heart, it said in dripping letters, *Miss You Already, Love Me.*

She finished getting ready for the day, dressing in a comfortable pair of jeans and sneakers. She was in her room selecting a top to wear when the telephone rang.

"Hello?" she said, picking the phone up from its cradle on the nightstand.

The line was dead. Linda regarded the phone for a moment, before hanging up and tossing it onto the bed.

It rang, again. She picked it up, turned it on and said, "Hello?"

Someone was on the other end, but wasn't saying a word.

"Hello?" Linda repeated. When she heard continued silence, but knew someone was on the other end listening, she disconnected the call. She dialed *66. A prerecorded message told her the incoming call was from outside the calling area. That meant it could be from a cell or pay phone.

She finished getting ready, impatiently eyeing the phone, as if daring the prank caller to call a third time.

With Ray at work, she did not want to spend the day home alone. She missed him and enjoyed the idea of their plans to do something in the afternoon together.

She ate a bowl of cereal while standing up at the counter, drank a glass of orange juice, then washed the bowl, spoon and glass.

She put the milk back in the fridge then stood by the closed door. It only took a fraction of a second to make her next decision. She opened the cupboard over the fridge and removed the bottles of alcohol.

She poured everything down the kitchen sink drain. If she and Ray were going to last, she did not plan to drink anymore. If he were going to spend time at her house, she was not going to have the stuff around. There was no need for it. She didn't need it. She put the bottles in a trash bag.

Feeling especially good about everything in general, thoughts of Joey Viglucci secluded deep in the recesses of her mind, she decided to go grocery shopping. She had promised to fix a special meal tonight for Ray, a testimony to the fact she was more than a halfway decent cook. To do so, she would need supplies. What supplies depended on what she planned to make. She thought Chicken French, or her Fettuccini Alfredo. Either required a perfect sauce for a successful meal.

As she picked up her purse and put on her winter coat she thought the Alfredo with Artichoke French as an appetizer. "I don't want to spoil him, though," she said out loud and laughed.

There were two new inches of snow on the ground. Hardly the storm the weather forecasters had been anxiously predicting. It was extremely cold out, though. The wind still seemed angry with the rest of the world. It demonstrated this by blowing at Linda from all directions at once. It picked up loose snow and sprayed it in her face relentlessly. She uselessly attempted to shield her face from the vicious attack. She was thankful to see Ray had been a gentleman and brushed the snow off her car before leaving. She took the trash bag full of empty bottles and garbage to the Dumpster on the side of the house, then hurriedly ran back to her car. She thought the exposed areas of flesh were going to cause immediate hypothermia.

She opened her car door, anxious to get out of the cold and into a place of refuge from the harsh and bitter wind. Instead she stood there, as if frozen. She stared at the plain white envelope on the front seat. Her mouth went dry, making it difficult to swallow.

She looked around her property. She did not see any footprints in the snow on the lawn. She did see two sets of footprints, presumably hers and Rays, coming off the front step, leading down the sidewalk to the car. The driveway, on the other hand, was a mess.

The snow was trampled. She imagined Ray brushing the snow off the cars, creating his prints and perhaps covering others.

She shut the car door and went back into the house. She used the cordless phone in the living room to call the investigator assigned to her case. "Hello," she said. "I know it's Saturday, but I need to speak with Officer Josaiah Valente, please?"

She was put on hold and decided to shrug off her coat. She bit her upper lip as she walked through her house, looking in each room. She expected to see an open window every time she walked into a room. Nothing looked out of order anywhere in the house. At the basement door in the kitchen, she stopped. She did not want to go down into the basement. She harbored a fear of basements from the time she was little, always envisioning a monster under the stairs, waiting to reach out between steps to grab her ankles as she ascended or descended the staircase. Most people hated to do laundry because it was time consuming, tedious task. Linda hated to do laundry because she hated going into the basement.

Her hand lingering over the doorknob, debating whether or not to inspect the basement windows, Linda nearly screamed as Officer Valente came on the line.

"This is Valente."

With her hand over her chest, catching her breath, Linda said, "Officer Valente? It's me, Linda Genova."

"Yes, Ms. Genova, what can I do for you?" he asked.

"I received another one, a letter. At least I think it's a letter. I went out to my car just now, I was planning to go grocery shopping, but when I opened my door I saw an envelope on my seat," she said talking too quickly, she knew. She couldn't slow down. She felt excited and apprehensive. Everything around her seemed to be moving in slow motion.

"Did you touch the envelope, Ms. Genova?"

"No. I left it. I came right in and called you," Linda said.

"Are you going to be home for a little while?" he asked.

"Well, yes, unless I can touch the envelope. Otherwise I can't get in my car," Linda said.

"No. I'd prefer you don't touch the envelope. I have to finish something up here. I promise I will be at your house as soon as I possibly can. All right, Ms. Genova?" Officer Valente asked.

"That should be fine. Thank you," Linda said and hung up.

Chapter 44

Ray stared at the note on his desk. It was dated with today's date. It had a time of ten minutes ago on it. Ray had started working the computer migration logging onto computer systems on the tenth floor, intending to work his way down the three floors of offices. He initially thought he could have all the computers migrated in four or five hours, but he now feared it might take the entire day. There were a lot of computers. Thankfully, most of the attorneys used laptops. He would migrate those systems on Monday.

The note said, To: Ray. From: P. Bierman. Ray did not know anyone else was at the office. Attorneys, he knew, worked long weeks. Their jobs were not nine to five. The box Urgent on the note was checked. Aside from the time and date in the upper corner, everything else on the note was blank.

The telephone rang. "Hartzman, Cross, Lacy and Bierman," Ray said, examining the note. "Ray speaking."

"Ray, it's Linda," she said. "How's work going?"

He could hear something in her tone of voice. She sounded preoccupied. "Linda? Is something wrong?"

"I got another letter from the secret admirer, I think. It's in my car."

"Did you call the police?"

"I did. They're on their way," Linda said.

"I need to work on a few more computers, and Bierman wants to see me," Linda said.

"Bierman's at work?" Linda asked.

"I guess so," Ray said. "But listen, as soon as I can, I'm going to get out of here. All right?"

"All right," Linda said. "I miss you."

"I'll come back over as soon as I can," Ray said. "And I miss you, too." He hung up.

Ray took the note and went over to Bierman's office. He felt an apprehensive knot in his stomach. The last time Bierman had wanted to see him it had been to chastise him for going bowling with Linda. As he walked, he kept thinking Bierman must have been following them. Bierman must know they spent the night together and wanted to fire him for violating the company's policy on dating.

That was ludicrous. If Bierman spent his time following them just so he could fire him ... the man would be half-crazy. Of course, Linda did suspect Bierman was the one harassing her with letters and flowers and phone pranks. If that were true, if he were that infatuated with Linda, then spending his evenings following his paralegal might not be implausible.

Ray kept running through scenarios in his mind. He wanted to be ready this time. If Patrick Bierman, big shot attorney, wanted to threaten him with his job, he wanted to be prepared. He was in love with Linda. A job with the firm didn't matter to him. He would quit in order to keep his relationship with Linda. He did not want Linda to quit. She had a career with the firm. He did not want to jeopardize her position. On the other hand, he had nothing to lose. He was three months sober and felt confident he possessed computer skills necessary to land him a competitive wage at a company within a reasonable amount of time. In other words, he would survive.

He didn't like Patrick Bierman. He thought he was self-important and pompous. To top it all off the guy was a sick pervert. Maybe, if Bierman did not have plans to harass him about his relationship with Linda, he would still quit. He wanted to give the guy a piece of his mind. He didn't want to threaten him, though the idea of putting some fear into his life, like the way he was terrorizing Linda, was appealing. Threatening a lawyer would be a foolish move. Bierman would know ways to make his life a living, or an imprisoned hell.

He decided to play it by ear.

As he approached Bierman's office, he saw the door was open. He knocked on the door as he entered. Bierman had a large, impressive mahogany desk. Everything about Bierman's office said impressive. Ray was not impressed.

Bierman sat in his high-back leather chair, facing the window. "Mr. Bierman?" Ray said, tentatively. Though everyone in the office spoke to one another in the familiar, calling each other by first name, he did not feel comfortable calling this man simply Patrick, especially now, when he anticipated some kind of deliverable wrath.

The chair did not spin around. "Mr. Bierman?" Ray asked, walking toward the desk. He started around the desk and stopped when he saw the chair was empty.

The pain came from nowhere, but shot through his back like a muscle spasm. The center of his back felt on fire. His shoulder blades thrust together, as if able to catch and contain the pain. He dropped to his knees. He fell to the floor, and rolled onto his back.

He did not recognize his attacker at first, the face so filled with hate and fury. He could not cry out as the knife that had been plunged into his back came down at his belly in full swing. He tensed his stomach muscles fruitlessly, hoping to stop the blade from penetrating. The tip of the blade sped through the layers of skin and muscle with ease. He felt blood work its way up his throat. He started to choke on it.

The note from Bierman was taken out of his dying hands.

The office door closed.

Raymond Telfer could not believe he was about to die.

The pain in his back and in his stomach burned. The blood was spilling out of the sides of his mouth, like a sink over filling with hot water. Ray needed a moment to figure things out. He couldn't concentrate. He decided to close his eyes, just for a moment, just so he could plan. He closed his eyes and the darkness consumed him.

Chapter 45

Linda stood by the picture window waiting for Officer Josaiah Valente to arrive. She kept wondering if she had been forgotten. Twice she picked up the phone, ready to call him again, but she reminded herself that it was a letter in her car, not a bomb. She knew he was working on Joey's murder, if only because of her entanglement in the matter. He was a police officer in a city full of crime. She knew she had not been forgotten, and understood she could not be on the top of his priority list.

It was nearly eleven when he pulled into the driveway. She waited for him at the front door. He was not what she expected. She thought he would be short and heavy. Instead he looked like he might be close to six feet tall. He was thin, but didn't appear scrawny. He had a red goatee with two small patches of gray at the chin. He wore Khaki slacks, a royal blue shirt, plain red tie.

He spent close to twenty minutes just looking at her car, the driveway and then following footprints around in the snow. Eventually he opened her car door and disappeared inside. She could not see what he was doing in the car. The snow was thick again on her windshield. When he emerged he held a brown lunch bag in his hand. He waved at her, closed the car door and walked up to the front step.

"How are you, Ms. Genova?" Josaiah Valente looked cold. His lips looked blue. "Can I come in?"

"Certainly," Linda said, stepping aside. They shook hands.

"A pleasure to meet you," he said, bowing a little as he did so.

"A pleasure," she said, unsure of what a more appropriate response might have been. "I made coffee while waiting. Would you like some?"

"Please. And I'm sorry it took so long to get here," he said by way of an explanation. He didn't need to tell her the specifics. As far as Linda was concerned, he didn't need to apologize.

"That's all right. I'm just glad you came. I must admit, I was surprised to get another one of these. I was pretty sure the problem was over," Linda said, leading the officer into the kitchen.

Josaiah Valente wrinkled his features, puckering his lips, squinted his eyes. "You did? And why is that?" he asked, setting the brown lunch bag down on the table.

Linda immediately knew what the officer was questioning. As she took out cups and saucers she let out a nervous laugh. "I don't mean because Joey died," she said. "I know that's what you must have been thinking, but that's not what I meant."

Valente said nothing. He waited in silence for her to continue. He looked at her with a penetrating stare. Linda smiled, trying to make light of a serious situation. "I think Patrick Bierman, the attorney, I think he was the one harassing me. I had a conversation with one of the senior partners at my firm. He assured me everything would stop if I called everything off."

"But you didn't call me," Valente said.

"Not yet, I hadn't, no."

"Hmmm."

Linda poured coffee.

"When was this?"

"A few days ago."

"Before Joseph Viglucci died?"

"I don't know. I believe so. We talked on Thursday at work. You called me Friday morning," Linda said. Friday morning was only yesterday. Linda thought it already felt as if weeks had passed.

Linda watched Valente, expecting to see something register in his expression. He was like a poker player. Nothing changed. He didn't cock an eyebrow, or purse his lips. He just watched her watching him.

"Cream and sugar?" Linda asked, looking to deflect the intensity of his watchful eyes. They made her uneasy and nervous. She knew she had no reason to feel this way. She was the victim.

"Please," Valente said.

"What about the letter?" Linda asked. "Are you going to open it?"

Valente asked, "You did not touch it at all, is that correct?"

"As soon as I saw it, I came in the house and called you,"

Linda said defensively. She heard it in her voice. It rose more than half an octave and threatened to crack. "Listen, I have no idea what you're thinking, but this doesn't feel right. As crazy as this might sound, I feel like a suspect in all of this."

Josaiah Valente lifted the cup to his lips, gently blew on the coffee before taking a sip. He closed his eyes, as if savoring the flavor, smacked his lips and let out a satisfying *ahhh*.

The way the officer could remain silent and ignore answering her question was unnerving. In fact, the last few weeks had been nothing short of unnerving. She thought she might be developing an ulcer. Her stomach felt as though it were burning. All the coffee she drank couldn't help. She put down her cup.

"Let me have a sheet of paper towel," Valente said, as if Linda had not been talking to him at all.

Linda handed the officer a sheet and watched as he laid it in the center of the kitchen table. From his pocket he removed a small leather rectangular pouch with a zipper. He opened it to reveal an array of tools on red velvet. He put the pouch on the table next to the paper toweling. From it he took out two pairs of tweezers. He poured the envelope out of the lunch bag onto the paper toweling, then picked up a corner of the envelope using one set of tweezers, and tore open the edge with the other. Linda was amazed how the man used tiny tongs like hands and fingers. Carefully, Valente extracted the paper from inside the envelope. He laid the envelope down on a corner of the paper towel, and the letter on to the middle of the toweling. The letter was folded in thirds. He unfolded it using both sets of tweezers.

In a complete silence that seemed to last an eternity, both Linda and Officer Valente read what was written on the letter.

Dear Linda,

If anyone had asked me, even a week ago, I'd have told them that, yes, it would work between us. I'd have said that our love would last forever, stand the test of time and all that other bullshit. But now ... now that I know what an insensitive bitch you are.

Now that I know what kind of a heartless person you are ... why would I want to spend my life with you? You don't care about me. You don't. I know that now and it's a shame. You,

Linda, you care about you.

Well guess what? I don't want you anymore. I don't want anything to do with you. You don't deserve me. You never did. I was just fooling myself. Who cares if you are beautiful? That beauty, my dear, will fade and when it does, you'll be alone. All alone.

And I don't want to hear you call me a quitter. I haven't quit. You quit. You disregard everyone else's feelings but your own. I can't work at a relationship like that ...take, take and take. You've got to give, even a little, give something—but I don't mean just to throw me a bone. That's more insulting. But this, all of this, it's too hard for me, too hard. And I don't need it.

I try and try, and you hurt me.

Well, now I'm going to hurt you.

Sincerely,
xxxxoooo

Valente let out a long loud sigh and sat down at the kitchen table. He took another sip of coffee. "This letter troubles me," he said. He leaned back in the chair and stared at the ceiling. "It really troubles me."

Linda took two steps back from the table, speechless. Someone wanted to hurt her. She found it difficult to breathe. She had never been threatened like this before. Her hands, shaking, kept moving up and down her belly.

Officer Valente got to his feet. "Don't worry. You're okay. You're just hyperventilating." He walked her to his chair and sat her down. "Take slow deep breaths."

Linda tried slow deep breaths. At first she didn't think it was going to work. She thought she might pass out. She closed her eyes and tried harder, concentrating on each breath. Eventually, she was able to bring it under control.

"I'm going to take this letter to the station. I'd like one of our forensic technicians to analyze it," Valente said. He used his thumb and finger to stroke the neatly trimmed hairs of his goatee. "I suspect we won't find prints on it this time either."

Linda looked at the letter again; her eyes drawn to the last sentence, *Well, now I'm going to hurt you.* Nobody left prints anymore. Everyone watched police shows and read detective novels. Criminals wore gloves, Latex, or otherwise. They bought reams of common paper from a chain store, much harder to trace. She supposed only an idiot left prints anymore.

"So what do I do? What am I supposed to do?"

"Do you have somewhere else to stay?" Valente asked.

"Why? You don't think I'm safe here?"

"I think you might be safer somewhere else," he said.

"Like where?"

"Somewhere other than here. Your family?"

"Don't have any. Not here."

"Friends?"

"I have a few."

"Would they let you stay with them a night or two?"

"I couldn't see why not," Linda said, thinking of Patty. She thought of Ray. She wouldn't ask Ray. "Yeah. I have friends I could call."

"I want you to call me, let me know where you are and leave me a number to reach you."

"You have my cell phone number," Linda said.

"I'll want both. An address, the name of the person you're staying with and a phone number," Josaiah Valente said. He finished his coffee in a gulp, as if it were lemonade served on a hot summer afternoon. "I've got to run. I don't normally work Saturday's you know."

"I'm sorry," Linda said.

"No. I was at the office. Doing work on a murder case," Valente said pointedly.

He stared at Linda for an extra long second before smiling. She wondered if he had done that on purpose. He had to be talking about Joey Viglucci.

"Keep in touch."

She showed him out, shut and locked the door. After calling Patty, she started packing.

Chapter 46

Linda knew she was going out of her mind. She could feel the mental screws loosening inside her brain. Things were beginning to rattle around up there. The few aspirin and cold glass of water she had taken nearly an hour ago did not seem to be helping any. Why should it? She did not have a headache. Taking the pills just felt like the right thing to do. There was nothing else to do. She had never felt so out of control of a situation. She did not like the helplessness she felt. Taking aspirin when she didn't have a headache was her attempt at taking control, as useless a move as it proved to be.

She had called and left two messages on Ray's answering machine at work. He had not returned her call. She did not want to bother him, knowing how busy he must be, but she did not want to be alone. She did not want to stay in her house any longer.

After Officer Josaiah Valente left she went up to her room and packed some things. While in her closet she looked for her silk pajamas. They were maroon red and her favorite. She checked her dresser drawers, to no avail. Realizing they must be in with the laundry, she settled on packing some nightgowns.

Every light in the house was on. Why having the lights on made her feel safe was beyond Linda. It was a sunny Saturday afternoon. If anyone broke into the house, it would make no difference if the lights were on or off. For some reason, it was consoling to be surrounded by light when otherwise alone.

When someone knocked softly at the door, Linda was not startled. She was thankful. In the kitchen she unplugged the coffee machine. She went to the front door and opened it, without looking out the window.

"Patty," she said, seeing her friend standing on the front step hugging herself.

Patty, without saying hello, opened her arms. Linda fell into them and the two women cried.

"This is so crazy," Linda said, when the hug ended. "I can't believe I'm being tormented like this."

Patty stepped into the house. "Forget it. Okay? I'm glad you called me. You're coming to my house tonight and you can stay with me for as long as you need. I have digital, we can watch movies all night long, or we can run out and rent something. I have popcorn. Whatever, all right?"

Linda hugged Patty again.

"Okay, okay," Patty said, scooping up two of Linda's three bags. "You have all you need?"

"I think so. I didn't bring my curling iron or hair dryer…"

"I've got those at my house. You're more than welcome to use them," Patty said starting out of the house. "Careful on the steps. They're icy."

Linda closed the front door, then opened it. "Patty I'll be right there," she called out. She went back into the house and changed the prerecorded message on the answering machine. "I'm sorry. I'm not home right now. Leave a message. I'll call as soon as I can. Ray if this is you, leave a message. I'll call you at home." She did not say where she would be staying. If the stalker called, she did not want him to know anything more about her. She peeled a sheet of notebook paper out of a coiled binder and wrote, *Ray, I will not be home today. I will call you at home. Don't worry about me, I'm all right*. She thought about how to sign the letter. She wanted it personal, but did not want to sound silly. Of course, they had already said they loved each other. But to write it…Hastily she wrote, *Love Linda*.

She took three pieces of tape out of the junk drawer near the sink. Outside, she taped her letter to the inside of the storm door, with the words facing out, so they could be read through the glass. She locked the front door. She put the bag she carried in the open trunk with the rest of her bags. She got into the passenger seat and fastened her seatbelt. "I feel like I'm moving away from home," Linda said as Patty backed out of the driveway.

"Don't be silly. This mess, all of it, is going to get cleaned up so quick you won't even remember any of it," Patty said.

Linda smiled to give her friend the impression agreed with that sentiment. Inside, she didn't feel that way. The façade might convince Patty, but she was not fooling herself. She would remember this, all of it, whether she wanted to or not.

* * * * *

Patty lived in a beautifully renovated Victorian, complete with a belvedere at the top of a cone peak. The house was a vibrant teal, framed in a sandy shade of tan trim. Linda loved the wraparound porch, complete with a chain-hung porch swing by the door. The property, outlined with tall pine trees and littered with century old Maples, presented the illusion of living in the country. The garage was detached and sat nearly twenty yards behind the house, designed and decorated in a miniature mirror image of Patty's home. "This place is so beautiful," Linda said. "I feel like I'm going to stay with royalty."

"You say that every time you come over," Patty said. "Well, not that royalty comment. That one's new."

"I've never stayed with you before."

"Good point," Patty said. She used a remote to open the garage. "They're calling for a bad storm tonight."

"They were calling for one last night, but we never got it," Linda said as the car pulled into the garage and the big door slowly closed behind them. "You got to wonder how these weather forecasters get their jobs."

Getting out of the car and walking toward the trunk with her keys in her hand, Patty shrugged, "I think I could be a weather person."

"You do, huh?" Linda asked, shutting the passenger door and going to the rear of the car. "Those people have to go to school and study meteorology and, what, astrology?"

"I don't think astrology has anything to do with it," Patty said. "Look at it this way, from October to March I'd predict that there's a good chance of snow. Most of the time, I'd be right. From April to June, rain. From mid-June through August, heat without the chance of rain. September to October, rain with leaves changing colors and falling from their branches," Patty said as if it were as simple as that. She lifted two of Linda's bags out of the trunk, leaving one for Linda to carry.

"Okay Patty Weather, how about when they predict storms?"

"Easy, I call Buffalo and Syracuse every night and see what the hell's happening at either end. If they're getting hit with strong winds and lots of snow, I'd tell my faithful viewers that there's a good chance we're in for much of the same," Patty said using her elbow to close the trunk.

"You know, in a simple way, your idea makes a lot of sense," Linda admitted, playing along with her friend's humorous fantasy.

"You bet it does. Let's not forget I'd be making more than a legal secretary could ever dream of making, and I'd be on television every day," Patty said, batting her eyelids.

"You'd make a good weatherman."

"Weather-woman," Patty corrected while leading the way out of the garage.

Upon opening the door, the wind gusted with brute strength, threatening to keep the door closed. "Feels like the bad weather's getting started early," Linda said.

"Let's get inside. I could use some coffee, Irish coffee," Patty said.

Linda pursed her lips, but said nothing. Irish coffee on a cold winter afternoon sounded wonderful. She had made a promise to herself not to drink anymore. A part of her wanted to drink, saying Ray would never know if she spiked a cup of coffee. But she would know. Her promising not to drink had nothing to do with whether or not Ray would ever find out.

They hurried toward the side door on the house. Patty handed Linda her things so she could unlock the door. Linda watched her pull open the storm door, then unlock three sets of locks using three different keys. Patty pushed open the door and hurried up a small flight of steps into the kitchen. A beep sounded every second. Patty punched a security code into her alarm system and the beeping stopped.

"How long do you have to disarm that thing?" Linda asked.

"Fifteen seconds," Patty said. "It doesn't sound like a long time, but it is. It takes one maybe two seconds to walk from the door to the box here on the wall, another two seconds to punch in the four digits to shut to countdown off. Get it?"

"I guess."

"When we go out, and I set it, we have thirty seconds. That time is needed, I think. Usually I set it, then realize I left my purse on the kitchen table, or the phone rings. There's always something that stops me from getting out the door. I can do it in thirty, but not fifteen," Patty explained, kicking her shoes off onto the welcome mat.

"What's the red bell?" Linda asked, setting her things down on the floor.

"Say someone breaks into my house, I hit that button it calls for the police and sets off the alarm in the house."

"What if you're not in the kitchen? What if you're up in bed?"

"I have another keypad in the hall at the top of the stairs," Patty explained. "Helps me sleep some nights. It's rough always being alone."

"You don't have to tell me about it," Linda said. She went back down the steps to shut and lock the side door. She came back up, took off her shoes and coat. Patty offered to take her coat. She hung both in the hall closet while Linda stood like a shy visitor in the same spot.

"Linda, I'm not going to tell you to sit down or ask you if you want something to eat. Sorry. Not that kind of host. You're either going to make yourself at home, or you'll starve. I guess as long as you don't pee on my ceramic tiles, I won't care too much," Patty said sincerely.

Linda took in a deep breath and sighed. "I won't be bashful."

"Good."

"I'm just not used to being somebody's guest, not like this, not under these circumstances," Linda said.

"What's that supposed to mean?" Patty asked.

"Well, it's not like we planned this slumber party. I can't help but feel like I'm being intrusive," Linda said. She knew she was going to cry. She could feel the lump burning in her throat as she fought to suppress it. Crying didn't make any sense. It wouldn't help solve anything.

Patty was beside her in a heartbeat and wrapped her arms around her. Since Patty was slightly shorter, Linda had to bow down some to accept the embrace. "I'm okay. I'm all right," Linda said. "I just … I appreciate this."

"Forget it. You'd do the same. I know you would. You would,

wouldn't you?" Patty asked, as if feigning uncertainty and insecurity.

Linda slapped playfully at Patty's arm. "You know I would."

"How about that Shamrock coffee I mentioned?" Patty asked, getting a coffee filter out of the cupboard.

"Sounds good, but I think I'll take mine black."

"Black?" Patty asked. "Too early in the day for you?"

Linda just smiled, using it as a way to avoid answering Patty's question. "Where will I be sleeping? Do you have an extra bed, or the sofa's fine."

"Sofa? Get serious. I have two guestrooms up stairs. Take your pick."

"You sure?"

"Stop. Sure I'm sure."

"All right, while you make the coffee, mind if I take these up to the room?" Linda said lifting the bags.

"Not at all."

Linda walked down the hall to the front of the house. She took the stairs to the second level. The stairs spiraled on to the belvedere. Linda tried looking to the top, but could not see. Instead, she walked down the hall. The first door on the left was the bathroom. Everything in it was wood trimmed, country style. A selection of magazines rested on a shelf above the toilet bowl. Everything looked immaculately neat and orderly. The next door on the left opened into a guestroom. Pink walls. Wood trim. A twin bed in the center of the room. A dresser with a vanity mirror angled across a corner along the east and north wall, near the window. Linda set her bags down. She walked across the hall to the first door on the right. It was identical to the room she had just left, except the walls were a soft shade of blue and the dresser with the vanity was in the northwest corner of the room.

Linda walked toward the last two doors along the hallway. One was a linen closet. The other opened into Patty's room. Linda had never seen it before. Pink walls. Wood trim. The furniture was white. The canopy bed looked beautiful. Stuffed animals were everywhere. The dresser top was filled with framed photographs. Linda walked into the room, amazed at the thickness of the cushioned carpet. She felt like she was walking on a sponge.

At the dresser she looked at the photos. Mostly, they were the same image, just in different sized frames, which Linda found odd. The photo that appeared in each frame was of a young, good-looking man with a brush cut, wearing a Marines uniform. In his arms was the cutest little girl wearing a pink dress. Next to the man was a woman who vaguely resembled Patty.

"It's my mom and dad, and that little girl is me when I was seven," Patty said, walking into the room.

"It's a nice picture," Linda said.

"It's one of the only really happy times I can remember."

"Why is that?"

"It was a time before my father ... never mind," Patty said, lowering her eyes.

"What?" Linda asked. "Patty, are you all right?"

She nodded, and forced herself to wear a smile, regardless of how thin it looked. "Coffee's just about done. I see you picked the pink room. Figured you would. I'll be downstairs. Get settled and come down when you're ready," Patty said, and left.

Linda figured they had the whole night and was sure they'd spend part of it talking. If Patty needed to talk, she'd be ready to listen.

Looking around the room, she realized something. The pink walls, the stuffed animals, the simple white furniture, even the canopy bed ... it all resembled a little girl's bedroom.

Back downstairs, as the coffee finished brewing, Linda realized she needed to call Officer Valente. He had wanted to know where she would be staying. "Patty, can I use your phone?"

Patty looked at Linda intently. "What did I tell you? Just use it. If you have to ask me, next thing you'll do is ask me to dial for you, or hold the phone to your ear while you talk. Told you already, not this host."

Chapter 47

Linda felt as if she had on a pair of earmuffs. Everything she heard sounded cloudy and filtered. Only one sound filled her ears. Her heart beating. It was beating fast and loud like a bass drum. Her mouth felt dry. She kept swallowing and swallowing, but there was nothing left in her mouth to swallow. Her hands shook. She tried to keep them interlaced and tucked between her thighs, but then her arms tensed up and quivered.

She knew Patty was driving as fast as possible under the conditions. The storm that had threatened for so long picked now to arrive. The roads were slick, perhaps hiding black ice under the camouflage of fresh fallen snow.

"So what did he say, exactly?" Patty asked.

When Officer Valente had told Linda that Ray had been stabbed—she felt her breath catch in her throat with a gasp. Valente went on to say he was in critical condition at the hospital and that it did not look good. She had been too upset to talk. She had managed to tell Patty that they needed to get to the hospital, that Ray had been stabbed. Nothing more. "That's all I know," Linda said. She watched as Patty maneuvered the car onto I-390 South. Ray had been taken to Strong. "Officer Valente is already there, said he'd meet me at the hospital."

"So Ray's still alive?"

"Valente said he was, said he didn't look good, or he said it didn't look good, I don't know. I can't remember now what he said, and there's a difference, isn't there? There's a difference between *he* doesn't look good and *it* doesn't look good," Linda said, waving her hands around with her fingers spread apart as though they might be webbed and used to fan herself.

"Okay," Patty said. "Let's stay calm and focused. All right? Ray's alive. That's the important thing. We need to concentrate on that for now. There is no sense thinking about anything else at this point. He's alive. That is the one thing we know for sure."

"You're right. You're right," Linda said, taking quick and shallow breaths. She tried to get her emotions under control. Getting hysterical was not going to help the situation. "I'm sorry. I was losing it."

"You don't have to be sorry. This is definitely a situation where losing it is, if not expected, then is at least accepted," Patty said. She switched on the wipers. Wet streaks stretched across the windshield, cutting visibility down considerably. "I can't see shit."

Linda looked out her own window. She could not worry about the drive to the hospital. She knew Patty would get them there. Her mind was trapped in a wintry storm of its own.

Whoever was stalking her was killing people.

The stalker had said he would hurt her. Did he mean he would hurt her physically, or emotionally by harming people she loved?

What kind of danger was she in?

Patty did not pull into the parking garage at Strong. Instead she drove into the emergency vehicle loop. "You get out here. I'll go park and meet you inside."

"Are you sure? You can head home. I'll get a ride," Linda said. "I'm ruining your entire weekend."

"Your boyfriend was just stabbed. I'd be here with you even if today was Super Bowl Sunday and I had tickets on the fifty yard line!" Patty said, trying to smile.

Linda knew Patty was being upbeat and optimistic for her sake. Still, Patty's demeanor reassured her, even if her motive was transparent. "Thank you."

"Forget it. Get in there. I'll go park."

Linda hated hospitals, but hated hospital emergency rooms more. There just always seemed a sense of dreaded anticipation from the moment you walked through the doors that whoosh open to greet you. Linda saw the front desk, the nurses behind it and the people all around her and felt claustrophobic.

In the waiting room a man sat alone. His arm was in a bloodstained, homemade sling. His injured arm looked limp, the hand just dangling out one end. A few seats down a boy, around ten, sat next to a woman who could have been his mom, if his mom had been fifteen when she had him. Neither looked injured. The boy sat with the heels of his feet up on the chair, hugging his legs and rocking back and forth. The woman seemed unable to focus. She kept looking around the room, but at nothing, at no one. She looked exhausted. She chewed on a small thread of skin near her thumbnail, spit it casually off her lip and then started chewing again. Across from them sat an old man with perfect posture. He kept his hands on his knees, his arms locked straight and stared at a clock on the wall as if hypnotized by the sweeping second hand. Near the opposite end of the waiting room were two women softly sobbing and hugging each other, either anticipating bad news, or anticipating worse news.

As Linda was about to approach the front desk, she spotted Officer Josaiah Valente. He stood at the end of the hallway near a vending machine. He was hunched forward, bending close to make a selection.

He stood waiting for a small cup to fill with coffee as she walked toward him. Her movement must have attracted his attention. When he saw her, he pointed to machine, silently offering to buy her a cup.

"No, thank you," she said. "Where is he?"

"Surgery. It's going to be a while," Valente said.

"What happened? How is he?"

"Strong," Valente said. "Apparently he was attacked in Patrick Bierman's office with Bierman's letter opener. Bierman's prints are all over the damned thing."

"Oh my God, Bierman?"

"It's possible," Valente said. "Somehow, Telfer managed to yank on Bierman's phone cord. Phone fell to the floor next to him. He dialed nine, one, one. He wasn't able to talk, really. The operator heard heavy breathing and gasping. The call was immediately traced and she dispatched an ambulance, police and the fire department."

Linda listened to Valente talk. She didn't want to have mental images of Ray suffering. She could not imagine someone hurting him. She could not believe he had managed to call for help. As Valente said, he *was* strong. "So now what? What about Bierman?"

"We tried contacting him at home. Apparently he moved out of his house a few weeks ago. All his wife knows is that he has an apartment in Greece, down near the lake. We sent police looking for him. He isn't home. We contacted his secretary, Carrie Waters, checking to see if he was out of town or something on a planned business trip, perhaps," Officer Valente said. He had a way of talking. Short, choppy sentences. His voice sounded like a monotone machine gun. Trrrt. Trrrt. Trrrt. But she liked it. Joe Friday style.

"And?"

"And she indicated he told her he planned a weekend get-away, maybe up to visit the casino in Niagara," Valente said.

"So if he's got proof he was in Canada?" Linda asked. She felt the hair on her arms and on the back of her neck stand on end. She did not feel well. She rubbed her stomach. To think a man she worked with for the last several years could be a cold killer was frightening.

"We're looking into it. Everything should be easy to check out. Like, you have to check into a hotel using your credit card. That creates a record that you're in Canada. Stop in at the casino, make a ruckus of some sort to establish witnesses who can identify you. Drive back across the border, back to Rochester in an hour and a half ... it's very doable and not at all far-fetched," Valente indicated. He blew on his coffee, a plume of hot steam bent and curled in frenzy with his breath, resembling the wild spirit of a ghost on the haunt. "I don't want to rule out Jason Kenmore. We sent police to his house. His wife and kids are distraught. The kids told an officer that their daddy went out last night. He hasn't returned. The wife, though it looked as if she hated admitting so, said her husband did that a lot, going out all night on the weekends. More so, she indicated, since losing his job over at MCT."

Kenmore. Bierman. Either man now posed a threat. Linda was frightened. Would they come for her? The police would have to find them sooner or later. *Sooner*, she hoped.

Linda saw Valente studying her. His eyes kept looking at her eyes, a concentrated stare. The weight of his stare felt immense. She looked away.

"Where are you staying? Could you write it down for me?"

Linda sat and took a pen and scrap of paper from her purse as a uniformed police officer came through a set of double doors.

"Excuse me a moment," Valente said, going to speak to the police officer in private.

Linda wrote down Patty's name, address and phone number. She also wrote her cell number down again. While she waited to hand Valente the information, she saw Patty come through the same set of double doors as the uniformed police officer. Linda stood up and waited as Patty walked by the police and over to her.

"How is he? Is he all right? Is he talking?" Patty asked. Her eyes seemed to scan Linda's face for answers, as if they might be written in code on her skin.

"No. He's not talking. He's in surgery. My God, Patty, they think it might be Bierman. Ray was stabbed in Bierman's office," Linda said, in a high pitched voice. She was close to hysterical, but tried to remain calm. The scale to balance her emotions was tipping. She could feel it. Calm was losing.

She took hold of Linda's hands, then looked at the paper. "What's this?"

"Your name and stuff. The officer wants it," Linda said. "I need to go to the restroom." Linda felt flustered. She was starting to sob. She knew she would not be able to control herself much longer. A nightmare was emerging all around her, closing in on her, and she felt trapped. There was nothing she could do—nowhere she could run to—to get away from it. "I just want to see Ray."

"Go to the ladies' room. Give me that paper. I'll give it to him. You just go to the ladies room," Patty said.

Linda went over to the ladies' room. Inside the small, compact sized room, she got down on her knees. She ignored the unsanitary situation, and let her face hover over the bowl. Her stomach muscles contracted and all at once she vomited, aware and alert to the fact she could not breathe as she did so.

Heaving, she reached for the roll of toilet paper. She tore of sheets and wiped the sickeningly acid tasting drool from her lips. She spit into the bowl and wiped chunks off her tongue. She dropped the tissue into the bowl and flushed it.

Clad in sweat, she washed her face in the sink. The room was too small. Again, she was overwhelmed by a sense of claustrophobia. It was too hot in the bathroom. She cupped her hands and filled them with water. She took a sip and gargled with the water in her mouth. She found a stick of gum in her purse. She unwrapped it the way a starving child might unwrap a candy bar. Chewing it, she could feel the sour taste being cleansed and replaced with hot cinnamon.

Looking at her reflection in the mirror, she was aghast. Her eyes looked sunken into her skull. Her flesh looked pale. Her hair, wet from washing her face in the sink, looked stringy and unkempt.

She used a brush to fix her hair, but when she saw it wasn't helping, ditched the effort. It didn't matter anyway. Right now nothing mattered, especially not her hair. Well, something mattered. Ray mattered.

Leaving the bathroom, Linda saw Officer Valente leaning against the wall talking on a cell phone. The other officer was not around. Patty was sitting in a chair near Valente, drinking soda out of the can.

"Are you all right?" Patty asked.

"I'm better," Linda said.

Valente was next to her. "Officer Valente, this is my best friend, Patty. Patricia Dent."

Patty and the officer said hello and shook hands. He seemed distracted.

"I have to leave. The doctor's have my cell number. They're going to call me when the surgery has ended," Officer Josaiah Valente said.

Linda saw it in his face. Though the man did not seem the type to let expressions register on his face, she saw it. Something else had happened. Something else was going on. Whatever it was, it had to do with her. "What is it? What's wrong?"

He sighed. "Jason Kenmore's body has just been discovered by a cleaning woman at a motel in the city."

It felt like a punch to the gut. Linda thought she might double over. She could still taste the bile in her esophagus. It burned like acid. The gum might take care of the mouth, but it was useless to the throat. "So what does that mean? Who does that leave? It leaves Bierman. My God … my God it's Bierman."

Chapter 48

At seven that evening a doctor came out into the waiting area of the emergency room dressed in aqua medical scrubs. Linda watched him look around the room. She had a feeling he was looking for her. Officer Valente had told Ray's doctor she would be waiting to hear an update. When they made eye contact, she slid forward on the chair, in anticipation.

"Ms. Genova, is it?" The doctor asked, pointing his finger at her.

"Yes?" She said and stood up. Patty, who had been carelessly flipping through magazine after magazine, stood up next to Linda and held her hand. Together they walked toward the surgeon, "How is he?"

"Mr. Telfer is in rough shape. He was injured pretty badly in two places, the back and stomach," the doctor said delicately, indicating the spots where Ray had been stabbed using both hands. "He lost quite a bit of blood. For a while, I thought we might lose him. He held in there," the doctor smiled. "It's going to be touch and go for the next twenty-four hours. He's in intensive care right now, recovering."

Linda felt hot tears. "Recovering? He's going to be all right?"

"At this point, it appears that way. I'll be checking in on him tonight and we'll take a good thorough look at him tomorrow, but for the most part, I think he'll be fine," the doctor said, a satisfied grin on his lips.

"Is he up? Can he talk? Can we see him?" Patty asked.

"Not tonight. He's has not awakened yet, and we don't expect him to," the doctor said.

"We won't wake him. We won't say a word," Linda said. Her eyes silently pleaded her case as tears streamed down her cheek.

"Two minutes and no more. Then you go home, get a good

night sleep and come back tomorrow," the doctor said firmly.

"Deal," Linda said. She felt tremendous. She thought she might explode with relief. She forgot about everything going on around her. She forgot about the stalker. Everything became Ray. He was going to be all right. He was not going to die. All she wanted in the world this doctor was about to grant her. She was going to be allowed to see him and little else mattered.

Following the doctor to the Intensive Care Unit, Linda kept squeezing Patty's hand. "He's going to be all right. I knew he was going to be okay, I did, I knew it."

Patty just kept shaking her head and smiling. "I don't know what to say. I'm just speechless. So much has happened…"

"I don't want to talk about that. None of that," Linda said. "I just want to see Ray."

Impatiently, she continued following the doctor with Patty at her side. The walk seemed to last forever. However, when she came to the ICU, her knees stiffened as if in bad need of oiling.

"Linda?" Patty said.

"I'm nervous. I'm not sure I can go in there," Linda said.

The doctor gave her a look—a smile—it felt reassuring. "You'll be all right," he said.

She was not sure what to expect. Patty squeezed her hand this time, lending her support and strength. Linda entered ICU. The doctor led her to a room where the nameplate was a strip of white medical tape. In blue marker it said, Telfer, Raymond. The doctor opened the door. Linda stood at the threshold for a moment. The room was well lit, whereas she expected a dark, gloomy room. It looked no different from any other hospital room she had ever visited. The walls were plain, eggshell white. There was a window. The only thing missing were chairs for visitors.

"Two minutes and not a second more," the doctor said and was gone.

Linda entered the room with Patty right behind her. Linda realized she had observed as much of the room as possible, without looking at Ray. She had less then two minutes left. She went to Ray's side. Tubes snaked out of his nostrils. A bag dripped clear fluid into a line running intravenously into the top of Ray's hand. His hair was a mess. She expected to see blood on his clothes, on his face, but there was none.

"Ray," she said tentatively. She looked over her shoulder at Patty, who stood against the wall near the door.

"The doctor said not to disturb him," Patty said. "He needs his rest."

"But I want him to know I'm here," Linda said. "He needs to know I'm here."

* * * * *

"I think you should go on home," the doctor on said. "It doesn't look as if your friend will wake up tonight. It's close to eleven, chances are he'll sleep until morning."

"We were told that," Linda said. She thought of Patty. At first Patty sat in a chair in the emergency waiting room flipping through magazines. Eventually she appeared to have looked through all of them, getting up and going from stack to stack set on tables around the room. After, she bought a candy bar and a soda pop. Linda noticed that for the past fifteen minutes Patty had done nothing but pace the hall, glancing at the clock on the wall each time she passed by it. "If I leave my number, will you call me it he wakes up? I don't care if it's three in the morning, or the minute I walk out to the parking lot."

"Of course. Leave the number at the front desk," the doctor said.

"I'll do that," Patty said and walked down the hall toward the exit. "I'll wait for you down there."

Linda thanked the doctor. "How's he looking?"

"Right now, he's sleeping."

"But you think he'll wake up in the morning, right?"

"That's the plan."

"Is there a chance he won't?" Linda asked. It was one of those questions where you already know the answer but you ask it anyway. Linda waited, holding her breath.

"There's always that chance. Your friend has been seriously injured. I swear it's a miracle that he made it this far. I don't see why he wouldn't wake up. The big plan's in God's hands. Not ours."

"You watch out for him while I'm gone. You'll do that for me?" Linda asked. She did not want to leave. If it weren't for

Patty she might consider spending the night in one of the uncomfortable emergency room chairs. Had she sent Patty home at the beginning of the day, she would have spent the night. Since Patty wasted the entire day waiting with her, she felt obligated to accompany her home. A good night's sleep wouldn't hurt. She'd be back right after breakfast. She planned to stand by Ray's bed. She wanted to be the first thing he saw when he woke up.

"We'll give him the best care available," the doctor said, giving Linda a reassuring smile.

"What's your name?" Linda asked. He impressed her as a man who cared.

"Hackey. Daniel Hackey," the doctor said.

"Doctor Hackey, will you watch out for him," Linda asked.

"I told you, we'll…"

"That's not what I mean. I am asking if you'll look out for him," Linda said. She didn't want to come out and say, I trust you. I like you. There was something authentic about his mannerism.

He continued to smile. He had heard it before, she knew. People must do it to him all the time, putting their faith and trust into his hands—not the hands of the hospital—but into the hands of Dr. Daniel Hackey.

"I will check in on him periodically throughout my shift," Dr. Hackey said.

Linda sighed with relief. "And you'll call?"

"Your number is at the front desk. I'll call even if it's three in the morning. If he wakes up as soon as you leave, I'll do you one better. I'll run out into the parking lot and get you myself," Dr. Hackey said.

"Okay," Linda said, laughing. "I guess a few hours of sleep will feel pretty good."

Chapter 49

They drove in almost complete silence to Patty's house. The roads were bad and visibility was terrible. At least six fresh inches of snow covered the ground. They passed cars marooned along the way. Linda sensed unexplained tension between them. She felt so tired and mentally worn out. She could not even imagine how Patty must feel spending an entire day in a hospital. "Thank you for staying the day with me," Linda offered. "I appreciate it."

"I know you do," Patty said, her tone snappy.

"Is something wrong?" Linda asked. She thought she had imagined the tension, but felt it now. "Did I do something wrong?"

Patty took a deep breath as she pulled into her driveway. "No. I'm sorry. I'm just feeling tense. I mean, I can't believe you don't feel the same way. I spent so much time thinking about everything going on, and none of it makes sense. None of it."

Patty pulled the car into the garage and shut off the engine. They sat in the car, protected in the garage from the wind as it whipped snowflakes as violently as a swarm of killer bees at anyone unlucky enough to be outside.

Linda shook her head. "I know what you mean. I feel it. God, do I feel it. I'm overwhelmed. I can't think about things anymore. Really, all I can think about is Ray."

"You love him that much?" Patty asked.

"I love him. There's something there between us," Linda said.

"Ray ... He's an alcoholic," Patty said. "You know you can't trust him. How can you want to get involved with someone like him?"

Linda was stung by the words.

"It doesn't seem to be a problem. He had some problems, we talked about them, but he's doing really well." Linda knew Patty was being protective, looking out for her, but she wasn't sure she liked it.

"Remember I told you a lawyer, not in our firm, told me about Ray's meetings," Patty said.

"Yes?" Linda asked. She felt her stomach muscles knotting.

"It was Patrick who told me," Patty confessed.

"He told you? Bierman told you?" Linda asked. "He told you, because he knew you'd tell me. He wanted to sabotage the relationship. He didn't want Ray and I going bowling together. That's why he wanted me to know about Ray's drinking. Patrick, that bastard, wanted to ruin anything that might be developing between the two of us. My God, Patty, he's obsessed. He's a sick and crazy man," Linda said.

"I guess," Patty said,

"And he's out there," Linda said, suddenly feeling a twinge of fear. The darkness surrounded them. Linda wanted to get out of the car, out of the garage and into the house.

"I doubt it," Patty said.

"You don't think so? You don't think he's out there? He might have killed Joey, he tried to kill Ray ... some cleaning lady found Jason Kenmore's body," Linda said, close to hysterics. Her hands were balled into tight fists and as she spoke she could feel the veins in her neck jetting out like tree roots bulging out of the ground.

Patty opened her door. The dome light in the car came on. "Patrick isn't coming for you."

Linda opened her door. "Patty, he killed Joey, didn't he. Patrick murdered Joey because he was jealous, or felt threatened."

"Joey never threatened Patrick, did he?"

"I don't mean he physically threatened him. Maybe he felt competitively threatened?"

"Competitively threatened. Linda, are you enjoying this, all this attention?" Patty asked. She shut her car door.

"How can you say that?" Linda asked. She shut her door, sending the garage into darkness. Linda walked around to the back of the car, keeping one hand on it the entire time.

She felt the cold wind laced with snow shrapnel as it slammed into her before she noticed the open doorway. A light came on outside the door. She heard Patty say, "There, that's better."

"Patty, how can you say that?"

"How can I say what? Careful you don't trip. It's still dark in here," Patty said.

Linda made it to the door and followed Patty out into the storm. She saw the shadow of Patty's home in the storm like a silhouette behind a thin shade. It seemed miles away.

"Follow me," Patty said, yelling. She reached out and touched Linda.

Linda put her hand in Patty's. She tucked her head down, chin to her chest. Like a two-car train they walked as quickly as possible toward the house.

Once inside, after Patty shut off the alarm, Linda asked, "Are you going to answer me?"

"Answer you, what? Linda what are you talking about?"

"You wanted to know if I was enjoying all of the attention," Linda said, huffing.

"Leave it alone. It was just a question. I didn't mean to upset you so much," Patty said.

"Yeah? Well you did."

"I'm sorry. I told you, I'm shot. It's been a long day, a long week. My mind feels like mush," Patty said, taking off her shoes and setting them neatly on the mat. "I'll wrestle you for a hot bubble bath."

Linda smiled and shook her head, putting her shoes on the mat, next to Patty's. "A bubble bath does sound great. You go first, really."

"Sure?"

"I'm positive. This way when you're done I can spend the rest of the night soaking." Linda thought about settling down in a hot tub of water. It would feel exactly like being home—without the wine. "So hurry up, I'm already anxious for my turn."

Chapter 50

Ray was tired; his eyelids felt heavy. He wanted to wake up, but seemed trapped in an incoherent space between being asleep and awake. He could not recall dreaming, but instinctively knew he had had a nightmare. Perhaps it was the dream-monster holding him back, keeping him from waking up.

With a cotton ball dry mouth, Ray felt his lips smack. Using every facial muscle he could muster he strained to open his eyes. He thought he could detect a dim light somewhere in his room. His eyelids fluttered. He smelled antiseptic cleaner, or urine. The acidic aroma assaulted his nostrils like a smelling salt. His eyes opened.

Feeling dazed and disoriented, Ray could not scream when he saw the man standing over him. His mind felt panicked, but he did not scream. Nothing felt right, the smells, the feel of the bed, his pillow.

"Where am I?" he asked, exerting himself to speak.

"I'm Dr. Hackey, Mr. Telfer. You're in the hospital."

The hospital? "Why? How did I get here?" Ray asked.

"You don't recall?"

Ray didn't want to close his eyes. It had taken him so long and so much energy to open them. The dim light in the room was bothering his eyes, though. Even though he felt like he had been asleep for years, he still felt tired. Sleep had a fisted grip on his mind and was trying to drag him back into its own world of dreams and make-believe.

As he became aware of the pain he felt like a dull throb throughout his body, he remembered. "I was stabbed…"

"That's right," Dr. Hackey said. "How do you feel?"

"Like a carved Thanksgiving turkey," Ray said, he laughed and coughed then groaned in pain. "It hurts to do that."

"To cough?"

"To breathe." Ray wanted to sit up.

He didn't want to think about it. It was the type of memory he wanted to forget about. He found it difficult to believe that someone actually stabbed him. "I came close to dying?"

"Close. Your record indicates you called nine one one, looks like you saved your own life."

He remembered that Patrick Bierman wanted to see him. He remembered going to Patrick's office. He remembered thinking the arrogant attorney was sitting in his big leather chair facing the window. Then he remembered the feeling of a knife being stuck into his back. "God, that hurt," Ray said. "I felt that blade pass through my skin ... I felt it scrape across things...Is it still today?"

"Have you lost any time? No. It's still Saturday and you should rest," the doctor said. "You are recovering from a very long and serious operation."

"But I am recovering?" Ray asked. He didn't feel like he was getting better. The pain in his body steadily became more prominent. He thought he might be dying, instead. "I'm in some pain."

"You are recovering, and I can give you a bit more pain killer, if you'd like," Dr. Hackey said.

"I like, I like," Ray said. "Was, did, has a Linda Genova been here?"

"Yes. Linda and another woman spent the entire day waiting. I finally convinced them to go home for some rest. Linda was very hesitant about doing so. In fact, she made me promise to call her if you woke up."

Ray smiled. "I love that woman, you know?"

"I guessed it was something like that," Dr. Hackey said. "I don't want to break my promise. I'm going to call her, but I'm going to instruct her not to return to the hospital until morning, because I'm instructing you to get some sleep."

"That makes sense, and you're the doctor," Ray said.

The doctor left the room. He seemed to return within seconds, but Ray could not tell if he had remained awake the entire time or if he had dozed off. "Did you call her, doc?"

"Actually, Linda's friend was supposed to leave the phone number at the front desk. The nurses on duty can't seem to locate it," Dr. Hackey said. "But don't worry, I'll find it and I'll call her."

"I have her number," Ray said. He closed his eyes tight, concentrating as he tried to recall it.

"She was staying with her friend," Dr. Hackey said.

"Sure, makes sense. The police in on this?" Ray asked.

"Yes. They're pretty involved. I just didn't want to get into that now with you," Dr. Hackey said. "There will be time for that tomorrow."

It came like a lightening bolt. It felt like one striking his brain. It did nothing to keep him awake, but for a moment, he felt charged. He hadn't thought about it, the who, the why. He felt like the stabbing happened years ago, not hours ago. "Doctor, the police. I need to talk to the police right away!"

Chapter 51
Midnight

The water was hot. The bubbles were oiled to make skin feel like silk.

She heard Patty crying and sat up straight in the tub, the bubbles falling off her breasts, leaving them exposed and cold. Linda pulled the plug at the base of the tub and stood up as the water drained. She reached for a towel and wrapped it around her hair. She used a second towel to quickly dry off her body. She tied it around her chest and stepped out of the tub onto the bathroom mat. Hanging on the door for her use was a pink, cotton robe. She put it on and tentatively opened the door. She passed by her room. Patty sat under the canopy, legs tucked beneath her, still wearing her own bathrobe. She held one of the pictures from off her dresser.

"Patty, are you all right?" Linda asked, not meaning to startle her friend.

Patty sprang up onto her feet. She tossed the picture back onto the bed. "Don't you knock?"

"I'm sorry. I heard you crying," Linda said.

"Done with your bath already?" Patty asked, as if choosing to ignore the scene that just unfolded. "Or you heard me crying and came out to see if I was all right? Well, I am all right. I'm fine. Go back and enjoy your bath."

Linda watched Patty hastily wipe away the tears. "Patty..."

"I'm all right, I'm telling you. Now go on, get, or I just might take another relaxing bath," Patty said.

Linda ignored Patty and walked into the bedroom. She could see Patty was hurting. Maybe they should have talked about it earlier, when Patty first indicated to Linda there had been a problem between her and her father. "Want to talk about it?"

"Talk about it? Talk about what?" Patty yelled. Then she laughed. Then she spun all the way around, staring up at the ceiling. When she collapsed to her knees crying, Linda sat next to her, took her into her arms, and rocked back and forth with her. "He was the greatest man, I thought. I always looked up to him ... what little girl doesn't look up to her Daddy?"

Linda felt something in her stomach twisting into a knot.

"But then it changed, it changed one night when my mother was out with friends," Patty said. "And he came into my room. I thought he was going to tuck me into bed, maybe read me a story. When he climbed into bed, I knew he was naked..."

Linda closed her eyes, feeling the burn as tears spilled down her cheeks. She did not want to hear anymore. So revolting. So unthinkable, unimaginable, she knew enough to make her feel violently ill. She controlled it as best she could. She would get sick, but not now. It had to wait. She could not comprehend living through any of what Patty continued to tell her. She wanted to close her ears and shut out Patty's voice. Instead, she held Patty tighter in her arms and rocked her back and forth a little faster. It almost felt as if she were trying to run, to get away. But they weren't moving. They weren't going anywhere. They were still seated on Patty's floor, in the middle of her child-like bedroom, reliving a nightmare together.

"He's in jail, you know. Not for what he did to me, but for murdering my mother. She came home one night, unexpectedly, and caught us. Caught him. And she went crazy," Patty said. She pulled out of the hug. She sat Indian style and rocked on her own.

Linda drew up her knees, and sat leaning against Patty's bed.

"I had a baseball bat in my room. I was Daddy's little girl, and since Daddy didn't have a boy, I was also his little boy. We played ball together. He coached my Little League team. So I had a baseball bat in my room, and when my mother ran out of the bedroom, he picked it up and followed her," Patty said. "I wanted to stay in bed and pull the covers over my head, but I couldn't. Instead, I got out of bed and ran after them. The only person wearing clothing was my mother. She was crying so hard, I didn't think she could see us anyway, not with all those tears in her eyes."

Linda just stared at Patty. Patty was talking, but it seemed more like she was talking to herself. She had to be separating herself from the memory, protecting herself from the pain of reliving it all. She was distant, but she kept talking, her voice taking on a frighteningly monotone pattern. Patty said, "When my mother picked up the phone, screaming that she was calling the police, my dad went at her with the bat. I was so scared. I was scared because I thought I was going to get in trouble for sleeping with my father. I thought the police were going to put me in jail. Then when my father swung the bat and it cracked into the side of my mother's head, I knew I wasn't in the kind of trouble my father was going to be in.

"I started screaming for him to stop, but he didn't. I watched my mother try crawling away from him. Her hand looked all arthritic as she reached out to me. I screamed for him to stop, but my dad hit her again and again in the head until the bat broke. Then he told me to go get dressed. Then he ran and got dressed. Then he came into my room and he told me to change into pajamas, not jeans. So I did, and he watched me. Then he told me to get in bed and go to sleep. He said he had some things to take care of and he turned off my light and closed my bedroom door.

"He didn't fool anyone. The police caught him a few days later when they found my mother's body in some shallow grave. A dog had dug part of her up," Patty said.

Linda felt the impact of the story. Molestation, witnessing murder, living with your father for a few days after watching him kill your mother, having your father arrested. "My God," Linda said, her mind spinning uncontrollably.

Patty started to cry again and Linda moved closer to hug her. Patty hugged Linda tightly and she could feel hot breath on her neck and chest.

* * * * *

Officer Josaiah Valente did not expect to spend his entire Saturday working. A murder always corrupted a forty-hour work-week and working on two homicides, well, forget about it. He might as well lease his house and move into the police station.

Locking up his desk, ready to go home for a few hours sleep, Valente groaned when his telephone rang. He debated not answering it. It was midnight. No one could know he was still at work. Whoever was calling could just think he'd already left for home.

By the fourth ring, as Valente was putting on his leather jacket, ready to leave, ready to walk away from the ringing phone, he looked up at the ceiling and asked, "Why me?"

Answering the phone, the officer on the other end talked excitedly. "Valente, you'd better get down here. We just impounded Kenmore's car. Sir, you better just come on down here."

"Can it wait until morning?" Valente asked. He could care less about Kenmore's car. He imagined a bag of dope in the glove compartment, a handgun under the seat. What ever it was, he would alter his report in the morning. Right now he just couldn't think anymore. His brain threatened to shut down. He wanted to get home and suck down a beer before he lost consciousness.

"We've got a body in the trunk."

A punch to the stomach. "I'll be right down."

Valente hung up, switched off his desk light and the telephone started ringing again. "I said I'll be right down," Valente said.

"I'm sorry. I was looking for a police officer named Valente?"

"That's me."

"This is Doctor Hackey, at Strong? I'm on the night shift and responsible for Mr. Raymond Telfer."

"He didn't make it?" Valente asked, not at all surprised. Telfer had not looked good. The doctors had told Valente it didn't look good. The man had lost a tremendous amount of blood. The internal injuries looked severe.

"No. The exact opposite, he looks good and he has woken up. He wants to see you. He says he knows who tried to kill him."

267

Chapter 52

Linda held Patty tight. Patty had stopped crying. Patty's hot tears were on Linda's chest, rolling down her skin between her breasts. Linda wondered if Patty had fallen asleep. Patty was breathing deeply. When Patty kissed Linda's chest, Linda did not realize what was happening. She tensed. Patty kissed her again, letting the kiss linger, her lips pressed against Linda's flesh.

"Patty…Patty what are you doing?" Linda asked, pushing Patty away.

"I love you, Linda. I'm in love with you," Patty said.

Linda, speechless, stood up, pulling her robe tight around her body.

Patty got to her feet, letting her robe fall open.

"Patty, those are my pajama's," Linda said, aghast, staring at the maroon red silk pajamas that were her favorite. "How did you get those? Where did you get those from?"

"I waited you know, Linda. I waited," Patty said. She reached between the mattress and the box spring and pulled out a knife that appeared to be caked in dried blood. "I detested Joey Viglucci. I hated the arrogant prick. You know that? You knew that. I might never have told you as much, but you knew how I felt about him, didn't you? Still, I let you have your fling. I never expected it would even last six months, but I was thrilled when it finally ended."

"Patty…"

"I was next, you know. I sent you those flowers. I was next. I waited my turn. I waited for the chance to take you out, to have you fall in love with me," Patty said, panting. She held the knife in one hand, the blade aimed at the ceiling. "Then Ray Telfer comes along and steps right into your life. He cut in line, Linda. That wasn't fair."

Linda thought she had known fear. She had known shit about

fear before. Fear quickly escalated to terror. She looked around the room. Nothing. There was nothing she could use to defend herself.

"Joey?" Linda asked.

"He was such an ass. I called him up, told him I wanted him. I told him I always wanted him. He invited me over," Patty said. "He was so disgusting. Men are disgusting. I hate men. There is not one man worth my time. None of them can be trusted. None of them care about women. They are simple minded and oh so easy to fool."

Joey was a simple-minded man. He did not deserve the fate Patty had dealt him. "Patty, you didn't...you..."

"I did. I let him climb into the Jacuzzi, then I dropped the CD player into the water with him," Patty said.

I should have known, Linda thought. The media coverage of the accident never mentioned a CD player or a Jacuzzi. It had just mentioned he'd been electrocuted, and yet when Patty had been at Linda's house, she had known exactly how Joey had died.

"And Jason Kenmore..."

"Same thing. He was easy to lure away. He thought he was meeting you."

"But Patrick? What about Patrick Bierman?"

* * * * *

"ID says Patrick Bierman," the police officer told Valente. They stood near the trunk of Jason Kenmore's car. Stuffed inside was the body of a man covered in blood. "Mean anything to you?"

"Yes. It means that Linda Genova's life could be in serious danger." Officer Josaiah Valente checked his pockets. He could not recall Linda giving him the address and telephone number of where she'd be staying. He checked his pockets to be sure. He had nothing. "Let me see your phone," Valente said.

"Right in the office," the officer said.

Valente dialed Linda Genova's number at the office and waited for the recording.

"Hello. You have reached Linda Genova, paralegal at the Hartzman, Cross, Lacy & Bierman Firm. I am away from my desk, or on another line. You can leave me a message at the tone, or if this is an emergency, you can reach my secretary, Patty Dent at...."

Josaiah Valente hung up and sat at the desk and logged onto the police computer.

Chapter 53

"Patty, you don't want to do this. You don't want to hurt me," Linda said. She was being backed into a corner. She needed to think of a way to distract Patty. "I never, never knew you felt this way. I swear, I never knew."

Patty looked hurt. "Didn't you ever think of me that way? Didn't you ever want to be with me the way I wanted to be with you? I mean, didn't you ever imagine us making love together?"

Linda wanted to tell her the truth, but couldn't. "Of course I did. All the time."

"You liar. What do you take me for? I'm not stupid. You never thought about me that way. When would you have? You are always thinking about yourself and about guys. You should know by now, you should understand how awful men are, how rotten they are. How can you not know that?" Patty asked.

"Not all men," Linda tried.

"Yes!" Patty pointed the knife at Linda. "Yes, all men!"

"If you love me, why do you want to hurt me? You don't really want to do this," Linda said.

"I do and I don't. I didn't know what to do, until Ray turned up alive at the hospital," Patty said thoughtfully.

"Ray," Linda whispered, crying. She did not feel strong enough to handle this. She thought she might crumble to her knees. She did not have the strength any longer to fight her adversary. She thought of Ray in a hospital bed. He had looked like he'd been in a peaceful sleep, while really, inside, his body fought for his life. Somehow, after being stabbed twice, Ray had managed to crawl to a phone and call for help. Linda knew she could not give up so easily. Crumbling to her knees would cost her her life.

"Ray. Ray. Ray," Patty cackled. "He's a worthless drunk, Linda, a useless alcoholic. I followed him to meetings. I followed him to his pathetic apartment. He has nothing. He'll amount to nothing, and he'll go back to drinking, and he'll hurt you. It's who he is. He'll break your heart because he's a drunk and because he's a man!"

Linda shook her head. "That's not true. No. That's not true."

"If Ray had died, you might have lived. I wanted to hurt you, to get rid of the filthy men in your life, but I wanted to save you, as well. I wanted to cleanse you of their disgusting ways. You and me, it would have worked," Patty said.

"It can. It still can," Linda said, fighting for her life.

"It could have. I think it could have. It can't, though. Not now. Ray's going to be fine, and he's going to tell the police. He'll tell them I tried to kill him. The police will come for me, and I don't want to be locked up again. I won't go back to being locked up, no way," Patty said.

Backed into a corner, leaning against the wall near the sliding closet door was a baseball bat. Linda saw it in her peripheral vision. It sat an arms-length away. "Patty, don't…" Linda begged, hoping to avoid an attack.

Patty sighed. "I really think we'd have made a great couple."

Linda thought she would not be ready to move. Everything happened in slow motion. Patty charged, thrusting out her arm, the blade poised, ready to strike. Linda, never looking away from the tip on the point of the knife, blindly reached for the bat as she attempted to jump out of harms' way. She cried out as the blade skinned her side, slicing through her flesh. Her towel fell away as Patty pulled back her hand, and raised it, ready to stick the knife into Linda's chest.

Holding the bat in the middle, Linda used it like a club. As Patty arched her arm toward Linda, Linda struck. She heard the solid crack as the bat connected with Patty's skull. Patty fell to her knees. Linda jumped over Patty, trying to run for the hallway. She had not thought the knife wound had been significant, but sudden pain erupted in her side as she ran.

She heard Patty scream, instinctively knew she was back on her feet and coming at her. Linda ran into the hall, stumbling into the wall. Right next to her face was the keypad for the security alarm. Linda pressed the red button to call the police. The second her finger depressed the button, an earsplitting alarm sounded at an inhuman decibel.

"Linda," Patty said, holding a telephone in her hand. She was at the threshold of her room. Her temple was cut, blood dripped down the side of her face, was matted into her hair. "The bat? After the story I told you, you decided to use a bat to defend yourself?" Patty asked, screaming to be heard over the sound of the screeching alarm.

Patty laughed. Linda trembled. She almost lost her grip on the bat. She moved both hands to choke hold it. She needed the bat.

"How ironic, don't you think? How freaking ironic can this get?" Patty asked.

Linda chanced a look to see how far she was from the stairs. She could make a dash for them, but did not like the idea of running down them with her back unprotected. Patty would get her. Her mouth and throat felt dry. Her legs felt paralyzed. She didn't think she would be able to run even if she had the opportunity.

The telephone rang. Linda looked at Patty. Patty looked at Linda with a mocking smile. "Who can that be?" she said to Linda, as she picked up the phone. Linda wanted to scream, but couldn't. She opened her mouth, but no sound came out. "Hello? Yes. My password? Baseball bat. Yes, it's a false alarm. Thank you."

The alarm stopped suddenly. The silence seemed unnatural. "Sorry. Looks like it's just you and me."

Linda ran for the stairs. She ran down three, before jumping down the rest of them. She kept envisioning Patty right behind her swinging the knife and sticking the blade into her back up to the hilt.

She thought for sure, as she was flying toward the floor, she had twisted an ankle. It happened all of the time in movies. But when she landed, she got to her feet and proceeded to run toward the kitchen. Adrenaline coursed though her body. Had she twisted or broken her ankle she was certain to feel it later. Right now, her body must have known that she needed to be able to run to have even the slimmest chance for survival.

Linda ran down the few steps to the side door.

She gasped, struggling to undue all three dead bolts.

"Linda," Patty said, standing at the top of the stairs.

Linda ignored her and tried to pull open the door. It wouldn't open. The door handle was still locked. She turned the tent shaped lock and pulled open the door, throwing herself out of the house and into the snow. She looked at the feet of a man standing in front of her. She looked up.

Officer Josiah Valente stood with his gun drawn.

Linda looked back to the house, through the storm door. Just on the other side of the door, stood Patty in Linda's favorite pair of pajamas. Blood covered her face. She was crying. The wet tears cleared a path through areas where the blood had already started to dry. "Patty," Linda called out.

Patty held the knife up to her own throat.

"Ms. Dent, drop the knife!" Officer Valente called out.

Patty Dent never looked away from Linda. She drew the blade across her throat and blood spilled down her neck like fruit juice spilling over the brim of a white cup. Patty put one bloody hand on the storm door glass as she stepped back. She closed the door.

Linda watched as Valente stepped past her and tried opening the storm door. "Ms. Dent?" He knocked on the door a few times. "Ms. Dent?" He smashed the glass with the butt of his revolver. He unlocked the door, turned and tossed Linda his cell phone. "Call nine one one."

Linda held onto the phone and watched as Valente struggled to open the door.

"Call nine one one," he ordered again, more urgently this time. He used his gun to shoot off the doorknob. He threw his shoulder into the door. It did not budge. He shot off the remaining dead bolts. He tried again to push open the door. It opened some, but something kept it from opening all the way.

Linda could see Patty's leg.

Before she could even turn on the cell phone, Linda closed her eyes and fell back into the snow.

Chapter 54
Tuesday, January 28

Ray was moved into his own room. He had a telephone and a television set with cable. Linda showed up with a bag of food from Nick Tahou's.

"Don't let the nurses know I'm feeding you this," Linda said putting the bags on the nightstand by his bed.

"I'll bet they know. I smelled the food coming down the hall," Ray said.

Linda leaned over the bed to kiss him. She loved his lips. She loved the way he kissed her. "I'm starving."

"Me too, but we should wait. Officer Valente was just here to see you. I told him you'd be right back. He should be here any second," Ray said. "How's your side?"

"I'm okay," Linda said. Patty Dent had cut her, but not badly. It hurt, but it didn't restrict Linda. "Doctor says you can get out of here on Friday."

"I'm ready now," Ray said.

There was a knock at the door. Ray said, "Come in."

Officer Josiah Valente walked in, dressed in street clothing. "Hello again, Ray."

"Detective," Ray said.

"Ms. Genova."

"How are you?" Linda asked.

"I'm wrapping some things up here, and I thought I'd bring you up to speed."

"I'd appreciate that," Linda said. She hated to know Patty had died. Despite everything that had happened, she was not actually angry with Patty. The woman was sick. Sad and sick. How could she be angry with someone who didn't know any better? Patty was not in control of her actions. She was handicapped, in a way, mentally unstable.

"The story she told you, Linda, was only half true," Valente said. "We were able to obtain her medical records from Colorado. Apparently, the father had been molesting her. The police believe the mother did arrive home early, or unexpectedly to catch father and daughter in the act."

Linda cringed. She held onto Ray's hand. He gave it a squeeze.

"When Patty's father started hitting her mother with the base-ball bat, Patty used a kitchen knife and stabbed her father in the back. She called the police. When the police showed up, she was wearing pajamas and in her bedroom with the door closed, pretend-ing to be asleep. When police investigators talked with her, they realized she was being abused. They had a rape counselor talk with her. When the woman inspected the child, got Patty to re-move her pajamas, her body was covered in her father's blood," Officer Valente said.

"Oh my God," Linda said. "And they sent her to jail for that, for killing her father?"

"She was never in jail, Linda. Besides, there isn't a jury in the country that would convict her. She's the victim through and through. She was, however, committed to a mental institution. That could be what she meant when she said she wouldn't go back to being locked up," Valente added.

"I can't believe this," Ray said.

"Well, there's more," Valente said. "In Denver, two years ago a woman was being stalked. It was circumstances very similar to yours, Ms. Genova. The woman kept reporting things to the police. Unfortunately, receiving anonymous love letters is not a crime. So at first, the police couldn't do much of anything. When this woman started dating someone new, the love letters took on an angry over-tone, becoming more sexually obscene and, eventually, threaten-ing."

"And what happened?" Linda asked. She almost had the feel-ing the officer was talking about her life. The sensation felt un-canny.

"The woman was murdered. The attacker broke into her house, chased her out into the cold and stabbed her to death," Officer Josaiah Valente said. "At the time, Patty Dent talked with the police, finger pointing. Patty swore her friend was trying to get away from the new boyfriend, that the new boyfriend couldn't take no for an answer, that he was a jealous man. Police searched the guy's house and found the knife in the new boy friend's car."

"But it wasn't him, was it?"

"We're looking into that now, ma'am, but I have a gut feeling there is an innocent man in jail."

Linda was crying again. She was crying for Patty. *What a life that poor woman led.* "So now what? What do we do now?"

"You go on living, Ms. Genova."

* * * * *

Linda heard from the New York State Division of Human Rights. Despite Jason Kenmore's death, the investigation continued. The state came back with a no probable cause. Linda was satisfied with the decision, though she felt guilty. Kenmore's family, a wife and three kids, were now alone. No money. Linda doubted the man had any life insurance outside of what the company had provided when he had been an employee. There was nothing she could do about it. Linda was not sure if the widow had any recourse. Maybe a civil action against Patty Dent's estate?

Linda resigned from her position at the law firm. She left without saying goodbye to anyone. She took the pension money she had earned as a vested employee and rolled it and her 401K into an aggressive IRA. She was confident that with her degree and training she would be able to find a job with close to any law firm she desired.

Ray sold his car for a few hundred bucks. He paid it to his landlord in order to break his lease.

They hired movers to load Linda's belongings into a U-Haul.

In Linda's driveway, dressed in jeans and a gray sweatshirt, Linda could not believe she was going to do it. "We're really moving to Florida, aren't we?"

"You'll love it. You okay with leaving your job?"

"Okay with it? I'm thrilled about it. There's nothing there for me. The partners exposed themselves. I saw their true colors. I don't want any part of that. Not anymore," Linda said, thinking she might work for a legal aid organization, really helping those in need of legal assistance. "Have you contacted Malcolm?"

"I did. He wasn't thrilled to hear I was moving, but when he heard I was headed home, I think he was somewhat relieved. I told him I'd keep in touch," Ray said. "I don't know. I don't think he believed me."

"Ray, we're not running away though, right? I need to know that. We're not just getting out of here and running away, right?" Linda asked.

Ray kissed her. "I'm not running from anything. Not anymore. You and I are starting over. We're starting a new life together."

"And you want your family in your life."

"They are so excited I'm coming home, I can't help but feel like the prodigal son."

"And me?"

"They can't wait to meet you. They love that we're moving to Florida and getting married."

Linda kissed him. "I love that we're getting married."

Hugging each other, Linda knew she was going to cry. She did not want to cry anymore. But this was different. These were the first happy tears she had cried … well, since Ray proposed to her. Not counting then, she could not recall when she had ever felt so hopeful.

The future might be unknown, but at least she had Ray now.

They would face life together.

She believed, together, they would make it through anything.

PHILLIP TOMASSO, III

MEET THE AUTHOR

Interviewer (I): What made you decide that you wanted to write?

Phillip Tomasso III (PT3): Growing up I suffered from a reading comprehension disability. This made me hate books. I did everything I could in school not to read. It wasn't until 7th grade that I read my first book from cover to cover. Our English teacher said we were going to read 4 books that year. All were by S.E. Hinton. The first was THE OUTSIDERS. After reading that, I was inspired. Aside from being just 16 when Hinton wrote that story, the author was also a young lady. It was much more difficult for women to publish then. (Hence, the initialed first name S.E.)

I started writing short stories and set a goal for myself, that I would sell my first novel before turning 30. It was July of 1999 that I signed a contract for my first novel, MIND PLAY. The book was released February 2000. I turned 30 that June.

I: Who are your favorite authors, and who influenced your writing?

PT3: There are so many. Obviously S.E. Hinton, then there is Stephen King, Dean Koontz, John Saul, Robin Cook, Lawrence Block, James Patterson, John Sandford, Lawrence Sanders, Jonathan Kellerman ... the list goes on and on and on ... I read roughly four books a month now. But there was a time, before turning 30, when I was reading four books a week. Over the years I've read many books that have inspired me, and many that were so bad, I tried to learn what it was about them I didn't like and then worked to make sure I didn't make the same mistakes in my writing ...

I write book reviews for a web-zine called Curled Up With A Good

Book (www.curledup.com). It's a great site. I get to select books I want to read and the editor sends them to me. They are not usually books by the best sellers. So in doing this job, I get the opportunity to read books by authors I might never have discovered, like Daniel Woodrell, Michael Kimball, Brian Rouff, Jess Walter, Justin Gustainis, Aaron Elkin, Karen Osborn, John B. Olson and Randall Ingermanson, to name a few.

I: Do you have a particular writing routine?

PT3:   Mornings. I get up at 2:30 AM Saturdays and Sundays and write until around 8 or 9, when the wife and kids start to stir. Otherwise, I'd have to take time away from them during the week, and that wouldn't be fair. As it is, nearly every weekend I drag them along to book signings at malls all over Western New York. (They're great though, supportive). I like to try to write a chapter per day. Then during the week I concentrate on plotting. I keep a notebook with me most of the time. Ideas come when I'm least ready for them. So the notebook comes in handy.

I: Where do you get ideas?

PT3:   Great question. No answer. They just come to me. I get a story idea, basically, beginning, middle and end. Then it is all I can do to get it down fast enough. I always know the end of the story, the Tomasso Twist, as I call it. And it is a matter of working toward that goal. I never use an actual outline. Too limiting, in my opinion. So far, I have been fortunate. I have not suffered from any writer's block and have a notebook filled with ideas still to write.

With ADVERSE IMPACT, the idea came to me, like other ideas. The fun part was deciding what my characters would be like. Especially Linda. I decided to plot the story around a paralegal, since I am a paralegal (for my full time career). I thought about making Linda lawyer, but the lawyer books are well represented by John Grisham and Scott Turrow. I thought it was time a paralegal write a legal thriller about a paralegal.

I: Are your characters based on real people or are they entirely fictitious?

PT3: Entirely fiction. I used to use the first names of friends and family. I have one great uncle, Uncle Bill. He's been begging me to be a character in a book. So I finally used his name, which is really Abelo. I told him about it, explaining that his character was to be the don of a Mafia family. He asked me what the name of the book was. I told him, Pigeon Drop. He said, "What's that? That's crap!"

But let me tell you, as soon as a book comes out and someone doesn't see their name ... if looks could kill. So I stopped doing that. My Uncle Bill (and Aunt Tubby) are the last to see their names – on purpose, in my work. (Sorry family).

I: How much research did you have to do?

PT3: Plenty. Except, I didn't know I was doing it. A lot of the book, aside from being about a stalker, is reflective of my day-to-day job as an employment law paralegal. My daily responsibilities are not much different from Linda's.

I also did research on the city. I want the facts to be accurate. I did a bit of research on the office building that Linda's firm works out of, to capture its history. That was fun. Some writers do not like doing research. I enjoy it. Sometimes the tough part is including what I've learned, without making it sound like a non-fiction documentary.

I: How long did it take you to write it?

PT3: I would say it took around eight months to write ADVERSE IMPACT. Then I pass the manuscript around to close friends and family and they rip it apart and mark it up with red pens. When I get the book back, it looks like it's bleeding to death. I work with everyone to hash out scenes that don't "feel" right, and brainstorm, and fix them ... the writing, re-writing never ends.

I: What are you working on next?

PT3: Well, I just finished writing the book I mentioned above, PIGEON DROP. It is a thriller about three grifters who con the Mafia by mistake and find themselves in a battle for their lives. (A little too dramatic? Actually it reads a lot like an Elmore Leonard novel, with James Patterson-size chapters. Loads of Quinton Tarentino dialogue).

In November, from Port Town Publishing, my first kid's chapter book will be released. It is entitled, KING GAUTHIER AND THE LITTLE DRAGON SLAYER. I will be using a pen name, though. Grant R. Philips. I do not want a nine year old to read King Gauthier and then rush out and by a copy of JOHNNY BLADE. So by using a pen name, I will keep my audiences separate, and happy—I hope.

I have an agent who is shopping around a middle grade novel, SOUNDS OF SILENCE. This is another Grant R. Philips title. It is the story of a 12 year-old boy who contracts a bad case of meningitis and becomes deaf. It is a powerful story (and if you want to talk about research ...)

I: What would you like readers to know about you and your book?

PT3: No animals or children were harmed in the writing of the novel. No, seriously. I hope people give my books a read. I put a lot of time into crafting the stories, and even though they are thrillers, the books have subtle messages to them.

I: Would you like to tell us a little about yourself?

PT3: Well, I work full time as an employment law paralegal for the Eastman Kodak Company. I am a freelance reporter for a small community newspaper. As I mentioned, I write book reviews for Curled Up With A Good Book, and teach creative writing classes, how-to-sell short story classes, and give presentations at a variety of locations like Barnes & Noble, libraries, and at Writers & Books.

I am married. My wife and I have three kids. Two boys, and the youngest is a girl. All three of our kids taking dancing lessons. The boys do a street jazz, and our daughter does tap. My kids are also very involved in sports, so I can't possibly coach them all, so I at least work at being an assistant coach. Except for the kids playing sports, I am not much of an outdoorsman. I like to be inside, air conditioning in the summer, heat in the winter.

I tried camping once in a tent. It rained. I'll never go again. But the kids keep my wife and I active. During the summer we are season pass holders to Six Flags at Darien Lake. Whenever we don't have a baseball game, we're there. I enjoy spending my time reading, writing, or watching movies (sounds boring ... but I like it).

Aside from enjoying being a writer, I like to point out how lucky I am to have the wonderful family and friends that I do. Without them, none of this is possible. My wife and kids are great, and supportive, and encouraging.

God bless.

Praise for other works by Phillip Tomasso III

JOHNNY BLADE

**"The Bloody Dagger Award" Honorable Mention (2002)
"One of the Best Mystery Paperbacks of 2002"
by New Mystery Reader Magazine**

"Almost every person who hangs out at Jack's Joint has an interesting story to tell and readers will find themselves wanting to hear it. The two lead police officers on the case are fascinating characters and should be featured in future books by Phillip Tomasso III. The villain is three dimensional, totally believable and pure evil. The romance between the reporter and the prostitute is sweet and charming. On a scale of one to ten, the plot scores an eleven."
> —*Harriet Klausner, Midwest Book Review*

"Johnny Blade quickens the blood. Tomasso's compelling characters lure you in and then lock the door as the screams begin!"
> —*S.J. Gaither, Co-Author of Black Moon*

"As a retired police officer, I felt that Mr. Tomasso had a law enforcement background because of his depth of police knowledge. This is cleverly written and displays a true writing artist. This book should easily fall into the classification of 'Best Seller'."
> —*Bobby Ruble, author of Have No Mercy*

"JOHNNY BLADE keeps your attention, and your emotions completely hostage until that last page. It is absolutely fantastic."
> —*Sue Hartigan, All About Murder Reviews* (5 Daggers)

"This book was an unexpected surprise … Tomasso weaves an intriguing tale of suspense that makes Johnny Blade hard to put down. The characters are well developed and real, without depending on gimicks or quirks to make them, or the story, interesting. I couldn't wait to see how the story ended...but hated to finish the book!"
> —*Overdue Book Club*

THIRD RING

Nominated for "The Bloody Dagger Award" (2002)

"Stephen King meet Sherlock Holmes. Something out of the ordinary, this book combines the intricacies of the occult with the intrigue of a good mystery. Sleuth Nicholas Tartaglia, along with an assortment of cohorts he acquires on the way, sets out to find a stolen book. His search becomes the search for a murderer, and ultimately he finds himself in search of a serial killer. Tomasso weaves each element of the mystery from the start, although the reader may not recognize the clues until the end. The use of witchcraft adds a twist that keeps this book from being just another mystery."
—*The Overdue Book Club*

"*Third Ring* is a cat and mouse game of the first water. Tomasso is wonderful at keeping the reader on his toes, and the edge of his seat. From the moment the reader meets Whine until the ultimate power of the Talisman is revealed, Tomasso exposes the reader to a world few have even imagined existed."
— Bobbi Duffy, *Inside the Cover Book Reviews*

"Third Ring is a tightly written, fast-paced private eye novel. Nick is an enjoyable character who relies on his instincts and street smarts to help keep a level head during an investigation."
—Jennifer Monahan Winberry, *The Mystery Reader*

"THIRD RING is a very well written fast paced thriller with more than just a few twists and turns. It combines the occult with intrigue, mystery, murder, and even has a little romance thrown in. Mr. Tomasso's characters are not only believable, and multi faceted, they are also intriguing. Some you will like, some you will hate, but all will grab your attention and pull you onto the next page and the page after that."
—*Sue Hartigan, All About Murder Reviews* (5 Daggers)

TENTH HOUSE

"Tenth House is without a doubt one of the best novels I've read in recent years."

—*M. R. Sellars, Author of Harm None and Never Burn A Witch*

"Phillip Tomasso's supernatural tale develops three-dimensional characters for a different style of detective series . . . where the unexpected prevails."

—*N.B. Leake, Write Time Write Place*

"Tenth House is meticulously detailed in both setting and character depth. The story will pull you in, shake you about, disturb you, keep you guessing and always wanting more. It delivers!"

—*Keith Rommel, BookReview*

MIND PLAY

"(Tomasso) crafts an engrossing and 'edge of your seat' tale of deceit, betrayal and murder. The story line and Mr. Tomasso's writing held my interest until the very end. He weaves a tale of mystery and suspense with dark threads of the supernatural ... a well-written novel with wonderful characters that come alive on the page ... I'll be waiting for Mr. Tomasso's next novel."

—*Nancy Mehl, The Charlotte Austin Review*

"Tomasso has a talent for building consistent characters and bringing them through some fast paced scenes."

—*Judi Clark, Mostly Fiction Review*

"Phillip Tomasso's supernatural tale develops three-dimensional characters for a different style of detective series ... where the unexpected prevails."

—*N.B. Leake, Write Time Write Place*

Printed in the United States
1279600001B/100-129